NORTHWE

Toward morning the win... hurricane force, buffeting the ... the canvas covers. Nate was constantly on the lookout for a suitable place where the settlers could make their stand. Finally, on a ridge, he was overjoyed to find a small spring sheltered by boulders just below the crest. With the vegetation burned away, there were few places the hostiles could take advantage of.

"This will have to do," Nate said, moving along the rim. Nodding in satisfaction, he moved to the west side and rose in the saddle to beckon the emigrants to join him. But as he raised his arm, he paused.

To the south, advancing at a determined dogtrot, was a long line of figures.

The Piegan braves were coming and they would be out for blood.

APACHE BLOOD

Nate was taken unawares when Chevalier suddenly lunged and stabbed at his chest. He threw himself to the right, sweeping his knife up, and barely managed to deflect the thrust.

"I almost had you, Grizzly Killer," Pierre said cockily. "And we've only just begun."

"We can still lower our weapons and shake hands," Nate said.

"Never."

"Tell me, Chevalier. What happens if I should only wound you? Will you let bygones be bygones? Can we go our separate ways in peace?"

"You will never know peace as long as I'm alive!"

"That's what I was afraid you'd say."

Other *Wilderness* Double Editions:
KING OF THE MOUNTAIN/
** LURE OF THE WILD**
SAVAGE RENDEZVOUS/BLOOD FURY
TOMAHAWK REVENGE/
** BLACK POWDER JUSTICE**
VENGEANCE TRAIL/DEATH HUNT
MOUNTAIN DEVIL/BLACKFOOT MASSACRE

GIANT SPECIAL EDITIONS:
ORDEAL
HAWKEN FURY
SEASON OF THE WARRIOR
PRAIRIE BLOOD
THE TRAIL WEST
FRONTIER STRIKE
SPANISH SLAUGHTER

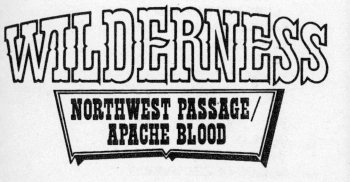

WILDERNESS

NORTHWEST PASSAGE/
APACHE BLOOD

David Thompson

LEISURE BOOKS   NEW YORK CITY

Dedicated to Judy, Joshua, and Shane.

A LEISURE BOOK®

May 1998

Published by

Dorchester Publishing Co., Inc.
276 Fifth Avenue
New York, NY 10001

ISBN 0-8439-4391-2

NORTHWEST PASSAGE

Chapter One

The piercing scream cut through the hot Plains air like a razor-sharp butcher knife through buffalo fat.

On one knee at the base of a low knoll, Nathaniel King tensed and glanced up from the fresh elk tracks he had been examining. The scream wavered eerily on a gust of wind. Before the last lingering notes died, Nate took three strides and vaulted onto his magnificent pied stallion. A tug on the reins and a jab of his moccasins brought the horse to an immediate gallop, and he raced off across the prairie toward the spot where he had left the pilgrims from the States.

Nate's first thought was that his greenhorn charges were under attack by hostiles, perhaps by a wandering band of Sioux, Arapaho, or even Blackfeet. There had been no sign of marauding war parties in the area, but a man could never be certain where Indians were concerned; they were as crafty as coyotes, as invisible as ghosts.

He clasped his Hawken firmly in his right hand and focused on the stand of trees sheltering the three wagons from the scorching sun. Oddly, he saw no hint of a commotion, and there should be a swirl of violent activity if a war party had struck. Not until he was 50 yards away did he see moving figures under the trees, some of them wildly waving their arms, and hear angry yells. Another 20 yards showed him the reason for the alarm.

A black bear was trying to clamber into one of the wagons.

Nate slowed and almost laughed aloud at the comical sight of the settlers prancing and dancing around the oblivious bear. It had its front paws braced on the side of the rear freight wagon, and was bobbing its big head up and down in the typical way a bear did when testing a breeze for scent. In this instance, it had no doubt been drawn to the wagons by the tantalizing odors coming from the food and other supplies piled high inside.

Black bears were seldom dangerous. A female with cubs would attack anyone foolhardy enough to approach too close, and a cornered bear was always likely to charge, but ordinarily they avoided humans like the plague. Unlike their fierce cousins, the mighty grizzlies, black bears possessed a mild temperament.

So Nate was not particularly concerned until he spied one of the Banner party, young Harry Nesmith, take aim with a rifle. "No!" he bellowed, and sped forward, seeking to avert potential calamity.

The rifle, a .50-caliber Kentucky, boomed.

Any hope of driving the hungry bear off without any trouble was dashed as the enraged creature dropped onto all fours and whirled, its gaping mouth wide in a vicious roar. It glared at the humans standing nearby, then abruptly charged a thin woman who stood immobilized with fear.

Nate was nearly there. Letting go of the reins, he used his legs to guide the stallion as he whipped the Hawken to his right shoulder, cocked the hammer, and took a hasty bead on the bear's head. Going for the heart or the lungs was unwise since a single ball in either often failed to bring a bear down. But the head shot, even if not fatal, might stun the black bear long enough for Nate to finish the unfortunate beast off.

The furious bear had only two yards to cover to reach the terrified woman when the Hawken cracked. In a whirl of limbs the brute went down, rolling completely over and smacking into the transfixed pilgrim. She flew to one side, landing on her back. The black bear was upright in the blink of an eye, snarling as it shook its head from side to side.

A heartbeat after squeezing the trigger, Nate was already grabbing for another weapon. His right hand streaked to one of the two smoothbore single-shot .55-caliber flintlock pistols wedged under his wide brown leather belt, and as the stallion came abreast of the bear he leaned down, lowered the barrel to within an inch of the bear's brow, and fired.

The black bear's head snapped to one side as if kicked by a Missouri mule. Then the bear blinked, tried to lift a paw, and sagged, its front legs buckling first. Snorting and spitting blood, it went prone.

Nate turned the stallion in a tight loop and leaped down before the horse came to a stop. Transferring the spent flintlock to the same hand that held the Hawken, he drew his other pistol, dashed up to the wheezing bear, which was struggling to rise, and dispatched it with a ball between the eyes. For a full ten seconds he stood still, inhaling the acrid gunsmoke, watching blood flow from the bear's wounds.

"Well done, King! I don't understand why my shot didn't do the trick."

The lighthearted words aroused Nate's anger. He spun, his features hardening, and strode up to Harry Nesmith. "Damn your hide!" he snapped, jabbing the flintlock into Nesmith's chest. The startled Ohioan stumbled backwards. "You had no call to go and shoot! We could have driven the critter off."

"Why are you so mad?" Nesmith responded indignantly. "We couldn't let that beast get into our victuals."

"Yes, King," interjected a deep voice to their right. "Why are you so upset?"

Nate shifted to face the leader of the group, Simon Banner. A tall, powerful blockhouse of a man who wore homespun clothes and a white hat, Banner constantly exuded a certain arrogance that rankled Nate no end. "Out here, Mr. Banner," he answered slowly, keeping his tone calm and level with a supreme effort, "we don't kill anything unless we absolutely have to. We don't ever waste game." He nodded at the dead black bear. "There was no need to kill it."

Banner scratched his bearded chin, then shrugged. "I still don't see what the fuss is all about. It's just a bear. We kill them all the time back East."

"Which is why there are fewer and fewer bears every year," Nate stated flatly. "You're not east of the Mississippi any longer, and it's time you owned up to that fact." He encompassed the prairie with a sweep of his arm. "Out here we do things differently. You might say we do as the Indians do. And Indians never kill animals unless they need those animals for food or their lives are in peril."

Banner made a sniffing sound. "We've only been together for a week, yet I can tell you admire the savages more than they rightfully deserve. They are heathens, after all."

It took all the self-control Nate could muster not to smash Banner on the mouth. "Need I remind you that my wife is a Shoshoni?" he asked gruffly.

"She is?" Banner replied in genuine surprise. "My word, King. I wasn't told."

For a moment Nate was inclined to doubt the assertion, until he reminded himself that the man who had arranged for him to serve as guide for this bunch, Isaac Fraeb, was a tight-lipped old cuss who never indulged in idle gossip. "Well, now you have been," he said. "So I'll thank you not to speak ill of the Indians again in my presence or I'll be obliged to show you better manners."

He sighed, his temper subsiding, aware that many Easterners shared Banner's prejudice through no fault of their own. When the government itself regarded Indians as little better than animals, it was only natural for those who believed in their government to feel the same way. Very few knew the truth. Very few had experienced what he had experienced. "Not all Indians are as bad as they're painted to be," he commented. "Some are as friendly as any white man who ever lived. And most are honest, upright people in their own way."

"How can heathens be upright in the sight of the Lord?" Banner asked quizzically. "Isn't that a contradiction in terms?"

"I suppose *you* would say so," Nate said. The man was, after all, the brother-in-law of a Methodist missionary, and as devout as a Quaker.

Suddenly a shrill reprimand was addressed at them both. "Isn't this a fine state of affairs? Here lies poor Cora, perhaps hovering at death's door, and all you men can think to do is argue over whether the bear should have been shot or not! Really!"

Alice Banner, her brown hair tucked up under her bonnet, stood over the woman who had been knocked down, a towel and a water skin in her hands. She clucked like an irate mother hen, then knelt and applied water to the towel. "Isn't Cora's life more important than your petty disagreements?"

Nate realized he had forgotten all about Cora Webster in the flush of anger that had seized him. Annoyed at himself, he stepped toward the unconscious woman, but the rest got there first. He let them tend her, studying their faces as they did, wondering what in the world he had gotten himself into by agreeing to hire out as a guide to these three brave couples on their way to the far-off Oregon Territory.

Simon Banner was easy to read, stubborn, proud, and hotheaded. His wife, Alice, was by contrast good-natured and always considerate of others, but feisty when crossed. Next, in terms of age, came Neil and Cora Webster, both pleasant enough but quite reserved, tending to keep to themselves even during the supper hour. Harry and Eleanor Nesmith were the youngest husband and wife, and it was the impulsive Harry who was directly to blame for Cora's condition.

Nate saw someone else hasten toward the clustered group, the last member of their little party, sixteen-year-old Libbie Banner. He rarely got to see her because her father made her stay in the family's wagon practically all the time. She was a blue-eyed blonde, endowed with the kind of full figure that drew suitors like honey drew ants.

He had initially been quite flabbergasted to find her with the group since there was little in the way of a social life awaiting her in Oregon. Very few settlers had gone out there so far; the last group had consisted of Methodist missionaries the year before. To his knowledge, there wasn't anyone else her age, or even close to it, living in the Willamette Valley. In effect, by taking her with them, her parents were banishing her to a life of loneliness. Or perhaps they were counting on more settlers arriving later on. He didn't rightly know and didn't feel it was his business to pry.

Now, as Libbie joined the others, Simon looked around and saw her. "Get back to the wagon, girl," he ordered sternly.

"But Mrs. Webster—" Libbie said in her musical voice.

"She's coming around," Simon said. "Cora probably just had the wind knocked out of her." He pointed at the first wagon. "Do as I told you and get back in there."

"Yes, Pa," Libbie said, her slender shoulders slumping as she did his bidding.

Nate's forehead creased in thought but he said nothing. Were he the girl's father, he certainly wouldn't treat her in the hard fashion Simon did. It was not his place, though, to intervene. Some parents, he knew, were much stricter than others. Simon Banner could do as he pleased. But given the man's disposition, Nate figured the poor girl must be going through living hell.

Cora Webster's eyelids fluttered. She abruptly revived and sat up, screeching at the top of her lungs, "The bear! The bear!"

"It's all right, dear," Alice Banner said, taking Cora's hands in hers. "You're perfectly safe. That horrible beast is dead thanks to Mr. King."

"It is?" Cora said, gazing around in wide-eyed bewilderment. Then she spotted the body. Exhaling in relief, she sadly shook her head and said, "I tried to get out of the way, but I just couldn't. It was as if I turned to stone."

"There's no need to explain yourself," Alice soothed her. "The sight of a charging bear is enough to petrify any soul."

Until that moment Neil Webster, a skinny man sporting a walrus mustache, had stayed to one side, allowing Alice to restore his wife to her senses. Moving nearer, he bent down and took hold of Cora's arm. "Come. I'll get you into our wagon where you can rest from your ordeal."

"Perhaps she should be examined for broken bones," Alice suggested.

"I feel fine," Cora said. "Truly. There's no cause to worry yourself on my account."

"We're all in this venture together, aren't we?" Alice responded. "We must stick together through thick and thin if we hope to reach the promised land safely."

Nate walked to his stallion. The "promised land" was the phrase most often used of late to describe the verdant splendor of the Oregon Territory. He had yet to visit the region himself, but if the tales he had heard from those who had been there were any indication, then the remote Northwest qualified as Paradise on earth. He began reloading his guns, starting with the Hawken.

Simon Banner cleared his throat. "We'll stay here another hour to give Cora plenty of time to rest."

"No, we won't," Nate said as he opened his powder horn. "We're leaving just as soon as all of you get on your wagons."

"What?" Simon said, turning. "Why, pray tell?"

"Because we're still five hours shy of South Pass. We're still in Sioux country, and they can't always be counted on to be friendly. Sometimes they are. Sometimes they're out for scalps."

Banner surveyed the sea of waving grass surrounding the stand. "Did you see some Sioux while you were scouting up ahead?"

"No."

"Then we're perfectly safe, hidden among these trees."

With the patient air of a teacher instructing a six-year-old, Nate explained while he worked. "On the prairie sound travels a long ways. At night you'll hear wolves howling and swear they're right outside your camp when they're far off." He began pouring the right amount of black powder into his palm. "A gunshot too can carry for miles if the wind is right. And since few Indians have guns, whenever they hear a shot they know white men must be responsible and they go investigate."

"So you're saying some Sioux might have heard our shots and be on their way here at this very moment?"

"You catch on quick."

The others cast nervous glances in all directions, except for Alice Banner, who made straight for her wagon, saying over her shoulder, "You heard the man, husband. Let's not dally. We've put too many miles behind us to end up as fly bait."

Her words galvanized everyone into action. Harnesses were checked, water skins and whatever else they had removed from their wagons were placed back on, and the husbands assisted their wives in climbing up.

Nate tucked the reloaded flintlocks under his belt, one on either side of his large metal buckle, gripped his rifle, and swung onto the stallion. All eyes were on him, and he could well imagine the picture he must present. Dressed in fringed, beaded buckskins, with a large butcher knife on his left hip, a tomahawk on his right, and his powder horn and ammunition pouch slanted across his broad chest, he looked every inch as wild and barbaric as the Indians they dreaded. His mane of black hair spilling from under his beaver hat only added to the impression. But anyone familiar with Indians would brand him as a white man right away; there wasn't an Indian alive who had the striking green eyes he did. "Head out and keep the wagons close together," he directed.

Pleasant thoughts of his wife and son filtered through his mind as he assumed the lead. Leaving them for extended periods, such as when he went off to trap beaver, was never easy. He always feared hostile Indians would find their cabin while he was away and slay them.

In recent years the trapping trips took him farther and farther afield, compounding his worry.

The life of a free trapper had changed dramatically in recent years, and he often wished things were like they were when he first started. In 1828, when he ventured into the Rockies with his Uncle Zeke, beaver were plentiful along every mountain stream and creek. Nine years later the relentless trapping had reduced their population drastically. If a man wanted to obtain prime pelts, he had to trek into isolated areas no one else had visited. And such areas were few and far between.

Some of the old-timers, including his best friend and mentor Shakespeare McNair, believed the days of the trapping fraternity were numbered. In McNair's case it hardly mattered since Shakespeare was getting on in years and was content to quietly pass his time at home with his lovely Flathead wife.

But to Nate the decline of the beaver trade meant a world of difference. He had a family to feed, clothe, and otherwise provide for. Supplying the necessities was still relatively easy; all he had to do was bring down a deer or a buffalo and they had meat on the table and hides for making clothes. In that respect, he lived much like his Indian friends.

Nate wanted more out of life, though. He wanted to be able to give his loved ones more than the simple necessities. He also wanted to set a nest egg aside for the future, for the days when he would be too old to trap or to do much hunting— provided he lived that long. And besides all that, he needed work, needed something to do to keep himself busy.

Jim Bridger, a man Nate respected highly, claimed many more emigrants would be heading to the Oregon Territory in the years to come, and that there would be a great need for reliable guides since most settlers "couldn't find their backsides with both hands and a mirror, let alone find their way to the Pacific Coast." And Bridger, Nate believed, was right.

Which was another reason he had agreed to take the Banner party to Fort Hall. They were going to pay him one hundred dollars for his services, a sizeable sum that would tide his family over until his next prolonged trapping trip. And if he found the experience agreeable, he might set his sights on hiring out again as a guide in the future. He made a mental note to buy old Isaac Fraeb a couple of bottles of whiskey to show his gratitude for being recommended for the job.

The creak and rattle of a wagon as it drew even with the stallion brought Nate's reflection to an end and he glanced to his right.

"I wanted to have a few words with you," Simon Banner said, flicking the reins with his brawny hands. His team, four sturdy horses well accustomed to hauling freight wagons, responded superbly.

"What about?" Nate asked.

"Do you think we'll reach Fort Hall on time?"

"We should."

"I don't want to be late. The man my brother-in-law is sending to meet us and take us the rest of the way might not wait around very long if we don't show up by the first of July."

"Don't worry, Mr. Banner. I'll get you there."

"But I *do* worry, King. I have the lives of my family and these other good people to think of. In effect we've put our fate in your hands, and I, for one, am still waiting to be convinced that you are every bit the able frontiersman Isaac claimed."

"If you're not happy with me, I'll ride off now and you can go your own way," Nate said. He looked at Alice Banner, touched his hand to his hat, and went to turn his horse.

"Now hold on!" Simon blurted. "I didn't mean to insult you, and I certainly don't want you to leave us alone out here in the middle of nowhere."

"Perhaps, husband," Alice said, "it would be best if you kept as tight a rein on your tongue as you do on the team."

Nate saw Simon flush scarlet and smiled at Alice. Of them all, she was the friendliest, the one he liked the best. She reminded him of an aunt back in New York, a practical, no-nonsense sort of woman who always spoke her piece and wasn't cowed by anyone.

"What lies on the trail ahead?" Simon asked quickly to cover his embarrassment.

"Past South Pass we'll make for the Green River. From there, we head northwest until we reach the Snake River area and Fort Hall."

"You make it sound so easy."

"It's not," Nate admitted. "There will be days at a stretch when we'll need to ration our water. Grass for the horses will be hard to find at times. There will be steep grades to deal with and deep rivers to cross. And every step of the way we'll have to keep our eyes peeled for Indians out to count coup." He stared at the white canvas top covering the bed of the wagon. "I never thought to ask. You folks did bring foofaraw, didn't you?"

"Bring what?" Alice inquired.

"Sorry, ma'am. Foofaraw is trapper talk for trade things like ribbons, beads, trinkets, and whatnot."

Alice laughed lightly. "What a funny term! You mountain men sure do invent colorful words."

Nate straightened. That was the first time anyone had ever referred to *him* as a mountain man. He'd heard and used the expression before, usually in reference to old coons like Shakespeare who had lived in the rugged mountains nearly all of their eventful lives. But he had never regarded himself as being a true mountain man since he hadn't lived in the Rockies half as long as most of the few old-timers still alive. He was a free trapper, plain and simple.

"I'm afraid we didn't bring much to trade," Simon Banner was saying. "No one told us we would need to."

The statement worried Nate. He hadn't thought to check their provisions when Isaac led him to where they were camped out on the prairie three days ago, and that oversight might cause problems later on if they hadn't brought all they should. "How many guns does your party have?" he asked.

"Each man has two rifles," Simon said, "and Harry and I each brought pistols along."

"Good. There's no telling when they might come in handy."

"Perhaps sooner than you think," Alice remarked, pointing due west.

Nate shifted, and there, riding hard toward them, was a band of six warriors mounted on sleek, painted war ponies. As he laid eyes on the band, the Indians whooped and waved their weapons overhead.

Chapter Two

No two Indian tribes dressed exactly alike or wore their hair in the exact same style. Although many Plains tribes and some mountain dwellers relied extensively on the buffalo for everything from their clothing to their cooking utensils and their lodge furnishings, they displayed an endless variety in making these items that never ceased to fascinate Nate. In one tribe the men wore loose-fitting, plain shirts, while in another the men went in for elaborate beadwork, in another long fringes. In one tribe the parflaches might be small and hand-painted; in another, large and adorned with bright beads. Even the cradleboards used by mothers to carry young children were unique with each tribe.

So it was that Nate recognized the band galloping swiftly toward him as a roving war party of Sioux. He hefted the Hawken and braced for the worst. Three wagons loaded with goods might be more of a temptation than the warriors would let pass. He was about to raise his hand, to use sign language to tell the Sioux not to get too close, when they angled to the north, still whooping and waving their bows and lances. He noticed a tall warrior in the lead held a long stick from which dangled three long locks of black hair, and then he understood.

"Simon, don't!"

Nate turned to see Simon Banner taking aim with a rifle. "You heard your wife!" he snapped. "They won't bother us if we don't bother them."

"How can you be sure?" Simon responded skeptically.

"See that man in the front?"

"The buck carrying that stick?" Simon leaned forward, his eyes narrowing. "What are those things hanging from it?"

"Scalps."

"My word!" Alice exclaimed.

"They're on their way back to their village after a successful raid on one of their enemies," Nate detailed. "Right now they're just taunting us, letting us know they're great warriors and that they're not afraid of us. But they don't mean any harm. They're in a hurry to reach their people so they can show off the scalps they took and tell about the coup they counted. The tribe will throw a victory dance for them, and they'll likely celebrate for days."

"How primitive," Alice said.

Nate was about to point out that victories won in battle were big events in Indian life when he spotted Harry Nesmith, perched on the seat of the second wagon, lifting the Kentucky. "No!" he roared, and goaded the stallion into a run that brought him to the wagon in seconds. "Don't fire!" he commanded. Then he gazed at the last wagon to verify Neil Webster wasn't about to commit the same mistake. "They'll leave us alone if we don't start anything."

In confirmation, the band was soon little more than black dots racing across the limitless expanse of verdant prairie.

"From here on out," Nate said to Harry, "no one will fire a gun without first getting my say-so. And that includes you, Nesmith. You're a mite too bloodthirsty for my taste. If you're not careful, you'll get us into a heap of trouble before this trip is done."

Young Nesmith bristled. "This is my gun," he declared, holding the Kentucky out over the edge of his seat, "and I'll shoot it any damn time I please."

Nate didn't waste time in further debate. He simply reached up, grabbed the Kentucky, and pulled with all the might in his arm and shoulder before Nesmith could think to let go. Which was sufficient to yank Harry clean off of the wagon seat and to send him sailing head over heels for a good dozen feet to tumble onto the ground with a resounding thud.

Cora Nesmith screamed.

Sliding down, Nate walked up to Harry, who had both hands on the ground and was attempting to stand. Without warning, without ceremony, he slammed the stock of the Hawken into the side of Harry's head and Nesmith crumpled like an empty sack of potatoes. Angry shouts from the right and the left made him look up.

Both Simon Banner and Neil Webster were converging on the spot.

"What's the meaning of this outrage?" Banner demanded rudely. "You're supposed to guide and protect us, not attack us!"

"True enough," Nate said, "but I didn't figure on having to protect you from *yourselves*. And I'm fed up with having every word I say tossed back in my face." He glared at the two pilgrims. "From here on out, all of you will do as I say when I say it. One more argument, one more time where one of you thinks he knows better than I do how to survive out here, and you'll be on your own. Savvy?"

"You don't mean that," Neil Webster said.

"Yes, he does," Simon stated, kneeling to examine Harry. "All right, King. We'll do things your way. But I want you to know I'm not accustomed to having any man tell me how to live my life."

Nate spun on his heels and stepped to the stallion.

"You're a hard man, King," Simon added.

"The Rockies make a man that way," Nate said, mounting. "Nature has her lessons to teach, and the man who fails to learn them doesn't last long. The wilderness is no place for weaklings, cowards, or pigheaded fools." He rode up to the first wagon, then stopped and looked back to observe Nesmith being slapped to life.

"Mr. King?" Alice said softly.

"Yes, ma'am?"

"Please forgive my husband and the other men. They're really decent, hard-working men at heart, and they don't bear you any ill will." She surveyed the unknown land to the west. "It's not easy taking the biggest step of your entire life, risking everything that you own and those you love the most, and not knowing how things will turn out in the end."

"If you don't mind my saying so, ma'am, your husband will do right fine with you by his side. Every hothead needs a wise woman like yourself to show him when he's making a fool of himself."

"Mr. King! I'm blushing!"

Grinning, Nate rode slowly forward. Soon the wagons were in motion again, and the next five hours passed uneventfully. Added to the rattling of the wagons and the dull thud of weary hoofs was the rustling of the wind through the high grass. Occasionally rabbits bounded away in bursts of incredible speed. Prairie dogs whistled shrilly to warn their fellows or chattered angrily at the intruders. Deer and antelope kept respectful distances.

Once a small herd of buffalo interrupted their grazing to watch the lumbering wagons go by.

Nate liked the plains, but nowhere near as much as he liked the mountains. Give him the snow-crowned peaks, the crystal-clear high country lakes, the virgin pine forests teeming with wildlife, and he was content. On the prairie he felt too exposed, too vulnerable. There were few places for a man to seek shelter if set upon.

Consequently, he was relieved when South Pass finally rose into sight. The mountains themselves had appeared much sooner, at first as vague blue shapes shimmering on the horizon. To the north lay the Wind River Range. To the south rose the Green Mountains. Between them lay the single most accessible pass through the entire chain of foreboding Rockies, a wide, gently sloping sandy saddle that wagons could negotiate with ease.

South Pass had been used regularly by Indians for ages; by white men ever since the early 1820's, when enterprising trappers had availed themselves of the gateway to enter the previously unexplored Green River country, which turned out to be a prime trapping region. The annual caravans bearing supplies from St.Louis to the various Rendezvous sites all relied on South Pass, and only the year before the caravan had included a number of wagons.

All this Nate knew well, and it was why he had guided the emigrants straight to the pass from their camp on the Plains. He was mildly surprised to note deep ruts in the soil left by the wagons that had gone over the pass the year before, and he idly wondered how scarred the earth would be if great numbers of wagons were to head westward in the years to come as Bridger and Shakespeare contended would be the case.

He was constantly alert for Indians. Availing himself of the slope, he turned in his saddle and scanned the prairie they were leaving behind. The endless sea of grass shimmered in the sunlight, stretching to the eastern horizon, broken only by scattered stands of trees and a knoll or two. There was ample game in evidence but no sign of Indians.

It would be a minor miracle if they reached Fort Hall without running into hostiles. The Green River country they were about to cross was a favorite stamping ground of the highly feared Blackfoot confederacy, consisting of the formidable Blackfeet themselves and their two allies, the Bloods and the Piegans. Of the three the Blackfeet were by far the worst, waging war as they did not only on all whites but also on every other tribe outside the confederacy. They were the bane of the Shoshones, Crows, and Nez Percé, all friends to the whites.

Nate had tangled with the Blackfeet on more occasions than he cared to count, and had no desire to go up against them again. If he should be killed, the pilgrims wouldn't stand a prayer. The Blackfeet would show no mercy, not even to the women. In fact, the women might suffer a worse fate than the men, who would undoubtedly be tortured before being slain. Some of the Blackfeet might be inclined to take the white women into their lodges, perhaps for the novelty, in effect banishing their captives to a life of perpetual slavery, to daily backbreaking toil, and much worse, to never-ending harsh treatment at the hands of the Blackfoot women.

Suddenly Nate heard a snort, then a low grunt, both from the other side of the pass. He was almost to the top, and he hefted his Hawken as he rode high enough to see the land unfold to the west. There were mountains and valleys and canyons galore. But much closer was a sight so unexpected that he reined up in astonishment.

Hundreds and hundreds of shaggy buffaloes were coming directly toward him.

He realized a large herd was on its way onto the prairie and the wagons were right in the path of the great brutes. If a stampede started, the settlers would be caught right in the middle. There was no time to swing wide and wait for the herd to pass because the foremost bulls were less than two hundred yards away. Something else had to be done, and quickly.

Nate wheeled the stallion and raced to the first wagon. "Buffalo!" he warned them, waving for the other wagons to close the gap. "Bunch up and sit tight. If the critters stampede, get in the beds of your wagons and lie low."

Nesmith and Webster brought up their wagons rapidly and positioned themselves on either side of Banner's wagon. No sooner did they stop than the first line of lumbering bison appeared.

Buffalo were completely unpredictable. A herd might flee at the mere sight of a man, or it might stand its ground until fired upon. Once panicked, a herd was transformed into an unstoppable force of Nature, rolling over everything in its way, covering scores of miles in uncontrolled flight. Indians used this trait to their advantage by driving herds over cliffs. In one day thousands of bison might be killed, providing enough hides and meat to last many months.

Individually buffalo were equally formidable. The bulls stood six feet at the shoulder and possessed horn spreads of three feet. Weighing upwards of two thousands pounds, they could bowl over a horse and rider with ease. And the cows were not all that much smaller.

Now a surging tide of brutes eager for the lush prairie grass swept over the rim of South Pass and down the gradual slope, venting a chorus of grunts, snorts, and bellows as they advanced.

Nate had moved into the narrow space between the Banner and Webster wagons, where the stallion couldn't be inadvertently gored. He didn't know how tightly the herd would press them and feared a stampede at any second. The pale faces of the settlers showed they shared his anxiety.

The buffaloes drew steadily nearer. Nate could see their nostrils flaring as they breathed, see their hairy sides rippling as they walked. The wind bore their strong scent to him, mingled with the dust raised by thousands of pounding hoofs. Already the leading ranks had become aware of the wagons and horses in their path, and the next moment those ranks parted, some bearing to the left, others to the right, giving the wagons a wide berth.

Nate hoped none of the women would cry out. Even a frightened whinny from one of the horses could set the bison into thunderous motion. He sat perfectly still and held the stallion the same way. On the wagon seats were six statues. Every member of the party was as rigid as a rock. Except for Libbie. He saw her peek out over her mother's shoulder, agog at the number of buffalo. If she only knew. This was a big herd, but it was nowhere near the biggest Nate had seen. Once, he'd sat and watched for a whole day as an unending stream of the great beasts flowed southward.

A passing bull suddenly bellowed and gave the wagons a wary look, then lowered its head and swung its wicked horns. But the swing was more of a defensive act than an outright attack, and neither horn came into contact with Webster's wagon or the horses.

Nate spotted calves here and there and heard their distinctive bawling. Usually born in May or early June, calves were able to stand 30 minutes after their birth, to walk within an hour or two, and within two days could join the herd on its travels. At two months their horns sprouted, as did their telltale humps.

The air filled with dust. Flies buzzed by. Harry Nesmith had a coughing fit until Nate glanced sharply at him. Around the wagons arose the ceaseless sounds of the herd. Minute after minute dragged by with awful slowness. Nate felt the stallion fidget and saw the teams doing the same. He wondered if he had miscalculated, if the herd was much larger than he thought. Then to his delight, the number of buffalo dwindled. Fewer and fewer went past. At the rear of the herd walked the old ones and the sick, the inevitable stragglers, those most likely to be picked off by wolves out on the prairie.

"Praise the Lord that's over!" Alice exclaimed when the last of the buffalo had gone by.

"I hope I never go through that again!" Neil Webster said. "Did you see the way those monsters were looking at us? I thought they'd charge us for sure."

Simon was staring at Nate. "Are there a lot of buffalo between here and Fort Hall? Will this happen again?"

"This was a fluke," Nate said, moving in front of the wagons. "Most herds in the mountains are small. But at this time of the year they like to head out onto the prairie, and that's when they form into big groups like the one we've just seen." He motioned for the wagons to resume rolling.

"If there *is* a next time, try to give us more warning," Simon commented resentfully. "We could have been killed."

Nate controlled his temper and rode to the crest. The ground was marred by thousands of hoofprints and droppings. Putting a hand above his eyes to shield them from the brilliant sunlight, he studied the lay of the land, reacquainting himself with the more prominent landmarks. He had a certain destination in mind, a valley watered by a bubbling brook, that he wanted to reach before dark.

The teams were exhausted by the time he called a halt, and when the men released the horses from harness, the animals plodded into the water and stood there drinking greedily. He watered his stallion before getting down to business, which entailed giving advice on how best to set up the camp.

With the sun sinking below the western horizon in a blazing display of vivid colors, a welcome cool breeze sprang up from the northwest. Soon Harry Nesmith had a crackling fire going and the women were busy preparing stew for supper. Nate had bagged a black-tailed buck the evening before, and there was enough meat left for a feast.

Nate sat on a log near the fire, a twig between his teeth, and listened to the conversations around him. As yet he was treated like an outsider and rarely invited to throw in his two cents worth unless they needed his opinion in his capacity as their guide. He didn't mind their attitude all that much. Years of living in the mountains, of being self-reliant and independent, had taught him that what others said or did could have no effect on him unless he let it. And he wasn't about to let a bunch of uppity Easterners upset him.

Alice Banner came over. "Mr. King, would you care for bread with your stew tonight? We have plenty, and I'm more than happy to share with you."

"You're a kind woman, Mrs. Banner. You remind me a lot of my wife."

"I do?" Alice said, smiling self-consciously. She was a robust woman, in her late forties or early fifties, and her hair, what little could be seen hanging from under her prim bonnet, was flecked with premature gray. "I gather you must love your wife very much."

"That I do."

"Do you find it hard . . . ?" Alice began, then caught herself. "What I mean to say is, do you like . . . ?" Again she stopped, and clasped her hands.

"Do I like being married to an Indian woman?" Nate finished for her. There was no sarcasm in her tone, no spite in her eyes, just simple curiosity, as well there might be in a woman who had lived her entire life in a sheltered farming community back in the States. "Yes, ma'am. I do. Winona is beautiful, caring, and intelligent. She speaks English better than I can speak her tongue, which says a lot because English is hard for most Indians to pick up."

"Speaking of English," Alice said, "I've noticed that you are a cut above most frontiersmen we've met. Many of them use atrocious grammar and the worst sort of profanity." She cocked her head. "You, I take it, are a literate man."

"I was born and raised in New York City," Nate said, and lowered his voice as if confiding a dark secret. "Don't let it get around, but I can read and write with the best of 'em. I'm a big admirer of James Fenimore Cooper."

"Cooper? Isn't he the one who writes those marvelous books about Indians and such? *The Last of the Mohicans* was one of his works, was it not?"

"You know your literature, ma'am."

"Not really," Alice said, and sighed. "I keep up on current events through newspapers and friends, but Simon limits our reading to the Bible. He believes that all other books are tainted by the Devil's influence."

"Even books like Cooper's? Nate asked. This was the first he had ever heard of such a notion and he didn't quite know how to take it.

"Especially those kinds of books. Simon says they offer a man's view of the world when what we really need to know is God's view." She glanced around and saw her husband moving toward the fire. "Now if you'll excuse me, I'd better finish with supper." Off she hastened.

Nate rose and stretched. He was a religious man himself, insomuch as he believed there was a God and he tried to live the Golden Rule as much as possible given the harsh nature of life in the wilderness, but the idea of being allowed to read from only the Bible struck him as fanatical. What about all the other great thoughts and beautiful sentiments that had been expressed by writers down through the ages? Didn't they count for anything?

He shook his head, grabbed the Hawken, and began to make a circuit of the camp. Stars had blossomed in the heavens. There were trees close at hand, aspens and others, and their leaves rustled in the wind. Cradling the rifle, he made sure the horses were all tethered, then turned.

From in the trees came a soft noise.

Nate was in a crouch in a flash, the Hawken leveled and cocked. A quick look at the fire revealed all three couples were accounted for. The noise was repeated over and over. It sounded like a low moan, as if someone was in pain. Puzzled, he worked his way into the trees and halted. Now it sounded like someone crying.

On cat's feet he stalked forward until he saw a familiar figure leaning on a trunk and sobbing uncontrollably. He rose and took a step backward, not wanting to intrude on her privacy, but his heel crunched down on a dry twig that snapped loudly and she whirled like a cornered animal, fear lining her features until she saw him.

"Mr. King!"

"Sorry, Libbie," Nate said. Something inside told him to keep his voice low so her parents wouldn't overhear. "I didn't mean to bother you. I'm leaving."

"I just needed some air," Libbie said, swiping at her damp eyes. She sniffled and gazed over his shoulder. "Is my pa hunting for me?"

"No."

Libbie nodded and dabbed at her eyes with her right sleeve. "I guess I'm more miserable over leaving all my friends and kin than I thought."

"I know how rough it can be," Nate said.

"Do you?" Libbie responded. She squared her shoulders and walked forward. "Life is rougher on some of us than on others."

"Strange words coming from one so young."

That stopped her. "Do you have to be an adult to know a broken heart? To have all your hopes and dreams ruined? To have the only true happiness you've ever known torn from you?"

"I reckon not."

Then she was gone, darting through the trees and to the wagons, coming on them from the rear so no one at the fire would notice. She vanished inside her parents' wagon in a swirl of blond hair.

What the dickens was that all about? Nate asked himself, moving into the open. He's seen her face as she went by, a face mirroring uncommon inner torment for a sixteen-year-old. True, by frontier standards a sixteen-year-old was considered a grown-up. But Libbie was from back East, and her parents were the sort to zealously safeguard their daughter from anything that might harm her. Hard as nails Simon Banner might be, yet there was no denying the man cared for his family.

Nate scanned the encampment, gazed to the south, to the north, and the east. And froze, a tingle of apprehension rippling down his spine. For in the distance, at about where South Pass should be, was a yellow pinpoint of light that could only be one thing.

It was another campfire.

Chapter Three

At night, when the pristine landscape was plunged in shrouding darkness, flickering campfires stood out like lighthouse beacons sweeping the sea, a certain lure for possible enemies. Which was why experienced frontiersmen and Indians alike took particular pains to build their fires where the flames couldn't be seen from any great distance. Only a fool who wanted to die advertised his presence in the wilderness.

Nate had picked their campsite wisely in that respect. The narrow valley in which he had called a halt opened to the east, and there were trees at the valley mouth that served as an effective screen from possible prying eyes. He always had the safety of the Banner party uppermost in mind when he selected places to stop.

But whoever had set up camp near the top of South Pass, he reflected, was just asking for trouble. The fire was high up where it could be seen for miles around. Since no Indian in his right mind would ever be so foolish, the fire must have been built by white men. Greenhorns, at that.

Nate walked to the fire, where the women were busy preparing the meal and the men were huddled together in conversation. "We're not alone," he informed them.

All six of them stopped whatever they were doing to look at him.

"What's that?" Simon asked.

"We have neighbors," Nate said, raising his right arm and pointing. Eleanor Nesmith gasped. One of the men muttered an oath.

"Indians, you think?" Neil Webster inquired anxiously.

"Not likely," Nate said. "But we'll know soon enough. I figure to ride back there and see who it is."

Simon turned. *"Now?"*

"I don't like the fact that they're right on our trail. It could be a coincidence. Then again, it might not. This is the perfect time to find out. I can get close to their camp without them noticing, and if they strike me as being unfriendly, I'll persuade them to stop following us."

"But if they're white men they must be friendly," Alice said.

"Not necessarily, ma'am. There are some nasty sorts out here who are worse than hostile Indians. Some years ago I had a run-in with a wicked bunch who went around killing trappers for their money. Another time I tangled with some white men who kidnapped my wife. And I shouldn't forget Crazy George, who took a fancy to human flesh and ate other folks."

The women were aghast.

"This Crazy George was a cannibal?" Cora Webster said, a dainty hand pressed to her pale throat.

"That he was," Nate confirmed. "He confessed to eating about eight people before he met his Maker. It seems he got started one winter when he was snowed in way up in the Rockies. He ran out of food, couldn't hunt game, and decided the only way he would survive until spring was if he ate the Indian woman who lived with him."

Cora appeared about to faint. "How disgusting," she said weakly.

"The man was clearly not in his right mind," Elizabeth Nesmith declared. She moved closer to her husband and he draped a protective arm around her shoulder.

"Why tell us this and scare the women so?" Harry Nesmith asked, his resentment transparent. "First you take me by surprise and almost cave in my skull, and now you're deliberately frightening the women. If you ask me, you're a poor excuse for a guide."

"I didn't ask you," Nate shot back. "And if I'd been trying to bust your head open instead of teaching you a lesson, you'd be feeding the worms right this minute." He nodded at the distant firelight. "I didn't tell you about my experiences just to scare you, but to let you know that some white men are as evil as can be so you'll be on your guard until you get to your destination."

"How nice of you," Simon said dryly. "But I'm more concerned about having you up and leave us at a time like this. What if something happens to you? How will we reach Fort Hall?"

"It's a two hour ride to the pass if I push my horse," Nate answered. "With luck I'll be back before midnight."

"I don't want you to go," Simon stubbornly persisted.

"Would you rather be taken by surprise by a pack of cutthroats out to steal everything you own?" Nate snapped, and when no one made a reply he pivoted and retrieved his saddle and Epishemore. His was typical of the square pieces of buffalo robes used by the trapping fraternity under their saddles to keep their mounts from being chafed. He walked to the stallion, and with a deft flip aligned the Epishemore on its back. Then he applied the saddle.

The settlers had followed him.

"At least take one of us with you," Simon proposed. "You might need help."

"I can manage quite well on my own," Nate said. "You'll be busy keeping watch here. Until I return, have a man on guard at all times. And remember to snuff out the fire after you're done with your meal."

"Be careful, King."

Nate glanced at him. Was Banner genuinely concerned about his welfare or only thinking of how hard it would be for the emigrants to survive on their own? He gave the man the benefit of the doubt. "Thanks. I always am." The Hawken clutched in his left hand, he swung up. "By midnight," he said, and rode eastward.

Despite the long hours of travel put in earlier, the stallion was rested and raring to go. "Come on, Pegasus," he said softly, using the name he had given the horse when it was presented to him by the Nez Percé. He gave the animal an affectionate pat on the neck. "Let's get this over with so I can get some sleep tonight."

He gave the stallion its head, feeling the cool air caress his face and fan his hair. His stomach rumbled, reminding him he should have snatched a bite to eat before leaving. Off to the right an owl hooted. To the left, deep in the forest, a wolf howled and was immediately answered by another.

Without the overloaded wagons to slow him down, he reached South Pass in half the time it otherwise would have taken. Had it been daylight he would have gotten there even sooner. But at night a rider had to be extra careful to avoid obstacles and holes that might harm his mount. So he held the stallion to a trot instead of going at a gallop.

The pungent odor of wood smoke tingled his nose as he entered pines to the south of the pass and slowly worked his way closer to the campfire. He tied Pegasus two hundred yards from his goal to prevent any horses in the camp from detecting the stallion's scent and acting up, thus alerting whoever was there.

Nate loosened both flintlocks under his belt, then crouched and stalked upward until he could see a pair of clean-shaven men seated in front of the dancing flames. Both were white, both wearing homespun clothes. Working his way to the last of the trees, he flattened and crawled to within 15 feet of the unsuspecting pair. They were eating heartily, chomping and slurping soup from tins. Four horses were tethered across the way.

"Tomorrow, you reckon?" the heftier of the duo suddenly asked.

"I don't rightly know," responded his lean companion.

"You'd better make up your mind soon."

"I will. But we don't want to rush things."

"You're not turning yellow, are you? Not after all he put you through?"

"No. Of course not."

"Then I say we do it tomorrow."

"We bide our time and wait for the right chance."

The hefty one shifted to stare at the lean one. "Damn it all, Brian! I knew you'd do this! I knew you'd drag my ass into this godforsaken wilderness and then get cold feet. If you were a real man you would have done what needs to be done long ago."

"Shut up and finish eating."

Nate guessed that neither man was much over 20 years old, if that, and as green as they came. They wouldn't live to get much older either at the rate they were going. He inched his way around until he was behind them, then rose slowly, the Hawken in both hands. The hammer made a loud click when he thumbed it back. "Not a move, gentlemen, unless you want some lead in your diet."

The hefty one started and dropped his soup, the tin clanging against a small rock bordering the fire. His companion, the man named Brian, stiffened with a sharp intake of breath. Neither made a play for their rifles, which were lying in plain sight beside them.

"So far, so good," Nate said, stepping closer. He slanted to the left until he could see their faces, and grinned when they gaped in surprise.

"Are you an Injun?" the hefty one blurted out.

"No, but thanks for the compliment," Nate responded. He wagged the Hawken. "You can keep eating if you want, but don't try to touch your rifles or you'll spring a leak."

"Who are you? What do you want?" Brian asked. He was a handsome youth with black hair and blue eyes. His skin was tanned, his chin cleft. A two-inch scar on his right cheek ran from below his right eye to the corner of his mouth.

"The handle is Nate King. Some hereabouts call me Grizzly Killer."

The hefty one gulped. "What kind of a name is that?"

"It's my Indian name, given to me by a Cheyenne warrior after I killed my first grizzly," Nate disclosed, stepping to within a yard of Brian and hunkering down, the Hawken leveled and steady. "The name stuck. Now the Cheyennes, the Shoshones, the Flatheads, they all call me Grizzly Killer." He paused. "Who might you two be?"

"I'm—" the hefty one began, but was promptly cut off by Brian.

"Don't say a word! We don't have to tell this guy who we are if we don't want to."

Nate leaned back. "You're not being very neighborly, young man."

Brian gave a bitter laugh. "You're a fine one to talk, mister, the way you sneak into our camp and hold us at gunpoint."

He jabbed a thumb at Nate. "And who are you calling young? Even with that beard of yours, you don't appear to me to be much over twenty-five, if that."

"All right. If you don't want to cooperate, I won't force you. But we have to palaver a bit before I cut out."

"Palaver?" the hefty one repeated.

"We need to have a talk," Nate translated, making a mental note to refrain from speaking mountain-man lingo when in the company of greenhorns. His whole vocabulary had changed remarkably since he departed New York City, and he now unconsciously spoke "mountainee jargon," as a trader at a Rendezvous had once referred to the trapper way of talking, as a matter of course. It was interesting, he mused, how a person adapted to new ways so completely that those who knew him in former times wouldn't recognize him if they saw him again.

"Talk about what?" Brian demanded.

"You two," Nate said. "Why are you trying to get yourselves killed?"

"You're crazy," the hefty one said.

"No, *you* are for building your fire near the top of South Pass, right out in the open where every Blackfoot within ten miles can see it. Or do you want a war party to pay you a visit come daylight?"

Brian glanced at the crackling flames, then out over the surrounding countryside. "We liked the view," he said softly.

"So do I, but it's not worth dying over," Nate said. "If you're smart, once I'm gone you'll move your camp down into the trees. And from now on don't camp out in the open like this."

He studied them for a minute. "I don't know what you two are doing here and it's not my rightful place to meddle. But unless you have a damn good reason, you should head for Fort Leavenworth or Independence or some other settlement just as fast as your horses will take you. Unless, of course, you're going to the Oregon Territory."

"Only part of the way—" the hefty one said, but his friend slapped his arm.

"Damn it, Pudge! Keep your mouth closed!" Brian snapped. "We don't know anything about this man. How do we know we can trust him?"

Nate was becoming annoyed. "I don't care if you trust me or not. I'm just trying to help you live a little longer." He lowered the rifle and crossed his legs. Since they wouldn't confide in him, maybe he could convince them to ride with the Banner party. He suspected there was some link between them and the settlers anyway, and this way he'd be able to keep an eye on them at all times and perhaps learn what they were up to. "At first I figured you might be cutthroats out to steal from a party I'm guiding to Fort Hall, but now I doubt whether the two of you could steal candy from a baby."

Brian's lips became thin lines.

"Face facts. Neither of you know much about the wilderness. You won't last a week in these mountains on your own. So here's an idea for you to consider. Why not join up with the group I'm guiding? There's safety in numbers, and you'd be treated to some fine home cooking every night."

"No," Brian said.

"Why not?"

"No."

"Some extra company on the trail is always welcome. What if one of you has an accident?"

"No."

"Brian, please," the one nicknamed Pudge said. "He has a good point. I would feel safer with them."

"Do you really think *he'd* let us ride along?" Brian countered.

"Who?" Nate asked.

"No one," Brian said sullenly.

"What's your connection to this group I'm with?" Nate probed. "Why are you following them?"

"None of your damn business. Now go away and leave us alone."

Nate recognized a hopeless cause when he confronted one. Pushing to his feet, he cradled the Hawken and thoughtfully regarded the pair. He doubted whether either of them posed a threat to anyone under his care, but he wasn't about to take unnecessary chances. "Since you won't be neighborly, I'm going to lay down the law. I don't want to catch either of you skulking about the people I'm with or I'm liable to shoot first and ask what you were doing later. If you want to pay us a visit, ride right up in the open where I can see you."

"You have no right ordering us around," Brian said.

"I reckon I am rubbing folks the wrong way lately, but it can't be helped. I have seven lives to think of." Nate nodded at each of them and walked off. "Don't forget about moving your camp," he said over his shoulder.

Neither of them uttered a word. Brian glared angrily, his fists clenched. Pudge appeared extremely upset, and if his expression was any indication he didn't want Nate to go.

Once Nate was back in the saddle, he glanced at the pair and saw them energetically preparing to relocate. A jab of his heels started the stallion westward. He pondered the incident as he rode, trying to make sense out of what they had said. There was little to go on. Apparently, though, Brian had a grievance against one of the emigrants. It would have been easy to force the young man to talk, but Nate balked at resorting to violence unless there was a clear and present danger to those under his care.

His best hope lay in mentioning the names of the pair to the pilgrims. The one who knew them might then provide whatever background there was to the affair. Resting the Hawken across his saddle, he rode at a leisurely pace until he came within a mile of the valley. It was then he saw the grizzly.

An immense black shape materialized to the southeast, moving northward. Nate reined up, his scalp prickling, and recognized the bear by its enormous outline and its distinctive shuffling gait. The monster was 70 feet away, at the very limit of his vision in the moonless gloom. Since the wind was blowing from the grizzly to him, it had not yet registered his scent. But the beast must have heard the stallion, so it might charge at an instant's notice.

He fingered the rifle, his eyes glued to the hulking form. Grizzlies were even more unpredictable than buffalo. Primarily nocturnal, they would attack anything that moved if they were hungry enough. And they were exceedingly hard to kill. He'd heard of a case where a grizzly had been shot 12 times, including balls in the head and lungs, yet still it kept coming.

Perhaps because he had ranged so far and wide over the plains and the mountains, it had been his misfortune to run up against more grizzlies than most mountaineers. So far he had always prevailed, but each time he'd barely escaped with his life. Trappers and Indians alike gave grizzlies wide berths, with ample cause.

Measuring over eight feet in length and standing four and a half feet high at the shoulders, grizzlies often weighed upwards of 1500 pounds. They were veritable behemoths, capable of slashing a man to ribbons with a single swipe of one of their huge forepaws. The mighty bears were, in every respect, the lords of their vast domain.

Nate's mouth went dry, his palms became damp, as he watched the bear pass in front of him and continue on. Thankfully, Pegasus stood stock still, not so much as a nostril flaring. The stallion instinctively sensed they were in great danger. Since grizzlies were capable of loping as fast as a horse over short distances, there was no guarantee Pegasus's speed would enable them to escape.

Nate heard the bear grunt a few times. Its ponderous head was close to the ground, perhaps following a scent. When the gigantic shape finally disappeared in the murk, he waited a full minute before goading the stallion forward. A quarter of a mile was covered at a gallop, then he slowed and looked back. There was no trace of pursuit. Nor did he see the campfire on South Pass. Brian and Pudge had done as he'd bid them.

Relaxing, smiling, Nate rode into the valley, passing through the trees and out into the open. The white canvas covering the wagons was a stark contrast to the inky night, and he made a beeline toward them.

Two hundred yards from the camp, Pegasus suddenly halted and gazed to the northwest. Mystified, Nate looked but saw nothing out of the ordinary. He lifted the reins, and was set to lash the stallion when he heard a low whinny. Squinting, he made out the forms of a number of horses heading northwest, and he immediately assumed some of the animals belonging to the pilgrims had strayed off.

Thinking he should catch them before they went too far, Nate angled to intercept the half dozen or so he could see. But he went just a few yards when he spied several figures walking with the horses. Puzzled, he stopped, wondering where Banner and the others could be taking the stock at that time of night. The answer, courtesy of a whispered string of words wafted on the wind, filled him with consternation.

One of those men had spoken in an Indian tongue!

The language was unfamiliar, so the Indians weren't Shoshones, Crows, Nez Perce, Flatheads, or Cheyennes. They might well be Blackfeet, in which case the odds of any of the settlers being alive were slim. But if there had been a fight, why hadn't he heard gunshots? Or had the raiders taken the whites completely by surprise and slit the

throats of all the men before a single rifle could be brought
to bear?

Nate hesitated, tempted to go after the stock but worried
about the pilgrims. Dismounting, he took the reins in his
left hand and hurried toward the freight wagons. The fire
had long since gone out. Now only the embers glowed dully. He halted 20 feet out to study the situation.

From inside the lead wagon rumbled the sound of
someone sawing logs. So at least one of them was still
breathing. Nate let the reins dangle and padded closer.
The wagons were all intact and there were no bodies
lying scattered about. He was almost to the Banner
wagon when he spotted what appeared to be a slender
log to one side. But he knew better. In two strides he
was kneeling beside the limp body of Harry Nesmith.
A hand to the man's throat revealed a slight pulse, and
a swift examination showed a nasty bump and a small
amount of warm blood on the back of Nesmith's head.
One of the Indians must have snuck up on Nesmith and
used a war club or a tomahawk to knock him out.

Nate swiveled, debating whether to awaken the rest of
the emigrants or to go after the stolen horses. The Indians
were still close enough to hear the commotion the pilgrims
were bound to make if he roused them, and he doubted
whether any of the party would be much help in a running
battle. It would be wiser, then, to try and recover the stock
alone before the Indians got much farther away.

He rose and stepped to Pegasus. Scores of yards off,
nearly to the forest, were the thieves and the horses.
Swinging up, he bent down to gather the reins in his hand.
Unexpectedly, the stallion shied.

Onrushing footsteps pounded on the earth.

Nate swept upright, twisting in the direction of
the noise, toward the wagons, and he was just in
time to see a lone warrior hurtle at him from out
of the darkness. His thumb was curling around the

hammer when the warrior leaped with arms outspread, and before he could fire the Indian slammed into him.

They both went down.

Chapter Four

The impact of the warrior's heavy body knocked the Hawken from Nate's fingers. He fell backwards, the Indian on top, a hand clawing at his throat. The dull glint of steel told him what the warrior's other hand was doing, and he barely got his arm up in time to deflect a vicious swipe that would have sliced his throat wide open.

Nate hit hard on his shoulders and rolled, heaving the warrior from him as he did. In a twinkling he was in a crouch and drawing his butcher knife. The Indian lunged and swung but Nate skipped aside and countered. He missed. They silently circled one another. The warrior feinted but Nate didn't take the bait.

Uppermost in Nate's mind was concern that another brave would come at him from behind while he was preoccupied with the man in front of him. It was hard to tell, but he believed the warrior was a Blood or a Piegan, the two tribes allied with the Blackfeet. All three were devoted to the extermination of all whites, so using sign language to try and convince his attacker that he was friendly would be a waste of time and would only get him killed.

The warrior closed and swung again. Nate darted to the right. He felt the man's knife nick his buckskins, and he thrust out, his blade biting into the warrior's side but not going deep. The Indian promptly moved back and hissed like an enraged rattler.

Nate knew the warrior was deliberately holding him at bay long enough for the other Indians to reach cover with the stolen horses. But he must get after them before they got to the trees. Since stealth and silence no longer mattered, he streaked his left hand to the left flintlock. His fingers were wrapping around the pistol when a shrill scream pierced the night.

The Indian involuntarily glanced at the wagons.

In that instant Nate pointed the flintlock and fired, the heavy-caliber gun booming and bucking. Hit squarely in the chest, the warrior was flung onto the ground. Nate didn't linger to confirm the kill. He dashed to Pegasus, wedging the pistol under his belt as he ran, and bellowed, "Indians! They're stealing the stock! Get up and grab your guns!"

The Hawken was lying at the stallion's feet. In a twinkling Nate scooped the rifle up. He swung into the saddle, turned Pegasus to the northwest, and galloped toward the trees. The horses were still in sight, but it was doubtful he could get there before the woods closed around them. Two Indians, one on either side of the stolen animals, were urging the horses on, yipping and yelling now that they knew they had been discovered.

Nate took a chance. He tucked the Hawken to his shoulder and sighted on the center of the Indian on the right. It was the best he could do given the range and the gloom, and he mentally crossed his fingers when he squeezed the trigger. For a second the cloud of gunsmoke obscured the target; then Pegasus swept

46 David Thompson

him onward and he saw the Indian prone on the ground.

The other warrior, the only one to be seen, had broken and was in full flight for the forest.

Without anyone to prod them on, the stolen horses came to a stop. Nate reloaded the Hawken, spilling some of the black powder before he poured enough down the barrel, and had the rifle cocked when he rode up to the one he had shot. A dark stain on the man's chest showed him where the ball had struck. The Indian's eyes were locked wide in death.

Circling around in front of the horses, Nate hunched low over his stallion's neck in case the lone survivor entertained the notion of taking revenge. Nothing moved in the forest. Speaking softly, he got the stock turned around and headed back toward the wagons, where a lantern had been lit and the emigrants were talking in loud, excited tones.

A few things were cleared up to his satisfaction. Now he knew why the Indians had not bothered to go after the sleeping pilgrims in the wagons. There had only been three warriors. Rather than risk someone sounding the alarm and having to face possibly superior numbers and the accurate guns of the white man, the three Indians had concentrated on getting away scot-free with the horses. One of them must have spotted him approaching and snuck up on him.

But not all his questions were answered. Why had there only been three hostiles? The only logical reason upset him tremendously for it meant the Banner party was now in dire peril. But it could have been worse. If he had not returned when he did, the whole bunch would now be stranded and without any hope of getting away.

"Look!" someone shouted. It sounded like Neil Webster.

"It's Mr. King!" This from Alice Banner.

Nate rode up and dismounted. Half of them were clustered around Harry Nesmith, the rest around the slain warrior. "Neil, I want you to take these horses and tie them good and proper to the wagons. We can't afford to lose a single one."

Webster opened his mouth as if to object, then thought better of the idea. "Whatever you say."

Simon Banner, who was on one knee beside the dead Indian and had a lantern upraised in his right hand, looked up. "Is this heathen a Blackfoot?"

"No," Nate said, going over to examine the body. The long hair parted in the middle and swept back at the front, the fringed buckskin shirt painted with symbols, and the style of moccasins confirmed his earlier hunch. "He was a Piegan."

"A what?"

"The Piegans and another tribe called the Bloods are close friends of the Blackfeet. Between them they pretty much control all the land between the upper Missouri and Saskatchewan Rivers."

Simon sighed in relief. "Thank goodness it wasn't the Blackfeet who hit us. None of us would be alive."

"You don't seem to understand," Nate said. "The Piegans and the Bloods are every bit as fierce as the Blackfeet. We're in for the fight of our lives after the one that got away tells the rest and they come after us."

Banner stood. "The rest?"

"We're nowhere near Piegan territory, which means there must be a war party in the area. These three were part of it. They were probably out scouting around when they saw our camp and they couldn't resist trying to steal our horses."

"How large do you think the war party is?"

"I've never known one to have less than ten warriors," Nate replied, gazing at Harry Nesmith. Eleanor, Harry's wife, was applying a damp cloth to his head and he was slowly reviving. The man was either incredibly lucky or had a skull as hard as granite. "Most have more. The biggest Blackfoot war party I ever heard tell of had sixty-nine."

Alice Banner, standing beside her husband, swallowed and fearfully stared at the woodland to the north. "Dear Lord! If there's that many we'll all be killed!"

"Not if I can help it," Nate assured her. He stepped nearer to Eleanor. "How is Harry?"

"He'll live, thank God," she answered, never taking her eyes off her husband. "The dirty cowards hit him from behind! They're worse than animals."

"They do what they have to," Nate said. He saw Libbie next to the wagons, a red shawl draped over her slim shoulders, her features downcast, and went over to offer an encouraging smile. "Are you all right?"

"Just dandy, Mr. King. I heard what you told my pa. How soon before the savages get here?"

"It all depends on how far their camp is from ours. I figure they'll come after us at first light, so they could show up at any time after that."

"Good."

Nate, surprised by the vehement bitterness in her voice, gazed into her eyes. What he saw there shocked him. "How can you be glad? If we get away with our scalps intact it will be a miracle."

Libbie stared at her parents, then said in a strained whisper, "I don't care. I don't care about anything anymore. If I die, so much the better."

"You're talking nonsense."

"Am I?" she retorted. "If you only knew! I deserve to die, Mr. King. It doesn't much matter to me whether I die at the hands of murderous Indians or of a broken heart. But one way or the other, I promise you I won't reach the Oregon Territory alive." With that she spun and climbed up into the Banner wagon.

Nate didn't know what to make of her attitude. Her sincerity was indisputable. But what could have so drastically soured such a young, lovely woman, on life in general and her future in particular? Something awful must have occurred, but for the life of him he couldn't think of what it might be.

"King?"

"Yes?" Nate replied absently, facing Simon, Alice, Neil, and Cora. The Nesmiths were huddled together on the ground.

"I told the others what you said about the war party," Simon declared. "We're all agreed that we should turn around and head back for St. Louis."

"And what about Oregon? What about those who are waiting for you out there?"

"Our lives are more important than reaching the promised land on time. If we head out at dawn, we should be able to reach the prairie well before the heathens show up. And on the prairie we can make better time than here in the mountains. We might be able to outrun the Piegans."

Neil Webster nodded in agreement. "At the very least we'll be able to see them coming. We'll have a better chance of defending ourselves."

"You're wrong on all counts," Nate said flatly. "In the first place, there is no way three heavy wagons can outrun the Piegans. Like the Blackfeet and the Bloods they usually conduct their raids afoot, but they can run all day if they have to and cover three times the territory a white man could in the same amount of time. If they want our hides they'll come after us no matter which way we go."

"Do you have any other objections?" Simon asked testily.

"You bet I do. In the second place, you'd be no safer out on the prairie than you are in the mountains. Piegans can sneak up through tall grass as easily as they can through pine trees, and they'd have your throats slit before you knew they were there."

"Do you have a better idea?" Neal inquired.

"Running scared isn't the answer," Nate told them. "To lick the Piegans, all we have to do is be craftier than they are. We have to outguess them every step of the way."

Alice Banner spoke up. "Do you really believe we can?"

"We have a fair chance," Nate said. "There's one thing you folks have to remember. In some respects Indians regard life as more precious than whites do. They grieve terribly whenever someone dies. Those who lose loved ones may be in mourning for months. Sometimes they chop off a finger or cut off their hair or do something else to themselves to show how much they loved the one who died."

"How barbaric!" Neil interrupted.

Nate ignored him. "They especially don't like to lose a man on a raid. It's bad medicine, the very worst kind of omen, if a war party returns bearing the news that some of the warriors died. The whole village goes into mourning."

"So what are you telling us?" Simon asked impatiently.

"That if we hold fast, if we put up a good fight and maybe kill two or three more of them, they might decide we're bad medicine and leave us alone."

Neil glanced at the dead Piegan. "But they've already lost men. Why would they bother us again?"

"They'll want revenge. And too, if they can take our scalps, if they can go back to their village with a lot of plunder, the loss of a few warriors will be easier to bear. Their people won't view the raid as a total failure." He peered up at the sparkling stars, noting the position of the Big Dipper. By his reckoning there were no more than five hours left until daylight. "If we can convince them that we'll sell our lives dearly and every scalp they try to take will cost them a man or two, they'll change their minds, turn tail, and leave."

"If we agree to go along with you, what do you want us to do?" Simon asked.

"Get set to head out right away."

"You want us to travel at night? Isn't that dangerous?"

"Not if we stick to open ground. I know this neck of the woods well, and I shouldn't have any problem finding a spot where we can make a stand. The important thing is to put a few miles behind us, to buy us some time."

"We'll talk it over," Simon said, and motioned for the others to join him as he moved to one side.

They were like frightened children, Nate reflected, ready to give up at the first grave hardship they ran into. If they were an accurate measure of the hordes of emigrants expected to one day flock to Oregon, then those untold thousands would fare better staying in the States. The frontier was no place for greenhorns, for those lacking courage. They had no idea of what they were getting themselves into. The wilderness was a harsh mistress, demanding the utmost from those who would dwell in her domain, and those who failed to take her seriously paid for their neglect with their lives. For the wild beasts and mankind alike, the unwritten law of the land was brutally simple: the survival of the fittest.

He walked to Pegasus, and happened to notice that Neil Webster had failed to tie up all the horses as he had directed. Maybe Nate was wasting his time trying to save these people. He certainly wasn't appreciated. Men like Simon and Neil thought they knew it all, thought they could do anything and everything without help from anyone else. And they resented being told what to do by someone who knew the realities of life in the wild better than they did.

Nate scratched his chin and stroked the stallion's neck. Perhaps this guiding business wasn't all it had promised to be. Was it worth the price of daily headaches over petty concerns, of having to put up with arrogant greenhorns looking down their noses at him, just so he could earn a few dollars? There were more important things in life than money. A man had his integrity to think of.

He saw Libbie peeking from the wagon and speculated on what could be bothering her. If she was so intent on dying, she might do something to give death a hand. It would be smart to keep an eye on her when possible so he could try and stop her from doing anything foolish. As if he didn't have enough to worry about.

After a minute Simon and the rest came back. The Nesmiths were now with them. Harry was pale and squinted in the bright lantern light.

"We've made up our minds," Simon announced. "We took a vote, and against my better judgment everyone has agreed to follow your lead. Our lives are in your hands."

"They have been ever since I took over from Fraeb," Nate reminded them. It was Isaac Fraeb who had initially agreed to take the emigrants from St. Louis to Fort Hall. And if Fraeb hadn't come down with a stomach sickness out on the Plains, Nate would be in his warm, cozy cabin with his wife and son right that minute. But Fraeb had become too sick to go on much farther despite trying every remedy known to whites and Indians alike. Isaac needed lots of bed rest, which he wouldn't get while acting as nursemaid for the pilgrims. So, gritting his teeth against the pain, Fraeb had ridden to ask the help of the one man he felt could handle the chore, namely Nate. And now Nate almost wished he had declined the offer.

"Do you want us to hook up the teams?" Neil inquired.

"Yes," Nate said. "We're pulling out in ten minutes." He looked at Nesmith. "Are you up to driving a wagon?"

"I'm a bit woozy," Harry said, gingerly touching his head. "And I have dizzy spells that come and go." He put a hand on his wife's shoulder. "But don't worry. Eleanor can handle a wagon as good as I can. We'll keep up with the rest."

"I hope so, for your sakes," Nate said.

The camp transformed into a whirlwind of activity as the men hastened to hook up their horses and the women filled all the water skins. Little was said. They all knew their lives were at risk, that every moment counted.

Nate took the lead, riding close to the Banner wagon. The settlers strung out in single file, a mere ten feet between the rear of each wagon and the lead horses of the next team. He took them out of the valley, then swung to the north, sticking to the open areas where the wagons made better time. They hugged the base of the mountains ringing the great basin they were in, and never strayed far from tracts of forest that would serve as their refuge should the Piegans appear sooner than Nate expected.

Traveling at night was a unique experience. The heavens were spectacular, as if a beautiful tapestry of radiant gems had been woven by divine fingers exclusively for human enjoyment. The sight was enough to take a man's breath away. And the cool breeze was a welcome contrast to the high heat of the day.

Some of the horses balked, being weary from their toils earlier, but a few cracks of a whip convinced them to forge onward. Occasionally wolves howled in the distance, or coyotes voiced their high-pitched yips. Owls, those nocturnal predators more rapacious than eagles, hooted frequently. Twice panthers vented rumbling snarls from near at hand. Every so often a rodent or some other animal would screech as it was caught in the grip of a stealthy prowler. And once, as the wagons passed a ravine, from within arose the unforgettable tremendous roaring of a grizzly. A few of the horses shied and the drivers had to calm them down before the wagons could proceed.

None of the night sounds were new to Nate. He lived with them every night, and knew them all. But he could tell the emigrants were a bit unnerved. Small wonder. It invariably surprised those who lived sheltered lives back in the States, those who conducted all their affairs while the sun was up and retired to their comfortable homes after dark, who lived in regions depleted of game, to learn that the wilderness was completely different. More animals were abroad at night than during the day, and many of them were meat-eaters that ventured out only under the cover of darkness to satisfy their cravings for raw flesh. That was why so few people ever saw panthers, bobcats, lynxes, wolverines, and the like; the animals roamed the land while the people were tucked safely in bed.

Nate held the Hawken handy, the stock resting on his right thigh, his thumb on the hammer, his finger on the trigger. It was rare for any of the big carnivores, other than grizzlies, to attack humans unless they were provoked, but he was taking no chances.

The bloodcurdling screams of the panthers underscored his hunger. Like most mountain men, he rated panther meat as downright delicious. Given a choice between a buffalo steak and a good cut of panther, ten times out of ten the mountaineers would pick the panther. Since he had not had a bite to eat since morning, he would have settled for any hot meal. Instead, he took out several pieces of jerked venison and munched on them.

Toward morning the wind picked up until it was near hurricane force, buffeting the wagons and violently shaking the canvas covers. The men had to wedge their hats down on their heads or lose them, and the women all securely tied their bonnets. Such high winds were common in the region, more so in early spring when warmer weather began to drive out the colder air.

Nate was constantly on the lookout for a suitable place to make their stand. There were plenty of gullies and ravines, but being caught in them would be a certain death warrant. He preferred high ground, somewhere with water and cover. While there were any number of hills and mountains slopes to pick from, none were ideal. There was either no water nearby or they lacked enough cover to suit him. He began to think he was being too fussy, and when the first streaks of pink and orange painted the eastern sky he resolved to find a spot soon no matter what.

Apparently Simon Banner was equally eager to stop, for he called out, "How much farther, King?"

"We'll call a halt before too long," Nate replied.

"I hope so. Our animals are on the verge of exhaustion. If the Piegans do show, we'll be stuck wherever they find us."

Shortly thereafter a ridge on the right drew Nate's attention. A gentle slope to the top was dotted with widely spaced trees, but the pines ended dozens of yards below the rim. Of more interest was what appeared to be a ribbon of water flowing down the west side. "Hold up!" he shouted, lifting his left hand. "I'll be back in a bit."

Pegasus galloped to the ridge and took the slope on the fly. Nate leaned forward to make the going easier for the stallion as its huge hoofs sent clumps of dirt flying to their rear. He made straight for the water and was overjoyed to find a small spring sheltered by boulders just below the crest. From the top he could see for miles in all directions. The opposite slope was charred black, the consequence of a fire triggered by a lightning strike on a gigantic tree that still stood, although the trunk was split down the middle and most of the limbs had been blasted off. With the vegetation burned away, there were few hiding places on the far slope the hostiles could take advantage of.

"This will have to do," Nate said, moving along the rim. The top consisted of an acre of flat ground, more than ample space for parking the wagons. Nodding in satisfaction, he moved to the west side and rose in the saddle to beckon the emigrants to join him. But as he raised his arm, he paused.

To the south, advancing at a determined dogtrot, was a long line of figures.

5656

6

They were too far off for Nate to note details, which weren't important anyway. He knew who they were. He knew the settlers had run out of time.

The Piegans were coming and they would be out for blood.

Chapter Five

Nate counted 14 warriors. He shifted his gaze to the wagons and wildly waved his arm, motioning for the emigrants to head for the hill, but his effort was wasted. The men had climbed down and were conversing next to Webster's wagon. Not one noticed him. And only one of the women, Alice Banner, was in sight. She was idly staring off to the west, admiring the view.

"Damn greenhorns," Nate muttered, putting his heels to the stallion. Pegasus raced down the slope and across the flat. The Piegans were still out of sight to the south but they wouldn't be for long, and once the warriors spied the wagons they would rush forward to attack.

The men turned as he pounded up. Simon Banner was the first to notice the anger on his face. "What's the matter, King? You look like you're fit to be tied."

"Didn't any of you dunderheads think to keep an eye peeled on me?" Nate rejoined. "While you stand here jawing, the Piegans are closing the gap. I saw them from up yonder. We have to get to the top of that ridge just as fast as you can whip your teams."

They needed no further prompting. Dashing to their respective wagons, they hastily climbed up and started urging their teams toward the ridge. Banner was in the lead, as usual, his whip cracking the loudest, his bellowing the harshest.

Nate hung back to cover them. He focused on the point where he figured the war party would appear. Not quite a minute later it did, and as he had foreseen, the Indians bounded through the high grass like panthers rushing hapless prey, their shrill war whoops and bloodcurdling shrieks rending the air.

The wagons had reached the bottom of the ridge and the horses were now toiling up the slope. They strained in their harnesses, their muscles rippling, their backs straight, their heads bowed, as they threw their entire bodies into their work, the heavy wagons making difficult a chore they normally could achieve with ease.

Halting, Nate tucked the Hawken to his shoulder and pointed the heavy barrel at the onrushing Indians. They saw him but, in testimony to their courage, none of them slowed. He sighted on the fleetest of the band, a strapping warrior armed with a war club twice the size most men could wield. Cocking the hammer, he touched his finger to the cool trigger, held his breath, and verified the sights were right where they should be. Then, and only then, he lightly squeezed the trigger.

The Hawken cracked, belched smoke and lead, and the foremost Piegan did a somersault and disappeared in the grass.

Nate's fingers were a blur as he reloaded. First he fed black powder down the barrel. Then, using the ramrod, he shoved a patch and ball down until both were snug against the powder. Finally, he cocked the rifle again and took deliberate aim. This time he was thwarted, however, when the Piegans, to a man, went to ground. One moment they were speeding toward him; the next they were gone, seemingly vanished off the face of the earth.

Grabbing the reins, he goaded Pegasus up the slope, staying behind the last wagon all the way to the top. There, he dismounted and took a position above the spring. Below, the Piegans were fanning out. He caught glimpses of them here and there as they darted from cover to cover. Behind him drummed footsteps.

"What should we do?" Simon Banner asked.

"One of you take the north side, one the east, and one the south. If you get a good shot, try and cut the odds. If not, don't waste powder. And if you see them getting set to rush us, give a yell."

Neil Webster surveyed the barren acre. "I don't much like being hemmed in like this," he commented.

"You can't call this being hemmed in when we can make a run for it any time we want," Nate said. "This high ground gives us the advantage since we can see them before they get too close. And it's easier to shoot downhill than it is uphill."

"I still don't like it," Neil said.

Once they had moved off, Nate eased down among the boulders rimming the spring. He dipped his hand in the cold water and drank his fill, then crawled out to where he enjoyed a bird's-eye view of the whole west slope. A hundred yards off an Indian dashed from one tree to another, too quickly for Nate to snap off a shot.

What would the Piegans do? Nate wondered. They were crafty devils, and they were bound to realize that an assault from all sides at once would cost them too many men. Their best bet, and one they would see in no time, was to make a mass rush up a single side of the ridge, counting on their superior numbers to overwhelm the defenders.

Which side would it be? Nate's brow furrowed as he tried to think like a Piegan. The east slope, where the lightning-spawned fire had burned off the vegetation, was out of the question since the Piegans would be easy targets. Which left three possibilities. The south side, though, was connected to a neighboring mountain by a narrow shoulder with few trees and boulders. On the north the ridge sloped steeply down into a notch. So the best approach was from the west, the very slope Nate was watching.

He figured it would take the Piegans a half hour or better to work out their strategy, and he made himself comfortable. Crossing his arms, he rested his chin on his right wrist. Far to the west several buffalo were grazing. To the southwest soared an eagle. The serene scene belied what was taking place on the ridge.

Minutes passed slowly. He constantly scanned the slope, but saw nothing. His every instinct told him the Piegans were sneaking closer and closer, but for the life of him he couldn't spot them. Grudgingly, he had to admit they were every bit as skillful as the Blackfeet and the Bloods, whom he had fought more times than he cared to recollect.

"Mr. King?"

The softly uttered words startled Nate. He twisted, stunned to see Libbie Banner sliding down toward the spring, a tin cup gripped firmly in her left hand. "Don't—" he began, too late. For a heartbeat later there was a loud buzzing noise and a streaking shaft thudded into the earth within an inch of her left leg. To her credit, she didn't sit there paralyzed with fear. Instead, she scooted among the boulders and crouched low, her breaths coming in great gasps.

Nate checked the slope, saw no hint of the Piegans, and moved back to confront her. "What the blazes are you doing here? Are you trying to get yourself killed?"

"Ma got a fire going and whipped up a batch of coffee," Libbie said, holding out the cup. "She thought you might like some."

Of all the harebrained acts Nate had ever heard of or witnessed, this one took the cake. He was about to tear into her, to give her a piece of his mind for foolishly risking her life over a trifling cup of coffee, but he held his tongue. Both Alice and Libbie had the best of intentions. They probably believed they were helping out, doing what little they could in the crisis. Sighing, he took the cup. "Thanks. Just don't ever do this again. I don't want your death on my conscience."

Her response was unexpected. "Why should you care one way or the other if I live or die? You hardly know me."

"True," Nate admitted after taking a sip. "But I gave my word I'd see all of you folks safely to Fort Hall and I aim to do as I promised."

"I hope you won't be too upset if one of us doesn't make it."

"You?"

Libbie nodded. "As I told you before, I have no inten- tion of reaching the Oregon Territory alive."

"Strange words coming from one so young. You have your whole life ahead of you. Why—"

"Please, don't," Libbie said brusquely. "I've heard all this already from my ma. The last thing I need is another long-winded speech about how I have so much to look for- ward to, and how I should be grateful to be alive."

Nate was surprised to learn that Alice knew how her daughter felt. It seemed to him that a girl would keep such a thing secret. "Does your father know you want to die?" he inquired.

Fleeting rage—or was it hatred?—rippled across Libbie's delicate features. "I would never tell him. He'd tan my hide good if he knew."

"A young lady your age is a bit too old to be spanked," Nate remarked.

"My pa doesn't think so. Until I marry, I'm his to do with as he pleases. And he's a firm believer in applying the rod of correction whenever I misbehave."

"Doesn't your mother object?"

"What Ma wants doesn't matter. In our family Pa rules. Every little thing has to be done just the way he wants or he sees red. If Ma objects, he slaps her around. He never talks things out. He treats us just like he does the horses." She paused. "No, I'm wrong. He treats his horses better than he does us."

"I'm sorry to hear that." Nate swallowed more coffee. "No woman deserves to be treated like property. When a man and a woman disagree, they should sit down and talk things out until they reach some common ground."

Libbie regarded him as she might someone from a foreign country. "Do you practice what you preach?"

"I try, but my wife isn't one for wearing her feelings on her sleeve. She keeps everything to herself, even when she's upset, so I have to pry things out of her. It tries my patience sometimes, I will confess. I'd much rather she'd come right out and speak her piece." Nate grinned. "Nicely, of course. No man can long abide being nagged."

"And you say I'm strange," Libbie said. "My ma told me that you're married to an Indian woman. And I've heard that Indian men treat their women about the same way my pa treats us."

"Not true," Nate said. "The men in different tribes treat their womenfolk differently. I'm an adopted Shoshone, and I can tell you from having lived with them off and on for years that the women in the tribe are always treated with respect."

"I had no idea. Too bad I wasn't born a . . ." Libbie began, and then her gaze strayed past him and her eyes became the size of saucers.

Furious at himself for being so stupidly careless, Nate whirled, sweeping the Hawken up as he turned. Two Piegans were at the boulders, the first in the act of drawing back his arm to hurl a lance. Nate fired from the hip. The ball smacked into the warrior's chest, dropping the man where he stood.

Undaunted, the second Piegan raised a tomahawk and charged, venting a nerve-tingling screech intended to freeze Nate in place.

Nate grabbed for a flintlock. His hand just touched the pistol when the Piegan reached him and the tomahawk arced at his head. Without thinking he threw himself to the right, and in so doing slammed his shoulder into a boulder. Pain coursed through his arm and down his spine. He tried once more to draw the flintlock but his right arm was temporarily numb.

Like a banshee the Piegan pounced.

From out of nowhere came a stream of dark fluid that struck the warrior in the face as he began to swing the tomahawk. Frantically the Piegan wiped his other forearm across his eyes to clear his sight.

That delay saved Nate's life. He drew the other flint-lock, pointed it at the Indian's belly, and fired.

At such close range the ball staggered the warrior, sending him tottering backwards. Gurgling, the Piegan sank to his knees. In a last act of fierce desperation, he raised his tomahawk to throw it, but his strength failed him. His eye-lids fluttered. He growled like an animal, then pitched onto his face in the dirt.

Nate scrambled up into a crouch. A glance at Libbie showed her holding the coffee tin he had dropped when he used the Hawken. Quickly he moved to the last boulder and peeked around it. Another pair of Piegans, evidently discouraged by the deaths of their fellows, were just seeking shelter behind pines lower down. He had a breather, and he used the time to reload his weapons.

The Piegans weren't pressing their attack. Perhaps, Nate reasoned, they had been probing to test the defenses of his small group. He hurriedly finished with the Hawken and began on the flintlock. Slight footfalls to his rear made him look over his shoulder.

"I've never seen anyone killed before," Libbie said weakly. "It's worse than I thought."

"It had to be done," Nate told her. "If I hadn't shot them, they'd now be taking our hair." He nodded at the top of the ridge. "You'd better sneak on back to the wagons. And tell your mother not to pass out any more coffee unless I say otherwise."

Libbie nodded. She glanced at the second Piegan he had slain, at the man's gut wound, and put a hand to her pale brow.

"Can you manage on your own?" Nate asked.

"I'm fine," Libbie said, but her dazed appearance made a mockery of the statement. She steadied herself against a boulder, then took a few steps.

"Hold up," Nate said, going to her side and taking her arm. "I'll escort you back." He disliked leaving his post, but he doubted she could safely scale the few feet of slope between the spring and the rim given her emotional turmoil. To those unaccustomed to the savage realities of frontier life, violent death could be extremely upsetting. Leading her to the boulder nearest the rim, he held her arm tight and suddenly burst from concealment, hauling her along with him.

An arrow whizzed from out of the blue and sank into the soil to their right.

Nate's back prickled until he was up and over and he had dropped flat. Libbie stayed close to him the whole time. Turning, he inched to the edge and peered down at the slope. The Piegans were still in hiding. But for how much longer?

Backing away, he took Libbie's hand and made for the wagons where the women were waiting. They had heard the shots, and all wore expressions of worry. Alice, her dress swirling about her ankles, ran to meet him halfway.

"What happened?"

"Two Piegans tried to jump us," Nate disclosed. "Your daughter is a bit rattled."

"The poor dear," Alice said, putting her arm around Libbie's shoulders. The girl stood docile, as blank as an empty slate. "As if she hasn't been through enough in the past few months." She led Libbie off. "I swear that if we make it to the Oregon Territory alive, I'll make it all up to her."

What did that mean? Nate reflected, and pivoted when Simon Banner and Neil Webster ran up to him. Before they could open their mouths, he tore into them. "Damn your hides! Don't any of you have the common sense God gave a turnip? How could you leave your positions at a time like this?"

"But we heard—" Simon tried to object."

"If the Indians were trying an all-out attack, I would have given a yell for your help," Nate declared. "And if they'd made it past me, you would have heard the women scream. Now you've left two sides undefended." He scanned the top of the ridge. "Where's Harry? At least he had the brains to stay put."

"He's on the north side," Simon said.

Nate looked in that direction, doubt creeping into his mind. Young Harry Nesmith was the hothead of the group, the rash one who always did things without thinking. It was odd that Nesmith should be the only man who hadn't come on the run upon hearing the shots. So odd, in fact, as to spark a disturbing premonition. He broke into a run, angling toward the north end of the ridge.

"What's the matter?" Simon asked.

"King, what's wrong?" Webster added.

Nate saved his breath for running. Shy of the edge he slowed and dropped into a crouch. On silent feet he moved to where he could see the upper portion of the notch and the slope below it. There was no movement, not so much as the flutter of a chipmunk's tail. Nor did he spy Nesmith. Lowering onto his elbows and knees, he carefully worked his way forward until his head poked over the edge. It was then he found the hothead.

Harry Nesmith lay on his back in a pool of blood between two huge boulders at the bottom of the notch. His blank eyes gazed lifelessly at the azure sky. Jutting from his chest were two deeply imbedded arrows.

Racked by guilt, Nate frowned and pulled away from the edge. He hadn't thought much of Nesmith, but he hadn't hated the man either. In any event, his personal feelings didn't really count. What did matter was his failure. He had promised to do his best to get all of the emigrants to Fort Hall, and now he had lost one of them.

Footsteps heralded the arrival of Simon Banner and Neil Webster, who both dropped flat.

"Where's Harry?" Simon inquired. "He should be right around here somewhere."

Nate jerked a thumb at the edge, then moved a few yards before standing and walking toward the wagons. His next chore weighed heavily on his heart. He would much rather face a horde of Blackfeet unarmed than do what had to be done. Eleanor Nesmith and Cora Webster were watching him approach, and he avoided meeting their anxious gazes until he was right in front of them.

"Something's wrong, isn't it?" Eleanor immediately asked. She stared northward. "Where's my Harry? Please don't tell me what I fear you're going to tell me."

Words were unnecessary. Nate merely looked at her, his sorrowful countenance conveying the message he couldn't bring his lips to utter.

"Oh, God!" Eleanor exclaimed, tears flowing from the corners of both eyes. "Dear Lord, no!" She spun, her hands covering her face, her shoulders quaking as she began sobbing uncontrollably.

"I'm sorry," Nate mumbled. Her grief was like a red-hot knife blade searing the core of his being. He felt as if he was directly to blame for the tragedy. Cora Webster put an arm around Eleanor. Overcome with remorse, not knowing what he could possibly say or do that would help, he moved to one side and bowed his head in thought.

He had to suppress his guilt and concentrate on their predicament or more lives would be lost. The Piegans were bound to attack soon. And with one man dead, defending all four sides of the ridge was now impossible.

"Mr. King?"

Nate looked around. Alice Banner was climbing down from the first wagon. "Yes?"

"Are we going to be moving out soon?"

"I don't rightly know yet. Why?"

"Libbie is in no shape to travel," Alice said, walking over. "She's just lying in there in a state of shock. All of this has been too much for her on top of everything else she's been through. She's so young, after all." A loud wail from Eleanor Nesmith caused her to stop and scowl. "I couldn't help but overhear about Harry. If you ask me, now we have two reasons to stay put for a while. Eleanor is in no condition for traveling either."

"We may not have much choice but to leave," Nate said.

"But if we do, who will drive the Nesmiths' wagon? Eleanor is too distraught."

"We'll figure that out in a bit," Nate said, scanning the ridge. The conversation had served to rouse him from his budding melancholy, and he realized he had better stop feeling sorry for what had happened and work to save the lives of the rest of the settlers. At the moment no one was keeping watch; the Piegans could be among them before they knew it. Hefting the Hawken, he ran to the west side and knelt near the rim. Below, a pebble or stone rattled loudly. He removed his hat, then rose up high enough to view the entire slope, and the moment he did a glittering shaft sped from behind a tree and nearly clipped his left ear.

Nate went prone and cocked the Hawken. Since the spring offered ideal protection and was their only source of water, he donned his hat once more and crawled close to the slope. He had to make a dash for the boulders and hope for the best. The Piegans had seen Libbie and him leave the spring, so the warriors might be expecting him or someone else to return. They would have the slope well covered.

Touching his left cheek to the grass, he slid out far enough for a quick glance. What he saw made him recoil in alarm. There were two Piegans at the spring! He glimpsed them crouched behind boulders. Now the Indians had control of the water supply, and any attempt to try and drive them off would result in certain death for some of the emigrants.

He heard a faint noise and risked another look-see. A Piegan was just disappearing behind a tree close to the spring. Others must have worked their way higher in his absence. Twisting, he saw Simon and Neil at the wagons and beckoned for them to hasten over. This time they were paying attention.

"What now?" Banner whispered when they got there.

"Spread out and get set. I have a hunch we're about to have some visitors," Nate said softly.

Neil Webster swallowed. "Shouldn't one of us stay with the women in case the savages make it over the top?"

"The women will have to fend for themselves. We'll be too busy," Nate predicted. As if on cue, a piercing war whoop sounded and was echoed by a dozen throats. He surged to his knees, aware they had run out of time and options, and beheld a ragged line of Piegans sweeping toward the crest. "Here they come!" he cried, wedging the stock of the Hawken against his shoulder. "Give them hell!"

Chapter Six

There were ten Piegans, all told, their painted features animated by the bitter hatred they bore all whites. Shrieking and waving their weapons, they bounded upward like agile mountain sheep. In their frenzied desire to count coup on their mortal enemies they paid no heed to their personal safety.

Nate took a bead on one of the pair rushing out from among the boulders bordering the spring. This time he went for a head shot, and his ball put a new hole smack between the Piegan's brown eyes. Lowering the Hawken, he heard Banner's and Webster's rifles crack as he whipped out a flintlock.

Arrows zipped past or arched overhead. He pointed the pistol at a charging warrior, then fired. The Piegan clasped his side, stumbled, and fell. To the left another Piegan had almost gained the top. Rising and taking four swift strides, Nate jammed the spent flintlock under his belt, grasped the rifle barrel with both hands, and swung the gun like a club.

The stock smashed into the Piegan's temple and the man toppled.

Yet another Piegan, lower down, whirled and ran.

Simon Banner and Neil Webster were embroiled in a life-and-death struggle with three warriors. Banner was using his gun in clublike fashion, holding two warriors at bay. Webster, however, was down, an arrow in his shoulder, grappling with a stocky Piegan who was trying to bash in his skull with a war club.

Nate sped to their aid, drawing his second flintlock en route. Without slowing he aimed at the stocky Piegan astride Webster and sent a ball crashing into the warrior's right ear. Then, discarding both the flintlock and the Hawken, he drew his butcher knife and his tomahawk and closed on the pair striving to slay Banner.

One of the Indians glimpsed him coming and spun to meet him. A war club swept at his face.

Pivoting, Nate blocked the club with his tomahawk and in the very next instant buried his butcher knife in the Piegan's torso. The warrior grunted and buckled, his legs as weak as runny pudding. Taking a breath, Nate threw himself at the third Piegan. The Indian was so intent on killing Simon Banner that he didn't see Nate's tomahawk swing in a loop that ended with the keen edge shearing off the back of his head.

Spattered with gore and blood, Nate faced the slope. To his amazement, their determined resistance had blunted the attack and the surviving Piegans were in full flight. He counted three warriors, one holding a hand to a bloody head.

"Alice!" Simon suddenly shouted.

Nate whirled and was dismayed to discover two Piegans were at the wagons. While most of the war party had kept him and the others busy, those two must have snuck up on the women from another direction. One was wrestling

Alice on the ground, trying to subdue her by pinning her arms. The second warrior had seized Eleanor by the wrist and was attempting to drag her off. Cora Webster stood with her back against her wagon, rigid with overpowering fear.

"Reload your guns!" he yelled at Banner, and sprinted toward the conflict.

The Piegan struggling with Simon's wife looked up and saw him coming. Letting go of Alice, the warrior stood and unslung a bow that hung over his left shoulder. In a smooth, practiced motion the Piegan drew an arrow from a quiver on his back and nocked the shaft to the sinew string.

Nate knew there was no way he could reach the warrior before the Indian loosed that shaft, and he tensed his leg muscles in preparation for throwing himself to one side when the Piegan let it fly. But help came from an unexpected source. Libbie Banner abruptly appeared in the Banner wagon, rising behind the front seat, a pistol clutched in both hands. She trained the gun on the Piegan's back and fired.

Struck between the shoulder blades, the warrior was thrown forward by the force of the ball tearing through his body. He tripped over Alice and fell to his knees, his stunned gaze on the blood-rimmed exit hole in his chest.

In seconds Nate was there. He drove the tomahawk into the Piegan's forehead, splitting the man's brow wide open, and spun toward the warrior trying to haul off Eleanor Nesmith. The Piegan was glaring at him, and when he started toward them the warrior flashed a knife from a hip sheath and plunged the blade into Eleanor's bosom.

"No!" Nate cried. A rifle cracked behind him, but whoever fired missed. The Piegan, smirking in triumph, spun on his heels and ran for the west rim. Nate reached Eleanor's side as she collapsed and he caught her in his arms, staring aghast at the blood streaming from the knife wound. She tilted her head and locked her eyes on his, eyes eloquent with a mute appeal he would remember for the rest of his life.

Eleanor's lips parted. She tried to speak, but all that came out was an agonized groan. Stiffening, she grabbed at his buckskin shirt, her bloodstained fingers smearing red streaks on his chest. Her movements weakened. In desperation she sucked air into her lungs, then frantically attempted to stand. Her legs wouldn't cooperate. Eyes wet with moisture, she glanced again at Nate, mustered a partial smile, and died.

Another shot sounded. Nate looked up to see the last Piegan vanish over the crest. Simon Banner was the one who had fired, and he now trotted to the west rim and shook his fist in the air while calling down the wrath of the Lord on the savages. Nate barely heard the words. He gently lowered Eleanor to the grass, closed her open eyes, and stood.

"Is she dead?" Alice Banner asked, coming up on his right side.

"Afraid so," Nate said ruefully. "First her husband, now her." He refrained from adding that given the way things were going, more of the emigrants might lose their lives before they reached Fort Hall. They'd be lucky if any of them made it.

"We'll have to give them a proper Christian burial."

At any other time and place the innocent statement would have been thoroughly appropriate, but right then and there, on the heels of the frenetic battle they had just been through and with the hostiles likely lurking below, it struck Nate as so ridiculous that he inadvertently laughed and shook his head.

Alice was horrified. "Mr. King! What, sir, can be so humorous at a terrible time such as this? Surely not the deaths of two fine people? Eleanor was a sweet, gentle soul who never wished ill of anyone."

"I'm not making light of Eleanor's passing," Nate said, but before he could offer an explanation both Simon Banner and Neil Webster came up, Webster doubled over with a hand gripping the arrow in his shoulder.

"Oh, no!" Neil said plaintively, staring at Eleanor. "Not both of them! So much for their dream of owning a prosperous farm in the promised land."

Simon hardly gave the body a glance. "What will happen next, King? Have we convinced the savages that they should let us be? You said that if we killed enough of them the heathens would give up."

"I said they *might* leave us alone," Nate corrected him. "Their next move is anyone's guess."

"What do we do then?" Simon snapped. "Stay here and wait for them to make up their minds?"

"No," Nate said, reaching a decision. "We'll leave as soon as you and I plant Eleanor. We dare not expose ourselves trying to get Harry, so I'm afraid his body must be left for the vultures. Alice and Cora will dig the arrow out of Neil."

"You want us to do *what*?" Alice Banner blurted out. She glanced dubiously at the shaft and slowly shook her head. "I don't know as how we can do it. Neither of us have much medical experience, and we've certainly never extracted arrows or bullets. Why, I'm afraid I'd faint halfway through."

Nate suppressed his disappointment. He should have expected as much, given that these were women who had never had to contend with hostiles before. In a way, his own wife had spoiled him. Winona was so marvelously self-reliant that he unconsciously expected all other women to be equally as competent, which wasn't the case. She could do anything and everything essential to life in the wilderness; she could cook, sew, skin game, tend injuries, cure sickness, ride like the wind, and perform a hundred and one other tasks in expert fashion. She could even fight like a wildcat when the occasion demanded. Until that moment, he hadn't quite appreciated how perfect she was for him. "Very well," he said. "I'll take the arrow out myself."

"Thank you," Alice said. "I'll help my husband bury Eleanor."

Neil Webster had to be helped to the fire. Nate got Cora busy boiling water. She had to be shaken a few times to snap her out of the abject fright that had seized her when the Piegans struck, but once she came around she applied herself diligently to the chore. She also climbed into her wagon and brought out several clean cloths to use.

Nate made Neil lie on his right side. Unbuttoning the homespun shirt, which was soaked with blood, Nate drew his butcher knife and cut a straight line from the top button to the shaft. Next, he peeled back the drenched fabric so he could examine the wound. The arrow had transfixed a fleshy part of the inner shoulder, below the collarbone, and gone completely through Webster's body. The barbed tip extended four inches out of the emigrant's back. "You're a lucky man," Nate remarked.

"Lucky?" Neil said, and grunted when Nate touched the arrow. "How do you figure?"

"The tip didn't strike a bone and wedge fast, as some are prone to do. Getting them out is a real chore. More often than not they break off when you try," Nate said, talking to keep Webster's mind off of the impending operation. It would be easier to extract the shaft if the settler was somewhat relaxed. He leaned over to inspect where the arrow had poked out Webster's back. "A friend of mine by the name of Jim Bridger got a couple of arrows in the back once, courtesy of the Blackfeet. One came out easy enough, but the head of the second one was hooked on a bone. So Bridger carried that arrowhead inside of him for three years, until he met up with a surgeon who could take it out." He smiled at Neil. "You're a heap luckier. I'll have this shaft out in no time."

"What will you use?"

"This," Nate said, holding up his knife. Twisting, he thrust the blade into the fire, letting the flames get the steel good and hot.

"Oh, God," Neil whispered.

"You'll do fine," Nate said, hoping he was right. Few jobs were more nerve-racking than trying to remove an arrow from a squealing weakling who wouldn't lay still so the job could be done right. "From the look of things, this arrow didn't have any poison on it."

Neil blanched. "Poison?"

"Yep. Some Indians like to dip their arrowheads in snake venom or stick them into dead animals. One nick can make a man as sick as a dog. Or dead."

"I had no idea."

"Indians can be nasty devils when they want to be, but most of them are as decent as any white men who ever lived," Nate said, gazing at the west rim. Time was of the essence. The Piegans had taken a terrible beating and just might take it into their heads to make another try at killing the emigrants. By all rights he should be keeping an eye out for them, but he was the only one who could remove the arrow. And if it wasn't extracted soon and the wound cauterized, Neil Webster might bleed to death.

When the water was boiling, Nate gave instructions to Cora. She knelt and lifted her husband's head into her lap, then took his hands in hers. Nate dipped a cloth in the water, being careful not to burn himself, and gingerly wiped the skin clean around the arrow, both on the front and the back. Neil flinched but held up otherwise.

"All set?" Nate asked.

"Get it over with."

Working swiftly, Nate snapped the arrow in half several inches below the feathers. Then he moved behind Webster, braced his feet on Webster's hips, and used the tip of his butcher knife to open the exit hole a half inch. Placing the knife down, he gripped the shaft with both hands, bunched his arm and shoulder muscles, and pulled with all his strength. The arrow hardly budged. Again he tried, and this time the shaft slid out an inch. By twisting it back and forth, he was able to loosen the arrow enough to pull it out halfway.

Neil Webster buried his face in his wife's dress but didn't cry out. He did groan repeatedly, and he trembled violently every time the shaft was twisted.

"We're almost there," Nate puffed, applying his sinews once more. He could feel the arrow sliding through the emigrant's flesh as, a fraction of an inch at a time, it slowly came out. Beads of sweat dotted his forehead when at long last he held the slender, dripping shaft in his left hand.

"It's out!" Cora exclaimed, and leaned down to kiss Neil on the temple. "Mr. King did it!"

"We're not done yet," Nate said, casting the arrow to the ground. Retrieving his knife, he held the blade in the flames to reheat the steel. Then he squatted in front of Webster. "You might want to grit your teeth," he advised, and when the emigrant did so, he touched the blade to the hole. There was a hissing noise and the odor of burning flesh assailed his nostrils. Webster stiffened and vented a low sob. Quickly, Nate moved around behind him and cauterized the exit hole as well.

Neil passed out.

"My poor darling," Cora said tenderly, stroking his neck. "He did all right, didn't he?"

"Yes, ma'am," Nate replied, rising. He saw his Hawken and the flintlock he had dropped during the battle lying where they had fallen and went to reclaim them, reloading his other flintlock along the way. A glance to the north revealed Simon and Alice Banner completing a shallow grave for Eleanor Nesmith.

Where was Libbie? In all the excitement, and what with having to operate on Webster, he had forgotten all about her. He looked at the Banner wagon, where he had last seen her, but if she was in there she was lying low. Stopping to bend down and pick up his discarded guns, he glanced to the south, and was amazed to behold Libbie strolling along the rim, a pistol in her right hand.

"What the hell!" Nate declared. He ran toward her, scanning the slope below, afraid one of the Piegans would be unable to resist such a tempting target. "Libbie!" he shouted. "Get away from there!"

She paid no heed and kept on walking.

Furious, Nate covered the distance swiftly, his arms and legs pumping. He jammed the pistol under his belt beside the other one. Libbie heard him as he drew close and started to turn. Grabbing her shoulder, he rudely yanked her back from the edge. "What in the world are you trying to do, girl? Get yourself killed?"

Her face the picture of sweet innocence, Libbie grinned and nodded. "Something like that."

"I don't understand you," Nate said, letting go. "One minute you save my hide, the next you're waltzing around in the open as if you're just asking for the Piegans to turn you into a porcupine."

"No such luck," Libbie said, her grin replaced by a frown.

Exasperated, Nate checked the slope. "I don't know why you're so all-fired set on killing yourself, but I won't let you do it. Not so long as I'm the guide of this outfit."

"You can't stop me."

"I'll do whatever it takes. If need be, I'll have your father tie you up until we reach Fort Hall."

"Pa would never do a thing like that."

"If he loves you, he will."

Libbie's next words were barely audible. "There are different kinds of love, Mr. King. Some are good. Some are bad. My pa would never tie me up because he doesn't care whether I keep on breathing or not. To him I'm vermin."

"You're talking nonsense, girl. All decent parents love their children."

"Not quite true. All decent parents love *decent* children. And I don't happen to qualify."

"What—?" Nate said, but she had turned and was trotting to the wagons. Utterly confused, he availed himself of the momentary free time to load the Hawken and his other pistol. To his relief, the Piegans appeared to have gone. At least he didn't spot any.

The surviving emigrants were gathered at the fire when Nate returned. They looked expectantly at him, every face betraying anxiety except for Libbie's. She was too downcast to care about their dilemma.

"We have two choices," Nate began. "We can stick it out here until we're positive the Piegans have left, or we can hightail it now, before they think to regroup and try again."

"I say we depart immediately," Simon stated. "But what do we do about the Nesmith wagon? Simply leave it for the heathens to plunder?"

"No," Nate said. "I suppose we should take it with us to Fort Hall. From there we can arrange for a letter to be sent." He stared at each of them. "That is, if Harry or Eleanor ever mentioned their kin to you."

"A brother of Harry's lives in New Jersey," Simon said. "At Trenton, I believe."

Neil, who sported a fresh bandage and was holding his left arm tucked to his side, faced the Nesmith wagon. "Wanting to do the right thing is all well and good, but who is going to drive this thing? I can't, and Simon will be busy with his own wagon."

"I will," Nate offered. "We cut out in five minutes."
He walked to Pegasus and brought the stallion over,
then used a length of rope to tie the animal to the rear
axle. A peek over the back loading gate revealed that
the Nesmiths had brought everything they would need
to start their new life in the Oregon Territory, and then
some. A chest of drawers, a stove, and a plow were
among the heavier items packed on the bottom of the
wagon bed. On top had gone cooking utensils, clothes,
flour, salt, a water keg, blankets, an ax, and much more,
all packed neatly and strapped down to prevent slippage
on the trail. He was inclined to toss out the plow and a
few other big items to make the wagon lighter, but there
wasn't time. The Piegans might surge over the crest at any
second.

He climbed on the wagon, leaned the Hawken beside
him on the seat, snatched up the traces, and released the
brake. Turning to see how the emigrants were faring, he
found all of them ready to go. Cora Webster was waiting
expectantly for the word to be given, her wounded husband, his face as pale as a sheet, next to her.

"I'll go first," Nate announced. "Stay close. If the
Piegans try to stop us, put your whip to your team and
make for the flatland. If they press us, try to discourage
them with a few shots."

"We know what to do," Simon Banner growled. "Let's
get on with it, shall we?"

Nate urged his team into motion and slanted to the west
slope. His experience with wagons was limited, and he
hoped he wouldn't make a mistake that would cause the
Nesmith wagon to flip over on the way down. He knew
enough to keep it pointed straight at the base of the ridge
and to be ready to use the brake lever should the speed
become too great. But the seasoned horses knew their
business and brought him safely to the bottom without
mishap.

The Piegans were nowhere in evidence. He suspected the war party had fled into dense forest to the south, which was the nearest heavy cover, and he scoured the woods time and again but saw no one. Once in the high grass he cracked the whip a few times and headed due west. In two hours they would come on a stream where he intended to call a halt.

Not having slept for so long, and being hungry enough to devour an entire bull elk at one sitting, he found himself becoming drowsy after going a mile. From then on he had to struggle to stay awake, but it was a lost cause. The rolling movement of the wagon lulled him into a dreamy, tranquil state. His eyelids became leaden with fatigue. He dozed off, snapped awake when the wheels hit a rut, then dozed off again. He was on the verge of slipping into a deep slumber when Pegasus whinnied.

A man living in the wild learned to rely on his horse for early warnings of danger. With its keen hearing and scent, a horse was almost as dependable as a trained watchdog. Those mountain men who lived the longest were those who early on learned to sit up and take notice when their trusted animals neighed in alarm.

Nate intended to enjoy a long life. So when Pegasus whinnied, his head shot up and he shifted in his seat to gaze at the stallion, which was in turn gazing off to the southeast. Leaning to his left, past the canvas top, he scoured the stretch of open prairie on that side and to their rear. He could still see the ridge and the mountain chain of which it was a part. Other than a flock of sparrows winging their way to the north, all was still. Whatever had pricked the stallion's interest was either hiding in the grass or else too far off to be seen. But not too far off to be smelled, since a sluggish breeze was blowing from the southeast.

He shook his head to dispel tendrils of weariness plucking at his brain. There was a chance the Piegans were dogging the wagons, waiting for another opportunity to strike so they could take their revenge. It pained him to think that a guard would have to be posted when the wagons arrived at the stream because he knew who would have to stand the first watch.

Facing around, Nate cracked the whip. And saw the leading edge of a storm front sweeping in from the west.

Chapter Seven

The roiling black and gray clouds unleashed their full elemental fury minutes after Nate and the emigrants reached a thin strip of trees bordering the east side of the gurgling stream. He had pushed the weary teams as hard as he dared in the hope of reaching shelter, all the while watching the swirling mass overhead as the sun was blotted out and the blue sky was transformed into a crackling cauldron that had threatened to explode in a deluge at any moment.

When the rain came, it came in great driving sheets, mercilessly pounding the canvas covers and the exhausted horses. Lightning flashed on all sides. Thunder boomed, seemingly shaking the very ground.

Nate didn't bother to unhitch his team for the time being. They were better off right where they were instead of being tied to nearby limbs or brush since they couldn't bolt while in harness. If lightning struck close to the wagon, the worst they could do was shy and prance in fright. If they were tied to trees, they might panic, tear the rope loose, and flee. Then he would have to spend hours rounding them up. And too, he didn't relish the thought of being soaked to the skin.

So he grabbed the Hawken and climbed under the wagon top to wait out the storm. Made of hemp and water-proofed with linseed oil, the canvas cover kept out most of the rain. There was a drawstring at the bottom for closing the opening, and he promptly did so. Now only a few drops spattered in now and then.

Nate worked his way to the rear. Outside, high winds shrieked past, violently shaking the canvas. He looked out and found Pegasus standing flush with the wagon. Water ran from the stallion's mane and tail. It also ran down both sides of his saddle, which he had neglected to strip off.

"Of all the stupid . . ." Nate muttered, and set the Hawken down. Bracing himself, he swung over the loading gate and hurriedly removed the saddle and his gear, placing everything in the wagon. By the time he climbed back in, he was dripping wet.

The emigrants were all in their wagons. He saw Libbie peering out and waved, but she made no response. Drawing the rear string so that both ends of the canvas were now sealed off from Nature's fury, he settled down on a bundle of blankets and rested his head on a soft pillow. A few minutes of peace and quiet would be nice, he reflected, and began to plot the course they would take once the weather cooperated. But total exhaustion engulfed him.

Almost immediately he fell asleep.

A tremendous crash of thunder abruptly awakened him. Nate sat up, blinking in surprise, unsure of where he was or what he had been doing. His mind felt sluggish, his body sore. Shaking his head, he pushed to his knees. One look at the possessions piled high around him sparked his memory and he recalled everything. How long had he slept? he wondered. And why was it so much darker than it had been when he drifted off?

Nate moved to the back and loosened the draw string. The storm still raged, although with diminished intensity. Gloomy twilight blanketed the landscape, and he realized night was not far off. He had slept for hours! Annoyed, he glanced at the other wagons. Both were lit from within by lanterns, and vague shadowy silhouettes played across the canvas tops whenever someone moved. The emigrants were warm and cozy, which was more than could be said for him. His buckskins were still wet, his skin damp, and he shivered when a gust of wind struck him.

Locating a lantern, he lit it. Next he stripped off his buckskins and wrung them out. Hanging them up to dry took but moments, and then he wrapped himself in a blanket and squatted next to the lantern, which gave off considerable heat as well as light. In minutes he was comfortably warm.

His growling stomach prompted a search for food. Eleanor Nesmith had packed enough jerked meat and other foodstuffs to feed an army. Included were a half-dozen biscuits she had baked two days ago. He hesitated before taking a bite, thinking of that young, vibrant woman who had been so full of life when she baked the biscuits and who was now feeding the worms. Such was life. People never knew from one minute to the next when the Grim Reaper would claim them, so it made sense to live each moment to the fullest. What would be, would be, and no amount of fretting about it ever extended anyone's life a single second.

He greedily devoured the biscuits. Jerky rounded out his meal, and he washed it all down with gulps of cool water. Coffee would have been preferable, but building a fire would have to wait until the downpour ended.

Nate resigned himself to staying by the stream until morning. In a way, the storm had turned out to be a blessing in disguise. A night's rest would do wonders for all of them, especially the horses. Which reminded him. Reluctantly, he donned his damp buckskins and went out.

The rain had slackened to a drizzle, the wind had died to a whisper. Taking Pegasus first, he tethered the stallion close to the stream where both water and grass were readily available. Working rapidly, he unhitched the entire team and took all of them over. Then he walked to the Banner wagon, but discovered that Simon had already taken care of those animals. The Webster horses were still hitched, though, so he tended to them. Before going back to his wagon, he stepped up to the Webster's and called softly, "How are you doing in there?"

Cora appeared, her features downcast. "Neil has a fever, Mr. King. He's resting right now, bundled up so he'll stay warm. But I'm worried about infection setting in."

"Don't be. I cauterized the wound good and proper," Nate said. "A fever is common in cases like this. By morning it should break and your husband will be fine."

"I hope so."

Nate touched a hand to his hat and went back. As he passed the Banner wagon, a gruff voice hailed him.

"King! So you're the one I heard. I take it we're staying put for the night?"

"We are."

"How's Neil faring?" Simon asked.

"He'll pull through."

Banner twisted his head to survey the darkening sky. "What are the odds the Piegans will come after us?"

"I'd say they're pretty slim. The storm wiped out our tracks, so unless they were close behind us when it hit, they have no idea where we are," Nate said.

"Good riddance, I say," Simon declared. "I take it we'll leave at dawn?"

"We will," Nate confirmed.

"Good. Let's pray we don't run into any more hostiles." Banner looked to the right and the left, then shrugged and closed the canvas.

What was that all about? Nate reflected, stepping to his wagon and climbing up. As his leg slid over the top he saw a huddled figure in the corner. The lantern light glistened off her golden tresses and revealed the earnest expression she bestowed on him.

"Please, Mr. King, come in. I need to talk to you."

Puzzled, Nate sat down opposite her. "Do your folks know you're here?"

"No. Pa thinks I'm answering nature's call," Libbie said, and grinned at some private joke. "He won't expect me back for five minutes or so, which is plenty of time."

"For what?"

"For getting your opinion on something," Libbie replied, resting her elbows on her knees and her chin in her hands. "I've come to respect you. You're not the uncouth lout my pa thinks you are."

"He said that?"

"Not in so many words, but I can tell how he feels. He's not very pleased at having you be our guide. He thinks you're too young, that you don't know what you're doing. And he blames you for the loss of Harry and Eleanor. He told my ma that we had better watch you like a hawk from here on out to make certain you don't make any more mistakes."

To hide his anger, Nate bowed his head.

"But I figure he's wrong," Libbie went on. "My pa makes a habit of misjudging people, so don't be upset. I can tell that you're a man who knows what he's about. Everything you've told us so far has turned out to be right. And you know these mountains like I know the back of my hand." She paused. "It wasn't your fault the Piegans found us. Those things happen."

Nate waited for her to get to the point of her visit. He hoped it would shed some light on her strange behavior, on why she was so eager to die.

"Mr. King, how do you feel about killing?"

"In what way?" Nate asked, recalling the Piegan she had shot to save his life. Was that what this was about?

"In every way."

He leaned back and took off his hat. "When I first came out here from New York City, I was shocked by it. Indians kill whites. Whites kill Indians. Both kill animals. Animals kill other animals. So much killing was hard to take until I came to see that it's part of Nature's way." He put the hat down. "If a panther wants to live, it eats deer or whatever else it can catch. If an owl gets hungry, it eats a rabbit. If an Indian wants to count many coup and be considered a great man in his tribe, he has to go out and kill his enemies. It's all part of life in the wilderness."

"So you don't mind having to kill?"

"Not when there's a reason. I have to eat, like everyone else. So does my family. And as a husband and a father I have a duty to protect my wife, my son, and my own hide the best I'm able," Nate said. He patted the hilt of his butcher knife. "Out here, Libbie, only the strong survive. It sounds harsh, but that's the way of the world."

"How many men have you killed?"

"I haven't counted them."

"Ever killed white men?"

"A few," Nate admitted.

"And it doesn't bother you? You don't feel guilt? You don't feel as if you've committed a sin?"

For a young girl, she was posing difficult questions. Nate toyed with the fringe on his pant leg before answering. "I've thought about all that. Many times. I know the Bible says, 'Thou shalt not kill,' but look at Samson and David. They were both mighty warriors and they killed time and again. Yet they were close to God." He sighed. "Have I sinned by killing others who were trying to kill me? Maybe. I don't rightly know. But I do know I wouldn't be here today if I'd let them kill *me*."

"Have you ever killed a child?"

Shocked, Nate glanced at her. "Heavens, no! Shooting a hostile out for my hair is one thing. Murdering children is another."

"Would you if you had to?"

"No."

"How can you be so sure?"

There was something about her tone that gave Nate pause. She had leaned forward and her eyes were boring into him as if she was trying to see into the depths of his soul. "I can't think of any reason for killing a child," he said slowly. "Even the Blackfeet don't do it. They adopt young ones into their tribe."

Libbie started to speak, but a shout outside made her straighten and gaze anxiously at the darkness that had claimed the countryside.

"Daughter? Where are you? Your supper is getting cold!"

"I have to go," Libbie said urgently. She scooted to the front of the wagon, then hesitated. "Thanks for taking the time to hear me out. Maybe we'll talk again sometime."

"Whenever you want," Nate said, and watched her step onto the seat. Her legs coiled and she jumped from sight. He heard her clear her throat as she walked toward her wagon.

"Here I come, Pa! Sorry."

Peering over the loading gate, Nate saw Simon Banner waiting for her. Simon offered his hand, but she refused to take it and climbed up on her own. Perplexed, Nate tied the canvas and pondered. Why had she been so intensely interested in the killing of children? Had a younger brother or sister died some time ago and she was trying to come to

grips with her grief? He wished they had not been interrupted so he could have gotten to the bottom of the mystery.

Another meal caused his drowsiness to return. He
rearranged some of the Nesmiths' belongings so he had
a flat space to stretch out, then spread the blankets and lay
on his back. The rain had almost stopped. Far to the east
thunder rumbled. He imagined that it must be raining on
Harry Nesmith at that very minute, and regretted they had
not had the time to bury the man beside his wife.

Presently he turned off the lantern, covered himself
with two heavy blankets, closed his eyes, and drifted into
a pleasant sleep.

Years of living in the wild had turned him into an early
riser. There were only so many hours in a day, and if a
man wanted to accomplish a lot he had to take advantage of
daylight while it lasted. Thus it was that the faintest of pale
tinges touched the eastern sky when Nate opened his eyes
and stretched. The long rest had completely rejuvenated
him. He jumped up, refreshed and eager to commence the
day's work.

His buckskins were not quite fully dry, but they would
be once he got outside and moved around. He dressed,
aligned his weapons as they should be, snatched up the
Hawken, and ventured out to check on the stock. All the
horses were accounted for, right where they should be. He
patted the stallion, then roamed among the trees in search
of dry timber for a fire. It took some doing, but he soon had
a blaze going.

The other wagons were still dark and silent. He moved
quietly so as not to awaken them. After all the emigrants
had been through, they deserved some extra rest. Taking
a coffeepot and coffee from the Nesmith larder, he treated
himself to a hot tin cup of the brew, adding a handful of
sugar for sweetening. Sugar was a rare commodity in the

mountains because the Indians never used it and the trappers could rarely afford it.

Gradually the world came alive. The horses moved to
the stream to drink. Birds chirped in the trees, sparrows,
chickadees, and jays all vying for the honor of the loudest
singers. Ravens flapped overhead. A rabbit hopped into
the open near the stream, but bounded off when one of the
horses snorted.

Nate sipped his delicious coffee, warmed himself by the
fire, and thought of how different life was in the mountains compared to the hectic existence of those who lived
in the States. Here a man could take time to smell the roses,
as Shakespeare McNair liked to say. He could relax and
enjoy the natural wonders all around him. There was no
one looking over his shoulder all the time, no one goading
him to work harder or faster as had been the case when
Nate worked as an aspiring accountant in New York City.

Here a man could take what life had to offer at his
own pace, a luxury for those burdened souls back East
who were constantly working more and more hours
to make more and more money so they could have
more and more things. His own father had been a
case in point, laboring ungodly long hours six days
a week so the family would prosper in a modest
way. To think that he had once wanted to follow in
his father's footsteps! Thank goodness his Uncle Zeke
had invited him to come West, where he had discovered that there was more to life than making money—
much more.

He finished his first cup of coffee, poured another. The
horses were grazing. On the other side of the stream a doe
stepped into the open, saw the horses, and ran off before he
could grab the Hawken and fire. He heard a rustling sound
behind him and pivoted on his heels.

Simon Banner, his hair disheveled, his expression that
of a man not quite fully awake, was emerging. He gazed

all around, then came toward the fire, scratching himself in various spots.

"Hello, King," he mumbled.

"Ready for a new day?" Nate asked.

"As ready as I'll ever be." Simon surveyed the trees. "Have you seen my daughter anywhere?"

"No."

"Where the hell has she gotten to this time?" Simon groused, and continued to the stream, where he knelt and splashed water on his face and ran his thick fingers through his hair.

Nate scanned the trees himself. With all of Libbie's crazy talk about wanting to die, he was concerned she might have taken her own life or simply wandered off to let Nature take its course. Then again, she might be tending to personal business. He swirled the coffee and downed the rest in large gulps.

"Still no sign of her?" Simon asked, returning from his ablution.

"Not yet."

"I swear that girl gets more contrary every day. Comes from having a sinful nature."

"Libbie?"

Simon nodded knowingly. "She seems all sugar and spice, but deep down that girl has a wicked streak a mile wide. Satan tempted her and she took the bait."

"I can't believe she's as wicked as you claim."

"That's because you don't know her like I do. You see the outside of a cup and think the inside is clean when it's not." Simon extended his hands close to the crackling flames. "I never thought I'd be saying this about my own flesh and blood; but Libbie is Satan's tool. If she would repent I could forgive her, but she won't."

Nate couldn't resist asking, "Is that why she's bitter toward you?"

"You've noticed? Ah, well, I should have expected as much," Simon said. "Yes, the girl despises me, and all because I try to live my life according to the Good Book. I'm stern, I know, but it's only to keep her on the straight and narrow. I don't want her to end her days in Hell."

"I doubt she will," Nate said to be cordial. "She has a good head on her shoulders. Eventually she'll marry a law-abiding man and raise you a passel of grandchildren to be proud of."

Surprisingly, Simon Banner turned beet red. "Maybe. But I doubt any God-fearing man will have her after what she's done."

"What did she do?"

Ignoring the question, Banner rubbed his hands together and turned away. "Now where in tarnation is that child?" He moved toward his wagon and shouted, "Libbie! Libbie, where are you?"

The yells were bound to awaken the others. About to chide Banner for being so inconsiderate, Nate changed his mind. It would soon be time to head out. He wanted to put as much distance behind them as possible before sunset. Not until then would he feel completely confident they had eluded the remaining Piegans.

"Libbie! Answer me!"

Nate stood and took the tin cup to his wagon. Placing it inside, he put a hand on his saddle, and was starting to lift it when a sharp cry rent the air.

"King! Come here, quick!"

Cradling the Hawken, Nate trotted to where Simon Banner was squatting well beyond the wagons, almost at the edge of the grass. "What did you find?"

"Take a look. Then you tell me."

The tracks were as plain as the nose on Nate's face, clearly embedded in the saturated soil. Four horses, two heavily laden judging by the depth of the hoofprints, had ridden up close to the camp from the east and a man had dismounted. Whoever it was had then approached the wagons but stopped ten feet off. Another set of footprints, smaller and dainty, undoubtedly those of a young woman, ran in a straight line from the Banner wagon to where the man had stood. Together the pair had stepped to the man's horse and mounted, and all the horses had made off to the southeast.

"Does this mean what I think it does? My daughter went with these strangers?"

Suddenly Nate remembered his encounter with the two greenhorns named Brian and Pudge at South Pass. In all the excitement of battling the Piegans, he had forgotten about them. But he would wager a year's catch of prime beaver pelts that the tracks in front of him were left by the pair and their animals.

The shouts had drawn the rest of the emigrants. Alice had a green shawl wrapped around her shoulders. Neil Webster was pale but held himself erect, Cora supporting him with an arm around his waist.

"Libbie has been kidnapped!" Alice now declared in stark horror. "Did the savages take her?"

"No, these were shod horses. Even I can see that," Simon answered, and glanced up at Nate. "Say, you never did tell us who had that fire going on the top of South Pass. Could they be the ones who took our girl?"

"There were two of them," Nate said. "Called themselves Brian and Pudge."

"Oh, God!" Alice wailed. "Not him!"

Glowering in unbridled rage, Simon rose and shook a fist at Nate. "Why didn't you tell us about them sooner? Do you have any idea what you've done, you fool?"

"If you'll recall," Nate said, keeping his temper with a monumental effort, "the minute I got back to camp, I had to stop some of the Piegans from stealing your stock. From then on we were kept busy just staying alive." He shrugged. "I forgot about Brian and Pudge."

"Of all the dunderheads who ever lived, you take the cake!" Simon practically roared. "Now, thanks to you, our daughter has been taken by those degenerates." Taking a step, he drew back his fist. "I should thrash you within an inch of your life."

And with that, Simon swung.

Chapter Eight

Nate exploded, releasing his pent-up feelings in a burst of fiery indignation. For days the emigrant leader had treated him as less than dirt, insulting him, mocking him, taunting him, and he had tolerated all he was going to stand. He blocked Simon's swing with the Hawken barrel, then rammed his right fist into Simon's mouth. Banner's lips split wide and the emigrant staggered. Unrelenting, Nate stepped in and landed a blow on Simon's cheek, then buried his fist in Simon's stomach.

"Stop it!" Alice screamed. "Please!"

Not in any mood to slack off, Nate delivered a sweeping punch to the chin that straightened Banner like a board. Slowly Simon crumpled into a limp heap, blood dribbling from his smashed mouth.

"How could you?" Alice yelled at Nate. She knelt beside her husband and tenderly took Simon's head in her hands. "Look at what you've done to him! And I thought you were a decent man!"

"I suppose you'd be happier if he had pounded me to a pulp?" Nate responded in disgust. Hefting the Hawken, he whirled and went to the horses. It would be a cold day in Hell, he mentally vowed, before he took a job as a guide again. Easterners had no respect for anyone but themselves, a fact he should have remembered form his years in New York. He led Pegasus to the back of the Nesmith wagon, leaned his rifle against a wheel, and hurriedly saddled up. After filling a parfleche with jerky, he rolled it in a blanket and tied both behind his saddle. As he gripped the reins to mount, he heard footsteps.

"Where are you going?" Neil Webster asked.

Nate swung up, then leaned down to scoop up the Hawken. "Where do you think?" he rejoined. "Someone has to fetch the girl back."

Cora exhaled in relief. "We were afraid you were leaving us to fend for ourselves." She forced a smile. "Not that we'd blame you after the way some of us have been treating you."

"I took the job of escorting all of you to Fort Hall, and that's what I aim to do," Nate said. He nodded at the Banners. "Do what you can to calm them down. And make damn sure that none of you try to follow me. I should be back by dark, but if I'm not, don't fret."

"Take care of yourself," Neil offered.

"Always," Nate replied, touching his heels to the stallion. Was their concern genuine, or were they only worried about what would happen to them if he failed to come back? He rode past the Banners and Alice turned spite-filled eyes on him, but she made no comment. Simon still lay unconscious.

Angling to the southeast, Nate stuck to the fresh tracks. His blood still raced, his temples pounded, and he was glad to be on the go again, to be doing something that would take his mind off the emigrants. Being away from them for a spell was just what he needed.

He stared at the tracks, concentrating on the task at hand. Brian and Pudge must have reached the stream in the wee hours of the morning, well after the rain had ended, since there was no water in any of the hoofprints, so they couldn't have more than a two-or three-hour lead. Burdened as they were with two pack animals, and with one of them riding double with Libbie, they should be easy to overtake.

Pegasus enjoyed being given free rein, and ate up the distance at a steady trot. Other than a few antelope and a solitary hawk, nothing else moved in the great basin between the Wind River Range and the Salt River Range.

The golden sun cleared the eastern horizon, bathing the landscape with warmth and light.

Nate speculated on the connection between Libbie Banner and the two men she was with. From the tracks, he gathered she has gone with them willingly and not been kidnapped as her parents claimed. There had been no evidence of a struggle, no sign of scuffed, distorted footprints as there would have been had Libbie put up a fight. Nor had she bothered to call out. So she must know one or both of them.

An hour out from the camp he was disturbed to find that Brian and Pudge had changed direction. Now they were going due east. Why? Doing so would take them into the Wind River Range, where the Piegans were most active. Worse, if they continued on the way they were going, they would soon be near the very ridge where the emigrants had fought the war party. Should the surviving warriors still be in the area, the three whites would be in grave jeopardy.

He brought the stallion to a gallop and pressed on until the range appeared. Then he slowed to give Pegasus a brief rest, fastening his gaze on the point far ahead where the tracks blended into the grass in the hope of spotting the four horses and their riders.

The ridge became visible, half a mile to the north. He rode faster, the Hawken resting on his thighs, one hand on the rifle with his thumb on the hammer. Perhaps Brian and Pudge, knowing that someone would come after them, were heading for the forest covering the high slopes with the intention of losing themselves in the dense trees.

The trail brought him to the base of a foothill fronting a majestic peak covered with glistening snow. He stopped to scour the pines and boulders above. Suddenly he caught the unmistakable scent of smoke and spied a thin gray tendril wafting skyward halfway up the hill. They had stopped and made camp!

Grinning, Nate moved toward the spot. He would have Libbie back with her folks by mid-afternoon. Bending low, he passed under a thick limb, then went around a cluster of boulders. Of its own accord the stallion halted and tossed its head from side to side while uttering a low whinny.

Something was wrong.

Nate climbed down, tied the reins to a bush, and stalked upward. A clearing came into sight. In the center was the fire, or the embers of one, glowing red and giving off the smoke that had caught his eye. Not a living soul could be seen, nor were the horses anywhere nearby. Had they spotted him and left? he wondered, creeping nearer. Or had they only stopped for a short while, just long enough to grab a bite to eat, and then gone on?

Disappointed, he made a partial circuit of the clearing before he ventured into the open. In the soft earth at the base of a tree he discovered a moccasin print, and in the clearing itself, not a yard from the fire, was a puddle of moist blood. His worst fear had come true.

A thorough search revealed that four Piegans had surrounded the camp, then pounced at an opportune moment. One of the whites, Pudge by the footprints, had gone down almost immediately, but Brian had resisted mightily before being overpowered. The Piegans would have struck so fast that it was doubtful either of them had managed to get off a shot.

He found where the Piegans had headed to the north-east, leading the horses. Evidently Libbie was mounted, but the two men had been compelled to walk behind the animals with a Piegan trailing and probably covering them with a gun or a bow. Drops of blood confirmed that one of them was wounded. If he had to guess, he would say it was Brian.

Sprinting to Pegasus, Nate mounted and rode in pursuit. He was an hour behind the war party at the most, and on horseback he should come on them before noon. Heedless of the limbs that tugged at his clothing and scratched his face, he held the stallion to a brisk clip.

He felt reasonably certain the Piegans wouldn't slay their captives right off. The whites would be taken to the Piegan village, where the men would be tortured before being killed and Libbie would in all likelihood find herself the unwilling mate of a prominent warrior, unless the Blackfeet women got their hands on her first.

It had taken Nate a long time to come to terms with the Indian way of measuring manhood and gauging courage in their enemies. Torture was the preferred means. Mutilation of captives was widespread, not due to a depraved desire to inflict suffering but as a means of putting a captive to the supreme test. If an enemy held up stoically under the worst treatment conceivable, then that enemy was regarded as truly brave and a credit to his tribe and would be put out of his misery quickly. But if a captured foe whined and pleaded and groveled, then he was mocked and scorned and allowed to linger in the most intense agony for as long as he endured the ordeal.

Not all tribes resorted to the barbaric practice. The Shoshones, Nate's adopted people, were less prone to mutilation than most of the surrounding tribes, but they would unhesitatingly torture any Blackfeet, Bloods, or Piegans they caught. With perfect justification, because those three tribes were the very worst offenders of all the Indians living in the northern Rockies and Plains. Shoshones who fell into their hands knew exactly what horrors to expect, which explained why the Shoshones as a people were utterly merciless toward those three tribes.

The tracks took Nate up and over the hill, down into a ribbon of a valley, and then toward rugged mountains. Occasionally he came on more drops of blood, but they were fewer and farther between. Which was a good sign. If whoever had been wounded collapsed and was unable to go on, the Piegans would dispatch him then and there after testing his manhood in some diabolically gruesome manner.

At the base of a towering peak the trail turned north-ward. Nate was thankful for the recent storm. The rain-saturated soil bore clear prints, so tracking was a simple chore.

A mile further on the Piegans had turned to the north-east again, passing between two mountains on a well-used game trail. Indians knew that animals invariably followed the path of least resistance when traveling, making game trails ideal avenues for crossing rough terrain. The trappers had readily learned the same thing, and experienced mountaineers relied heavily on such trails when exploring new country.

There was another reason for the practice. Often game trails led to water, and water was precious to man and beast alike. Nothing lasted long without it. The man who stuck to a deer or elk trail could be confident that somewhere along the way there would be good drinking water.

Nate saw elk, deer, and mountain sheep tracks as he rode. There were also prints of smaller animals, such as rabbits, skunks, and porcupines. Mixed in with the tracks of the plant-eaters were the distinctive paw prints of panthers and bobcats. Because of the great number, he figured there was a lake or a river ahead.

His hunch proved correct.

Beyond the mountains unfolded a virgin valley lush with spruce, fir, and aspen trees. Dominating the center of the valley was a shimmering blue lake, toward which the game trail meandered through the underbrush. A carpet of pine needles muffled the thud of the stallion's hoofs.

Nate rode cautiously, his sixth sense telling him the Piegans were not far off. As he drew near the lake he heard gruff voices speaking in an Indian tongue he did not know. Halting, he slid down and worked his way along until he could see the lake and the shore clearly. There he found those he was after.

Three of the four Piegans were standing near the water, talking. The fourth, armed with a rifle taken from Brian or Pudge, stood guard over the captives. The two men and Libbie all had their hands bound behind their backs and were seated on the ground close to the horses. A large red stain on Brian's right shoulder confirmed he was the one who had been wounded earlier.

Lying down, Nate took aim at the Piegan holding the rifle. Then he paused, debating whether he should shoot. There was no chance of missing, but could he drop the rest of the Piegans fast enough to prevent any of them from reaching the three whites? The answer was no. And he wouldn't put it past the Piegans to use the captives as shields, or else to kill them out of blatant spite.

Reluctantly, he held his fire. He must await a better time. If some of the Piegans should go off to hunt or leave for some other reason, he would have the captives freed in no time. If he had to, he'd wait until dark, until most of the warriors were asleep, and then make his move.

At that moment Brian spoke. "Would it hurt to give us some water, you bastards?"

None of the Piegans paid him the least regard. The one acting as guard was gazing off to the north.

"Water!" Brian snapped. "We're all thirsty." He nodded at the lake. "All we want is a few sips. Is that too much to ask?"

The guard looked at him but made no response.

"At least let *her* have some," Brian persisted, indicating Libbie. "She's a woman, you savages! She deserves to be treated decently."

"You're wasting your breath," Pudge said softly.

"If I could only get my hands free," Brian said, straining against the rope around his wrists. His face became scarlet from his exertion and his veins bulged.

"Please don't," Libbie said. "You'll start bleeding again, and you've already lost too much blood as it is."

"I feel fine."

"You're a terrible liar. No man can take a knife in the shoulder and then act as if nothing happened. You should be resting comfortably in bed." Libbie glanced at the Piegans by the lake. "If they keep on pushing us as hard as they've been doing, all of us will be worn to a frazzle when we get to wherever we're going. But you'll be the worst off. So please, for my sake, conserve your strength."

"For you, dearest, anything," Brian said with a smile.

Nate's eyes narrowed. Had he heard correctly? Had the greenhorn just called Libbie his "dearest"?

"Don't say that," she replied. "It's my fault you're in this fix. If you hadn't come after me, we wouldn't be staring death in the face." She sadly shook her head. "You should have left well enough alone."

"Oh?" Brian said sarcastically. "I should have stayed back in the States while the woman I love was being taken against her will to the Oregon Territory? I should have let your father have his way when we both know he's wrong? When we both know that what he did was the most vile thing any person has ever done?"

Libbie closed her eyes, her mouth curling downward. "I don't want to talk about that."

"You must come to terms with it one day. Better now than ten years from now. It's enough to drive someone insane."

"Brian!"

Brian studied her tormented features, then scowled. "I'm sorry," he said, "but I can't help how I feel. If it wasn't for you, I'd put a ball in your father's head."

Tears poured down Libbie's cheeks and she doubled over as if in pain, her forehead resting on the grass.

Pudge angrily stared at Brian. "Now look at what you've done! Why must you upset her so at a time like this? Hasn't she been through enough already?" He made a clucking sound in reproach. "You're my best friend, so believe me when I say that sometimes you act as bad as these lousy Injuns."

The captives fell into a moody silence. Nate watched them, trying to piece together the little information he had gleaned. Now he understood why Libbie had gone willingly with the pair. From the sound of things, her father had nipped her romance with Brian in the bud and dragged her off to the promised land despite her wishes.

He saw the three Piegans walk over to the fourth, and after a brief discussion the captives were hauled to their feet. Libbie was bodily lifted onto a horse, the tallest of the warriors climbed on the other mount, and presently they were all moving around the west side of the lake. One of the Piegans handled the packhorses while the other two walked on either side of Brian and Pudge.

Nate ran to Pegasus and followed. He stayed in the trees, always keeping the party in sight but never, ever exposing himself to their view. Miles of forest fell behind them. The sun climbed ever higher. He wasn't worried that the Piegans would reach their village before nightfall since Piegan territory lay two or three days to the north-east, which would allow him plenty of time to effect a rescue.

He *was* worried, though, about the Banners and the Websters. Left long on their own, they might get into trouble. A fire built too big or random shooting was all it would take to attract any Indians within miles of their camp. And being as close to the stream as they were was also a danger since hostiles might decide to swing by for some water. To put his mind at ease he had to free Libbie and her friends that very night and try to be back at the wagons by early the next day.

The Piegans had ascended a rise and were now going down the far side.

Nate waited a few minutes to be on the safe side, then rode to near the top and slid down. Letting the reins drag, he moved to the top and slowly raised his head high enough to see the land below. What he saw about gave him a fit.

The party he was trailing had stopped in a meadow one hundred yards away. All of the Piegans were waving their arms and whooping and laughing at 12 *more* Piegans approaching from the south. This new group was likewise excited by the meeting, and soon the newcomers reached the meadow, where much hugging and smiling took place. The newcomers then turned their attention to the captives, some stroking Libbie's golden hair while others prodded and pushed Brian and Pudge. Brian flew into a rage and kicked one of those baiting him, at which point he was rendered unconscious by a war club to the back of his head.

Sinking down on his haunches, Nate rested his chin on his knees and felt a wave of helplessness wash over him. Saving Libbie and the greenhorns from four Piegans would have been difficult enough; saving them from 16 would be next to impossible. But he wasn't about to give up. As his mentor, Shakespeare, was so fond of repeating, "Where there's a will, there's a way."

Only in this case, the way eluded him. Sneaking into the Piegan camp after dark, after most of the warriors dozed off, was certain suicide. The Piegans would be doubly alert since they were in the wild where an enemy might discover them at any time, and a single light sleeper would prove his downfall. He must come up with a better plan.

Crawling back up, he watched the Piegans tie Brian's arms and legs to a long pole, which two of the stoutest warriors then carried between them as the combined bands hiked in the direction of their own country. Pudge was ringed by men with lances who delighted in jabbing him every so often. Libbie, placed back on her horse, was momentarily spared further indignities.

Nate went to Pegasus. There was nothing he could do for the time being except stay close and pray for a miracle. Instead of going over the top of the rise, where he was bound to be spotted, he rode to the left down the slope, entered the trees at the bottom, then adopted a course parallel with that taken by the Piegans. Bolstered by their combined numbers and elated at the spoils they were bringing back to their people, they were making enough noise to scare off every animal within half a mile. Laughter and singing carried on the wind.

The shadows lengthened as the sun banked toward the western horizon. Occasionally Nate caught glimpses of the war party, but for the most part he relied on his ears to mark their progress. The proximity of so many humans had silenced the wildlife; for over an hour he didn't hear so much as the peep of a bird.

A mountain crowned with two peaks jutting skyward like the twin horns of a bull turned out to be the Piegans' destination for the day. A sparkling creek bordered its base, and on the near bank the Piegans pitched their camp. The majority erected five conical log and brush forts, a customary practice of their tribe and their allies when on the trail, while several went off after game.

From under the sheltering branches of an overhanging pine, shielded by limbs that drooped to within a foot of the ground, Nate observed everything the Piegans did. The hunters had marched to the south, so he need not fear discovery by them. He saw Libbie, Brian, and Pudge shoved into a fort close to the creek, which gave birth to a daring idea.

Twilight claimed the mountains when the hunters returned bearing a large black-tailed buck. The deer was butchered by a skilled Piegan who took five minutes to do what would take the average trapper half an hour to accomplish. Presently they were all gathered around the fire to take part in the feast, except for a lone warrior who stayed in front of the conical fort containing the captives.

Nate crawled to where he had hidden Pegasus in thick undergrowth. He wedged the Hawken into his bedroll for safekeeping, then drew his tomahawk and his butcher knife and returned to his vantage point. The darkness deepened. The sun sank beyond the far mountains. In the rosy glow of the fire the faces of the Piegans gleamed dully.

He imagined they were doing as the Shoshones would be doing under similar circumstances, swapping tales of their exploits since leaving their village. The four who had survived the battle with the emigrants had a lot to tell, so he wasn't at all surprised when their conversation dragged on until almost midnight.

At last the Piegans began turning in. Only a few, at first, went into the forts. Then a few more. And so it went until all of them were inside save one who had taken the place of the man who had stood guard over the captives since sunset. Left unattended, the fire dwindled to low, sputtering flames.

Nate let more time pass before crawling from under the pine to the bank of the creek. Taking a breath, he eased into the shallow water, shuddering in the sudden cold, and turned toward the encampment. Just as he did, the Piegan on guard looked in his direction.

Chapter Nine

Nate froze in place, the gently flowing water soaking the front of his buckskins from his neck to his moccasins. Had the Piegan somehow heard him? He doubted it, since he had made no noise whatsoever. Holding the butcher knife and the tomahawk close to the water, he watched the Piegan scan the forest. The man didn't act as if he suspected there was an enemy about. On the contrary, after a minute the Piegan stretched and yawned, then strolled to the stream and knelt to drink.

Thirty yards away, Nate fought off an impulse to shiver and waited for the guard to move back to the fort. The creek, fed by snow runoff from the high peaks above, was liquid ice. Staying in the water too long would render his arms and legs numb. He would have no chance of freeing the others.

Finished quenching his thirst, the Piegan stood, wiped his mouth with the back of his hand, and walked back to the conical fort. He took up a position in front of it, then sat down with his legs crossed, his back to the fort.

Nate snaked forward, keeping his weapons above the water, using his elbows and his knees to propel himself, moving first one limb, then the other. The fire was now so low that its feeble glow bathed only the nearest forts. The one containing the captives stood shrouded in shadows.

He dared not go too fast for fear of making a splash that would be heard by the guard, yet he dared not dally either, or the cold would take its toll on his circulation. Hugging the near bank where the darkness was heaviest, he drew within ten yards of his goal.

The Piegan had set down his lance and had rested his elbows on his knees. He appeared bored, and was having trouble staying awake. Now and then his head bobbed, but he drew himself up again each time.

Nate stopped directly behind the fort where the three whites were held. Like an enormous salamander crawling onto land, he inched onto dry ground and paused to let the water run off his clothing. Warily, silently, he moved to the rear of the fort, then rose into a crouch. Gingerly taking a step, he moved to the right until he could see the back of the guard.

The rest of the camp was deceptively still. Should the guard sound the alarm, the Piegans would pour from the structures armed to the teeth and ready to fight to the death. From within a fort to the right arose loud snoring.

He glided toward the guard, his right hand firmly gripping the tomahawk. A single blow should suffice if delivered to the proper point. He saw the Indian's shoulders droop, took another step. The warrior was almost asleep. Raising the tomahawk overhead, he lifted a leg and carefully placed his foot down.

A twig snapped.

Muffled by Nate's wet moccasin, the snap was barely audible. But it caused the Piegan to jerk his head up and around, his right hand streaking for the lance by his side.

Nate was braced and ready. As the warrior turned, he swung, driving the tomahawk downward with all the power in his arm. The sharp blade bit into the Piegan's forehead above the right eye and split his skull like an overripe melon, burying itself inches deep in his head. Blood spurted. The Piegan gasped, clutched at the tomahawk, then broke into violent convulsions.

Nate held onto the tomahawk handle with both hands. Afraid the thrashing would awaken some of the other warriors, he glanced at the closest forts. The guard's arms went suddenly limp, then the man slumped forward, his eyes locked wide, his mouth contorted in a grimace.

Satisfied the guard was dead, Nate put a foot on the Piegan's shoulder and wrenched the tomahawk loose. He wiped the blade on the Indian's leggings, then padded to the fort and squatted in the opening. Inside lay three inky forms. Entering, he moved to Libbie, conspicuous by her long blond hair even in the gloom. From the way she was lying, he gathered her ankles and wrists were bound.

"I saw what you just did, mister," she abruptly whispered. "You look vaguely familiar. You are a white man, aren't you?"

"It's Nate King. I've come to free you."

A startled exclamation burst from the figure on the left. "Thank God!" Pudge declared. "I thought we—"

Nate reached the greenhorn in a single stride and clamped a hand over Pudge's mouth, gouging the hilt of his knife into the man's lips in the process. "You damn fool!" he snapped. "Do you want to set the Piegans on us?"

Pudge, the whites of his eyes the size of walnuts, vigorously shook his head.

Nate listened intently but heard nothing to indicate any of the warriors had heard. "I want all of you to keep quiet," he directed softly, releasing his hold on the greenhorn. "When I cut you loose, don't make a sound." Moving behind them, he quickly sliced through the ropes. They rose to their knees, all three rubbing their wrists and ankles to get their blood flowing again.

Outside, an owl hooted.

Edging to the opening, Nate surveyed the forts. Had that been a real owl or a signal? With Indians it was hard to tell. Some of them were so expert at imitating animals that it was impossible to know which was the real thing and which was not. He detected no movement. Twisting, he regarded Libbie and the two men. "We're going to try and reach the trees without being discovered. When you go out the entrance, turn to the right until you're at the creek. We'll follow it north into the woods."

For the first time Brian spoke. "What about our horses?"

"They're on the south side of the camp. I'll swing around and get them after all of you are safe."

"I don't like leaving them. Without our horses we wouldn't last a day in these mountains."

"Just do as I say and you'll come out of this still wearing your scalps," Nate said. He went out first, crouched until certain it was safe, then motioned for the others to emerge. Pudge was the last, and he grunted as he squeezed through.

His face reflecting his anger, Nate touched the keen point of his butcher knife to the heavyset man's fleshy cheek. Pudge blinked, then nodded his head once in understanding. Frowning, Nate gestured for them to move around the fort. He trailed them, keeping watch on the other log structures. The fire, now mere fingers of flame, revealed very little.

Instead of wading into the creek, Nate stuck to the water's edge. He was afraid one of them—most likely the clumsy Pudge—would inadvertently splash around or slip on a wet rock and arouse the war party. The soil bordering the creek was soft, cushioning their footfalls nicely, and soon they were in the sheltering forest where he halted.

"My horse isn't far," he disclosed. "I'll take you to him, then go after your own animals."

"How did you find us?" Libbie asked. "How did you know we'd been captured?" She paused. "Did my father send you?"

"We'll talk about that later," Nate said, and rose to head for Pegasus. A hand fell on his shoulder.

"Our supplies, King," Brian said. "I saw the savages remove our packs. We have to get them back."

Nate had witnessed the same thing. "The Piegans put all of your equipment in one of their forts. We have no hope of sneaking in there and getting it out, so you'll just have to make do."

"Without food? Without weapons? What chance will we have to survive in this wilderness?"

"You should have thought of that before you left the settlements. These mountains are no place for green-horns," Nate responded, and shrugged to dislodge the man's hand. He hurried through the underbrush until he came on the stallion, whispering to it as he approached so the horse wouldn't spook or whinny.

"Can I talk now?" Pudge asked.

"Go ahead," Nate said.

"I'm in your debt, King. I don't know how I can ever repay you, but I will someday. I swear it. If not for you, we'd all be goners."

"You have my thanks too," Brian said, but without a trace of heartfelt warmth or conviction.

Puzzled by the man's bitter attitude, Nate slid his knife into its sheath and tucked the tomahawk under his belt. If the situation was reversed, he'd be over-joyed at being saved from certain death. Brian, oddly enough, seemed to resent what had happened. Nate decided to get to the bottom of the matter later, after they had put enough miles behind them for them to be truly safe.

Removing the Hawken from the bedroll, Nate held the
rifle in the crook of his left elbow and grasped the reins in
his right hand. "Try not to make much noise if you can
help it," he advised, casting a meaningful look at Pudge,
and hiked to the southwest.

"I thought you were going after our horses," Brian said.

"I will, once we're due west of the Piegans."

"What difference does that make?"

"If something goes wrong, I don't want to have to swing
around the Piegan camp to make good our escape. I want to
be able to cut right out. And west is the direction we have to
go to take Libbie back to her folks."

"Oh."

They covered ten yards in silence. Then Brian commented starchily, "If you were a gentleman, King,
you'd let Libbie ride your horse. Or don't good
manners count for much in these stinking mountains
of yours?"

"Brian, what has gotten into you? How can you talk to
Mr. King like that?" Libbie upbraided him.

"It's all right," Nate said to forestall an argument. "He
has a point. But my stallion has become a contrary cuss
and won't hardly let anyone ride him but me. Not even my
wife, who has a way with animals. If I tried to put Libbie on
him, he might make a ruckus the Piegans would hear."

"*You're* married?" Brian asked.

"Of course. Why are you so surprised?"

"Is your wife a white woman or a squaw?"

Nate stopped abruptly and whirled. Unconsciously, he
leveled the Hawken. "I would be extremely careful were
I you," he said coldly. "I won't abide anyone insulting my
wife. The last man who did is dead."

The others resembled statues. Brian stared at the rifle
barrel for a few seconds, then smiled wanly. "I meant no
disrespect," he said softly. "After all that's happened, I
guess I'm not my normal self."

"Please, Mr. King," Libbie chimed in. "I know Brian as well as I do myself. He doesn't hate all Injuns like some men do. And he doesn't make a habit of going around insulting people."

"That's nice to know," Nate said dryly. He resumed walking, and speculated on what would happen when they rejoined Libbie's parents. Simon wasn't the type to forgive and forget. The girl and her friends might wind up wishing they had never been rescued.

Over a hundred yards from the Piegan encampment, Nate halted and tied the stallion's reins to a low branch on a spruce tree. "This is where you wait," he announced. "If you hear shooting, head west."

"Which way is that?" Pudge asked, gazing in blatant confusion at the myriad of stars sparkling in the firmament. "How can you tell which way is which once the sun sets?"

"You learn to read the heavens, just like the Indians do," Nate said. He pointed at a group of seven familiar stars that every boy learned about at an early age. "Do you know what that is?"

"Sure. The Big Dipper," Pudge answered.

"Good. Now pretend you draw a line straight out from the two stars that form the bottom of the dipper. Do you see that star all by itself?"

"The real bright one?"

Nate nodded. "That's the North Star. Face it and hold your arms out from your sides. Your left arm will be pointing to the west."

"Amazing," Pudge said, grinning. "I'll never get lost again knowing this."

"Stay alert until I get back," Nate said, and began to walk off.

"Hold it, King," Brian said. "Surely you're not planning to leave us defenseless? Can't you leave at least one of your guns here?"

The request, while reasonable, bothered Nate. His every instinct warned him not to trust the man.

"For Libbie's sake, if for no other reason," Brian added. "What if you're caught? How will we protect her? With our bare hands?"

"I suppose you're right," Nate admitted reluctantly, and stepped over to the blond beauty. "Here. Hold onto this for me," he said, offering the Hawken.

"Are you certain you won't need it?" she asked.

"No. It's best if I have my hands free anyway," Nate said. Hastening into the murky forest, he cautiously skirted the quiet camp until he was hidden in a dense thicket south of the conical forts. A tendril of white smoke wafted upward from the seemingly dead campfire. The slain guard still lay where he had fallen.

All four horses had been secured by lengths of rope to trees flanking the camp. There was abundant grass, and two of the horses were grazing contentedly. The third had lain down, while the fourth was drinking from the creek.

Would they neigh and give him away? Nate wondered, moving from concealment. He stepped lightly to one of the grazing animals, which looked up, chomping noisily, but betrayed no fear. Nor did the second horse he gathered up. The third, the one trying to sleep, snorted and shook its head in annoyance at being disturbed. He patted its neck and scratched behind its ears until it grew calm. Then he unfastened the rope to the fourth horse and led the animals into the trees.

Behind him the Piegans slumbered on.

He was delighted at his success. By first light, when the war party would awaken and find the guard, his little group would be ten miles or better from the creek. Being on foot, the Piegans had no hope of catching them.

Nate reflected on the issue of the two greenhorns in depth. What should he do about the troublemakers? They weren't part of the emigrant train, and it was highly doubtful Simon Banner would want them tagging along. Knowing Banner, Simon might shoot them on sight. But could they be persuaded to head back to the States? He doubted it. Libbie and Brian were in love, and young lovers were notorious for taking rash risks wiser heads would avoid at all costs. Brian had already stolen Libbie from her folks once; there was nothing to stop him from trying again.

It would help immensely if he knew why they had done what they did. Clearly, they had known one another before the Banners left for the promised land. Had Libbie's father forced her to break off with Brian? If so, on what pretext? Did that explain why she hated Simon so much and why she had wanted to die?

There were so many questions and so few answers.

The greenhorns and Libbie were eagerly awaiting him. Brian, he saw, now held the Hawken, and the first thing Nate did upon rejoining them was to walk up and say flatly, "My rifle."

Brian hesitated. "You have two pistols. I'd like to hold onto it for a while."

"My rifle," Nate repeated, extending his right hand, palm up.

"It's only fair that we share your weapons. What if we're attacked? Shouldn't we be able to defend ourselves?"

Nate made no reply. He simply waited, his features flinty, until, with a sigh of displeasure, Brian gave the Hawken to him. Then Nate mounted Pegasus. "I hope all of you can ride bareback," he said.

In a smooth, lithe motion, Libbie vaulted onto one of the other horses and held the rope rein in her left hand. "Don't worry on my account, Mr. King. I was raised on a farm, remember? Before I was seven I could ride like the wind."

Pudge stepped up to an animal and tentatively stroked its mane. "I never have been much of a rider and I've never gone bareback, but I'll do the best I can." Swinging up, he balanced himself and nodded. "All set."

His face a mask of resentment directed at Nate, Brian climbed onto yet a third horse. "I'll hold my own," he declared. "And I'll watch out for Pudge."

"Then let's go," Nate said, taking the lead to the last horse in his left hand. "By nightfall we'll be back at the wagons."

"Do you have any idea what will happen when we get there?" Brian asked testily. "Libbie's father will shoot Pudge and me on sight."

"I won't let him," Nate promised.

"You don't know Simon like we do," Brian said. "He's mean. No, worse than that. He's downright wicked. The man has no consideration for anyone else, and he's not above killing when he feels it's right. The world would be better off without him."

"Those are mighty strong words," Nate remarked, glancing at Libbie in the expectation of her speaking up in her father's behalf. She sat glumly astride her mount, her posture the picture of dejection.

"Every word is true," Brian insisted.

"Maybe," Nate allowed. "But the important thing is that Simon wants his daughter back. And since I agreed to guide the whole family to Fort Hall, I have to see to it that she's returned to her folks no matter what my personal feelings on the matter might be."

"You don't think much of her pa either, do you?"

"I've met nicer people in my time," Nate confessed, and urged Pegasus forward. "Enough jawing for now. This isn't the proper time or place, not when the Piegans might show up at any time."

That got them going, and for the next three hours they rode hard across the benighted landscape, most of the time through thick forest where low limbs and logs posed constant obstacles. When, at length, they entered a wide, grassy valley, Libbie goaded her horse up alongside Nate's.

"Mr. King, I wanted to say that I'm sorry I've put you to so much trouble on my account. But I also want you to know that I would do it again if I had to. Brian and I are going to be married the first chance we get, and I won't let anything stand in our way. Not even my pa."

"I take it you've changed your mind about wanting to die?"

"Brian changed my mind for me. He says we can't allow the past to poison the future. We have to be strong, to do whatever it takes to bring us true happiness." She paused. "There comes a time in a person's life when they have to do what is best for them, not what their parents might think is best for them. Don't misunderstand. We should all honor our fathers and mothers, just as the Good Book tells us to do. But we have to cut the ties if the ties are strangling us." Again she paused. "Does that make sense to you?"

"Perfect sense."

"When I was young I was a dutiful girl. I always did as my folks wanted, and they never had any complaints." Libbie gazed skyward. "I thought they were the most loving, kindest parents a girl could have."

"Something changed your mind?" Nate prompted when she fell silent.

"Yes. I made a mistake. A big mistake, to be honest. But I thought I could count on their love and understanding to help see me through the hard times. I was wrong."

"Is that why you despise your pa so?"

"If you only knew!" Libbie declared, her voice husky with repressed emotion. "He did something so terrible, so disgusting, that I'll bear the scar inside of me for my entire life."

Now was the moment of truth. Nate looked at her, hoping she would finally reveal the key to unraveling the mystery, but Brian came abreast of him on the other side.

"If it bothers you so much to talk about it, dearest, then don't." Brian nodded at Nate. "And there's certainly no need to tell *him* everything. Some secrets are best kept secret."

"I just thought he should know after all we've put him through," Libbie said.

"All he needs to know is that we don't want to go back to your father," Brian said. "How about it, King? What will it take to change your mind?"

"Simon and Alice are counting on me to return her safe and sound," Nate said.

"Even if she doesn't want to be taken to them? Don't her feelings count?"

Nate glanced to the right at the greenhorn, who rode with the makeshift rope rein in his left hand and with his right arm dangling out of sight on the far side. "I have a job to do and I aim to do it."

"What if I paid you to let us go our own way?" Brian proposed. "The savages took all the money I had on me and scattered it on the ground. But I still have several hundred dollars in a bank account. Every penny of it is yours if you'll ride on back to the Banners and tell Simon that you couldn't find us."

"I won't lie. Not for you. Not for anyone."

"What can it hurt? A little white lie?"

"Out here a man is only as good as his word. You might think it strange, but we take great stock in always being honest with folks, in always telling the truth."

Brian studied Nate in the dim light. "Yes, I can see that trying to change your mind is a complete waste of time. I'm sorry, King, that it had to come this. If there was some other way, I'd gladly take it."

"What are you talking about?" Nate asked, and too late saw out of the corner of his eye, Brian's right arm arc up and around, swinging a long, dark object at his head. He

tried to raise his arm to block the blow but was unsuc-
cessful. Tremendous pain exploded in his right temple and
scores of bright dots appeared before his eyes. Vaguely,
he heard a scream. Then a second blow connected and
the pain became a tidal wave that swamped his mind and
plunged him into abysmal darkness.

Chapter Ten

The sun revived him.

Nate first became aware of the sensation of heat on his face. His cheeks felt warm enough to fry an egg. He also heard the wind shriek past and the rustling of the high grass. Opening his eyes proved a twofold mistake; the bright glare of sunlight hurt them terribly, forcing him to squint, and pounding waves of agony rocked his head. Wincing in torment, he held a hand above his eyes to shield them from the sun and slowly pushed up on one elbow.

He was lying in the middle of the valley, exactly where he had fallen, ringed by an ocean of grass. The position of the sun told him he had been unconscious for seven or eight hours. He touched his temple and felt dried blood.

Rising to his knees, he took stock. The others had taken Pegasus with them. His rifle was gone, as was one of his flintlocks. They had left him a single pistol, but stolen his powder horn and bullet pouch. Thankfully, they had not thought to appropriate his knife or his tomahawk. Close by lay his crumpled, bloodstained beaver hat. Beside it was a broken branch three feet long and as thick as his wrist, also bloodstained.

Nate leaned over to pick up the hat. He had only himself to blame for being left high and dry, since he had failed to keep watch on the others as they negotiated the tracts of woodland during the night. Obviously, Brian had spotted the branch and either hung over the side of his mount to grab it, or else had stopped and taken but fleeting seconds to arm himself. If Nate had stayed more alert, the greenhorn wouldn't have been able to take him by surprise.

He placed his hat loosely on his head, and had started to shove to his feet when faintly to his ears came the sound of voices. Indian voices. Twisting, he rose high enough to peer over the top of the grass, and beheld a sight that made his pulse jump.

Just entering the eastern end of the valley was the Piegan war party, strung out in a line in typical fashion, the foremost warrior bent over to better read the sign.

Nate lowered to his hands and knees and scooted to the north, crawling as rapidly as the intense hammering between his ears allowed. He'd figured the Piegans would give up since they had no hope of catching quarry on horseback, but they were a persistent bunch. Perhaps they counted on their former captives stopping to rest. Or the loss of one of their own might have fired them with resolve to seek vengeance.

They were still far off, which gave Nate time to crawl to the closest trees and stand. He knew when they came on the spot where he had fallen they would plainly see what had happened and would realize that one of those they sought was afoot and not much ahead of them.

Turning westward, Nate ran. He gritted his teeth and clenched his fists, resisting the pain as best he was able. To help firm his own resolve he thought of Brian and what he would do to the treacherous vermin when he found him. Because he would find him. No matter how much time was required, nor how far afield he had to range, even back into the States if need be, he would track him down, recover Pegasus and his other possessions, and pay the greenhorn back in kind for the cowardly blow to his head.

At the west end of the valley the trees on the north and south side blended together into a sprawling stretch of pristine forest. Under different circumstances he would have enjoyed the lush scenery. Now he concentrated on making the best time, on avoiding downed trees and thickets that would slow him down.

A flurry of shouts to his rear was evidence the Piegans had found where he had been knocked off his stallion. In a minute they would be after him. Conditioned by the harsh land in which they dwelled, they were as sleek as deer and as muscular as panthers. No white man could hope to match their fleetness unless he was also mountain-bred or as crafty as a fox.

Nate would have to rely on his wits. He covered a quarter of a mile, then saw a mountain on his left. Making toward it, he found a ravine slicing into the underbelly of the mountain and penetrated a hundred yards into it. A 30-foot-high wall on his right, latticed with erosion-worn cracks, afforded the hand-and footholds he needed to climb to the top.

He trotted 50 yards, then angled down the slope and resumed his westward flight. The detour would only slow the Piegans a bit but every bit helped.

All his years in the mountains was paying off in one respect; so far his lungs were holding up remarkably well. Few people in the States were aware of the strain high altitudes put on the human body. Many a trapper, on first venturing into the Rockies, discovered to his chagrin that his body turned traitor. Lungs used to dealing with sea-level altitude had to work much harder a mile or more up, and until a trapper adjusted to the drastic change he had to contend with chronic shortness of breath and difficulty with breathing after strenuous exertion. A few trappers whose bodies were for some unknown reason unable to make the adjustment were compelled to return to the States to sustain their health.

He was doing fine. A mile of steady running had left him only slightly winded. In the forest behind him rose a chorus of excited yips and whoops. The Piegans must be gaining despite his utmost effort.

Casting about for another way to slow them down, Nate spied a cliff composed of solid rock to his right. It was part of a low peak bordering the valley. Sprinting over to the base, he halted and took a few precious seconds to catch his breath. The cliff could be climbed with difficulty, but he had no intention of doing so. Instead, he glanced over his shoulder at the footprints he had made on his approach. He had deliberately slammed his feet down so that each moccasin print was complete and clear.

Now he had to focus every atom of his being on the ruse. Taking a breath, he also took a step backwards, placing his left foot directly down on top of the left footprint he had made just before he stopped. Then he quickly took another step backwards, this time setting his right foot down in the second-to-last track he had made. Ever backwards he went, each stride precise. He must be careful not to smudge the footprints or to leave two impressions. Doing so would be a dead giveaway the Piegans would instantly spot.

Walking backwards, he entered the trees. Next to a cluster of weeds he bunched his leg muscles and jumped, sailing over the weeds and breaking into a sprint the moment his feet touched the ground. How much time had he bought himself? Five minutes? Ten? It all depended on whether the Piegans fell for his ploy and believed he had scaled the cliff.

Not a minute later he heard an uproar when the Piegans came to the base of the rocky height, their impassioned yells echoing hollowly in all directions. They knew they were close behind him, and probably imagined he would soon be in their grasp. Some would climb up, others would flank the cliff on both sides. He heard nothing to indicate that they were aware of his scheme and in hot pursuit.

He allowed himself to relax slightly. His lungs now ached abominably; his arms and legs were becoming sluggish. He had to stop to regain his strength before he was too weak to lift a foot. A stand of aspens afforded the ideal hiding spot, and he moved into the center and knelt.

Nate would have given anything for ten hours of uninterrupted sleep, a luxury he was unlikely to savor for quite some time. He steadied his breathing and leaned against a trunk. As soon as he caught his breath he had to be on his way. To delay was to invite disaster since the Piegans wouldn't stay fooled by his strategy forever.

Fatigue made his limbs feel leaden. He closed his eyes and sagged. His face felt flushed and he was perspiring freely. Mopping his brow, he thought of the scream he had heard when Brian struck him. That must have been Libbie, which meant she had not been expecting the attack. He was glad. He liked her, and he didn't like to think she had been a willing party to such a dastardly act.

Straightening, Nate moved out of the aspens and hiked westward. He figured the others would head in that direction until they came to the Green River Basin. Then they would turn southeast and make for South Pass. His wisest course of action, therefore, might be to return to the emigrants and use one of their horses to catch Libbie and her friends.

Quite by accident he found fresh hoofprints, and recognized those of Pegasus among them. So he was on the right trail. He began trotting, his arms swinging loosely, pacing himself so as not to wear himself out prematurely.

Alternately trotting and briefly resting, he covered another mile. His buckskins were damp with sweat and clung to him like a glove. The sounds of the Piegans had long since faded, and he congratulated himself on outfoxing them.

A green meadow opened out before him. He ran through the tall grass, feeling it swish around his legs. Suddenly a feral shriek cut the air to the rear. Startled, he whirled and nearly tripped over his own feet at the sight of a lone stocky Piegan rushing out of the trees. The warrior waved a war club overhead and increased his speed.

Spinning, Nate ran for all he was worth. Had the Piegans discovered his trick already and were they now all close behind him, or was there only the one man? If he knew the answer to that, he would know whether to use his flintlock or not. The shot was bound to alert the rest, so he didn't want to employ the pistol unless he was positive the entire war party had given chase, in which case it didn't matter if they heard.

Nate decided to save the ball for when he really needed it. He drew his knife on the run and held it close in front of him so the pursuing warrior couldn't see it. He gripped the blade, then intentionally slowed, pretending to be on his last legs, bending over as he glanced over his shoulder to mark the Piegan's advance.

Sensing an easy kill, the warrior was ten yards off and closing like an avenging wraith. His mouth curled in a triumphant grin and he held the war club ready to swing a crushing blow.

Nate slowed to almost a walk. Surreptitiously watching the Piegan, he waited until the man was less than ten feet away before he uncoiled with stunning swiftness and threw the knife. Practice made perfect, as the saying went, and Nate had practiced such a toss on countless occasions.

He'd even won a few knife-and tomahawk-throwing contests at the annual rowdy Rendezvous where the trappers competed in everything from foot races to wrestling to hopping competitions.

The blade caught the Piegan in the chest over the heart and sank in clean to the hilt. He abruptly stopped, dropped his war club, and grabbed the knife. Venting an enraged growl, he tore the blade out, held it in his right hand, and sprang at Nate. But he only took two strides. Then his knees buckled and he sprawled forward to lie still, blood trickling from the corner of his mouth.

Nate knelt to pry his knife from the warrior's fingers. He wiped the blade clean on the grass and stood. In the woods bordering the meadow erupted a series of strident whoops, and he glimpsed painted figures gliding through the trees. So the whole war party was after him! Turning, he slid the knife into its sheath and fled for his life.

Now that the Piegans had him in sight they would run all out; they wouldn't slow down until they overtook him. His main worry was being struck by an arrow. Indian boys were instructed early in the use of the bow, and by the time each boy became a full-fledged warrior he could hit a human-sized target from horseback at a full gallop.

He came to the end of the meadow and plunged into pines. Not a moment too soon. Buzzing like a provoked hornet, a shaft sped out of the blue and thudded into the ground within inches of his left foot. He weaved to the right, then the left, putting as many tree trunks as possible between the Piegans and him.

Unbidden, a terrifying thought entered his mind: He was going to be slain! Outrunning the Piegans was impossible. It was only a matter of time, of mere minutes, before the fastest among them was nipping at his heels.

Frowning, Nate shook his head, dispelling the gloomy notion. Where there was life, there was hope! And so long as he had a single breath remaining in his body he would fight for his survival with all the strength he could muster.

Another arrow clipped a branch to his right. A third streaked over his shoulder and hit a tree.

Nate looked back. Three or four of the Piegans were well ahead of the pack and rapidly narrowing the gap. Of them, two held bows. If only he had his Hawken! But he didn't, and no amount of wishful thinking would change the stark reality of the imminent death confronting him unless he could come up with something fast.

But *what?* What could he possibly do to evade the determined Piegans? All his tricks had failed him and he could think of nothing new.

An arrow snatched at the fringe on his right sleeve. Nate glanced over his shoulder to see one of the bowmen was now 15 yards away and nocking yet another shaft. On impulse he drew the flintlock, halted, and spun. The warrior was raising the bow when the pistol cracked, and the Piegan clutched at his face, then toppled.

The other warriors immediately sought cover.

Nate continued his frantic flight. He would gain a few seconds on them. Perhaps, on second thought, even more. Now that the Piegans knew he had a gun, they would be more cautious and go a trifle slower. Thank goodness they had no way of knowing he was out of ammunition and the flintlock was useless!

He spent over two minutes in running flat out, until his body throbbed with agony and he found the taking of a single breath to be an excruciating ordeal. He was close to the end of his endurance and he knew it. The yips of the pursuing Piegans reminded him they were on the verge of catching him, but there was no reserve of energy for him to draw from that would enable him to pull ahead, nor was there any way of eluding them.

His legs weighed a ton. Despite his wishes, his body slowed of its own accord. His legs refused to cooperate. His lungs screamed in protest. Inhaling raggedly, he stumbled into a clearing and stopped. The least he could do was sell his life dearly. With that in mind he started to draw his tomahawk and butcher knife. Then he froze, wondering if his ears had deceived him.

He'd heard a low whinny.

Looking up, he was stupefied to see a horse walking toward him. And not just any horse; it was Pegasus! The stallion bore dozens of scratch marks on its belly, flanks, and legs, and it was coated thick with sweat.

"I'm seeing things!" Nate blurted. But the apparent apparition came right up to him and touched his neck with its muzzle. He could feel its warm skin, smell its body. "Pegasus?" he said softly, reaching up to touch the stallion's mane.

A cry of baffled rage came from the throat of the first Piegan to spy the animal.

Nate galvanized into motion. Gripping the reins, he swung into the saddle and brought Pegasus around sharply. At a stroke of his legs the stallion plunged into the woods. He hunched low in case one of the warriors tried to bring him down with an arrow, and he hadn't gone five yards when two shafts narrowly missed his head. Then Pegasus reached a gallop and the war party swiftly fell far to the rear.

It had all happened so incredibly fast that Nate feared he was dreaming. Perhaps he had fallen and struck his head and was only imagining the stallion had arrived at the very last instant to pull his hide out of the fire. But the rolling gait of the big horse and the feel of the immensely powerful animal between his legs reassured him that this was real.

Dazed, he rode several miles before he thought to slow down. He was safe. The Piegans could trail him all they wanted, but they'd never catch him now. All thanks to Pegasus.

Leaning forward, he stroked the stallion's neck and spoke soft words of affection. In the past there had been horses he'd liked, some he'd even been quite fond of, but none held a candle to his gift from the Nez Percé.

It was strange. When he'd first received the stallion, the horse had willingly let his wife and son climb on and had taken them for many a pleasant ride. His best friend, Shakespeare McNair, had also ridden Pegasus once. But the more time Nate had spent with the animal, the more it came to regard him as its sole master. Eventually, Pegasus would only let Nate climb up. When others tried, the stallion would snort and kick or rear.

Nate had never known a horse to become so particular, and had mentioned as much to McNair. The aged mountain man had claimed to have known of two or three other horses that had developed exceptional attachments to their owners, and Shakespeare had been of the opinion that it was a blessing in disguise. "No one," Shakespeare had said, "will ever be able to steal this critter. If they try, they'll wind up on their backsides in the dirt."

Was that the explanation for Pegasus turning up at the right place at the right time? Had the stallion broken away from Libbie and the greenhorns and returned to find him? It was the only logical reason that he could see. So Shakespeare, as usual, had been right. Having a superbly devoted animal like Pegasus was a blessing. Never again would he—and he grinned at the thought—look a gift horse in the mouth.

He rode for another hour, until a stream beckoned, then finally halted. Pegasus was parched and gulped the water in great draughts. Sinking to his knees, Nate cupped a mouthful to his dry lips and sipped.

His bedroll and parfleches were still tied to the stallion. Since one of them contained the jerked venison and pemmican Winona had packed, he need not worry about having to waste time hunting game. And since his spare ammunition and black powder were stored in the other, his pistol was no longer useless.

After drinking his fill, Nate attended to the first order of business reloading the flintlock. After the stallion slaked its thirst, he mounted and rode leisurely westward. As much as he wanted to catch up with Brian, he was not going to ride Pegasus into the ground doing it. That Pegasus was weary was self-evident. Nate would have to stop in a while so they both could rest and recuperate.

An hour and a half later he ascended a hill and reined up in a dense group of pines. Confident the stallion would hear or smell anything or anyone that approached, he secured the reins on a tree next to a patch of grass, then crawled under the tree, curled up into a ball, and was immediately asleep.

This time it was a cool breeze from the northwest lightly caressing his face and rattling nearby tree limbs that brought him around. He sat up, rubbed his eyes, and turned.

Pegasus was cropping grass a few feet away.

Crawling out, he straightened, then stretched. His body ached from head to toe, but he was alive and glad to be so. The sun had set hours ago and now a half-moon bathed the countryside in a pale light.

"Ready to travel?" Nate asked, stepping to the stallion, which lifted its head and rubbed against him like an over-sized dog. Climbing up, he rode down the hill and bore due west.

Munching on jerky satisfied his hunger. He felt invigorated and raring to tangle with the polecat who had laid him low. Now that he had time to think, he dwelled on the fact his prized Hawken had been stolen, and could barely control his anger. Next to a free trapper's horse, his most important possession was his rifle. Stealing one was a certain death warrant.

Back in '23 a man by the name of Hugh Glass had set the example for all mountaineers. Severely mauled by a she-bear protecting her cubs, he was left to die by the party he was with, abandoned in the most remote region of the mountains without so much as a knife to his name. His associates, certain he would die, took everything he owned but the clothes on his back. Through sheer will-power Hugh Glass survived, and then he commenced an odyssey that became legendary.

Living on berries and the carcasses of game killed by wild beasts, laying low when hostiles came near and avoiding the numerous grizzlies that appeared, Old Glass, as the trappers called him, traveled hundreds and hundreds of miles until he eventually caught up at Henry's Fort with the men who had deserted him. There he learned that one of the party, the man who had taken his rifle, had headed back toward civilization.

Unfazed, Old Glass went on, covering hundreds more miles, going far down the Missouri to near the mouth of the Platte, and there at Fort Atkinson he caught up with the man. Glass would have killed him too, if not for the fact the former trapper had enlisted and wore the uniform of the United States Army. The commanding officer intervened, talking Glass out of seeking revenge, but when Glass cut out for the wilderness again he held his own rifle in his gnarled hands.

Nate could understand Glass's determination. A good rifle often saved a man's hide again and again, so it was only natural for a trapper to come to regard his rifle more as a friend than as merely a lifeless piece of wood and metal. Some mountaineers got into the habit of talking to their rifles like they did to their horses, and no one made light of them for the habit.

Those living in the States seldom understood such a way of life, but to those who experienced the rigors of mountain living such behavior was perfectly all right. And as attached as the whites became to their horses and their guns, they were outdone by the Indians, many of whom would take cherished war ponies into their lodges at night if they feared a raid by an enemy tribe. A prominent Shoshone warrior went so far as to bring his war pony in whenever it rained.

A sharp nicker from Pegasus shattered Nate's idle reverie, and he looked around for the source of the stallion's alarm. He readily found it.

Ten feet off to the left, crouched on a giant log, was an equally giant panther.

Chapter Eleven

Nate instantly reined up and drew the flintlock. He cocked the pistol but held his thumb on the hammer, waiting for the big cat to make the first move. A single shot might not down it, and he didn't want to fire unless he had no choice.

Its pointed ears laid back, its long tail twitching back and forth, the panther uttered a piercing snarl.

Still Nate refused to shoot. He hoped the panther would leave him alone and elect to go seek prey elsewhere. It was rare for the reclusive predators to attack humans, so rare that many Indian tribes regarded panthers as timid. Unlike grizzlies, which would go after any intruders in their domain, more often than not panthers would flee at the first whiff of human scent.

The cat tilted its head, then growled and slowly backed off the log until just its head was visible. In a blur of speed it whirled and vanished in the underbrush.

Nate listened, but heard no sound other than the wind. Not surprising, since few creatures could move more silently than panthers. Carefully lowering the hammer, he tucked the pistol under his wide leather belt and resumed his journey.

Traveling at night was risky business. There were more meat-eaters abroad, heightening the odds of running into one. And a man had to constantly be on the lookout for potential dangers to his mount, such as prairie-dog burrows or other such holes that could cripple a horse in the blink of an eye.

But Nate had no intention of stopping. This was his chance to gain on the greenhorns and Libbie. The trio had not enjoyed a moment of rest since their capture, so they must have been utterly exhausted when they made camp. They'd sleep until dawn, perhaps even later. And he would use those hours to make up the time he had lost.

He thought of Shakespeare's prediction that one day the vast territory west of the Mississippi River would be overrun by men just like Simon Banner and the greenhorns. It was inevitable, Shakespeare had said, because Americans were a restless race who always liked to see what lay over the next horizon. That wanderlust, combined with the need for more and more land as the population grew and grew, would lure countless emigrants westward.

Lord, he prayed McNair was wrong! If emigrants did come by the thousands, it would spell an end to the way of life he knew. The Indians would not stand still for having their land occupied by farmers and ranchers and the like. Warfare would be widespread. And Nate shuddered to think of what would happen to the game now so marvelously abundant. Just as back in the States, the wildlife would be killed off, hunted to near-extinction by those who could see no further ahead than their next meal.

Already beaver were hard to find thanks to the diligent trapping of only several hundred whites. And the mountain buffalo had been drastically thinned out to supply food and blankets for the trappers. The effect of a mass migration would be like that of a plague of locusts, chewing up the land and killing off practically all the wildlife in its path.

Nate gazed fondly out over the sea of trees intermittently eclipsed, as it were, by gigantic islands of stone and dirt, the majestic Rockies that so stirred the souls of those who chose to dwell among them. He never wanted the paradise he had found to change. Should the prediction come true, he would be strongly tempted to join with the Indians in opposing the white onslaught.

Time went by. His thoughts drifted. Toward daylight he reached the basin and turned to the southeast. Searching for tracks could wait until the sun rose. He was positive Libbie and the two men were making for South Pass, so all he had to do was make a beeline for it.

Now he brought Pegasus to a gallop. His eyes roved the region before him seeking a telltale pinpoint of light, although he doubted he would spot one. Any fire left unattended since the evening before would now be extinguished.

A pink and orange tinge graced the eastern skyline when he saw the smoke. Arising from the other side of a hillock a mile away, the gray column signified his hunt was at an end. He slowed to a walk as he neared the base of the small hill and palmed the flintlock.

One of the three must be awake, Nate deduced. Perhaps they had taken turns keeping watch. Reining up, he swung down and moved around the hill until he could see their camp. First he saw the four horses tethered to scrub trees. Then he spied a crude lean-to, the open end facing to the south, away from him. Near it was the fire, beside which squatted Pudge.

Dropping into a crouch, Nate threaded through the grass. He figured Brian and Libbie were still asleep in the lean-to. Well, they were in for a rude awakening! Keeping low, he advanced to within a dozen feet of the fire.

Pudge had the look of someone who was thoroughly miserable. His hair was a mess, he needed a shave, and his homespun clothes were bedraggled. Wedged under his belt was Nate's other pistol. He yawned, then muttered to himself as he warmed his hands.

Nate could see through the gaps between the slender branches forming the wall of the lean-to. Glimpses of golden tresses told him Libbie was lying nearest the back, so Brian must be at the front. Stealthily rising and tiptoeing forward, he came up behind Pudge and lightly touched his flintlock to the greenhorn's head. "Don't make a sound," he warned.

Gasping in fright, Pudge went rigid.

"Did you really think I wouldn't find you?" Nate asked softly, and leaned forward to grab the stolen pistol. Then he moved around to where Pudge could see him. The greenhorn swallowed and looked as if he wanted to dig a hole to hide in. "Give me one good reason why I shouldn't shoot you here and now," Nate said.

"Please, Mr. King," Pudge blubbered. "It wasn't my idea to knock you out and steal your things. Brian did it all on his own. I'm sorry it happened. I truly am."

"Not as sorry as you're going to be. I'm of half a mind to take Libbie on back to her folks and leave the two of you here afoot."

"You wouldn't!"

Nate glanced at the lean-to and raised his voice. "All right, you two! Rise and shine! Company has come calling." He trained both pistols in their direction. "And I want your hands where I can see them or one of you might end up eating lead for breakfast."

He saw Libbie sit up, and grinned at the shock both she and Brian must be experiencing. A moment later she stepped into the open, smoothing her dress down and gazing in amazement at him.

"Mr. King! You're all right! Thank God!"

"As well as a horse like few others," Nate added, wagging a pistol to beckon her closer. He stared at the lean-to, eagerly waiting for her beau to emerge. The prospect of paying Brian back made him tingle with anticipation.

"I'm so glad you weren't hurt," Libbie said sincerely. "I was totally against what Brian did to you, and I tried to get him to revive you and bring you along but he refused to listen."

Nate was wondering why the bastard had yet to appear. He peered at the wall of the lean-to but saw no one moving within. "Where is the no-account varmint?"

"Right behind you!" snapped the gleeful voice of the other greenhorn. "And I've got your rifle pointed at your spine. So if you know what's good for you, you'll drop those pistols and turn around."

For a few seconds Nate hesitated. His reflexes being what they were, he was confident he could step to one side, spin, and fire before Brian got off a shot. Then he heard the distinct click of the Hawken's hammer being cocked. Unfortunately, Libbie was in front of him. If Brian did manage to fire, or simply squeezed the trigger as he fell, the ball might accidentally strike her. Or possibly Pudge if the shot went wild. And he had no grudge against either of them.

"I'm waiting, King," Brian said. "I don't want to shoot you if I can avoid it, but I'll be damned if I'm letting you take Libbie back to her pa. Now put down those pistols!"

Reluctantly, his every instinct telling him he was making a great mistake, Nate lowered the flintlocks to the earth and released them. As he straightened, Brian laughed.

"You mountain men aren't as tough as you're made out to be. We hear all these fantastic stories about how your kind can lick dozens of Injuns with their bare hands and kill grizzlies with just their knives, but it's all hogwash. This is twice I've gotten the better of you."

"Don't remind me," Nate said, his temper soaring. Pivoting, he stared down the barrel of his rifle.

Brian beamed and nodded at the hill to his rear. "I was up yonder keeping watch when you showed up. In another five minutes Pudge would have relieved me." Giving Nate a wide berth, he walked to Libbie's side. "You're too persistent for your own good, Mr. King. What am I going to do with you?"

"I won't have you hurting him again," Libbie declared. "You never should have struck him in the first place."

"What choice did he leave me?" Brian countered. "You were there. I tried to talk him out of taking you back but he wouldn't listen. I even offered him every dollar I have, yet he refused to accept it." Brian scowled. "I didn't like taking unfair advantage of him anymore than you did, my love. Can I help it if he's too thickheaded for his own good?"

Pudge stood and joined them. "What are we going to do with him, Brian?"

"We let him go," Libbie said quickly.

"That would be dumb," Brian declared. "He'd only follow us until he found some way to take us by surprise, then he'd force you to go with him. Is that what you want?"

"No," Libbie answered.

"How about if we take his horse and leave him here?" Pudge suggested. "He'd never catch us."

"That's what we figured before," Brian said, "but that pied nightmare of his tore loose and took off on its own." He glared at Nate. "Your stallion about caved in my head. We'd stopped for a short rest and I was leading it to water when it tore the reins from my hands and ran away. I tried to stop it but it reared on me and knocked me down."

"Pegasus knows a polecat when he sees one."

"Funny man," Brian barked, and nudged Pudge with his elbow. "Get something to tie him with and do it as tight as you can. I don't want him giving us any more trouble."

While he was covered by the Hawken, there was nothing Nate could do as Pudge took a lead rope off of one of the horses and came over to bind him. Pudge used Nate's knife to cut off a piece.

"Sorry again, Mr. King," the hefty youth apologized, then pulled Nate's arms behind his back, looped the rope about Nate's wrists, and secured it with three knots. "There. All done."

Smiling smugly, Brian lowered the Hawken and let the hammer down. "Have a seat, King," he said in a mocking tone, and gestured at a spot near the fire. "I'd offer you some coffee, but I'm afraid we don't have any since you wouldn't try to reclaim our supplies from those savages."

"Don't treat him so, Brian," Libbie scolded.

Nate eased to the ground and crossed his legs. Once again he had taken the greenhorns too lightly and paid for his folly. Once he got free, he would not make the same error in judgment a third time. Glumly, he stared into the crackling flames and resigned himself to being their prisoner for a while.

"Pudge, go try and catch his stallion," Brian directed. "It's grazing on the other side of the hill."

"Why me?" Pudge responded.

"Because I'm not letting Libbie out of my sight," Brian said, sitting across from Nate. "Take the two flintlocks if it will make you feel any better."

"You bet it will," Pudge stated, gladly scooping up both guns. He took a few strides, then paused, fingering the weapons and gazing anxiously out over the open land to the south and west. "What if there are Injuns watching us?"

"I doubt it, or Mr. King wouldn't have walked into our camp the way he did," Brian said. "We're safe. Don't worry."

"Are you in your right mind? I won't stop worrying until we're safe at Fort Leavenworth," Pudge asserted. Bracing his round shoulders, he tramped off to do Brian's bidding.

"Do you really believe you'll make it all the way to Fort Leavenworth with no food and no water?" Nate casually asked. "A person can die of thirst and hunger on the prairie just as easily as from a hostile's arrow or lance."

"Not if that person knows where to find water and game," Brian said.

"And you do?"

"No. You do."

Libbie looked from one to the other. "What are you getting at, dearest?"

"Simply this. Mr. King here must know the Plains as well as he does the mountains. If we take him with us, he'll have to lead us to water and game if he doesn't want to die along the way. So I propose we make him our unwilling companion until we reach civilization."

"And what then?" Libbie inquired.

"Why, we let him go, of course. What can he do then? We'll explain everything to the officer in charge at Leavenworth and I'm sure he'll see things our way. And since the Army has no jurisdiction out here, King can't press charges." He chuckled. "Have no fear. Once we're at the fort, we'll be safe. The Army isn't about to let him murder any of us."

"But it's not right to drag him across the prairie against his will."

"Then give me a better idea," Brian said.

Libbie opened her mouth, closed it, opened it again. "I don't have one," she confessed.

"I do," Nate addressed Brian. "Allow me to take Libbie

to her folks. Pudge and you can ride along and I'll convince Simon to let the two of you join us."

"We've discussed that before and I told you what would happen," Brian said. "No thank you, mountain man. My way is the best."

Further argument would be useless, Nate realized. The younger man had his mind made up, and that was all there was to it. Nate had to exercise the patience of a Shoshone warrior until his chance to turn the tables came, and come it would. Traversing the prairie would take weeks. During one of the times when Brian slept, Nate would teach the arrogant greenhorn just how resourceful mountain men could be.

"Mr. King," Libbie said, "it would have been best for everyone if you had gone back to my folks instead of coming after us. Why didn't you leave well enough alone?"

"And let your true love get the best of me?"

"I see. Your pride was wounded."

"No, my head," Nate corrected her. "You don't see at all, Libbie, because you were born and bred in the States. You don't know that out here a man is measured differently than he is back there. In the States a man is a success if he has a lot of money and power." Nate noticed Brian yawning. "Out here a man is measured several ways, and one of the most important is the measure of his courage. The indians count coup to settle who is the bravest. For free trappers like myself, our reputations take the place of counting coup, although quite a few of us do that at times."

"*You've* counted coup?" she said in surprise.

"Many times," Nate admitted. "I'm an adopted member of the Shoshone tribe. If I didn't count coup, I wouldn't be considered a warrior. I wouldn't be allowed to sit in the councils with the men."

Brian threw back his head and cackled, then glanced at Libbie. "Don't this beat all! Your precious mountain man is as much a savage as those red devils who took us captive."

"It's not like that at all," Nate said harshly. "It's more like earning rank in the army. An Indian starts by going out and stealing a few horses or killing an enemy or two, and in so doing he qualifies to be a warrior. He continues to advance in standing in his tribe by adding to the brave deeds he's done. Eventually he works his way up to become what you might call a Little Chief. And after stealing a certain high number of horses and taking a lot of scalps, he may even earn the title of Great Chief."

"How quaint," Brian commented.

Nate would have slugged the man if his hands were free. Since he had Libbie's thoughtful attention, he went on. "Becoming a warrior is the most important goal in a young Indian's life. If he hasn't done any brave deeds by the time he's twenty, then he's not allowed to take part in councils and has to do the same work as the women. In some tribes the women even get to order him around. No man wants to suffer such a fate." He paused. "So Indians don't count coup just to see who can be the most savage. They do it as a measure of their manhood."

"I think I understand," she said.

"Who cares what Indians do?" Brian interjected. "They all deserve to be rounded up just like cattle and put wherever the government wants to put them. That's what President Jackson said and I believe him."

"You would," Nate muttered.

Brian bristled and started to lift the Hawken; then his gaze went past Nate and he stood. "Where's the stallion?"

"I couldn't get close," Pudge announced. "It saw me coming around the hill and took off like a bat out of hell. Chasing it would have been a waste of time." Walking up beside Nate, he looked down and grinned. "That's sure some horse you've got there, Mr. King."

"Believe me, I know."

"Enough talk," Brian said curtly. "Let's mount and head for South Pass. I know we're all hungry and we haven't eaten since we left the Piegan camp, but by nightfall, with some luck, I'll bag something to eat."

"I hope so," Pudge said. "At this rate, when we get back home folks will change my nickname to Skinny."

It was Pudge who helped Nate get on one of their horses. Brian put out the fire. Libbie went into the lean-to and did whatever women do so that when she came back out she was as radiant as sunshine and her clothes were hardly ruffled at all. And she did it all without a drop of water or the use of comb and brush.

Brian assumed the lead, Libbie riding by his side. Pudge had to lead the animal bearing Nate. They bore to the southeast, holding their horses to a trot that rapidly ate up the miles. Several times Pudge looked at Nate and seemed about to speak, but he always glanced away moments later without saying what was on his mind.

Over an hour after leaving camp, Pudge looked at Nate yet one more time, then suddenly looked startled and pointed to their rear. "I'll be damned! Take a gander at that!"

Twisting, Nate saw Pegasus five hundred yards off, following them. The stallion was cleverly matching their gait and speed. By staying that far out, it could easily avoid being caught should Brian or Pudge go after it. Nate grinned and wished he had the stallion under him instead of the bay he was on.

"What the hell!" Brian declared, having looked over his shoulder at the yell from Pudge. Reining up, he turned his horse and glared at Pegasus. "It's that contrary cuss again! For two cents I'd blow its brains all over the prairie." He raised the Hawken and sighted down the barrel.

By then Nate was almost abreast of Brian's mount since Pudge had not yet stopped. He didn't know whether Brian would really fire, and although the range was too great for any degree of accuracy, he wasn't going to risk his stallion being struck through sheer dumb luck. So as he came even with Brian's mount, he leaned to the side and used his legs to propel himself like a human battering ram at the greenhorn.

Engrossed in taking a bead, Brian was caught off-guard. Nate's head slammed into his side, throwing him off balance, and together they toppled from his horse onto the grass.

Nate landed on his left side and rolled. He heard Brian curse, then surged upright, applying his shoulder against the ground for leverage. As he straightened he lashed out with his right foot, catching the sluggish greenhorn in the pit of the stomach. Brian doubled over, sputtering and wheezing, and Nate followed through with a second kick to the tip of Brian's chin that stretched the younger man out like a board.

"Mr. King, don't!" Libbie wailed. She had drawn rein ten yards ahead, but now she goaded her horse toward them.

Nate quickly sat down, tucked his knees to his chest, and straining mightily, worked his bound hands up over the back of his legs until they cleared his feet. Close by lay his Hawken. Although his wrists were tied, his fingers were loose enough to permit him to grab the rifle and point it at Brian.

"No!" Libbie cried, stopping mere feet away.

Disregarding her, Nate managed to cock the Hawken and touched a finger to the trigger. He was forced to hold the gun awkwardly, but there was no doubt in anyone's mind that he could fire if he was so inclined.

Blinking several times, Brian groaned and rose on his elbows. "You bastard," he said, blood trickling from the corner of his mouth. "You almost broke my jaw."

"I tried my best," Nate countered, backing up to give himself room to maneuver should one of them come at him. That was when he noticed Pudge. The hefty green-horn had swung around but had not drawn a flintlock. Instead, Pudge was staring to the southwest, his forehead knit in perplexity. Overcome by curiosity, Nate shifted in the same direction and felt the short hairs at the base of his neck prickle. A mile off was a long brown line resembling for all the world a brown wave rolling across the basin.

"What the dickens am I looking at?" Pudge asked.

"It's a buffalo stampede," Nate answered, "and they're heading right this way."

Chapter Twelve

"Dear God!" Pudge blurted out in horror.

"What do we do?" Libbie asked.

"We get out of their path or we get trampled," Nate said, and stepped up to her horse. "I need your help. Climb down and cut me loose. And hurry."

"No!" Brian roared, pushing off the ground and taking an unsteady stride, his fists balled at his waist. "Don't you dare listen to him, Libbie!"

Pivoting, Nate leveled the Hawken. "Not another step, polecat," he warned, "or I'll put a ball through you." His steely tone stopped Brian cold. The greenhorn made no response, his eyes pools of simmering hatred.

Suddenly they all heard the sound of distant drumming, like thunder rumbling far off.

"You'd better hurry," Nate reminded Libbie.

She needed no further persuasion. Jumping down, she used his own butcher knife to slice through the ropes, and tossed them at his feet when she was done. "Which way do we go?" she then asked apprehensively.

The same question was uppermost in Nate's mind. The buffalo were spread out over a half-mile front and were now only three quarters of a mile off. It was a small herd, but trying to outflank it would be a risky proposition. If one of their horses flagged, its rider was doomed.

When buffaloes stampeded, they stopped for nothing. Nothing at all. Which was why Indians often surrounded a herd, provoked a stampede in the direction of a convenient cliff, and drove hundreds of the dumb brutes to their deaths. Afterward, there was always plenty of meat for everyone in the village and much rejoicing.

"What got them going?" Pudge wondered.

"Anything under the sun," Nate said, about to issue instructions when he remembered something he had to do. Hastening over to Pudge's horse, he extended his right hand. "Both of my pistols. Now."

"Yes, sir. Whatever you say," Pudge said, transparently glad to comply. "Just save us from those monsters, will you?"

Nate pointed to the northwest, at part of the range of hills and mountains forming the eastern boundary of the Green River Basin. The nearest foothill stood less than a mile off. "Ride for your lives," he advised. "When you reach the trees, don't stop. Make for high ground and the herd should pass you by."

"Should?" Libbie said.

Pudge wasted no words. His legs flapping against his mount, he slanted toward the closest foothill, dust rising in large puffs from under the flying hoofs of his animal.

"You too," Nate said, running up behind Libbie's horse and giving it a smack on the rump. In a flash she was racing after Pudge.

"What about me?" Brian asked. "I suppose you'll take the other two horses and leave me here to be crushed to a pulp."

"You take them."

"What?" Brian said, as if unsure he had heard correctly.

"You take them," Nate repeated, and sprinted madly toward Pegasus. The stallion had halted four hundred yards away and was staring intently at the swelling line of onrushing bison. "Pegasus!" Nate shouted, waving his arms. "Come to me! Come on!"

If the stallion recognized him, it made no move to obey. Perhaps fascinated by the fury of the stampede, it simply stood there and stared.

"Pegasus! Don't just stand there, you simpleton!" Nate bellowed, his limbs flying, running as he had seldom run before. Pegasus looked at him but didn't move. Of all the times for the stallion to be fickle! "Come on, darn you!" he yelled. "Or we're both goners!"

At last Pegasus moved to intercept him, but at a walk, not a trot.

"Faster, damn you!" Nate urged. Well past the stallion he could see the front ranks of buffaloes, their shaggy heads low to the ground, their massive bodies partially obscured by the thick dust cloud swirling from underneath them. Was there time for him to mount and reach the hills before the herd did? It would be close. Too close.

Pegasus moved faster, reaching a trot in seconds.

When the stallion was almost upon him, Nate swerved two steps to the right, let the big horse come alongside, and vaulted into the saddle while Pegasus was still in motion. The Hawken clutched tight in his left hand, he worked the reins and his legs and was immediately speeding for the sanctuary of the inviting green hills.

Pudge was hundreds of yards ahead. Libbie rode close in his wake. Brian, astride their third horse, was halfway between Nate and the others. The last horse, the bay, had been left exactly where it had stopped after Nate jumped off it. He glanced at the abandoned animal but did not veer from his course; any further delay would prove too costly. The bay would have to fend for itself.

The thundering of the herd grew and grew, until looking back Nate could see the wicked, curved horns of the leaders and imagined he could also see their brooding dark eyes and their flaring nostrils. Pegasus was galloping as fast as Pegasus could go and still the herd appeared to be gaining. Nate bent forward, his heart beating wildly in time to the driving rhythm of the stallion's hoofs. *Go! Go! Go!* he shrieked in his mind.

Repeatedly he glanced at the buffaloes, fearful he had gotten underway too late. On his next glance he saw the bay break into a run. Belatedly, it had realized the urgency of fleeing. That most basic of creature instincts, self-preservation, sparked the bay into a mad dash for its life, a dash that it lost not a minute later.

The first squeal was almost humanlike, so much so that it chilled Nate's skin. He saw the front rank of bison overhaul the terrified horse, saw the bay go down amid a swirl of hoofs and tails and slashing horns. Some of the foremost buffaloes tried to jump over the obstacle, and failed. Those behind the leaders never wavered, never parted even slightly. Their hoofs reduced the bay to a pulpy mass in the time it would take a man to pull on his boots.

Nate graphically knew what to expect should he suffer the same horrendous fate. Like the wind he rode, and like a raging storm the stampeding herd pursued him. He set his eyes on the first hill to the exclusion of all else. If he went down, it wouldn't be for a lack of trying.

Each second became an eternity. The buffaloes didn't gain any more ground, nor did they lose any.

Pudge was the first among the trees, and as Nate had directed he headed straight for the crown of the hill. Seconds later Libbie did likewise.

Nate had given that advice because he had witnessed stampedes before, and knew from prior observation that herds invariably broke in half at the base of hills and mountains to sweep around on either side rather than go up and over the crest. He counted on these buffaloes doing the same.

But could he reach the top before them? Despite the stallion's superb performance, the bison would be so close at the bottom of the hill that if the stallion stumbled just once on the slope the herd would be on them before Pegasus recovered. So Nate opted to change his tactic.

Presently the hill loomed before him. With a jerk of the reins he cut sharply to the left, hugging the bottom. To his rear a tremendous din of earth-shaking proportions drowned out all other sound. The ground itself seemed to tremble. He glanced upward and glimpsed Brian racing up the slope. Libbie and Pudge were lost among the trees, and he hoped they would reach the top safely.

He dared to look at the herd just as the seething mass of unstoppable brutes reached the hill. As he had expected, the buffaloes parted, some bearing right, some left. But, to his consternation, not all imitated the example of those in the foremost ranks. A large bunch in the middle of the mass went straight up the hill, straight toward Libbie and the greenhorns!

His hope of evading the herd was now diminished. He'd intended to go around to the far side, then angle up the slope. But if he did so now, he'd run smack-dab into the portion of the herd going up and over. So he must come up with another brainstorm, and do it quickly.

Pegasus flew to the opposite side. Already a few buffaloes had appeared at the south end. Instantly Nate cut to the left, bearing due east, barreling into pines and brush that crackled as he plowed through.

The two prongs of the herd were sweeping around the hill as the third bunch rumbled over the top.

Faintly, Nate heard a scream. Or was it his imagination? He tried not to think of what might have happened to

Libbie if she had been caught in the open. He couldn't do her any good anyway, not unless and until he saved his own skin.

The swiftest buffaloes were not more than 30 yards behind him. They charged into the forest with the force of a tornado, smashing aside anything and everything in their way.

Nate weaved among trunks and hurdled logs while casting about for a means of escape. He anticipated the stampede would lose its momentum before too long. The trick was to stay alive till then. Bearing to the left, he sought for the end of the foremost line of bison, but saw only beast after beast after beast.

On and on he rode, losing sight of the hill because of the canopy of limbs overhead. Without warning the trees thinned and he found himself in a narrow valley. Heading up the center, the wind rushing past his face, he searched for a way out of his predicament. *Any* way out would do. He wasn't fussy.

The valley bore to the right, meandering between a pair of jagged peaks, one of which threw an enormous shadow across the valley floor.

"Yea, though I walk through the valley of the shadow of death," Nate thought to himself, and suddenly stiffened on seeing that which promised to make the quotation come true. Two hundred yards ahead reared a rugged bluff. The valley was a trap!

To the right and left were steep slopes, so steep Pegasus would not be able to climb either without falling. To his rear arose the constant rolling thunder of the herd. A hasty glance showed him the buffaloes had him completely boxed in.

Of all the rotten times for his luck to run out! Nate reflected, desperately scanning the slopes and the bluff. He was not at all ready to meet his Maker; he had a wife and son depending on him for their sustenance. And of all the ways to be killed, being caught in a stampede had to be one of his least favorite. It would be much better to die in bed wearing a smile on his lips, and nothing else.

He was almost to the bluff. The bison had slowed, but not enough. They promised to sweep right up to the bottom of the bluff, and in the process to bury him beneath tons upon tons of hurtling sinew and muscle.

Then Nate spotted the game trail where the bluff and the slope on the right blended together. It wasn't much of one, a winding ribbon stretching from the valley floor to near the top of the peak, but he was in no mood to quibble. As the old saying stated so well, beggars couldn't be choosers. Either he took the trail or he died.

Incentive like that took him up the slope faster than was prudent. Pegasus slipped, faltered, and was on the verge of falling when Nate hauled on the reins and shifted his balance, giving the stallion help enough to carry it forward. From there on up he was compelled to take the ascent slowly, his gaze riveted on the herd below.

The buffaloes were moving at a trifle of their previous speed when the leaders came to the bluff and halted. Those pressing so tightly together in the main body of the herd did the same, and within moments what had once been a panicked horde of bison resembled more a peacefully grazing herd of tame cattle.

Nate climbed steadily. The only tracks on the game trail were those of bighorn sheep, and he marveled that the big stallion could negotiate the same terrain. Toward the top the going became exceedingly difficult. Pegasus slipped time and again, but never fell.

"You can do it, boy," Nate coaxed, and wasn't disappointed. Not quite an hour after commencing the ascent, they came to where the trail led over the crest and down into another valley. Pausing, he surveyed the tranquil herd, then gazed to the west at the distant hill where he had last seen the greenhorns and Libbie. Were any of them still alive?

The descent took half the time of the climb. Once at the bottom of the spacious valley, he turned toward the hill. He felt weary and slumped in the saddle. Having pushed Pegasus so hard in fleeing from the buffaloes, he let the horse take its sweet time, although he was sorely tempted to gallop the entire way.

The countryside lay entombed in silence when he arrived. None of the usual wildlife was present, every animal that could having fled at the onset of the onrushing herd. Eventually the birds and squirrels would come out of hiding and the forest would resume its normal pattern of life, but for the time being it was as if he rode across an alien landscape devoid of life.

"Libbie?" Nate called out at the base of the hill. "Are you up there?"

The only answer was the sighing wind.

Most of the hill was a shambles. From top to bottom the buffaloes had flattened the underbrush, uprooted and flattened trees, and scarred the earth with their iron hoofs.

Nate rode upward, scouring for sign. At the top he halted. The west slope was in the same condition as the east. Broken limbs lay everywhere. Bent and snapped trees made a mockery of Nature's design. "Libbie?" he repeated, to no avail. He started down slowly, his eyes roaming over the blistered slope, then reined up on spying a large lump of bloody flesh off to the left.

The general outline baffled him until he detected the wispy vestige of a tail and realized he was staring at the hindquarters of one of the horses. The animal had been literally torn apart. Moving closer, he saw a torn leg, then another, both ruptured, the cracked bones exposed. Scattered bits of grass, pine needles, and clods of dirt partially covered the horse's head, but not enough to conceal the pulverized flesh and the bulging eyes.

Nate had seldom seen such a revolting sight, and his stomach churned. The implications were even more upsetting. If a horse had gone down, so had its rider. So which one had paid the ultimate price for foolishly trying to grapple with the wilderness on its own terms when all three of them were woefully ignorant of the basics of wilderness survival? Which one would have been better off staying in the States, where the worst a man had to contend with was an occasional marauding black bear or a poisonous snake?

He saw a leg jutting from out of a smashed thicket and at first mistook it for part of a tree trunk. Then he saw the shoe and the homespun pants, both coated with dried blood. Inwardly, he was relieved. The horse had not been Libbie's. "Please let it be Brian," he said to himself, stopping beside the mangled mess lying in the midst of shattered limbs and crushed leaves. "Please."

But it wasn't.

Pudge had fallen onto his back and had never had the chance to rise. Hundreds of driving hoofs had reduced his body to the consistency of pudding. Strangely enough, except for a pair of slash marks on his right cheek and a lot of grime, his face was intact. His eyes were wide open, his mouth the same, his tongue poking out. He had screamed as death claimed him, but it was doubtful he had heard it over the din of the herd.

Nate climbed down and gathered up enough branches and brush to cover the greenhorn's head. It was the least he could do. No, not quite, he promptly corrected himself. There was one more thing. Pudge deserved to go properly.

He stood for a moment with bowed head, trying to think of the right words to say, but except for a passable knowledge of the Psalms and the words of Jesus, he wasn't much good at quoting from the Bible. Feeling uncomfortable, he tried anyway.

"Forgive him, Lord, for being a dunderhead. He had no business being out here. But he came because his friend did, and, if I recollect rightly, 'Greater love hath no man than this, that a man lay down his life for his friends.' If that's the case, then Pudge here died the way a man should, and I hope his soul makes it to your side. Amen."

Mounting, he grimly resumed his search. The others must have suffered a similar grisly fate. He dreaded finding Libbie, but he wouldn't stop until he did. She also deserved to have a few words spoken over her remains. He would leave Brian for the vultures and the coyotes.

An hour of intensive hunting, crisscrossing the slope again and again, produced no results. He stopped at the bottom and scratched his chin. If Libbie and Brian had been trampled, he should have found some trace. Since he hadn't, both must have somehow survived. Then where had they gone?

The obvious answer drew his gaze to the southeast. "Damn, not again," he muttered, and broke into a gallop. The pair had a two-hour head start. If he overtook them by noon he would be fortunate.

Once Nate rode clear of the ground torn up by the bison, he immediately spied two sets of fresh horse tracks leading in the general direction of South Pass. Brian had wasted no time. Nate figured they had cut out the minute the buffalo had passed over the hill. Or the minute after they'd found poor Pudge.

A rare, cold hatred seeped into Nate's soul. He imagined what it would be like to seize Brian in his hands and throttle the life from the bastard. The greenhorn had been an unending source of trouble ever since they met. And now, once again, Brian was bucking the wishes of Libbie's parents and trying to get her out of the territory at all costs. The idiot! Didn't he realize the pair of them stood little chance of crossing the prairie alone and unarmed?

He wondered what she saw in the man. Brian was handsome, he supposed, but a flashing smile wasn't everything. Inner qualities counted for more, qualities like courage and devotion and loyalty. And a dash of common sense, which Brian evidently lacked.

This time he would not go easy on them. He would truss Libbie up, if need be, and throw her on her horse. If Brian objected—and Nate hoped he did—then Nate would thrash Brian within an inch of his life. Possibly closer. Libbie must cease acting like a child and do what was best for the Banner family.

The hours elapsed slowly. From the depth and spacing of the tracks, Nate gathered that Libbie and the greenhorn were riding their animals into the ground. They had yet to learn that he would catch them no matter how fast or how far they rode.

Noon came and went.

Since his throat was parched, he knew Pegasus was equally thirsty. So when he came abreast of a hill known to have a year-round spring on its north side, he strayed from the trail to give them both a short rest. The ice-cold water was delicious and he drank to his heart's content. Pegasus was still drinking when he leaned against a boulder and rested the Hawken in his lap.

He thought of the Banners and the Websters, who must be besides themselves by now over his prolonged absence. Were they waiting for him to return, or in their impatience had they continued westward? If so, they might well be dead, meaning all his hard effort was being wasted. Time would tell.

Given the ability demonstrated by the emigrants, Nate sincerely hoped that great numbers of them would *not* flock to the promised land, for their own sakes. Many, far too many, would perish before they ever saw the crashing surf of the Pacific Ocean. And a line of bleached bones would be the only legacy they left behind.

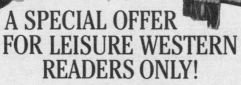

A SPECIAL OFFER FOR LEISURE WESTERN READERS ONLY!

Get FOUR FREE Western Novels

Travel to the Old West in all its glory and drama—without leaving your home!

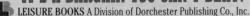

GET YOUR 4 FREE BOOKS NOW—
A VALUE BETWEEN $16 AND $20

Mail the Free Book Certificate Today!

FREE BOOKS CERTIFICATE!

YES! I want to subscribe to the Leisure Western Book Club. Please send my 4 FREE BOOKS. Then, each month, I'll receive the four newest Leisure Western Selections to preview FREE for 10 days. If I decide to keep them, I will pay the Special Members Only discounted price of just $3.36 each, a total of $13.44. This saves me between $3 and $6 off the bookstore price. There are no shipping, handling or other charges. There is no minimum number of books I must buy and I may cancel the program at any time. In any case, the 4 FREE BOOKS are mine to keep—at a value of between $17 and $20! Offer valid only in the USA.

Name_____

Address_____

City_____ State_____

Zip_____ Phone_____

Biggest Savings Offer!

For those of you who would like to pay us in advance by check or credit card—we've got an even bigger savings in mind. Interested? Check here. ☐

If under 18, parent or guardian must sign.
Terms, prices and conditions subject to change. Subscription subject to acceptance. Leisure Books reserves the right to reject any order or cancel any subscription.

GET FOUR BOOKS TOTALLY *FREE*—A VALUE BETWEEN $16 AND $20

PLEASE RUSH
MY FOUR FREE
BOOKS TO ME
RIGHT AWAY!

Leisure Western Book Club
P.O. Box 6613
Edison, NJ 08818-6613

Or would it?

Nate remembered all the quaint if sparse settlements along the frontier where hard-working men and women eked out spartan existences by wrestling day in and day out with a harsh land that fought them every step of the way. Drought, insects, hostiles, floods; all these the hardy breed of settlers took in stride, refusing to give up in the face of cruel adversity.

Perhaps he had misjudged them. He still didn't want thousands of greenhorns to invade the Indian lands, but he now knew that if they did, they would come to stay. The Indians would be unable to drive them off, and in the long run the prairie and the mountains would become just another stepping-stone on the path to American's conquest of the continent.

A buzzing bee intruded on his reflection and he stood. What had gotten into him? It didn't do for a man to ponder weighty matters when he should be tending to business. Pegasus was done, so he climbed up and headed out, bearing, as ever, to the southeast.

When the dots appeared, Nate didn't quite know what to make of them. There were two, on the horizon, not moving at all. Whatever they were, they must be big. He doubted they were buffalo or elk, which left a single, troubling, likelihood.

Riding closer, he distinguished the silhouettes of a pair of horses. That spurred him to ride at a gallop until he was within 50 yards of the pair; then he slowed. They were the horses Libbie and Brian had been riding, but there was no trace of the lovely girl or her beau.

Puzzled, suspecting the handiwork of hostiles, Nate cocked the Hawken and rode to within 20 feet, then drew rein. Sliding down, he warily advanced. The horses simply gazed at him. He saw that the high grass all around them had been trampled down but bore no evidence of hoof marks. Something other than the horses must have been responsible. Glancing to the right and left, concerned he was blundering into a trap, he strode toward the animal Libbie had been riding. He had a yard to cover when suddenly something grabbed hold of both his ankles and he was brutally slammed to the earth.

Chapter Thirteen

Nate had to let go of the Hawken and throw out his hands to cushion the impact. The pressure on his ankles relaxed, but was instantly replaced by something encircling his knees, and looking down he saw that Brian had seized hold of him and was trying to keep him pinned to the ground. He also saw how he had been tricked. There was a shallow depression, not more than a foot deep but at least 12 feet long, that the devious greenhorn and Libbie had used as their hiding place; had lain down in it earlier and then covered themselves with flattened grass. If he had been more attentive, he might have figured out their ploy. Nate wanted to kick himself. He had stupidly walked right into their trap, and they had him right where they wanted him.

Now Libbie was also emerging from concealment, her fair features etched with the same somber desperation as Brian's. "Get his pistols!" Brian screeched.

Shocked to find Libbie working in concert with the greenhorn, Nate belatedly made a grab for his right flintlock. But Libbie reached him before his hand could close on the gun and grabbed his wrist.

"Please, Mr. King!" she cried. "Don't resist and we won't hurt you!"

Nate could feel Brian clawing higher, toward his waist, and he streaked his left hand down, grasping the other pistol. Again, though, Libbie thwarted him by grabbing his wrist.

"Please!" she pleaded.

Thinking only of what would happen should Brian gain possession of one of his weapons, Nate wrenched his arms up and out, tearing loose from Libbie, and threw himself to the left, away from her, trying to roll but unable to do more than twist because of Brian's hold on his legs. He kicked out, or attempted to, his leverage limited by the weight of the greenhorn's body.

Libbie lunged at his knife.

Nate shoved her aside and she tripped and fell. Bending forward, he delivered a punch to the side of Brian's head. The greenhorn abruptly let go of his legs, surging upward and snatching at one of the flintlocks. Nate pounded him again. Suddenly Brian vented an inarticulate snarl of rage, dived at his throat, and wrapped both hands around his neck.

Together they rolled over and over. Locked face-to-face, they fought as men driven.

Nate felt Brian's fingers gouging into his windpipe, cutting off his air, and he whipped a right that cracked hard on the greenhorn's chin. But Brian clung fast. Another blow rocked him and his grip slackened slightly.

"Stop it, please!" Libbie wailed.

Neither man heeded her. Brian, beet red, his veins bulging, was trying with all his might to throttle the life from Nate. For his part, Nate gasped for air and struggled to pry Brian's steely fingers off his neck. He was amazed at the man's strength. It was as if Brian had inexplicably become as strong as ten men.

Nate hurled himself to the left, then immediately reversed direction in an effort to throw Brian off balance. He was only partially successful. Brian's body slipped to one side, but the man's fingers remained locked on his throat. Already Nate's lungs were burning in anguish. He began to feel light-headed and knew he must get air to them and get air to them *now*.

If there was one lesson Nate had learned from his Shoshone friends about mortal combat, that lesson could be summed up in two words. Anything goes. When a warrior's life was on the line, he did whatever it took to prevail. Biting, scratching, kicking, they were all done in the heat of intense battle when the difference between time and eternity hung in the balance. So it was that Nate entertained no compunctions about snapping both hands up and gouging his thumbs into Brian's eyes, digging his nails in as far as he could.

The greenhorn yelped and released his hold as he tried to protect his precious sight.

At the very moment that Brian's hands fell from Nate's neck, Nate rolled yet again, to one knee, and rammed his right fist into the greenhorn's face. Brian toppled, groaning and sputtering, his hands pressed to his eyelids.

"You've blinded me! You've blinded me!"

Taking deep breaths, Nate shoved upright and drew his flintlocks. "I doubt it," he muttered. "Now on your feet." He took a step and prodded Brian with his toe.

"I can't see, I tell you!"

Libbie stood a few yards off in an apparent daze. "We were so close," she said softly. "So close."

"You would never have made it to the settlements by yourselves," Nate responded. "I'm doing you a favor by escorting you back to your pa."

"If you only knew," she said.

Nate stared at Brian. Curled in a fetal position on the ground, the greenhorn was vigorously rubbing his eyes and whining pathetically. "I told you to stand," Nate declared, and delivered a light kick to the man's side. "You'd better listen. It wouldn't be wise to get me any madder than I am."

"Damn you!" Brian rasped, tears of anguish rolling down his cheeks. Lowering his hands, he pushed unsteadily to his feet. He cracked his eyelids, squinted at the world around him, and sniffled. "Lord, it hurts."

"But you can see, can't you?"

Brian glowered.

"Can't you?" Nate demanded, pointing a pistol at the greenhorn's midsection.

"Yes! No thanks to you!"

"Next time I'll slit your throat. Would that make you happier?" Nate said sarcastically, and moved closer to Libbie. "I'm disappointed in you," he informed her. "I thought we were friends."

"We are," she said.

"Then why did you help him?"

"I had to."

"Why?"

She averted her gaze, her hands clasped at her waist, her shoulders trembling.

"Why?" Nate persisted.

"Leave her alone!" Brian declared, stepping nearer. "She's been tormented enough. But if you take her back, her torment will never end." He held out his hands as would a beggar desiring alms. "If you have a spark of decency in your soul, you'll forget this happened, mount up, and ride off."

"We're all going back," Nate said.

Brian drew himself up to his full height and opened his watery eyes a bit more. "The only way you're taking her back to that bastard is over my dead body."

"Don't tempt me."

"I mean it," Brian said, clenching his fists. "I don't care if you kill me. My life isn't important. Libbie's welfare is." He took a menacing stride. "So drop those pistols or else!"

"You're insane," Nate said, training both guns on the greenhorn's chest.

"I know what I'm doing," Brian stated gruffly. He took another pace. "What will it be, King? Do you allow us to leave, or will you have the murder of an innocent man on your conscience for the rest of your life?"

"I'm taking her to the wagons," Nate said, and cocked both flintlocks.

His eyes alight with passionate zeal, Brian paused and coiled to spring. "If not for your meddling, she would be safe right now. We'd be well on our way east. And Pudge, dear Pudge, would still be alive. He was the best friend I had in the whole world, and he died because of you."

"I had no part in his death. He was killed in the stampede. Those things happen all the time out here."

"Do they now?" Brian said bitterly. "But if you hadn't shown up at our camp when you did, if you hadn't delayed us further by attacking me when I went to shoot your horse, we wouldn't have been anywhere near that herd when they stampeded. We'd have been miles from the spot." He gazed sadly skyward and spoke to the clouds. "Why did it have to be Pudge? I saw that he was about to ride into a low limb and I yelled but he couldn't hear me. He went down and didn't move, and I had no chance to reach him before the bison did. I barely had time to get behind a boulder!"

There was no doubting the sincerity of the greenhorn's remorse, but Nate refused to accept responsibility for the tragedy. "If you're going to place blame, place some on yourself. If you hadn't spirited Libbie from her folks, *none* of this would have happened."

"I knew you wouldn't understand," Brian said, and unexpectedly leaped.

Nate was almost caught by surprise. Almost, yet not quite. He shifted to the right, so that Brian missed tackling him, and rammed a flintlock into the man's temple. Brian fell prone, stunned.

"No more!" Libbie screamed, dashing over and throwing herself protectively on top of the one she loved. "I can't stand to see him hurt! Please don't hit him again!"

"That's up to him."

She looked tenderly at the greenhorn, then caressed his brow. "You wouldn't despise him so if you knew the truth. And I think it's time you were told."

"No!" Brian blurted out in a whisper. "Don't!"

"Yes, beloved," Libbie said. "It's the only way. If he knows, he may agree to let us go."

"He has no right to know!" Brian disagreed. "It's our burden, and ours alone." Grunting, he rose on an elbow and raised his other hand to touch her cheek. "Let the past be buried. Every time you dig it up, every time you relive the nightmare, you're only adding to your misery."

"We *must,*" Libbie insisted, and slowly rose to stare Nate straight in the eyes. "Mr. King, I don't blame you for any of this. You had no idea when you agreed to guide us that you would be working for a murderer."

"A murderer? Your father?"

Libbie nodded.

"Who did he kill?"

"Our child."

Nate glanced at Brian, who was as white as milk, then back at her. "I'll admit your father isn't the most tolerant man I've ever met, but a murderer? How do I know you're not making this up so I'll go along with what you want?"

"Not quite a year ago I gave birth to a healthy baby girl," Libbie disclosed, her lower lip quivering. "I'll admit I made a mistake. I should have waited to be in the family way until after Brian and I were married, but I couldn't help myself. I love him so much." She stopped, her voice breaking, and coughed. Do you have any idea how people in the States regard a woman who has a child out of wedlock, Mr. King?"

Nate nodded, but she seemed not to notice.

"They regard her as sinful. To them, she is no better than a common prostitute. People shun her. They go out of their way to avoid her. Even her church congregation wants nothing to do with her, and her family ends up sharing the blame," Libbie said, tears flowing freely. "I know. I saw it happen to a cousin of mine."

There was no need for words so Nate made no comment.

"I would have gladly faced all that," Libbie went on. "With Brian by my side, I would have faced anything. But my pa never liked Brian. Pa refused to let me see him, so I had to sneak away whenever I could." Her voice broke again. "When I became in the family way, Pa saw red. He beat me within an inch of my life, then vowed that no daughter of his was going to give the family a bad name by acting like a whore. He warned Brian to stay away from me or he would kill him. And he made me a prisoner in our own house. Once I was so big that it showed, he wouldn't even let me use the outhouse except at night."

Tears were pouring down Brian's face.

Libbie dabbed at the tip of her nose with her sleeve. "Ma helped me deliver, and as soon as the baby came out, Pa took her."

"Took her?" Nate repeated.

"Yes." Her tears were a virtual torrent now. "I never did find out where until a few months later when I came on a mound of dirt at the back of our property."

"Dear God."

"From then on, Pa wouldn't let me out of his sight. He was worried I'd, soil the family name again. He was also scared someone might find out what had happened, so he decided we should move somewhere else and start all over. He sold our farm, and off to the promised land we went."

Nate let down the hammers on the flintlocks and tucked them under his belt. His throat was oddly constricted. There was also an itching sensation in his nose as he stepped up to her and put his hands on her slender shoulders. "You should have told me sooner."

"Now will you let us go in peace?"

"You'll never make it alone."

"We have to try."

"You don't have any guns. You don't have any supplies."

"We'll make do."

"And what about the hostiles? What about the grizzlies and all the other wild beasts?"

"God will watch over us."

The lump in Nate's throat grew, and he had to cough himself. "Why not go to Oregon? I'll make certain your pa doesn't bother you."

"We can't, and you know it."

"Then I'll find a spot in the hills where you can stay until I get back. I'll see you safely to Fort Leavenworth, and I won't charge you a penny."

Libbie smiled. "You're a kind man, Mr. King. I've always known that. But what about your family? And we both know Brian and I would be hard pressed to live off the land. We'd be better off heading east."

"There has to be another way."

"There isn't."

For all of ten seconds Nate racked his brain. At last, his soul heavy with sorry, his mind ablaze with indignation, he uttered a heartfelt, "Damn!" Then, again, so softly the word was barely audible. "Damn."

They saw him coming from a long way off, and were waiting in a state of nervous agitation when he reached the wagons. The Websters hung back. But Simon and Alice hurried up to him and the former gripped his arm as he dismounted.

"Speak, man! Where the devil is she? Don't tell me you couldn't find them?"

Nate stared at Banner's hand until the man removed it. Wearily, he tied Pegasus to a wheel and leaned back. "I found them, all right," he announced, "and I'm afraid I have bad news."

"Please, no" Alice breathed.

"You'll have to go on to the Oregon Territory by yourselves," Nate said.

"But what about Libbie?" Simon roared. "Is she alive? What could have happened to her and those two degenerates who took her?"

"The Piegans," Nate said.

Both husband and wife recoiled, aghast.

"Tell me it's not so!" Simon declared.

"I wish I could," Nate responded. "They ran into the rest of the same war party that attacked us."

For a fleeting second Simon's countenance reflected profound sorrow, then the sorrow was replaced by hate so overwhelming that he flushed scarlet and clenched his fists until the knuckles were pale. "It's all *their* fault! That sinful Derrick boy and his fat friend! They stole our precious girl out from under us and got her killed by their stupidity! If they were still alive I'd beat their brains out!" Spinning, he stalked off toward the stream, raining blows on everything in his path.

Nate watched him go, then looked at Alice. She was studying him from head to toe, her brow knit in deep thought.

"I've always taken you for a remarkably careful man, Mr. King. One of the most careful men I've ever met."

"Thank you."

"Yes indeed. So I find it quite surprising that you seem to have lost some of your effects while you were gone," Alice said, and pointed at his waist. "For instance, I could have sworn you once carried a knife with you."

"I dropped it somewhere."

"Oh. And did you also drop one of your pistols? I seem to recall you had two, not one."

"I lost it while going through thick brush. Don't fret yourself. I have another one at home."

"Thick brush, you say? Is that where you lost your powder horn and ammunition pouch as well?"

"I don't rightly know. It's not important. I have plenty to spare in my parfleche."

"Do you now?" Alice said, glancing at the stallion. "Why, you've apparently lost one of *those* as well. Didn't you have two before?"

"They never do stay on very well no matter how tight you tie them," Nate said.

Alice Banner's eyes were moist but sparkling with an inner light as she leaned forward and whispered, "Have no fear. Your secret is safe with me. I doubt my husband will even notice." Straightening, her cheeks and chin trembling she said huskily, "Bless you, sir. I only pray she finds the happiness she so truly deserves at long, long last."

"So do I, ma'am. More than you'll ever know."

APACHE
BLOOD

Chapter One

They were only ten miles along on their journey when their huge black dog spied the hostiles.

It was late morning. The party of five, consisting of two brawny, bearded men, two lovely Indian women, and one grinning boy vibrant with excitement, had just crested a low ridge. Before them, extending from north to south, ran the long emerald line of rolling foothills that bordered the majestic Rocky Mountains to their rear.

In the lead rode a strapping young man sporting a mane of black hair that flowed past his broad shoulders. His alert green eyes swept the foothills and the well-nigh limitless prairie beyond, but he detected no movement. Satisfied, he started down the ridge, and it was then that the dog voiced a low growl.

Nathaniel King reined up sharply and glanced at the mongrel, which was gazing intently to the southwest, its thin lips curled up over its tapered teeth. "What's got you riled, Samson?" he asked softly, and stared in the

5

same direction. Instantly he saw them, not quite a mile away, seven or eight riders moving between a pair of foothills, heading for the plain. He could tell they were Indians, but they were too far off to note details of dress and hair that would enable him to determine the tribe to which they belonged.

"Utes!" declared the white-haired man behind him. "A war party out to count coup, I reckon."

Nate snorted. "You're guessing, Shakespeare. You'd have to be an eagle to see them clearly from here."

The elderly mountain man gave a snort of his own. "That's the trouble with you young cubs. Your don't use your senses—your eyes, ears, and nose—like you should, the way animals do. That's because your brains are always half asleep," he said, and launched into a quote from his favorite playwright. "Care keeps his watch in every old man's eye, and where care lodges, sleep will never lie. But where unbruised youth with unstuffed brain doth couch his limbs, there golden sleep doth reign."

Despite himself, Nate chuckled. His mentor's passion for the writings of William Shakespeare was legendary among the trapping fraternity, which explained the nickname bestowed on McNair years ago by his friends. "If you say they're Utes, I'll believe you," he responded. "You're seldom wrong."

"What do you mean by *seldom*?" McNair demanded.

Nate was watching the band below. Utes often attacked whites on sight, and he had to be ready to get his family to safety. Fortunately, the warriors were moving to the east, their backs to the ridge. Unless one of them turned completely around, he and his loved ones were safe. Even so, his left hand gripped the Hawken resting across his thighs a bit tighter.

Like most free trappers, Nate was a walking arsenal. In addition to the rifle, he carried a pair of single-shot

.55-caliber flintlocks tucked under his wide brown leather belt. On his right hip, in a beaded sheath, was a large hunting knife. Wedged under his belt above his left hip was a tomahawk. And slanted across his powerful chest was a powder horn and an ammo pouch.

"Should we take cover, Pa?" inquired the boy, seated astride his roan a few yards from McNair.

"No, Zach," answered Nate. "We hold still until they're gone. Remember what I taught you about how much easier it is to see something that's moving than something that's not?"

"Yep," Zachary said. "And I've been practicing, Pa. The other day an old she-bear walked right by me and didn't bat an eye. She figured I was a tree or a bush, I bet!"

"Oh? I thought I told you to stay away from bears. Grizzlies will tear you to pieces, boy. And even black bears can be mean when—"

"The Utes," Shakespeare interrupted urgently.

One look showed Nate why. The band had stopped for some reason, and the last several warriors were still visible in the gap between the hills.

Suddenly the warrior bringing up the rear stretched and idly surveyed the surrounding countryside. He scanned both hills, then twisted to admire the snow-crowned Rockies.

"Keep your horses still," Nate cautioned the others, and hoped the swishing of their animals' tails wouldn't give them away. There was no way to stop their mounts and the four packhorses from moving their tails. But at such a distance, the odds of the Ute noticing were slim. It would take someone with sharper eyes than McNair to spot such slight motion.

His own horse, a superb gelding distinguished by black leopard spots on a dusky background, was holding itself as rigid as a statue. Pegasus was the name he had given it, in remembrance of a mythical flying steed he had often read about as a child. The gelding was a gift from the grateful Nez Percé, bestowed after he helped them fight off a Blackfoot war party.

Few white men owned a Nez Percé horse, although most would give a year's wages to do so. This was because the Nez Percé had been breeding their Palouses, as the breed was commonly called, ever since the days of the Spanish conquistadors. Now, few horses could match a Palouse for speed and endurance. They were highly prized by all men who knew their horseflesh.

Pegasus, in fact, had been the object of much envy from Nate's fellow trappers at the annual Rendezvous. Some had made generous offers to buy him, but Nate had refused them all. Pegasus was the best horse he'd ever owned—the best he had ever seen—and he would rather part with an arm or a leg than the gelding.

So now, as the Palouse stood stock still as if sensing their danger, he affectionately touched his hand to its neck and whispered, "Good boy!" He saw the Ute warrior face front again, and moments later the band vanished into dense forest.

"Do you reckon that one saw us?" Zachary asked.

"I don't rightly know," Nate said uncertainly.

Shakespeare voiced his thoughts. "If he did, he wouldn't let on. He'd wait until they were out of sight, then tell the rest. And as sure as shootin', they'd decide to shadow us and ambush us when we least expect it."

"Maybe you're wrong," Zach said with the typical optimism of the very young. "Maybe all they'd want to do is trade. We have plenty of supplies we can do without."

"Trust me," Shakespeare said. "They wouldn't settle for a few fixin's when so much more could be theirs for the taking."

"Like the horses and stuff?"

"And stuff," Shakespeare replied grimly.

The mountain man's underlying meaning was plain to Nate, who studiously avoided glancing at the two women behind his son. Both his wife and Shakespeare's made no comment, but he knew they both understood. Both had lived all their lives in the Rocky Mountain region; both were fully aware of the harsh realities of life in the savage wilderness.

He tapped his heels on Pegasus's flanks and began the descent. After going ten yards he looked back and smiled at Winona, the Shoshone beauty who had claimed his heart the very first time he ever laid eyes on her, although he had been too stubborn to admit as much for a short while thereafter. She had on an attractive buffalo hide dress she had made herself, as she had all of the family's clothing. Her raven hair, which hung past her hips when she was standing, swayed with every stride her mare took.

"I do declare!" Shakespeare said with a grin. "You are the darnedest one for making cow eyes that I ever did see!"

"And you never do?" Nate retorted.

"Not on your life. A growed man like me has too much dignity for such tomfoolishness."

Light laughter burst from the lips of the woman riding beside Winona. Blue Water Woman, a full-blooded Flathead, was more than twice as old as Nate's wife but hardly showed her age. A few streaks of gray in her hair and small telltale wrinkles at the corners of her lively eyes were the only evidence of her added years. She pointed at McNair, then said in slightly accented English, "If I was given a prime beaver pelt every time you bend the truth, husband, I would have more than have been caught by all the trappers who ever lived."

"He makes cow eyes too?" Nate asked, enjoying the slight crimson tinge on his friend's full cheeks.

"I tell you, Nate," Blue Water Woman said. "One of the reasons I became his wife is because he makes better cow eyes than any man I have known."

"Women!" Shakespeare muttered. "They are all but stomachs and we all but food. They eat us hungerly, and when they are full they belch us."

Unfazed, Blue Water Woman replied, "When it comes to belching, husband, you outdo a gorged buffalo."

Tickled by their banter, Nate grinned as he rode to the bottom of the ridge and swung to the southeast. It pleased him to see McNair bested. Blue Water Woman was one of the few people who could hold their own against Shakespeare in a battle of wits, which perhaps helped explain why they were so happy together.

Nate checked the gap once more. The Utes appeared to be long gone, but he wasn't taking any undue chances. For the next hour and a half he repeatedly searched for any sign of the band.

"I can hardly wait to get there," Zachary commented as they wound among the foothills toward the plain. "How long will it take us again?"

"That depends on a lot of things, young'un," Shakespeare said patiently, although the same question had been posed a half-dozen times since they left Nate's cabin. "It depends on how well the horses hold up, on the weather, on the water situation, and on whether we run into a lot of hostiles."

"Do you think we'll see Comanches?" Zach asked, fearfully accenting the last word.

"We might," Shakespeare said, "but I'm more worried about running into Apaches. They make the Comanches look like a ladies' sewing circle."

"They do? But Rafe Bodeen says the Comanches are the fiercest Indians this side of the Rockies. He says they can scalp a man so he never even notices his hair is missing.''

"Bodeen?'' Shakespeare exclaimed. "Why, he's the biggest liar who ever donned britches. And what would he know about the Comanches anyway? He's never been south of Long's Peak.''

"But he's heard tell all about them,'' Zach objected. "He told me so himself.''

"Rafe Bodeen is a braggart who loves to hear himself jabber and to fill the heads of little boys with tall tales,'' Shakespeare said. "Why, if Rafe wasn't a human he'd be one of them there sperm whales.''

"Tell me about the Apaches,'' Zachary prompted.

"Another time.''

"Please, Uncle Shakespeare.''

Nate looked over his shoulder and saw McNair's grizzled features soften. The mountain man liked being regarded as Zach's uncle, even though they weren't kin. And much to Nate's delight, Shakespeare enjoyed teaching Zach all the things a growing boy should know if he hoped to one day make a go of it in the mountains. Since Zach wasn't the only one who still had a lot to learn, Nate listened, engrossed, as the mountain man talked.

"The Apaches aren't like any tribe around. They keep to themselves high in the mountain country around Sante Fe and on down toward Mexico. Those who know say the Apaches have lived there forever, and none of the other tribes have been able to drive them out. Truth is, the other tribes are a mite scared of them.''

"Even the Comanches?''

"Even the Comanches, though you'd have a dickens of a time making one own up to it. You see, Zach, the Apaches are warriors through and through. They love to go on raids to kill and plunder, and they're not too particular about who they raid. Whites, Mexicans, other Indi-

ans, it's all the same to them." Shakespeare paused and
gazed thoughtfully at the remote horizon. "They're not
at all like the Indians you know, the Shoshones and the
Flatheads and the like, who organize war parties every
now and then to teach their enemies a lesson or to steal
horses. The Apaches live to make war and nothing else.
They don't care much about buffalo hunting or fishing
and whatnot. To them, war is everything."

"Gosh," Zach said.

"Don't get me wrong, son," Shakespeare went on.
"I regard them highly. In their own way, the Apaches
are a noble bunch. They admire courage more than anything else. Which is why when they capture a man, they
like to torture him. Not because they're more bloodthirsty
than most. No, the torture is their way of measuring how
brave a man is. If they think he's brave, they'll put him
out of his misery quickly."

"And if they don't figure he's brave?"

"Then they'll keep on doing what they're doing until
he dies. They're not ones to show mercy to cowards."

Zach had moved his roan closer to Shakespeare's white
horse. "Have you ever seen an Apache up close?"

"Fairly close, once, more years back than I care to
think about."

"What happened?"

A shadow seemed to pass over the mountain man's
face. "It was on my first trip to Santa Fe. Our caravan
was camped a day shy of the town when some Apaches
snuck into our camp and took one of the women, a wife
of one of the traders. She screamed as they were hauling
her off and we all ran to her rescue."

Zach was practically glued to McNair. "Did you save
her?"

The answer took a full five seconds in coming. "No,
we didn't. Tried our hardest, mind you, but the devils

had too much of a head start. We caught a few glimpses of them as they glided off like ghosts, but that was all.''

"And the lady?"

"I'd imagine she became the wife of an Apache warrior. She might even still be alive, though the odds are against it. White women don't take well to Indian living. They're too soft.''

They rode in silence for a while, Nate pondering his friend's words and wondering if he had made a mistake in agreeing to this trip to Santa Fe. The journey had been Shakespeare's notion, the first lengthy break any of them had taken from their daily responsibilities since a similar trip to St. Louis a while back.

Ordinarily, the mere thought of the time and expense involved would have been enough to convince Nate to decline. But much to his surprise, Winona had expressed interest. And when Blue Water Woman also wanted to go, the die had been cast.

Perhaps, he reasoned, spring had something to do with it. The regal Rockies were aglow in the verdant splendor of springtime, with the tall trees and the high grass daily turning greener while the wild creatures resumed the active pace of their lives that had been disrupted by the bleak winter. After months of bitter cold and little food, the wildlife throbbed with vitality once again. The steep slopes echoed to the sharp cries of birds of prey and the strident calls of ravens and jays. Coyotes yipped on occasion, while at night the howls of wolves wafted eerily on the wind.

Spring transformed the mountains from a barren domain of snow and stone into a lush paradise. The buffalo resumed feeding in great herds out in the open. Deer and elk were in abundance. Panthers prowled the thickets. Bears were ever in search of food, shuffling over hill and down dale. And a man had only to breathe in the cool, crisp, invigorating air to feel alive in the depths of his being.

The rekindling of life on such a grand scale was bound to have an effect on those who had been cooped up in their small cabins or lodges for months on end. Whites and Indians alike were eager to get out in the sun again, to hunt, fish, and frolic to their heart's content. Winona and Blue Water Woman were no exception. They'd longed for a break in their daily routine, and what better way than to take a trip to distant Santa Fe, a trip few Indian women ever got to make, a trip they could proudly tell their grandchildren about in the decades to come?

Nate was equally thrilled at the prospect of seeing new country and spending time in the leading center of the Mexican province of New Mexico. Santa Fe, he had been told, was founded by the Spanish way back in 1610, and since then it had grown and prospered remarkably well to where it now served as a focal point of trade between the United States and Mexico. Large caravans from the States regularly carried a wide variety of trade goods there. Trappers and mountain men frequently paid Santa Fe a visit to kick up their heels and squander their hard-earned money.

All of that was appealing, but Nate still had reservations. They would have to journey hundreds of miles through territory only Shakespeare had ever visited, and once south of Bent's Fort they ran the very great risk of encountering hostile bands of Kiowas, Comanches, or Apaches. The thought of them made him wish he had left his wife and son at home, but he knew trying to convince them to stay behind would have been a hopeless task. When Winona set her mind to something, she was as immovable as a giant boulder.

Nate was brought out of his reflection by another question from Zach.

"Uncle Shakespeare, what did you mean by white

women are soft? Do Ma and Blue Water Woman have harder skin 'cause they're outside a lot?''

Somehow McNair kept a straight face. "No, Stalking Coyote," he said, using Zach's Shoshone name. "White women are soft because, generally speaking, they're lazy. At least the well-to-do ones are. They'd rather have servants make their meals and mend their clothes and grow their vegetables than do it themselves. Instead of making their own dresses, they go to stores to buy the fanciest finery they can afford. When they need shoes, they buy them. When they need a new winter coat, they buy it." He sighed. "They're pampered from cradle to grave, so it's no wonder they don't last long when they wind up in the hands of some warrior."

"There must be something they can do right," Zach said.

"True. I reckon I'm being too finicky about their habits. They *do* know how to spend money better than most other folks."

"Some of them are awful pretty. I saw some in St. Louis, remember?"

"That you did, but I figured you were too young to notice their eyelashes and such," Shakespeare said with a snicker.

"What's so funny?" the boy asked.

"You take after your pa," Shakespeare replied, and quoted again, "You are a lover. Borrow Cupid's wings and soar with them above a common bound."

"What's that mean?"

"It means," Nate interjected, "that your uncle better put a rein on that tongue of his before it gets him in deep trouble."

"God shield I should disturb devotion," Shakespeare declared.

Zachary frowned. "I'll be happy when I'm older so I can understand what you say."

"Don't count on that, son," Nate told him. "I'm full-grown and half the time I don't have the slightest idea what he's babbling about."

"Babbling?" the mountain man blustered. "What fire is in mine ears? Can this be true? Stand I condemned for pride and scorn so much?"

Nate knew better than to debate the point when Shakespeare was in one of his infamous moods. McNair could quote the English bard at a drop of the hat and rant on for hours at a stretch if not cut short. As if to prove him right, Shakespeare pressed a hand to his chest in a perfect mimicry of a stage actor and commenced reciting some of his favorite lines.

"To be, or not to be. That is the question. Whether 'tis nobler in the mind to suffer the slings and arrows of outrageous fortune, or to take arms against a sea of troubles, and by opposing end them. To die, to—"

"Husband dearest," Blue Water Woman interrupted.

"Yes, my sweet dove?" McNair responded grandly.

"Much more of that and our horses will start dropping like flies. Maybe you should wait to entertain us until we stop for the night."

"Ouch. You've cut me to the quick, wench."

"Do you want me to make a salve of beaver oil and castoreum so you'll heal faster?"

The two women tittered.

"Do you see?" Shakespeare addressed Nate. "Do you see what happens when you teach your wife English too well? She turns on you like a rattler the first chance she gets."

Everyone was in such fine spirits that Nate temporarily forgot all about his concerns for their safety. He continued making for the edge of the prairie where the going would be easier, though they would be close enough to the forest-covered foothills to swiftly seek cover should hostiles appear. Beside Pegasus walked Samson.

He marveled again at the good fortune that had resulted in his becoming a free trapper. When he looked back at his past, at his one-time plan to be an accountant in New York City, he had to chuckle at his foolishness. If not for the many strange twists and turns his life had taken, he would still be there, spending his days seated at a desk instead of getting out and about, dealing each month with mountains of clerical work rather than admiring Nature's handiwork, dying a little more inside with the passing of each day, his soul withering away like a parched plant for lack of the things that mattered most in life.

A dense tract of undergrowth materialized on his right and Nate swung left to go around it. He absently peered into its depths, thinking he might spy a black-tailed deer he could shoot for their supper, but as his eyes roved over the tangle of branches and leaves he saw something else entirely, a massive dark shape that moved a few feet in his direction and then stopped. Alarmed it might be a bear, he reined up.

Suddenly the shape moved again, this time crashing through the brush in a twinkling and dashing out into the open where it halted to balefully glare at the intruders, its nostrils flaring, its short tail twitching.

Nate started to raise his Hawken, then thought better of the notion. A single ball seldom sufficed to drop a two-thousand-pound bull buffalo.

Chapter Two

Of all the wild creatures teeming in the untamed land between the mighty Mississippi River and the pounding surf of the Pacific Coast, none were larger or more formidable when provoked than adult buffaloes. Standing six feet high at the shoulders, with a horn spread of over three feet, buffaloes were capable of bowling over grizzlies, panthers, horses, or men with astonishing ease.

Normally buffaloes paid little attention to humans. A man could ride up close to a herd and watch them graze without fear of being charged. If concealed and upwind, a hunter might down any number of the shaggy brutes without the rest so much as batting an eye. But once the buffaloes realized what was happening, the peaceful herd became a rampaging horde of destructive behemoths.

Rare was the mountain man who came on a bull all by itself. Buffaloes were led by their instincts to gather together into herds of varying sizes. Now and then a cow with a newborn calf might be seen hurrying to catch up with the main body. But solitary bulls were an oddity.

Now, as Nate met the unwavering stare of the heavily breathing bull, he noticed that its coat lacked the usual healthy luster, that one of its horns had broken off near the tip, and that there was a wicked gash in its left rear leg exposing part of the bone. This was an old male, he realized, well past its prime. Perhaps it was ailing as well as injured. Whatever, it had fallen behind the herd to which it belonged and been unable to overtake them. So, all alone and perhaps sensing it would be at the mercy of the first hunters or wolves to come along, the bull had sought sanctuary in the thicket.

What would it do? Nate wondered, and shot a hasty glance at the others. They were all as motionless as he. Zach was wide-eyed. Shakespeare had a thumb on the hammer of his rifle but wasn't trying to bring the gun to bear. Samson, thankfully, was calmly staring at the bull.

Nate waited, tense with anticipation. About 15 yards separated Pegasus from the brute. At most he would be able to get off one shot if the monster attacked. The bull was sniffing the air while scrutinizing them, apparently undecided whether they were harmless or not. A few more seconds of silence, he thought, might convince it to turn and reenter the thicket.

Then Samson snarled.

The effect on the old bull was electrifying. It snorted, tossed its head, and broke into a lurching rush, lowering its head as it pounded straight at Pegasus.

In sheer reflex Nate snapped the Hawken to his shoulder, took a hurried bead, and fired. The blast was echoed by three others. For a moment it seemed as if thunder had peeled. The bull staggered, surged erect, and kept coming, and it was all Nate could do to wrench on the reins and get Pegasus out of the way. He saw the bison's good horn sweep past the gelding's side, missing by inches, and his right hand darted to a flintlock.

Already the bull was going after another victim, angling sharply at Shakespeare, whose white horse reacted with a frantic jump to the side that would have done justice to a pronghorn antelope. Again the bull missed, pivoted on its hoofs, and spied Zach.

The boy sat rooted in place, his mouth slack, his arms limp.

"Move!" Nate bellowed, aiming at the brute's ear. He cocked the hammer and squeezed off his shot just as the bull charged. To his left Shakespeare also fired a pistol.

At the twin retorts the buffalo stumbled, its legs scrambling for a purchase, and rose to its full height. Zach had collected his wits and was desperately striving to goad the roan into motion, but the panic-stricken mount refused to cooperate. Once more the bull closed, but much slower this time.

Nate moved to intercept the monster, intending to put Pegasus between the bull's horns and his son. As much as he loved the gelding, he loved his son more, and would gladly sacrifice the one for the other if there was no other choice.

Out of the corner of his eye he saw Winona galloping forward, her fingers flying as she shoved her ramrod home. She had the same idea he did, and she was nearer. His heart seemed to leap into his throat as she stopped in front of Zach and swept her rifle up. Exactly as he had taught her, she fixed the bead on the bull, cocked the gun, and fired, all in the span of a second. Her ball smacked home, loud enough for all to hear, and the next instant the brute was going down in a whirl of limbs and tail to slide several yards to a final rest almost at the very hoofs of her mare.

"Damn, that was close!" Shakespeare breathed.

Nate barely heard him. He was vaulting from the saddle and running up to the bull, which was down but not dead, its eyes fluttering and its sides heaving as it feebly struggled to stand yet again, the spark of life unwilling to relinquish its hold on the aged, torn hulk of a body. His second flintlock streaked clear. In a blur, he touched the barrel to the beast's side and sent a lead ball directly into its lungs.

Snorting in fury, the bull tilted its enormous head and took a swipe at the human gnat causing it so much pain. But its head had only swung a few inches when the bison abruptly stiffened, grunted, and collapsed, its tongue protruding from its mouth. Blood began dribbling from its black nose.

"That did it," Shakespeare commented.

Gulping air, Nate took a step backwards. His right hand was shaking uncontrollably. Inwardly he quaked at how close Winona had come to meeting her Maker. A glance into her eyes showed she was experiencing similar feelings. "Nice shooting," he remarked, and was shocked at his strained voice. He quickly coughed, licked his lips, and added, "I didn't know you could reload that fast."

"Nor did I," Winona said in such perfect English that anyone in the States who heard her speaking in the next room would have no idea she was a Shoshone. She had an exceptional gift for learning new tongues. Shakespeare, who had spent many years teaching not only Blue Water Woman but many other Indian friends the white's man language, had been amazed at how readily and thoroughly Winona learned it. She was, Shakespeare believed, a natural-born linguist. "I don't know how I did it," she mentioned.

"I do," Shakespeare declared. "Your blood was pumping like a geyser and you weren't thinking of anything but the safety of your young coon. I've seen folks do amazing things when their loved ones were in danger." He started reloading his rifle. "Why, once I saw a Crow woman lift a tree that had been blown down during a storm and landed on her lodge, pinning her little girl. I was in a lodge across the way, and I ran right over with several warriors. The trunk of that tree must have weighed hundreds of pounds, yet she had it off the ground when we got there and we pulled her girl out. Later when she tried lifting the tree, she couldn't even budge it."

Nate set to work reloading his own guns, glad to have something to do. Only a greenhorn left his weapons unloaded for longer than was absolutely necessary. In the wilderness a man never knew when danger might strike, as the attack of the bull buffalo had so vividly demonstrated. McNair himself had once put it best: "An empty gun is the sure-fire sign of an empty head."

Young Zach, who had not uttered a sound since the buffalo appeared, cast a tormented gaze at his father. "I'm sorry, Pa. I truly am."

"For what?"

"I'm yellow, Pa. I was scared clean through." Zach bowed his head in shame and added in Shoshone, "My spirit is sick."

Nate was in the act of pouring the proper amount of black powder down the Hawken barrel and he kept on pouring, only slower, giving himself time to think on how best to respond to his son's declaration. He had seen the fear on Zach's face, and he knew how upset the boy must be.

The matter wasn't to be taken lightly. Courage was one of the cardinal virtues of a Shoshone warrior, as young Zach was well aware. The driving ambition of every boy in the tribe was to one day prove his bravery in battle and then to be asked to join one of the prestigious warrior societies. Those who showed cowardice became social outcasts; they weren't permitted to share in many of the traditional activities of the men. Every boy acutely dreaded that happening to him.

"I've been scared quite a few times myself," Nate said, and smiled reassuringly at Zach. "Usually it's been when, like now, something happened so fast that I didn't have time to think. If, for instance, a grizzly should come charging at you from out of nowhere, you're first reaction is to run to another part of the country just as quick as you can go." He paused to cap the powder horn. "So being afraid every so often is perfectly normal, son. Don't let it get you down. There will be other times when you'll be put to the test and I know you'll do just fine."

"How do you know?" Zach inquired.

"I can answer that one," Shakespeare said cheerily, moving his mare over next to Zach. He gave the boy a hearty clap on the back and said, "You'll do fine because you're the son of Grizzly Killer, the man who has killed more grizzlies than any white man or Indian who ever lived. Never forget that some of your pa's blood flows in your veins, son. One day you'll be as well known as he is."

Under the mountain man's friendly influence, the boy brightened and nodded.

"I will, Uncle. One day I'll be as famous as Pa. No one will ever dare call me yellow."

McNair glanced at the bull. "Well, now we have to decide what to do about this critter. We already have enough jerked venison, pemmican, and other victuals to last us clear to Santa Fe. But we sure as blazes can't let this critter lie here and rot. I say we make camp here for a day or two and dry as much of the meat as we can, then tote it with us. Our pack animals can carry the extra weight with no problem."

"But why go to all that bother?" Nate asked, displeased by the delay it would cause. "Wolves, coyotes, and buzzards have to eat too."

"Wolves and coyotes didn't kill it. We did. That makes it our responsibility, as you well know," Shakespeare noted.

One of the cardinal unwritten rules of wilderness life was to never let good meat go to waste. Nate sighed and reluctantly nodded in agreement. "I reckon a day or two won't hurt."

Winona had dismounted and walked up to the bull. Reaching out, she placed a hand on the huge carcass and closed her eyes.

"Are you all right?" Nate asked, joining her.

She held still for a full ten seconds. Then she lowered her arm and gave him a look that radiated sheer love. "I was thanking the Great Mystery for the life of our son," she said softly so none of the others could hear.

He smiled and leaned closer to kiss her lightly on the cheek. Words were not needed. Their eyes eloquently conveyed their emotions.

"Now don't start with that cow-eyed business again," Shakespeare playfully chided them as he swung to the ground. "We'll never get this bull carved up with you two acting like you're courting."

Soon they were all busy at various tasks. Nate and Shakespeare rolled up their sleeves, pulled their butcher knives, and commenced removing the bull's hide, being careful not to tear it so later it could be made into a fine robe. Winona and Zach collected dry wood and built a small fire. Blue Water Woman took care of the horses, removing the saddles and packs and tethering the animals where they had plenty of grass to graze on.

Nate pondered as he worked. Here they were, barely started on their long journey, and already they were losing valuable time. He hoped it wasn't an omen of things to come. Then he reminded himself that he was viewing the matter as a white man would and not as an Indian. Whites, especially those living in New York and other cities back East, were always scurrying about like so many mice, always on the go, always trying to cram as many activities as they could into each day. They lived a hectic existence, rushing here and there and everywhere, Time their harsh taskmaster.

Indians, however, were vastly different in their outlook and way of life. They seldom rushed anywhere, unless it was to rush into battle should an enemy be sighted near their camp, or to rush off after buffalo if the village was in need of meat and a herd should be spotted nearby. Generally, though, Indians went about their daily activities at a sedate pace, completing each chore properly and patiently before moving on to the next. When they ate their meals, they ate slowly. When they tanned hides, they took their time. When a horse needed breaking, it was done over a period of days, not hours. In almost all things Indians did, they worked at a relaxed pace. The precious moments of each day were savored, not gulped at a single draught. Time was of no consequence in this regard, and as a result they were the masters of Time and not the other way around.

This train of thought made Nate realize how foolish his annoyance had been, and he consciously willed himself to relax and enjoy the interlude. He even whistled as he sliced away, and suddenly he was conscious of being watched.

"What, pray tell, has put you in such fine fettle?" Shakespeare wanted to know. "A while ago you were acting as if you had a burr up your backside."

"It feels good to be alive," Nate said simply.

"That it does," Shakespeare concurred. "As there comes light from heaven and words from breath, as there is sense in truth and truth in virtue, that it does."

"More William S.?"

"Of a sort."

It took them well into the afternoon to butcher the bull

to their satisfaction. By then Winona and Blue Water Woman had set up a crude framework of trimmed branches on which to hang the thin strips of meat. Everyone pitched in to help, and soon the job was done.

Five thick, juicy masses of prime bull meat were saved for supper, and so toward sunset the two women unpacked their cooking utensils, both owning a number of tin pans, cups, plates, and whatnot obtained at a previous Rendezvous, and started cooking the meal. Winona dug out her coffeepot, and was walking to the fire when she stopped and glanced at Nate.

"Have you seen Zach?"

Nate looked in all directions, but the boy was gone. He recalled seeing Zach and Samson heading into the forest to the north of their camp shortly after the meat was hung out to dry, but he'd thought nothing of it at the time. Boys loved to go exploring, and Zach was no exception. Grabbing his rifle from where it rested on his saddle, Nate hiked toward the tree line. Zach knew enough not to stray far, and Nate was confident he would find his son quickly.

At the edge of the trees he came on their tracks and followed them into the pines. True to form, the boy had wandered from one attraction to another, first a partially rotted log, next a tree that had been struck by lightning, and so on, meandering ever deeper into the solitude of the woodland. At length Nate spied a hill ahead. Sure enough the trail led him to its base. Above him, scattered about the slope, reared dozens of large boulders, some bigger than his cabin.

"Zach?" Nate called.

There was no answer.

"Zachary!" Nate yelled. Once more no reply was forthcoming, and he became irritated that the boy had strayed off much farther than was wise. He cupped a hand to his mouth to try a third time. "Zachary King!"

From somewhere near the top of the hill came a sharp yip.

"Samson?" Nate said, and began ascending. He heard a louder bark. Going around a boulder, he saw the great black dog standing 40 yards away near what appeared to be a rock ledge.

"There you are. But where's Zach?"

Concerned, Nate hurried. Samson barked several times, as if urging him on. When he was still ten feet off the dog whirled and dashed onto the ledge, then turned and barked again. "What's got you so worked up?" Nate asked.

The ledge turned out to not be a ledge at all, but rather a spot where long ago the ground had buckled and cracked, creating a narrow fissure that extended deep down into the earth. On either side of the fissure was a shelf wide enough for a person to stand on. Nate stood on the rim and scanned the top of the hill. "Zach? Where are you?"

"Down here, Pa!"

The muffled response, coming as it did from under Nate's very feet, made him stiffen in shock, then drop to one knee. He could see 20 feet down into the fissure but no further. Beyond that the sunlight didn't penetrate. "Zach? Are you hurt? What happened?"

"I'm scraped up some," was the answer. "I was trying to see what's at the bottom and I slipped."

The opposite wall was as smooth as glass, the near wall rough and laced with cracks. "Can you climb back out?" Nate inquired, trying not to betray his anxiety. He had never liked enclosed spaces, and the thought of his son trapped down there gave him the jitters.

"No. I've tried, Pa, but my left leg is stuck."

Nate's mind raced. He could climb down himself, although it would be a tight squeeze, but what if he also became wedged fast? "You hang on, son. I'm going back to the camp for some rope and some help. I'll be back before you know it.''

"Okay, Pa."

"I'm leaving Samson here so you'll have some company."

"Hurry, please. I'm afraid my leg will slip free and I'll fall the rest of the way."

"You're not at the bottom?"

"No, sir. I think the bottom is a long ways down yet. I dropped a stone but I didn't hear it hit."

"You just hang on," Nate reiterated, rising. He motioned at Samson to stay, then whirled and went down that hill as if he had wings on his feet. Horrifying images of Zach plunging into the depths of the fissure lent speed to his legs. When he burst from the trees the others were gathered around the fire, sipping coffee. They had only to take one look at him to shove to their feet in apprehension.

"What is it?" Shakespeare asked.

Nate told them as he rummaged in the packs and located the length of rope he always included in his supplies. Spinning, he started back and the three of them fell in alongside him. He glanced at Winona, about to tell her that someone should stay with the horses and their provisions. The set of her features changed his mind. She had just as much right to be there as he did.

It seemed to him that they were moving at a snail's pace. Since he was the fleetest of foot, he swiftly pulled out ahead, weaving among the pines and vaulting all obstacles with ease. The hill broke into view and he raced upward, the soles of his moccasins digging into the soil for a firm purchase. Samson, obediently, had not budged.

"Zach?" Nate shouted.

"I'm here, Pa."

"I've got some rope. I'll be down there in no time," Nate said, and scoured the shelf for a projecting rock or an adequate boulder to which he could secure the rope. There were none. The nearest boulder was five feet below the fissure on the right. Dashing over, he made a loop, and was tying it when Shakespeare, Winona, and Blue Water Woman reached the shelf.

"Tarnation!" Shakespeare exclaimed. "How the devil did he manage to fall in there?"

Nate was too busy to reply. Once the rope was attached, he moved back to the rim and handed his Hawken to Winona. "Keep an eye that the rope doesn't come loose," he cautioned.

She stared into the fissure. "Perhaps I should be the one to go down, husband. I am smaller than you."

"I can make it," Nate said, and stepped to the very edge. Balancing on his heels, he took up the slack and prepared to go over the side.

Shakespeare suddenly seized the rope to play it out slowly and gave a bob of his chin. "Don't fret none. I'll hold down this end. You just make damn certain you don't get yourself stuck or we might never get you out."

On that optimistic note Nate lowered his right leg down, then his left, bracing his feet against the inner wall. Gradually he eased lower and lower, straightening as he went, until his head was below the rim. He could feel the smooth wall brushing against his back and his heels. To say it was a tight fit was the understatement of the century.

He swallowed hard and kept inching downward. The close press of the walls jangled his nerves and set his teeth on edge. Waves of fear pounded at his brain but he refused to succumb. That was his son down there, and he would do whatever was required to save the boy, just as would most any other Shoshone or white father. Parents since time immemorial had been laying down their lives to protect their offspring. Such caring self-sacrifice was one of the most basic of human instincts in those who had not fallen into the mistake of loving themselves more than they did their own children.

"Zach?" he called to get his bearings as he sank into the gloom below.

"Over here, Pa."

Nate peered to his left, waiting for his eyes to adjust to the dark, and worked his way ever lower. A minute later he spied Zach's upturned grimy face lined with worry. Grinning, he said casually, "You beat all sometimes, son. I swear I'm going to start putting a leash on you so you won't wander farther than you should." He expected Zach to laugh. Instead, the boy frowned.

"Be real careful, Pa. I think I heard something earlier."

"What?"

"Something was moving around."

"All the way down here? You're loco," Nate joked, and then froze because he heard something himself, a slight scraping noise to his right. He looked, and barely made out the outline of a ledge that couldn't have been more than three or four inches wide, which wasn't very wide at all, but still more than wide enough for the large rattlesnake that was slowly crawling toward him.

Chapter Three

How the snake got down into the fissure hardly mattered. The sight of its distinctive large triangular head and its thick body patterned on the back with dark diamonds bordered by a lighter shade sent a chill rippling through Nate. He imagined he could see the snake's markings clearly, but of course he couldn't in the shadowy confines of the crack. He did hear the sibilant hiss of its flicking tongue and a faint rattle as its tail moved along the thin ledge.

"Pa?" Zach asked, having sensed that something was wrong.

Nate made no reply. With a start he realized the thin strip of stone on which the snake was crawling ran right past his face, angling upward toward the rim. Holding himself rigid, his breath catching in his throat, he watched the reptile glide closer.

"Pa? What is it?"

The rattler, head held low, drew abreast of Nate, and

31

he could see its slender tongue testing the air. Its eerie eyes were fixed straight ahead, its scales rippling as it climbed. He kept waiting for the deadly serpent to crawl out of sight so he could relax.

Unexpectedly, just then, with the fine particles of dust suspended in the air, Nate felt an urge to sneeze. The impulse was nearly overwhelming. Yet he dared not let go of the rope to clamp his nose shut or his forearm would brush against the rattlesnake. Nor dared he sneeze, for the rattler might turn on him in the blink of an eye and strike.

In despair Nate bit down hard on his lower lip, his teeth digging deep into his skin. Intense pain seared through him, pain he hoped would suffice to take his mind off sneezing. The tingling in his nose slacked off for a few seconds, which was all the time needed for the rattlesnake to slide into the darkness and be gone.

Unable to control himself any longer, Nate sneezed so loud that more dust swirled off the wall and enveloped his face. He began coughing, which caused the rope to shake violently, and his sweaty hands started to slip. Girding his muscles, he held fast until he could inhale without difficulty.

"Pa?" Zach said, sounding greatly concerned.

"I'm fine," Nate answered. "Just saw a snake." He resumed lowering himself down. Reflecting on the close call, he realized there might be many more rattlers in the fissure. Some snakes liked to hole up in cool, quiet places during the heat of the day. Sometimes hundreds or even thousands congregated in a single den. It was possible there were hordes of rattlers somewhere at the bottom, and he worried what would happen if either of them should plummet into the fissure's depths.

"My left leg is falling asleep," Zach remarked.

Yet another worry, Nate thought, scowling. If the boy's circulation was being cut off, there might be internal damage to the leg. He shifted so he could slide down next to his son, and tensed his left arm to bear all of his weight as he tried to squeeze his right arm around Zach. Nothing doing. The walls narrowed at the very spot where Zach was stuck, and it was well they did. On either side was a bit more space, enough so that the boy would have plunged all the way to the bottom had he missed that spot by a matter of inches either way.

"I'm sorry, Pa," Zach said softly.

"We all have accidents from time to time," Nate said, and let it go at that. Which struck him as ironic. If he had pulled a harebrained stunt like this on his own father, he would have received a tongue-lashing to beat all tongue-lashings and a whipping that would have left him unable to comfortably sit down for a month. And, truth to tell, if he had never left New York, if he had married someone there and raised a different family, he would probably have acted the same way if his son did something similar.

But living with the Shoshones had changed him. Living as an Indian had altered his perspective on life. Indian parents rarely resorted to physical punishment. Stern words, yes, and discipline that involved extra work or the denial of favorite pastimes, but not spankings or slappings or beatings with a rod. Indian parents regarded incidents like this one as educational. The only way for a child to learn, they believed, was for that child to go out and experience life. If the child committed a foolish act, then the child suffered the consequences and learned never to be so foolish again. Certainly there were risks in allowing children to learn so much for themselves, but the gains outweighed the risks, the gains being that Indian children matured more quickly than their white counterparts, acquiring a practical wisdom that stood them in excellent stead the rest of their lives.

Nate eased lower and attempted to get his arm around

Zach's legs. There wasn't enough extra room for a finger, let alone his whole arm. Frustrated, he went even lower until he was below his son. Bracing his back against the rear wall for extra support, he put his right palm against the sole of Zach's left moccasin and pushed.

"Ow!" the boy cried out.

"This will likely hurt a bit," Nate said, "but it can't be helped." Once more he pushed, and felt the wedged leg give slightly.

"Don't fret about me, Pa," Zach said through clenched teeth. "Do what you have to."

Pride swelled Nate's heart. He pushed harder, working the foot back and forth as much as he was able, and gradually the leg loosened. Dust cascaded onto his face, forcing him to avert his gaze. His left shoulder and his back were hurting, but he paid them no heed. Patiently he continued moving his son's foot until the leg abruptly slipped free to one side.

Instantly Zach, who had been clinging to the wall with clawed fingers, started to slid down. Nate lunged upward, looping his right arm about Zach's waist, and arrested the fall. "Hang on tight," he advised. Then, hugging his son close, he commenced his ascent.

"We're coming out!" he yelled.

The rope leaped upward of its own accord, hauling him toward the welcome light overhead at twice the speed he could manage on his own. Once or twice his back bumped the wall, and once his elbows were jarred, but the discomfort was a small price to pay for being swiftly pulled to the surface. There he found not only Shake-speare but also Winona and Blue Water Woman had helped to get him out.

"Thanks," Nate said, rising to his knees and lifting Zach upright. There were tears of gratitude in the boy's eyes.

"I won't ever do anything like that again, Pa. I promise."

"Let's hope not," Nate said. "I'd rather wrestle a grizzly than be hemmed in like a pea in a pod."

Winona stepped up and gave Zach a hug; then she examined his left leg. The boy's leggin was torn and his skin scraped badly, but there was scant blood and the bone was unbroken. The only comment she made while conducting her examination was, "You must remember to be more careful in the future, my son. Sometimes I think you are as accident-prone as your father."

In the act of rising, Nate had opened his mouth to deliver a witty retort when he saw Samson standing with head held high and ears erect, staring in the direction of their camp. He twisted, gazing out over the trees, and saw the thin spiral of smoke that indicated the location of their fire. He also heard, faintly on the wind, a series of high-pitched whinnies.

"Something is in our camp!" Shakespeare bellowed, and was off the shelf like a shot, sprinting down the slope with great leaps, a human bighorn in action.

"Bring the rope!" Nate said, and followed his mentor, scooping up the Hawken first. At the base of the hill he could hear the agitated horses clearly, and he prayed a panther wasn't after them. Or worse, a grizzly. The loss of a pack animal wouldn't be so bad, but if one of their mounts should be ripped apart they would be forced to turn around and head home.

A glance back showed Winona and Blue Water Woman trying to undo the knots he had made when he tied the rope to the boulder. Good, he reflected. They would be delayed getting to the camp, which should give Shakespeare and him time to deal with whatever was spooking the horses before they got there.

For an old-timer, McNair was incredibly spry when

he had to be. Ten yards ahead he darted around an evergreen and jumped over a log.

Nate willed himself to catch up. If a wandering grizzly had struck their camp, it would take both of their rifles to bring the monster down. Single shots hardly ever did the trick. More often than not, a grizzly would be shot seven, eight, nine times and still keep coming, its lungs perforated and its innards shot all to hell, yet still able to tear a man to shreds with a single swipe of its mighty paw.

He glimpsed the end of the trees at the same moment he drew even with McNair. Past the pines on the right were the tethered horses, some prancing in place as if their hoofs were on fire.

"I hope it's not those Utes," Shakespeare said.

That hadn't occurred to Nate. The band was in the area, though, and might have spotted the smoke, a careless oversight on their part that never would have happened if they hadn't become distracted by Zach's plight. He lifted the Hawken, ready for a bloody battle, and charged from cover.

Standing next to the rack of drying buffalo strips was the intruder.

Nate and Shakespeare dug in their heels and halted side by side. A whiff of rank odor hit Nate a second later and he scrunched up his nose. His thumb on the hammer uncoiled. Under no circumstances would he shoot, and risk having to take two or three baths a day for six months to erase the even worse foul smell that would ensue.

Sniffing daintily at the meat, a large skunk walked slowly around the rack, then ambled close to the fire. The flames weren't to its liking, so it shuffled toward the horses. Several tried to pull their picket pins out in their efforts to get away from the brazen creature. Others shook their heads and snorted. The skunk, oblivious to the commotion it was so innocently causing, again changed course, moving toward the forest.

Nate's eyes widened as he saw it coming his way. Should he run or stay still? He heard Shakespeare whisper to stand fast, so he did. The skunk paused to paw at the earth briefly, then resumed its evening stroll. Suddenly it caught their scent and halted.

Ordinarily a skunk was no threat. Unless afflicted with rabies, skunks either gave humans a wide berth or ignored them entirely. And while nocturnal by nature, they were not averse to coming out before sunset when the whim struck, as this one had done.

Nate could see its dark eyes swiveling from Shakespeare to him and back again. What was it thinking? he wondered, watching it closely. There was no evidence of the telltale ring of drooling saliva common to animals with hydrophobia, so his only worry was the oily, fetid musk contained in glands in the animal's backside. A grown skunk could spray ten to 15 feet with astounding accuracy. Often it went for the eyes, since the musk would blind anyone or anything long enough for it to get away. Many an unwary Indian and trapper had found out the hard way just why the lowly skunk was shunned by fierce panthers and savage grizzlies alike.

Seconds passed. The skunk didn't move.

Then there was a crashing in the brush and a black form hurtled into the open and stopped between Nate and Shakespeare. Samson no sooner saw the intruder than he lowered his hairy head and vented a warning growl that would have scared any other creature half to death.

Not so the skunk. It chattered like an irate squirrel, stamped its small front paws, raised its hind legs, and arched its bushy tail.

''Move!'' Shakespeare shouted.

No prompting was needed. Nate dived to his left,

springing as far as he could go. Over his shoulder he saw Samson take a step, and he started to yell, to tell the dog to sit, to stay, but he was too late. The skunk had already spun. From its rear end shot a jet of vile liquid that splashed squarely onto Samson's brow.

The dog recoiled, blinked, and snorted. Backing away, Samson frantically rubbed a paw across his nose, then rubbed his forehead on the grass. Neither helped. Turning, he vigorously shook his head and wheezed while staggering a few feet.

Prone on the ground, Nate faced the skunk. A healthy one was capable of unleashing five or six shots of musk in swift succession, and he had no desire to be its next target. The intruder, however, had no further interest in them. It was walking to the west with the peculiar rolling gait common to its breed, head and tail held proudly on high, not the least bit concerned about reprisals.

"Damned arrogant critter!" Shakespeare muttered. "Why the Good Lord saw fit to make them, I'll never know."

"Maybe they're supposed to keep the rest of us humble," Nate quipped, and was immediately sorry he had spoken because he inhaled a few stray tendrils of musk lingering in the air. Coughing and gagging, he stood and moved farther from Samson. The hapless mongrel, meanwhile, had fallen to the ground and was rolling back and forth in a frenzied bid to rid himself of the offending stench.

"Want me to shoot it and put it out of its misery?" Shakespeare asked, wearing a lopsided grin.

"Don't you dare!" yelped a shrill voice. Zach raced out of the woods to crouch in front of the mongrel. "No one harms my dog! Ever!"

"I was only joshing," Shakespeare said.

"You weren't funny," Zach declared, and tried to

stroke Samson's neck. The dog, ignoring him, wouldn't stop rolling. "Pa, what are we going to do?"

"Give him a good dunking in the first stream we find."

Zach leaned forward, his hand outstretched. "We can't . . ." he began, and gasped, his face contorting into a mask of utter revulsion. Doubling over, he covered his nose and mouth and hacked uncontrollably.

Nate took a breath, held it, and dashed to his son. Grabbing Zach around the waist, he carried the boy to the fire and gently set him down. "You'd better wait a spell before you try to pet him. He's not fit company for man or beast right at the moment." Looking up, he saw Winona and Blue Water Woman giving Samson a wide berth.

"What happened?" the latter asked, her eyes twinkling with inner mirth. "Don't tell us the famous Grizzly Killer was routed by a skunk."

"If word of this ever gets back to my people," Winona threw in, "Grizzly Killer will have to change his name to Smells Bad."

The two women laughed.

Knowing the futility of trying to respond to them, Nate walked to the horses and verified each was still firmly tethered. Next he checked the meat rack to see if any of the strips had been tampered with. All was in order. By the time he got back to the fire, Blue Water Woman was preparing fresh coffee and Winona sat with an arm draped on Zach's shoulders.

Shakespeare was trying to cheer the boy up. ". . . have days like this, son. Every one of us. It's the bad days that help us appreciate the good days more. Why, I remember one time your pa and me were out trapping beaver. Danged if he didn't get himself attacked by a black bear, a grizzly, and a Ute, all on the same day."

"At least I didn't get myself caught by a Blackfoot war party like someone I could mention," Nate interjected.

"Who?" Zach asked.

Shakespeare coughed and quickly went on. "That's not important. What matters is that you don't let a little accident now and then get you down in the doldrums." He rested a hand on the boy's arm. "This is in thee a nature but infected, a poor unmanly melancholy sprung from change of fortune."

"What?"

Sadly shaking his head, Nate squatted and picked up a tin cup. "I do wish you'd use common English with him, Shakespeare. He never understands when you warble like the bard."

"Warbling, is it now?" the mountain man responded a bit testily. He quoted from another play. "When a man's verses cannot be understood, nor a man's good wit seconded with the forward child, understanding, it strikes a man more dead than a great reckoning in a little room. Truly, I would the gods had made thee poetical."

Nate shrugged. "I never was one much for rhyme and all that. Give me a Cooper novel any day and I'm content."

"James Fenimore Cooper," Shakespeare spat, and reverted to the trapper vernacular. "That long-winded varmint! He's more in love with words than he is with life. Old William S., on the other hand, was a man who knew people. Knew the way they think, knew the way they act. He saw right through them and wrote the truth. Cooper? He's a literary flash in the pan compared to William S."

"I've read all of Cooper's books and I don't recollect coming across a lie in any of them," Nate countered. As with many of the free trappers, reading was one of his favorite pastimes, especially during the long winter months when the cold and the snow drove everyone indoors. A good book helped pass the hours pleasurably. Naturally, every trapper had an author he liked more than other writers, and heated arguments over the merits of each often arose. Some, like McNair, were partial to Shakespeare, although none had gone to the trouble he had to memorize all of a dozen plays. Some preferred Byron, some Scott. A few would read the Bible and nothing else. Nate often thought that many of the good citizens back in the States, who tended to view trappers as illiterate savages little better than the Indians those citizens despised so much, would have been shocked to learn the truth.

Leaning back against his saddle, he sipped his coffee and contentedly watched Winona and Zach talking in low tones. The boy was happier, and under Winona's influence he would soon be his old indomitable self. Children were like that. They bounced back from hard times faster than adults, maybe because they weren't so set in their ways and could take things more in stride. Children were like saplings, bending whichever way the wind blew but seldom breaking. Adults were like trees in their prime, able to bend, but more likely to snap if the wind blew too strong.

He thought about the events of the day—the run-in with the old buffalo, the incident at the fissure, and lastly the encounter with the roving skunk—and grinned. Life in the wilderness was rarely dull. Seldom did a day go by when something unusual didn't occur. It was just one of many fascinating aspects about the wilderness that had so appealed to him when he first ventured west. Unlike city life, where a person suffocated under the drudgery of a daily routine, where each day was almost an exact duplicate of the one before, life in the Rockies was an unending series of adventures big and small. A person felt *alive* in the wild.

Shakespeare, who had been gazing to the south while

drinking coffee, now stood and came around to Nate and knelt.

"Come to declare a truce?" Nate asked, and grinned.

"No," McNair said, shaking his head. He stared into the fire and spoke so quietly his lips barely moved. "Didn't it strike you as strange that our horses got so worked up over a skunk?"

"Not really," Nate said, wondering what his friend was getting at. "The critter must have wandered around the camp for a while before we got back. They didn't like its scent, is all."

"I thought so too until a minute ago," Shakespeare said. "Then I saw our other visitor."

"What other visitor?" Nate asked, sitting up so abruptly he spilled some coffee onto his lap.

"Take a gander at the trees south of us. Be casual about it so you don't spook him."

Placing the cup down, Nate stretched and shifted so he could scan the forest. He half expected to see a Ute lying in ambush, but for half a minute he saw no one. Then, as his brain sifted the random patterns of lengthening shadows and dying patches of sunlight, he saw a vague shape lying on the thick low limb of a spruce tree. It took a moment for the outline to become clear, and he whistled softly. "I'll be damned," he muttered.

"It must have been sneaking up on the horses when they picked up its scent," Shakespeare guessed. "It was the cause of the ruckus we heard when we were up on the hill. That skunk just happened to show up when we did."

"We can't let it sit there until dark," Nate said. "First chance it gets, it'll try for our stock."

"Do you want to do the honors or should I?"

"My rifle is handy," Nate said, picking up his Hawken. The women and Zach were watching him, puzzled. He cocked the hammer, then rose into a crouch. "Too bad we can't use any more meat," he mentioned.

"I know," Shakespeare said. "Panther meat is the best there is."

Nate pivoted on his heels, pressed the stock to his right shoulder, and aimed at the limb on which the powerful predator crouched. Steadying the barrel, he lightly touched the trigger, took a breath, and squeezed.

At the loud retort a tawny panther leaped clear of the limb and alighted on all fours in a crouch, its tail waving wildly, its ears flattened in anger. A feral snarl rumbled from its throat. For a moment it seemed about to attack, but the moment passed and the big cat spun and bounded into the forest, blending into the shadows with a skill not even the most seasoned Indian warrior could hope to match.

It all happened so rapidly that none of them got more than a glimpse of the magnificent animal. Nate slowly lowered his rifle and listened in vain for sounds of the creature's passage through the underbrush.

At length Zach laughed and said, "We sure are seeing a lot of critters on this trip. Maybe, if we're lucky, we'll see a grizzly soon."

"Bite your tongue, son," Nate said. "We're supposed to have fun on this trip, not fight for our lives every step of the way. I'll be happy if we don't tangle with anything else from here on out."

Little did he know what lay in store for them.

Chapter Four

Bent's Fort on the Arkansas River was actually a gigantic mud castle. There was nothing like it anywhere west of the Mississippi. Fort Union, situated where the Missouri and Yellowstone Rivers met, and Fort Pierre, on the northern Plains, were two of the bigger centers of the fur trade, but they could hardly hold a candle to the fort built by the Bent brothers and their good friend Ceran St. Vrain.

The front wall alone was 14 feet high, 137 feet long, and nearly four feet thick. The side walls ran for 178 feet. Huge towers had been constructed at the northwest and southeast corners, and each was constantly manned by alert guards who could effectively use the field pieces that had been brought in at much expense and with considerable hard labor to duly impress any and all hostiles.

Bent's Fort was an impregnable fortress. The whites knew it and could sleep soundly within its sheltering walls at night. The Indians also knew it, both the friendly tribes and the hostiles, so the latter didn't bother to waste the lives of their braves in trying to overrun it. The Comanches and Kiowas and others accepted its presence as inevitable, but many resented it all the same.

The fort almost qualified as a thriving colony. Up to two hundred men could be comfortably garrisoned there at one time, not to mention upwards of four hundred animals. Just inside the north and west walls were large corrals to accommodate the animals.

Nate had heard much about Bent's Fort, and was eagerly awaiting his first sight of the post. From a low rise he got his wish, and on spying the high adobe walls he broke into a smile. All of them did. He lifted his reins and started forward, but a word from Winona stopped him and he turned. "What's wrong?"

"Nothing, husband. Blue Water Woman and I must get ready."

"Get ready for what?"

"We must make ourselves presentable."

"You look fine to me," Nate said, and heard Shakespeare cackle as the two women rode off to be by themselves.

"For a married man, you sure have a lot to learn about womenfolk," the mountain man declared. "They're not about to wear their everyday dresses into the fort. It's fanfaron time, and there ain't a thing we can do but sit here and twiddle our thumbs until they're ready."

"What's fanfaron, Uncle Shakespeare?" Zach inquired.

"A French word, little one. Showing off, you might call it."

"What does Ma want to show off?"

"Ask me that question again in fifteen years and I'll tell you."

"Pa's right. You always talk in riddles."

"I try, boy. I try."

When the wives returned they had on their very finest ankle-length dresses made of the softest buckskin and gaily decorated with beads, fringe, and even a few tiny bells that jingled as they moved. They had plaited their hair and each wore a brightly colored ribbon; Winona's was red, Blue Water Woman's blue.

"My, oh, my!" Shakespeare exclaimed, doffing his beaver hat to them. "You beautiful ladies look fit for a Washington banquet. You'll be the talk of the fort."

"We would be pleased if it was so," Blue Water Woman said coyly.

Zach fidgeted in his saddle. "Can we go now? We've been waiting here for hours."

"It only seems that way," Nate mumbled, and assumed the lead. They had to swing around to the south side of the fort since the main entrance was located there. Along the way he saw a middling encampment of Indians close to the Arkansas River, 20 lodges arranged in a half-circle. "Arapahos?" he wondered aloud, knowing that tribe did extensive trading at the post.

"Cheyennes," Shakespeare answered.

Nate recalled hearing that it had been Cheyennes who had helped the Bents pick the site after William Bent had saved the lives of a pair of their warriors. Strategically placed at a crossroads of Indian travel, the fort now did a booming business with all of the tribes in the region. The Indians received guns, knives, tools, and trade trinkets in exchange for buffalo hides and other pelts. The Bent brothers and St. Vrain, all scrupulously honest, had acquired an unparalleled reputation for fairness so that even tribes who normally shunned the whites, such as the Gros Ventres and the Utes, routinely traveled to Bent's Fort to barter.

It had been several years since Nate last saw any Cheyennes. He had been meaning to seek out one of them for quite some time, a prominent warrior called White Eagle,

the man who had bestowed the name Grizzly Killer on
him after he slew his first monster bear by a sheer fluke.
That name had stuck, and now Nate was known far and
wide as the white who had slain more grizzlies than any
man alive. Not that he'd planned it that way. Somehow,
he seemed to attract grizzles the way a magnet attracted
iron. The truth be known, he would much rather attract
rabbits or squirrels.

The main gate was wide open, and both whites and
Indians were freely coming and going. Perched on the
wall above the gate was a belfry where a lookout sat. At
the first sign of hostiles he would sound the alarm and
rouse the entire garrison. This worthy now leaned forward to study their party. "Are my eyes playin' tricks
on me, or is that none other than Shakespeare McNair I
see?" he called out happily.

"Kendall?" the mountain man responded.

"None other," said the lookout, a strapping fellow in
a red cap. "I'm workin' for the Bents now, and finer
booshways you can't find anywhere."

"It's been a while," Shakespeare said. "How's the
family?"

"Lisa is as feisty as ever. And Vail is the apple of her
dear mother's eye. I'll introduce you later after my stint
here is done."

"I'll look for you."

They were about to pass through the gate when Nate
realized the nearest whites and Indians were looking his
way and some of the whites were scowling. He faced
straight ahead, acting as if he had no idea why they were
perturbed. Samson was certainly oblivious to their dirty
looks. He felt sorry for the mongrel because it still
smelled like day-old garbage after a dozen baths or better.

Once past the iron-sheathed gate, Nate gazed at a spacious inner court ringed by small whitewashed guest
rooms. Over to one side stood a well. There were also

offices, meeting rooms, warehouses, wagon sheds, rooms for the staff, and more, just as Shakespeare had detailed there would be. Although Nate had never set food inside the fort before, he felt as if he knew it as well as he did the interior of his own cabin.

There were Indians in abundance; Cheyennes and Arapahos and Osage and even a few Kiowas. Mingled among them were free trappers, Frenchmen from St. Louis, and voyageurs from far-off Canada. Altogether, it was as motley and colorful a gathering of humanity as anyone was likely to see anywhere west of the last Missouri settlement.

Nate made for a hitching post, running a gauntlet of frank stares. He began to dismount, then stopped in surprise on seeing a black woman emerge from a nearby doorway and scour the court for a moment before disappearing back inside.

Shakespeare grinned. "That's Charlotte, the cook. Stay on her good side, Nate, and you'll eat pumpkin pie and slapjacks as tasty as any offered in the fanciest home in New York City."

The ringing of a heavy hammer on an anvil drew Nate's attention to a blacksmith shop at the southeast corner of the fort, and when he turned back to the hitching post there stood a man with a receding hairline and aquiline features who was dressed in a fine black suit.

"As I live and breathe!" the man exclaimed, coming around the post and advancing on McNair with his hand extended. "Shakespeare, you old coon! What brings you to our neck of the woods?"

"Howdy, Bill," the mountain man said, swinging down and shaking heartily. "It has been a while, hasn't it?"

The man nodded. "I figured by now some Blackfoot would have your hair hanging in his lodge."

"I'm too ornery to let them get me," Shakespeare said. He proceeded to introduce Blue Water Woman, Winona, Zach, and finally Nate to the stranger. "This here is William Bent," he concluded.

"I'm delighted to make your acquaintance," Bent said. "Make yourselves at home here. If you're staying overnight, I'll arrange guest rooms for you."

"We'd be in your debt," Shakespeare said.

"Not at all. What are old friends for?" Bent responded, and moved off with a cheery wave.

"You didn't tell me that you knew one of the Bent brothers," Nate remarked.

"I know all three of them."

"Is there anyone you *don't* know?"

McNair, grinning, tied his horse to the post. "You have to remember that there aren't all that many white men in these parts. Sooner or later you'll meet most of them if you get around enough." He paused. "Bill and I go back to the time he was trading up in the Northwest. He was having a hard time making ends meet because of competition from the Hudson's Bay Company. There was many a time we'd sit around sharing whiskey and I'd listen to him describe his woes."

"Well, he doesn't have many woes now," Nate said, surveying the whirls of activity all around them. Here and there clusters of Indians were engaged in trade talks with members of the fort's crew. That the talks were effective was testified to by the enormous piles of prime pelts being prepared for transport by caravan to St. Louis, pelts easily worth several thousand dollars on the open market. The Bents and St. Vrain, he deduced, must be making money hand over fist. They'd soon be incredibly wealthy if they weren't already.

After Nate and Shakespeare assisted their wives down and secured all the animals, they all strolled around to

see the sights. Over Zach's protest Nate left Samson tied
with their horses. The dog whined and pawed at the rope,
but Nate refused to take the mongrel along and upset
everyone within sniffing distance.

They saw lusty free trappers drinking and laughing.
They saw proud Indians strutting about wearing new
blankets draped over their shoulders or adorned with new
trinkets. Toward the north end of the square, as they
completed their circuit, a peculiar series of subdued
cracking sounds could be heard. It gave Nate pause and
he scoured the square for the cause.

Shakespeare, who never missed a thing, pointed at the
roof of a building visible beyond the trader's room right
in front of them. "Billiards," he disclosed.

"Here?"

"Bill and his brothers have spared no expense in providing all the comforts. Do you play?"

"Of course. Every boy in New York City can play by
the time he's twelve. At one time I was rather good."

"Is that a fact? Then we'll have a match later. Our
wives should find it interesting."

"Say, Pa," Zach said, tugging on Nate's sleeve.
"What's that man doing to Samson?"

Turning, Nate beheld a trio of stern voyageurs ringing
the hitching post. A hefty specimen in buckskins and a
blue cap was angrily addressing Samson while jabbing a
thick finger within inches of the dog's face. Nate hurried
over, fearing trouble. Voyageurs were a hardy, independent lot, as befitted men who made their living trapping
the most remote regions of Canada. Occasionally some
drifted south into the Rockies, but it was unusual for any
to be as far south as Bent's Fort.

"Is there a problem, gentlemen?" he politely inquired,
stopping close to the post.

The three scrutinized him from head to toe, their dark,
seamed features impassive.

"And who might you be?" demanded the one in the blue cap.

"I'm the man who owns this dog," Nate informed them. "Has he bothered you somehow?"

"You're damn straight he has, American."

"How?"

"Hell, take a breath," snapped Blue Cap. "The bastard stinks like dead fish." He spoke a sentence in French.

"I don't understand," Nate said.

"I asked if your dog is part skunk," the voyageur translated, his companions all smirking.

Nate struggled to control his surging temper. Voyageurs, he reminded himself, were renowned for their arrogance; they tended to look down their noses at their American counterparts, always acting as if they were better trappers and, therefore, better men. Better meaning tougher. All trappers took pride in being hardy souls. Voyageurs just went overboard.

"Maybe we should skin this ugly beast," the spokesman taunted.

"We can sell the meat to the Cheyennes," suggested another. "They love to eat dogs." Chortling softly, he bent over and reached for the mongrel's neck.

Samson wasn't about to let a stranger touch him. Bristling, he lunged, his great jaws snapping down on the Canadian's wrist, his teeth piercing the buckskin and digging deep into the man's flesh.

Shrieking in agony, the man threw himself backwards, tearing his arm loose and ripping his sleeve in the process. Large drops of blood dripped from the puncture marks. "Damn him!" he roared. "Look at what the son of a bitch did to me!"

The man in the blue cap, cursing a blue streak, drew a pistol and pointed it at Samson's head. "I'll teach this cur to mind its manners."

Everything transpired so quickly that there was no time for Nate to think, no time for him to do other than that which he now did—step in close and swat the pistol barrel aside with the stock of his Hawken. The flintlock discharged, the ball smacking harmlessly into the ground. "That will be enough!" he declared.

But the voyageur in the blue cap had other ideas. Enraged at Nate's interference, he suddenly sprang, swinging the pistol at Nate's forehead. Nate ducked under the blow and retaliated by driving the Hawken into the pit of the voyageur's stomach, doubling the man in half.

Strong arms abruptly clamped around Nate from behind, pinning him in place. "I've got him!" cried the other uninjured voyageur. "Bash his brains out, Pierre!"

Nate saw the one in the blue cap straighten and raise the flintlock overhead. Instinctively Nate lashed out, ramming his left foot into Pierre's knee. Pierre screeched and crumpled. The man who held Nate, roaring like a madman, drove forward, slamming Nate into the hitching post, and it felt as if a mule had kicked Nate in the gut. His lungs emptied in a great whoosh and he saw stars before his eyes. Dimly, he was aware the voyageur had drawn him backwards and was tensing to slam him into the post once more.

He mustn't let that happen! Twisting sharply, he succeeded in throwing the voyageur off balance. The man's arms slackened for a moment, and in that span Nate exerted all of his strength and wrenched himself free. Whirling, he glimpsed the voyageur clawing at the hilt of a butcher knife. Nate's fist stopped that, rocking the voyageur on his heels. A second blow dropped the unconscious Canadian in a heap.

Not until that moment did Nate hear the loud shouts on all sides and see men rushing from every direction. He backed next to Samson and held the Hawken level.

A few yards away was Shakespeare, covering the man Samson had bitten.

"What the devil is going on here?" asked an irate man with the bearing and dress of an aristocrat as he pushed his way through the crowd to the front. "Everyone knows the rules. No shooting is permitted in the fort. Nor will we tolerate fighting."

Shakespeare stepped up to Nate. "Don't lay an egg, Ceran. My friend Grizzly Killer didn't start the trouble." He bobbed his head at the Canadians. "They did."

"McNair?" said Ceran St. Vrain. "When did you get in?"

At that juncture William Bent hastened up from the other side and glared at the man named Pierre. "Shakespeare is telling the truth, Ceran. I happened to see what happened from the blacksmith shop." He jabbed a finger at Pierre. "You, Chevalier, have gone too far this time. You persist in imposing on our hospitality when we've warned you to behave."

"No one tells me what to do!" Pierre said, wincing as he cradled his knee with both hands.

"There you are wrong," Bent said calmly. "We will have your leg looked at, and then you and your friends will be escorted from the fort. Should you try to return, the lookout will be under my personal orders to shoot you on sight."

"You wouldn't dare!"

From out of the throng came Bent's employees, rugged Frenchmen and others armed with rifles, pistols, clubs, and knives. Fully a dozen strong, they stood on either side of William Bent, and all it took was one look at them for every man there, and particularly Pierre Chevalier, to realize they would gladly tear into anyone who in any manner threatened their employer.

"You were saying?" Bent said.

Pierre, his face beet-red, put both palms on the ground

and pushed upright. He tottered unsteadily for a bit, then shoved his pistol under his belt. "I'm not fool enough to stick my head into an open beaver trap," he said.

"You will gather your belongings and vacate the premises within the hour," Bent directed.

"If you insist," Pierre said bitterly. He glanced at Nate, hatred seeping from every pore. "This isn't over, Grizzly Killer. Not by a long shot. You will see my friends and me again soon. Very soon."

"Chevalier, why don't you do us all a favor and go jump in Lake Winnipeg?" Shakespeare asked.

The general laughter only further fouled Pierre's mood. "Have your fun, McNair. We'll be paying you a visit too. You had no call butting into this affair."

The crowd parted as the three Canadians were escorted into a nearby building, four fort employees carrying the one who was unconscious. With the excitement over, the rest of the gathering gradually dispersed.

William Bent and Ceran St. Vrain lingered.

"I wouldn't take Chevalier's words lightly, my friend," Bent told McNair. "He's not one to forgive a slight. He wears his hatred like most men wear clothes, and he can be as devious as a fox when he wants to be."

"I know all about him," Shakespeare said. "Don't worry. We'll be on our guard once we leave here."

"Which will be sooner than you expect if you are involved in any more disturbances," Ceran commented. "You always did have a knack for being in the thick of things."

"And you always did wear your britches too tight," the mountain man replied.

St. Vrain wasn't amused. "If you will excuse me," he said formally, and made for the building where the voyageurs were being tended to.

William Bent sighed. "You shouldn't have done that,

Shakespeare. I know the two of you never have gotten along very well, but he is my partner. I must put up with his stuffy attitude every damn day. Now I'll have to listen to him gripe about you for the next week or two.''

"Is that all? I'll have to insult him again before we go."

"You're incorrigible," Bent said, turning. He inhaled deeply, then walked in a tight circle around Samson, examining the dog carefully. "Let me guess. He tangled with a skunk and lost. And you had the gall to inflict him on us?"

This last was addressed at Nate. "We couldn't very well leave him out on the prairie to fend for himself."

"Why not?" Bent asked half seriously.

From between Winona and Blue Water Woman, both of whom had been standing quietly close at hand, stepped Zach. He ran up to Samson and affectionately threw his slender arms around the huge canine.

"Don't you worry, boy. I won't let anyone harm a hair on your head," he declared.

"There's your answer," Nate told Bent.

A warm smile curled the trader's mouth and he nodded knowingly. "I see your dilemma. Very well. The dog can stay, but you'll have to keep him in your room so as not to provoke another fight."

"Fair enough."

"Now come along and I'll show you where you'll be staying," Bent said.

The guest rooms, while small, were comfortably furnished. Most, they were informed, were currently empty, but that would soon change as the Bents were expecting a large caravan from Missouri any day now. During the spring and summer months an unending stream of wagons passed through en route to Santa Fe.

Bent stayed and chatted while they unsaddled. He lent

a hand in stripping their supplies off the pack animals, then graciously extended an invitation for them to join him and his wife for supper that evening.

Nate had only to see the spark of joy in Winona's eyes to accept. He walked outside with Bent and thanked him for the offer.

"My pleasure. It will make my dear wife happy. She so enjoys the company of other women." Bent stopped, glanced at the doorway, and lowered his voice. "I couldn't help but notice that both Winona and Blue Water Woman were carrying rifles earlier. It's most unusual to see women armed like that. Are they good shots?"

"The best. Shakespeare and I taught them ourselves. We figured it would come in handy if we're ever attacked by hostiles again. Four guns speak louder than two."

"Quite true. Wait until my wife hears." He took several strides, then cast a somber look of warning over his shoulder. "You might need four guns, my young friend, if Pierre and his bunch ever come looking for revenge."

Chapter Five

The large caravan from the States reached Bent's Fort the next morning a few hours after sunrise, and everyone turned out to see the heavily laden wagons arrive; trappers, mountain men, voyageurs, employees, and even the entire population of the Cheyenne village by the river.

Zach, perched on Nate's broad shoulders to get a better view over the heads of men in front of them, wiggled in glee and chattered constantly about the size of the wagons and the people he saw. This was a new experience to him and he enjoyed it with typical boyish zeal.

All the women at the fort, including Charlotte the cook, were splendidly dressed in their prettiest attire. Anyone unfamiliar with Indians ways would never suspect that the Indian wives of the free trappers, who stood so demurely by the sides of their spouses, were actually showing off. Gaily adorned in their finest buckskin dresses as they were, the wives were doing the exact same thing their wealthy white counterparts in high society did when they donned expensive gowns to attend formal balls and other social functions, proving once again that the two cultures might be outwardly different, but that in their hearts the two peoples were very much the same, a fact few realized to the detriment of both.

There were 110 wagons in the wagon train and close to two hundred men, traders and muleteers combined. All were well armed. Caravans had to be strongly protected against hostiles, most notably the wily Comanches and the fierce Apaches.

At the head of the column rode two men, the wagon boss and one other. William Becknell was the man in charge, a veteran of the Santa Fe trade who was widely hailed as "the Father of the Santa Fe Trail" because of a shortcut he'd discovered some years back.

When trade between the States and Santa Fe commenced, the caravans left Independence, Missouri, and struck off westward along the Arkansas River until they reached the approximate spot where Bent's Fort would later be built. From there they traveled southward along the edge of the mountains, through Raton Pass, and then eventually westward again until they hit Santa Fe. This Mountain Route, as it became generally known, was long and arduous.

Becknell had sought a shorter route. One year, instead of following the traditional trail, he made a bold and daring decision to leave the established route two-thirds of the way to the cutoff to Raton Pass and strike directly southwestward across the blistering Cimarron Desert. He almost didn't make it. His party ran out of water, so to survive they cut the ears of their mules and drank fresh blood to quench their thirst.

This new route, the Cimmaron Cutoff as it was called, shaved a hundred miles off the Mountain Route and became equally as popular with the traders. But there were many who refused to take it. They were unwilling to contend with the brain-baking heat, the roiling clouds of alkali dust that choked men and animals alike, and the deceptive mirages that led caravans off course. Then too, the Comanches were more apt to strike wagon trains taking the desert route than the mountain route.

So for years now both trails had been in regular use. The U.S. government helped out by paying two tribes, the Osage and Kansas Indians, who inhabited the central Plains, to leave the caravans alone, and by sometimes sending military escorts who would stay with the caravans until they reached Mexican territory.

This particular wagon train lacked a dragoon escort, Nate noted as he surveyed the line from one end to the other. He looked again at the man who rode beside Becknell, a dashing Mexican with a wide-brimmed white hat, a waist-length dark blue jacket that hugged his lean form, and matching blue pants that flared out at the bottom. Around the man's middle was a bright red sash, partially covering his white shirt. Tucked under that sash were two polished flintlocks.

"I've never seen his like before, Pa," Zach mentioned. "Is he from Santa Fe, you reckon?"

"He might be," Nate allowed.

"Gosh, he sure is a dandy."

"No more so than your mother," Nate recklessly joked, and received an elbow in the ribs for his wit.

Since the fort couldn't possibly hold so many wagons, the traders parked outside, dividing up into four groups and forming four protective circles. Afterward, they let their stock of mules, oxen, and horses loose to graze inside each ring, a standard precaution in case of an attack by hostiles.

Nate kept an eye on William Becknell during the activities. Bent had told him that Becknell invariably took the Cimarron Cutoff nowadays, but in this instance the wagon train was carrying a load of medical supplies,

ammunition, and other provisions for the post, which
necessitated taking the old Mountain Route.

Not being one to look a gift horse in the mouth, Nate
waited until he saw Becknell and the Mexican dandy
walking toward the iron gate. Then he excused himself,
leaving Winona and Zach with Shakespeare, and moved
to intercept the pair. Both halted at his approach.

"Mr. Becknell?" Nate said, offering his hand. "I'm
Nate King, and I'm sorry to impose on you but I was
wondering if my party can join your caravan to Santa
Fe?"

The legendary wagon master scrutinized Nate from his
beaver hat to his moccasins. "A mountain man is always
welcome, sir. You're all fine shots and a few more guns
might come in handy should the Comanches pay us a
visit." Becknell admired the Hawken. "How many are
in your party, Mr. King?"

Nate told him.

"Shakespeare McNair is with you?" Becknell said,
sounding delighted. "Why, I haven't seen that old buzzard in seven or eight years. I should have known he'd
be alive and kicking."

"You know him too?"

"Who doesn't? That man has a knack for getting
around."

"Don't I know it," Nate said. "One of these days I
expect I'll hear he's been to China and back."

Both Becknell and the Mexican laughed. The trader
indicated his companion and said, "Where are my manners? Allow me to introduce a very good friend of mine,
Francisco Gaona. His family is very prominent in New
Mexico. He came north with me after my last trip to see
some of the States for himself."

"My pleasure," Nate said, shaking hands. The Mexican's hand was firm, hinting at latent strength.

"Mine also, *señor,*" Francisco said, a hint of amusement in his eyes as he examined Nate's outfit. "Perhaps you would do me the honor of eating supper with us tonight? You are the first . . ." he paused ". . . mountain man I have met, and I would like to learn more about those who live as you do."

"My family would be glad to join you," Nate responded. He agreed to meet them at six o'clock, and promised Becknell he would bring McNair along.

The rest of the day was spent in mingling at the fort and with members of the caravan. Zach asked a million questions, wanting to know where the mammoth wagons were made and how much weight they could carry and why the front wheels were smaller than the rear wheels and why some wagons were pulled by mules while others were pulled by oxen, and on and on and on.

Nate answered as best he could, explaining that the wagons were made in Conestoga and Pittsburgh and other places, that each could carry up to ten tons of trade goods, that the front wheels were smaller so the wagons could make tight turns without difficulty, and that whether a man used mules or oxen was a matter of personal choice.

Shakespeare didn't help matters by snickering at some of the questions and suggesting some more for Zach to ask, such as why were mules so stubborn and were boy oxen stronger than girl oxen? McNair had no idea how close he came to being shot in the foot.

At the appointed hour Nate, his family, and the McNairs met Becknell, Gaona, and others from the caravan for a hot meal at the fort. They were joined by William Bent and Ceran St. Vrain. Charlotte outdid herself, treating them to succulent buffalo meat, biscuits, potatoes, beans, countless cups of rich coffee, and more.

It was after the meal, as they all sat around the long table chatting and, in the case of many of the men, smoking on their pipes, that an incident took place Nate never forgot for as long as he lived.

He was listening to Becknell talk about the unbeliev-
able profits to be made in the Santa Fe trade. He heard
how a recent caravan had transported $35,000 worth of
goods there and returned to Missouri with $190,000 in
gold, silver, and prime furs. It set him to thinking about
how hard he had to work just to make ends meet, and
how he was lucky if he made $2,000 dollars in any given
year.

Preoccupied with his thoughts, he failed to notice the
three men who crept in through a side door, until he
heard the click of a gun hammer being pulled back and
he gazed around in surprise to see the three voyageurs
he had tangled with the day before not three yards away
with their rifles trained on the group at the table.

Pierre Chevalier wagged his gun at Nate and smirked.
"So we meet again, *mon ami*? But not as you would
like, eh?"

Everyone was frozen in place. William Bent was the
first to recover and he rose in indignation, snapping,
"What the hell is the meaning of this, Chevalier? You
were warned to stay away from this post."

"So we were, Bill," Pierre said. "And I intended to
do as you so unjustly wanted." He took a step closer to
Nate. "But then I was watching through my telescope,
waiting for this pig to leave the fort so we could finish
the business between us, and I saw him talking to Becknell. Now why would he do that? I asked myself. And I
wondered if maybe he was planning to hook up with the
caravan and travel to Santa Fe." The voyageur scowled.
"I couldn't take the chance of that happening. Getting
close to him then would be too hard to do what with
the men of the caravan ready to shoot at anything that
moves."

"So you snuck back in here?" Ceran St. Vrain said.
"How dare you!"

"It was quite easy. All we had to do was blend in with

one of the groups from the caravan and your lookout never spotted us.''

Bent jabbed a finger at the front door. "Leave, now, and there will be no hard feelings.''

"I'm afraid I can't,'' Pierre said, focusing on Nate. "This is just between the two of us. My friends will make certain no one interferes.''

Nate, holding a cup of coffee in his right hand, stared down the barrel of Chevalier's rifle and wished he was sitting straighter so he could get at his flintlocks. Keeping his voice level, he asked, "Are you going to kill me without giving me a chance to defend myself?''

"Not at all,'' Pierre answered. "This will be a fair fight, I assure you.''

It was then that Francisco Gaona stood, his hands hanging loosely at his sides. "Pardon me, *señor,* but this man is a friend of mine and I can not stand by and do nothing while you impose your will on us.''

Chevalier looked at the Mexican as if he was inspecting a new animal species for the very first time. Snorting, he said with contempt, "No one asked your opinion, greaser. Sit down and keep your mouth shut until this is over.''

Gaona's features darkened perceptibly. He glanced at the men on either side of Chevalier and an odd smile creased his lips. "I do not like having guns pointed my way. Kindly have your *amigos* lower theirs or suffer the consequences.''

The voyageurs exchanged glances and laughed.

"What can you do?'' Chevalier asked disdainfully.

"This,'' Francisco said, and moved, his hands invisible as he swept both pistols from his sash, cocking them as he drew. The two shots boomed as one. Chevalier's friends were hit, each in the shoulder. Both staggered and dropped their rifles as the balls ripped through them. Both clutched at their wounds, one falling to his knees.

Belatedly, Pierre uttered a bestial growl and pivoted to aim his gun at Francisco, but as if by magic Francisco had transferred his right-hand pistol to his left and a smaller pistol had blossomed in its place, pointed at Pierre's head. Pierre turned to granite.

"You will be so kind as to drop your rifle, *por favor*," Francisco said.

Chevalier hesitated. His thumb, which rested on the hammer of his rifle, twitched for all to behold. Everyone knew he was tempted to shoot. All he had to do was cock that hammer and fire. Then he took a good look at Gaona's smaller pistol and saw that it was already cocked. His face crimson with suppressed rage, he lowered his rifle to the floor, then straightened. "Now what, you bastard?"

"What happens next is up to Señor King," Francisco responded.

Nate slowly rose, all eyes on him. He set down his cup and stepped clear of the chair. Since he was the one Pierre had challenged, what happened next was entirely up to him. He could ask Bent to have Pierre thrown off the fort again, but doing so would leave the greater issue unresolved. And as sure as people loved to gossip, there would be talk. The trappers and others would learn what had transpired and they would spread the word to those they met. Within a few months everyone living in the Rockies would know that he had refused to stand up to Chevalier and his courage would come into question. He dared not let that happen. Of all human virtues, the Indians and the mountain men alike valued and respected courage the most. If he wanted to be able to hold his head up at the Rendezvous, he had to answer the challenge in the only way possible. "How do you want to do this?" he asked.

The voyageur smirked and reached behind his back.

Out came a large butcher knife, the blade gleaming in the lantern light. "Will this do?"

Nodding, Nate removed his pistols and placed them on the table beside Winona. For an instant her gaze caught his. He could practically feel her soul reaching out to him and his resolve faltered, but only for a second. Pulling his knife, he confronted his adversary. "Ready when you are."

"Now just hold on!" Bent declared. "Since I'm part owner of this post, I have a say in what goes on here. And one of our ironclad rules is that there will be no fighting on the premises."

"We can make no exceptions," St. Vrain added.

"Very well," Pierre said. "First take care of my friends. Then let's take this outside the walls where we'll have all the room in the world. How say you, King?"

Nate nodded.

Soon a mass exodus ensued, with word of the fight spreading like wildfire among all those at the fort and, thanks to swift runners, those at the wagons and even in the Cheyenne village. Scores and scores of people poured through the gates and streamed from the camps and the lodges. They formed into a gigantic crescent with the open end at the front of the fort. Inevitably, bets were placed, with men shouting back and forth as they offered and accepted odds.

Of all this activity Nate was barely conscious. He was thinking of Winona and Zach and what would happen to them should he lose. And lose he might. Pierre Chevalier was not to be taken lightly. No matter how well Nate fought, a single slip or mistake could cost him his life. What would happen to his loved ones then?

Such worry wasn't new to him. A free trapper never knew from one day to the next whether he would be alive to greet the following dawn. Every time he ventured forth on a trapping trip, he couldn't help but speculate on whether he would see his cabin again. The grim nature of life in the often-savage wilderness dictated that every man must stay constantly on his guard or risk forfeiting the life he held so dear. Hostiles, grizzlies, disease, accidents, they all claimed trappers at an appalling rate. Some old-timers claimed that out of every five men who boldly ventured into the Rockies, only one would ever make it out again.

His only consolation was that should he perish, life would go on. Winona and Zach would eventually recover enough to get on with their lives. Winona, unfortunately, would be compelled by necessity to remarry. Single women were at a decided disadvantage in a warrior-dominated society; only the men were permitted to hunt buffalo, the staple of Indian life.

Nate bowed his head, girding himself, banishing his morbid thoughts. Long ago he had learned that if a man wanted to win a fight, he had to *believe* he was going to win it with every atom of his being. Attitude was all-important. As with every aspect of life, a positive outlook invariably meant the difference between success and failure.

A hand fell gently on his shoulder, and he looked up into the kindly face of his mentor. They knew each other so well, they had been through so much together, that words weren't needed. The hardships they had endured had forged their friendship into an unbreakable bond. Still, Nate spoke. "If anything should happen to me, watch over Winona and Zach."

"Do you think I'd do otherwise?"

They were standing just outside the gate. Nate surveyed the crowd and felt self-conscious. He hadn't meant for the dispute to become so public an issue. Off to one side were Bent, St. Vrain, and Becknell in earnest conversation. Chevalier stood waiting a dozen yards away. "Keep your eyes on the crowd," Nate said. "Pierre might have other friends."

"Don't fret. If anyone so much as touches a weapon, he's dead."

Nate steeled his will and strode forward. He heard Zach calling his name, but he refused to look back. Now, more than ever, he mustn't weaken.

Pierre also heard. "Isn't that your brat, King? Don't you care that soon he'll be crying over your grave?"

"Go to hell."

"One day, Grizzly Killer, I undoubtedly will. But today it is your turn. And maybe, afterward, I will stop by to see your wife."

Right then and there Nate would have attacked, but the three traders suddenly joined them.

"We want several things made clear," Bent declared. "None of us approve of this feud. You're setting a bad example for the other trappers, and I wouldn't be surprised if in the future we have to work a lot harder to maintain order."

"You make me want to cry, *mon ami*," Chevalier said in mock sorrow, then roared with laughter.

"I fail to see the humor," Bent stated testily.

"So do I," St. Vrain said, and looked at Nate and the voyageur. "Must you resort to this drastic step? Can't we sit down like gentlemen and discuss the matter? Perhaps we can avoid bloodshed."

"Save your breath, Ceran," Pierre snapped. "This is a matter of personal honor with me. If you had fire in your veins instead of ice, you would better understand."

Nate knew the traders were wasting their time if they hoped to prevail on Chevalier to change his mind. He was going to tell them as much when a lean, gray-haired stranger dressed in homespun clothes walked from among the spectators and came toward them.

"Who is this?" Pierre asked.

"Crain, a trader in dry goods," Becknell revealed. "This is his first trip to Santa Fe."

The lean man smiled and nodded at each of them, then turned to the wagon master. "Bill, what is going on here? I've just been informed that these two men will fight to the death with knives. Surely such a barbaric practice won't be countenanced."

"I'm afraid it will," Becknell replied.

"We can't permit it, I tell you. We're civilized men, not primitives like those Indians over there."

"Get back with the rest, Mr. Crain," Becknell advised. "If you don't care to watch, return to the wagons. There's nothing you can say or do that will alter matters."

"But whoever wins will be guilty of murder! We have a legal right to stop this atrocity before it goes any further," Crain declared. "Gather enough men and we can lock these two up until they've cooled down."

"I'm afraid you're mistaken about our legal authority in this case, Mr. Crain," William Bent interjected. "You see, there is no law here, not in the sense of an organized legal system such as exists back in the States. There isn't a law officer within hundred of miles of this spot."

"But . . ." Crain began.

Bent held up a hand. "Let me finish. You're like a lot of men when they first head out this way. You mistakenly think that the same rule of law applies west of the Mississippi that applies east of it, and you're wrong. Out here a man is his own law."

"That's anarchy!" Crain blurted.

"It's freedom, sir. True freedom. Back in the States a man gives up his right to do as he pleases. In exchange for false security, he lets the government run his life, lets himself be ruled by the dictates of politicians instead of the dictates of his own mind and heart." He paused. "If these men want to settle their dispute with knives, out here they have that right.''

''I've never heard such foolishness,'' Crain said in disgust, and glanced at Nate and Pierre. ''If you two simpletons are so intent on killing yourselves, go ahead.'' So saying, he stomped off, his back as stiff as a board.

Chevalier grinned. ''There are jackasses everywhere, it seems.'' Sobering, he hefted his knife and faced Nate. ''But enough talk, eh, King? Let us, as they say, get down to business.''

Then, unexpectedly, Pierre attacked.

Chapter Six

Nate had expected the voyageur to wait until the three traders were out of harm's way before beginning the fight, so he was taken unawares when Chevalier suddenly lunged and stabbed at his chest. Only his pantherish reflexes saved him. He threw himself to the right, sweeping his knife up, and barely managed to deflect the thrust. Their blades rang together. Continuing to move, to circle, he sought an opening.

Bent, St. Vrain, and Becknell were walking rapidly away.

"I almost had you, Grizzly Killer," Pierre said cockily, lowering into a crouch and holding his knife close to his waist. "And we've only just begun."

Refusing to respond, to break his concentration, Nate circled and waited. He did as Shakespeare had taught him, fixing his eyes on Chevalier's knife. When it flicked out, he backed up. When it slashed at his body, he twisted and dodged. When it arced high, he ducked low. And all the while he looked for his chance.

Many of the onlookers were yelling and cheering. To the trappers this was the equivalent of high entertainment, of the sort they frequently witnessed at the Rendezvous and other gatherings when men who had too much to drink took offense at an imagined or real slur. Only, those fights were usually conducted with fists or as simple wrestling matches.

By their very natures, the trappers and mountain men—those old-timers who no longer trapped for a living but made ends meet as best they could whether living by themselves in a remote cabin or among whichever Indian tribe they happened to favor—were a lusty, hardy bunch. They lived hard, loved hard, fought hard, wringing the most life had to offer out of each and every moment. Regret wasn't in their vocabulary.

So Nate took no offense at the playful shouting and goading of the bystanders. He shut out the noise, focusing on Chevalier, his knife extended, edge out, for a quick swipe. But he purposefully didn't swing as often as he could have. He gave the impressions of being timid, of being unwilling to overextend himself and risk injury. There was a reason behind his behavior, which soon became apparent.

Pierre grew increasingly confident the longer the fight went. He grew bolder, darting in closer and closer in his eagerness to bury his blade into Nate. His swings weren't quite as controlled, his movements a bit less precise.

Still Nate held back. Several times he might have scored, but he passed up the opportunities. He craved a decisive win. If he merely nicked his foe, the voyageur would become cautious and be more difficult to defeat.

"What's taking you so long, Chevalier?" someone in the throng called out above all the rest.

Pierre's cheeks reddened and he growled. Taking a step rearward so he was beyond Nate's reach, he snapped, "Did you hear that, King? That's what I get for going easy on you."

"We can still lower our weapons and shake hands," Nate said, breaking his silence.

"Never."

Nate stopped circling. He had to be certain. "Tell me, Chevalier. What happens if I should only wound you? Will you let bygones be bygones? Can we go our separate ways in peace?"

"You will never know peace as long as I'm alive!"

"That's what I was afraid you'd say," Nate said, and feinted. Pierre countered, Nate evaded the knife, and they resumed circling. A lightning strike at Nate's right wrist would have connected if Nate hadn't leaped out of the way.

The voyageur's eagerness was giving way to impatience, and impatience was wedded to recklessness. Pierre attempted to disembowel Nate. Failing, he cursed, shifted, and drove his knife at Nate's neck.

Gliding in and under the blow was child's play. In front of Nate was Chevalier's unprotected abdomen, and with a swift thrust Nate ripped the man's buckskin shirt and the skin underneath, but not severely. Pierre, horrified, pressed a hand to the wound and backed away, shock slowing him down.

Nate took another long stride and saw the voyageur's knife sweep at his neck. Jerking aside, he felt a puff of air as the blade flashed past. Then, pivoting sharply, he whipped his knife upward and plunged it into Pierre's knife hand.

Chevalier howled. His weapon fell as he wrenched his hand loose, causing blood to spray all over him and the ground. Agony etching his features, he tried to flee.

But Nate wasn't going to let him. He pounced, raining

the knife down on Pierre's face, using the hilt not the blade to batter the voyageur's cheeks and lips. Chevalier staggered, then raised his arms to ward off more blows.

Nate was relentless. He slammed his left fist into Pierre's stomach, and followed through with a left to Pierre's chin. Down the man went, crashing onto his back, stunned yet not out. Pierre rose on an elbow and grabbed at Nate's legs with his good hand, which was a mistake because in so doing he exposed that hand to Nate's knife, and paid for his oversight when the bloody blade pierced his palm.

Arching his spine, Chevalier wailed like a wounded wolf. "No more! No more!"

Heedless of the appeal, Nate tore his knife free and stood over his enemy. He gripped the front of Pierre's shirt and elevated the butcher knife overhead for a death stroke. Pierre froze, eyes wide in terror. The crowd fell deathly still. All Nate heard was a roaring in his ears, the roaring of his blood as it raced through his veins. He had Chevalier right where he wanted him. All it would take was a single stroke and the voyageur would never bother anyone else ever again. His arm was poised and tensed for the kill.

Suddenly a single voice broke the silence, the plaintive call of a young boy in turmoil. "Don't, Pa!"

Tense seconds passed. Slowly Nate's muscles relaxed and his arm dropped. He shoved Pierre flat on the ground, then straightened. "You can thank your lucky stars, fool, that I'm raising him to believe there's a God in Heaven."

"What?" Pierre blurted out weakly, not comprehending. "What's that you say?"

Nate felt an odd weariness flood through him, and with it a feeling of immense satisfaction. Turning away, he saw his wife and son and stepped toward them. The great cheer that burst from scores of lips stopped him, and the next moment he was inundated by people pressing in

from all sides to congratulate him and clap him on the
back. He nodded numbly and let them buffet him this
way and that, until abruptly a white-haired raging bull,
pushing through to his side, scattered those in front with
a warning.

"Let him pass, damn your hides, or there will be hell
to pay!"

They parted, made meek by Shakespeare's wrath, and
offered no interference as the mountain man escorted
Nate over to Winona and Zach.

William Bent appeared out of nowhere. "You did fine,
King. Real fine. No one will hold this against you, and
once the word gets out, even Chevalier's friends will
leave you alone."

"Let's hope so," Nate said, about to drape his arm
around Winona's shoulders when he saw that he still held
his knife, the blade dripping blood. Crouching, he wiped
it clean on the grass, then stuck it in his sheath.

Francisco Gaona came over, his hand outstretched. "I
would like to offer my congratulations also, *señor*. I have
seen many knife fighters in my time and you are one of
the best."

"I could say the same about you with pistols," Nate
replied, shaking hands, impressed by Francisco's sincerity. He found himself liking the Mexican more and more
as time went on.

"Much practice, *señor*," Francisco said. "My *padre*
gave me my first *pistola* when I was but ten years old."

Small fingers touched Nate's own, and he looked down
into the anxious upturned face of his son. He smiled
reassuringly and gave Zach's fingers a tender squeeze.
"Everything is all right now."

"I was scared again, Pa," the boy said softly. "Only
this time I was scared for you."

"That makes two of us."

Shakespeare cleared his throat, rubbed a hand in

Zach's hair, and announced, "What say we cut short this palaver and go in for some drinks. I'm buying."

"Will wonders nerve cease," Nate declared.

They weren't the only ones desirous of quenching their thirsts. The room was packed. Many of the patrons saw fit to recount the fight over and over, with those who had won money extolling Nate's skill while those who had lost debated the mistakes Chevalier had made and related how they would have fought differently to insure they won.

Bent and St. Vrain secured a corner table. Nate let McNair buy him a whiskey, although he would rather have gone with Winona, Blue Water Woman, and Zach to their guest rooms. He took a tentative sip, and winced as the burning liquid scorched a path down his throat.

"Strong stuff," Shakespeare said, grinning. "Bent here doesn't believe in watering his drinks down like some shady tavern owners I've known do." He winked at Nate. "Of course, I can't say if he does the same for the Indians."

"I'd never cheat a customer," the trader said indignantly. "Everyone knows that, which is why even the Kiowas trade with me. They know they'll get a fair deal." He tipped his drink. "Honesty is always the best policy."

"An admirable trait, to be sure," Francisco commented, and gazed at Nate and McNair. "So perhaps it is only fitting that I be honest with the two of you."

"How so?" Shakespeare asked.

"If I may be so bold, *señor*, I would like to ask why you are going to Santa Fe?"

"Because it's a hell of a lot closer than Paris," Shakespeare joked. "Actually, because we're in need of a frolic and Santa Fe is as friendly a city as you'll find anywhere."

"Not anymore," Francisco said soberly.

"I'm afraid he's right," Becknell chimed in. "Santa Fe isn't like it was back when you were there last. The attitude of the authorities has changed, and so has that of many of the people."

"Some of the people," Francisco amended.

"Care to enlighten us?" Shakespeare said.

William Becknell sighed. "It all started several years ago. I began to notice that a few of the people I deal with weren't as hospitable as they used to be. One or two avoided me. Then pretty soon it spread. I was puzzled at first, until I realized that they had been seeing us at our worst for years and that sooner or later this was bound to happen."

McNair nodded thoughtfully. "I understand."

"Well I don't," Nate said, wondering about the implications for their visit and the treatment his family would receive.

"It's like this," Becknell elaborated. "Since I first opened up the Santa Fe Trail, caravan after caravan has paid Santa Fe a visit with just one purpose in the minds of the traders who go there. Namely, to get rich quick, to reap enormous profits they couldn't possibly earn anywhere else." He paused. "It's greed, pure and simple, and greed never fails to bring out all that's ugly in us."

"When the traders and wagoners get there," Shakespeare said, taking up the explanation when Becknell stopped, "they tend to cut loose a mite more than they should. They drink, they gamble, they spend their nights with the painted ladies. In short, they just raise sheer hell."

"Who can blame them?" This from Bent. "After traveling over eight hundred miles through hostile Indian country, and having to contend with a burning desert part of the way, no wonder they're ready for some fun and relaxation."

"But now some of the citizens of Santa Fe have grown tired of the rowdy behavior," Becknell continued. "They regard us Americans as more of a nuisance than a blessing."

"Then why don't they just come out and say that they don't want any more caravans to pay them a visit?" Nate asked.

"It's not as simple as that," Becknell answered. "They need the goods we bring. They can't get them anywhere else. So they tolerate our coming, but the authorities have put a stop to the wild celebrating. And a lot of the common people avoid us when we show up. They won't have anything to do with us."

Francisco Gaona, who had been attentively listening in uncomfortable silence, now spoke. "Not all the common people, *señor*. Many of us realize we owe a great debt to you Americans. Before your caravans started coming, we had to travel many hundreds of miles to the south through the heart of Apache country to buy those things you now bring to us, and often we had to pay more than we pay you." He folded his hands on the table. "No, you have done us a great service. I think part of the problem is that my own government has become too greedy and they resent that the traders are unwilling to pay more."

"What do you mean?" Nate inquired.

It was Becknell who answered. "The authorities in New Mexico have the power to charge us whatever customs duties they want to impose, most of which goes into their own pockets. To keep the duties reasonably low, we have to pay bribes. Lots of bribes. Everyone from the governor all the way down to the customhouse clerks wants their share." He scowled. "Most of us resent having to give up a portion of our hard-earned profits for the benefit of crooked petty officials and his obesity, the governor."

"How does all of this apply to us?" Nate asked. "We're not going to Santa Fe to trade."

"The bad feelings are so general that some of the mountain men who have gone to Santa Fe for a good time have found themselves tossed into jail if they step the least bit out of line. A few have been set upon by local rowdies," Becknell replied.

"Please don't think badly of my people," Francisco said quickly. "We are not all like that."

Nate, disturbed by the news, took a swallow. Dare he take his family into the middle of such a powder keg? What was to stop the New Mexican authorities from throwing him in jail if he inadvertently did something wrong?

Shakespeare didn't share his misgivings. "Thanks for the warnings," the mountain man told Becknell and Francisco, "but this doesn't change our minds none. If we're on our best behavior we won't be bothered. And I really would like to see Santa Fe again. I have a few friends living there who I haven't seen in a coon's age."

"And you, *señor*?" Francisco asked Nate.

"I'll talk it over with my wife, but I'd imagine she'll want to keep on going if Blue Water Woman and this old buzzard aren't turning back."

"Excellent. Then perhaps you will do me the honor of staying at my *hacienda* during your visit? It is only fifteen miles outside of the city."

"We wouldn't want to impose," Nate said.

"Nonsense. Having you and your family as guests would be a treat for my own family. It would not be an imposition at all." Francisco looked at McNair. "My invitation holds true for you also, *señor*."

"Then I reckon we'll take you up on it. Maybe you can help me track down some of my old friends. One of them is named . . ." Shakespeare suddenly stopped to stare intently at the entrance.

A general hush fell over the room, silencing every man there. Nate looked around, and was shocked to see Pierre Chevalier framed in the doorway. The voyageur wasn't wearing a shirt. Both his hands and his abdomen had been heavily bandaged. His black and blue face was badly swollen. His lips were puffy. He spied Nate and advanced, saying nothing to those who voiced a word of greeting.

"Not again," Shakespeare muttered.

Chevalier halted a yard from Nate and gave a curt nod. "I'll keep this short, American. I know enough to admit when I've made a mistake, and I'm man enough to own up to it. I challenged you and you beat me, fair and square. So as far as I'm concerned, the matter is settled."

Nate was too flabbergasted to say a word.

"How about you?" Chevalier asked. "If you insist on satisfying your honor, I'll meet you wherever and whenever you want once my hands have healed."

"My honor is satisfied," Nate said, finding his voice.

"Good. Then there will be no hard feelings between us." Chevalier nodded, smiled, and departed.

"Well, I'll be damned!" Shakespeare exclaimed after the voyageur was gone and murmuring broke out all around them. "He's more of a man than I figured."

"Can you trust him?" Francisco asked.

"I hope so," Nate said.

"Whether you can or whether you can't, by this time tomorrow it won't matter," Becknell mentioned. "We'll be well on our way to Santa Fe by then."

"I'll drink to that," Nate said, and did so.

To their right rose green foothills that served as mere footstools for the towering Rockies beyond. To their left stretched the well-nigh limitless prairie, a sea of grass teeming with buffalo, antelope, and deer.

Nate admired the scenery on both sides as he rode

southward at the head of the four long lines of wagons. In front of him were William Becknell and Francisco Gaona. His family was on one side, Shakespeare and Blue Water Woman on the other. Across his thighs rested his Hawken.

Long ago they had lost sight of Bent's Fort. Bent and St. Vrain had come out to wish them well and make them promise to stop by on their return trip; then the pair had stood and waved every so often as the lumbering wagons rolled off. Eventually the fort had become a black dot in the distance, and ultimately had vanished in the haze.

The burning sun made men and animals alike lethargic. The wagoners had to crack their whips repeatedly to keep their mules and oxen going. At the rear of the columns rose a cloud of choking dust, which explained why Nate had graciously accepted Becknell's invitation to ride up front with him.

"Say Pa," Zach said. "I've been meaning to ask you why they have the wagons strung out in four rows instead of one?"

Becknell overheard and turned in the saddle. "It's a precaution, son, in case we have to move fast should hostiles attack. At the first sign of them, I give the order and the muleteers form the wagons into a big square."

"Gosh. Do you think we'll be attacked?" Zach asked.

"I doubt it," Becknell said. "Even the Comanches will think twice about raiding a wagon train this size."

"What about the Apaches?"

"They're a different story entirely. I've had those devils slip right into our camp and slit the throat of some poor unfortunate while he slept."

"You have?" Zach said, aghast.

The trader promptly realized his mistake and hastened to add, "But that hasn't happened in three or four years, as I recollect. Most Apache activity is now concentrated south and southwest of Santa Fe, not in the mountains to the north.''

"Do you post guards at night?"

"Lots of guards.''

"If you need help, let us know. Samson and I want to do our share of the work.''

"I'll keep you in mind,'' Becknell promised.

The Father of the Santa Fe Trail, from long experience, knew exactly where the best spots to make night camp were situated, spots where there was plenty of water for everyone and sufficient forage for the stock. This first night they halted at the base of a high foothill. After the square was formed, the mules, oxen, and horses were let loose to graze and cook fires were started.

Winona and Blue Water Woman were the only women in the entire company, and the muleteers went out of their way to treat them both with the utmost courtesy. Where normally the wagoners used five swear words in a six-word sentence, they now conducted themselves like perfect gentlemen in the presence of the ladies. As the pair strolled around the encampment they were treated to polite bows or the touching of hats in the most exaggerated civil manner.

Nate came on Shakespeare squatting by a fire and heard his friend's throaty chuckles. "What has you amused?'' he wanted to know.

"I'm thinking of how happy these muleteers will be to reach Santa Fe. I expect that city is going to be in for a fit of cussing like none other in human history.''

"Why do you say that?''

"Because these muleteers can no more curb their tongues for long than a grizzly can curb its appetite. They'll have a lot of catching up to do when they get there.''

Twilight enveloped the land when the evening meal

was completed. Becknell, Francisco Gaona, and several wagoners came over to socialize. They were all listening, enthralled, to Shakespeare tell about the time he was captured by the Blackfeet, when a skinny muleteer bearing a rifle approached.

Becknell saw the man and stood. "What are you doing here, Mullins?" he demanded. "You're supposed to be on guard duty."

"That I am, sir. But I figured this was more important."

"What is?"

"The fact we have company calling, sir."

"Company?" Becknell said. "Damn it all, man. For once can't you get right to the point? Who would come visiting us out in the middle of nowhere?"

"Why," Mullins said, "who else, sir, but a pack of murdering Comanches?"

Chapter Seven

There were only four of them, four young warriors whose proud and fearless bearing was in stark contrast to the nervous fidgeting of the two dozen muleteers and traders who held rifles fixed on the quartet. Their bronzed faces were painted for war, and they were variously armed with lances, bows, knives, and one inferior old flintlock of the type often traded to the northern tribes by the Hudson's Bay Company.

Nate stayed close to Becknell as the wagon master pushed through the line of whites. He saw the tallest of the Comanches scrutinize him, then gaze past him to stare at Shakespeare.

Without preliminaries the tall warrior's hands moved in sign language. "This is Comanche territory. You are not wanted here."

Becknell went to lift his hands, then hesitated. "Where's Shultz?" he asked a nearby muleteer. "He speaks sign better than I do."

"Allow me," Nate volunteered, stepping forward. He translated the Comanche's words.

"What's this devil up to?" Becknell mused aloud. "He knows that we know this is Comanche land and that we're going through whether they like the notion or not."

"Let's find out," Nate said, facing the tall warrior. "What is it our Comanche brothers wish? Why do they honor us with this visit?" he signed.

Surprise flickered across the warrior's features. "No white man has ever called a Comanche his brother before," he responded, his hands flowing gracefully as he formed the signs. "Who are you?"

"I am called Grizzly Killer."

"How is it that you have an Indian name?"

"My people are the Shoshones."

The Comanche's dark, fathomless eyes raked Nate from head to toe. "You do not look like any Shoshone I have ever seen."

Smiling, Nate answered, "They are my adopted people. My wife is Shoshone. My son is being raised to honor the Shoshone ways."

"You are one of those who lives in the high mountains and catches beaver for their hides?"

"Yes."

"I have heard of such men."

A strained silence ensued as the tall warrior surveyed the wagons and the stock within the square. At length he signed, "I fought Shoshones once. They fought bravely, as men should fight. They have my respect and you have my respect." He made a gesture of contempt at the line of traders and muleteers. "These others are less than dogs, but they may go their way in peace." He uttered a piercing yip, and all four of them wheeled their war ponies and dashed off across the prairie into the gathering darkness.

"What was that all about?" Becknell asked, perplexed.

Shakespeare stepped closer. "It's my guess they're
part of a large band and they were fixing to raid us later
tonight. Those four came in to look us over, to count our
guns and horses and see where we might be vulnerable.
But now they've changed their minds. If not for Nate,
some of us would be pushing up buffalo grass come
morning."

"What did he do? I didn't catch all of that between
them?"

Nate walked away as McNair explained. He found
Winona, Zach, and Blue Water Woman waiting anxiously to hear what had happened, so he simply informed
them that the Comanches weren't going to cause any
trouble.

"That's good to hear, Pa," his son said. "But it's the
Apaches I'm worried about. I hope they don't give us
any trouble either."

"You're getting yourself worked up for no reason,"
Nate assured him. "I'd never let the Apaches get you.
You know that. You're as safe as if you were back home
in our cabin."

Winona gave him a long, hard look, but she said nothing.

The next couple of weeks tended to bear Nate out. Their
days passed uneventfully, and their nights were undisturbed. Because Becknell was taking the Mountain Route
and not the Cimarron Cutoff there was ample water all
along the way. Twice they did see Indian smoke signals
in the distance, but the Indians left them alone.

When, at last, the wagon train negotiated the Sangre
de Cristo Mountains and crested a last low rise, before the
overjoyed wagoners unfolded the sprawling whitewashed

city they had traveled so far to reach. At the sight of their destination the traders and muleteers whooped in delight, fired their guns, and waved their hats.

Nate was equally thrilled on seeing the many flat-topped roofs crowning the neatly arranged adobe-brick buildings. He squinted in the bright sunlight at patches of green on many of the roofs and said aloud, "I'll be darned if that doesn't look like grass."

"It is, *señor*."

Turning, Nate found Francisco Gaona riding beside him. "I've never heard of grass roofs before."

"The roofs themselves are made of heavy timbers," Francisco revealed. "On top is piled a thick layer of earth, then grass seed is spread around and let to grow."

"Amazing."

"There is a method to our apparent madness, *señor*. You will find that it gets very hot here, hotter by far than anywhere you have ever been, and the earth helps keep the rooms cool during the heat of the day. For this same reason the walls of our buildings are much thicker than those in your country."

The rutted track they had been following merged into a road bearing westward into Santa Fe. At the side of the road, watching the wagons go by, stood an old man dressed in a plain white cotton shirts and pants. A straw sombrero protected his head from the sun. He was holding a rope lead in his left hand, and strung out behind him were six burros laden with large bundles of chopped mountain scrub pine.

"Firewood?" Nate asked.

"*Sí*," Francisco answered. "Yes, it is firewood. *Piñon*, we call it. At this time of year the days are hot but the nights are cold. That old man will sell all he has gathered in the city."

Further on they encountered two riders heading into the mountains. Both were well dressed in expensive clothes and sombreros. In addition, gaily colored blankets with slits in the center for their heads had been draped over their shoulders.

At a question from Nate, Francisco said, "Those are called *ponchos,* my friend. And those men are *caballeros.* 'Gentlemen,' I believe you would say in English."

The *caballeros* called out greetings to Gaona as they went by, and he returned the favor.

Soon they were close enough to see people moving about along the streets. Nate marveled that there were so many, until he remembered the city boasted a population of three thousand. When all the surrounding ranches and other estates were taken into account, there were close to four thousand local inhabitants.

Zach rode up on Nate's right side. "Isn't this wonderful, Pa?"

"It's an education," Nate said.

The road entered Santa Fe from the east. Many of the pedestrians stopped to stare, while the rest just went about their business. Nate and his companions started to cross a wide street, and as Nate glanced to his right he spied a huge church silhouetted against the background of the snowcapped Sangre de Cristo range.

"That is our cathedral," Francisco said, sitting straighter in the saddle. "If you like, we will go there during your stay."

The innocent proposal gave Nate pause. For some reason it made him feel oddly uncomfortable. Maybe, he told himself, it was because he hadn't attended church in years, not since that day long ago when he left New York City for the unknown lands beyond the frontier. Zach, he realized with a start, had never set foot in a house of worship. Doing so might do the boy some good. "We'd be pleased to go," he said.

Suddenly an immense plaza opened up ahead, and Becknell led the wagons toward the customhouse situated at the north side of the public square. Along the south side was a row of shops. On the east side farmers had spread out blankets on the ground and were busily peddling vegetables, melons, bread, and more. A long, low building on the west side of the plaza was distinguished by a tall flagpole in front, from which hung the Mexican flag.

"That is the governor's palace," Francisco mentioned when he saw where Nate was looking. Then he added rather ominously, "It is also the prison."

The square bustled with activity. Nate saw chicken vendors carrying their birds in large wooden cages. There were oxen pulling carts containing sacks of grain. Horsemen rode at their leisure. Dark-haired women sashayed about in the shade. At each corner of the square sat a large cannon. And, to his delight, Nate spotted a man-sized sundial positioned at the very middle of the plaza.

Winona and Blue Water Woman were gazing at everything in awe. This was something no other Shoshone or Flathead woman had ever experienced, and they would have much to tell their relatives and friends when they next visited their respective villages.

Zach stared at one new sight after another, giggling in childish glee.

"If you have no objections, *señor*," Francisco said, "I would like to go to my *hacienda* to see how my family is doing. Tomorrow or the next day, after we are well rested, we will come back to Santa Fe."

Since Nate had already arranged with William Becknell to meet the trader in one week in front of the customhouse to begin their trip back, he was free to do as he pleased. He put Gaona's proposal to his family and friends and they all agreed.

It was late afternoon when the sprawling estate with its tilled fields and large herds of cattle and horses being

tended by skilled *vaqueros* came into view. Francisco
had spent the ride telling them about early Spanish settlements in the region, and how the Mexicans had carried
on after winning their independence in 1821.

Nate was picking up more and more Spanish words as
they went along, but he couldn't begin to compete with
Winona, who only had to hear a word spoken once and
be told its meaning to always use it correctly from that
time on. Zach also learned readily. Shakespeare, it turned
out, was already fairly well versed in the language. Blue
Water Woman, much to Nate's satisfaction, had to work
as hard as he did.

Francisco was given a tremendous welcome. *Vaqueros,* servants, and family members streamed from all
directions. A beautiful woman in a fashionable blue dress
swept into his arms and tearfully kissed him. A young
girl of ten joined them, and for a minute no one else
disturbed these three as they tenderly embraced.

Then Francisco cleared his throat and introduced his
newfound friends to his family. "This is my beloved
wife Maria and my daughter Juanita."

The weary travelers were escorted inside while their
horses were tended to by servants. Nate gratefully accepted a glass of fruit juice. As he slowly sipped they
were given a grand tour, and he was greatly impressed
by the many immaculate rooms with their simple but
expensive furnishings.

After being afforded the means to wash off the dust of
the trail, they were seated at a long table and treated to
a sumptuous feast fit for a king. There was wine, beer,
tequila, juice, milk, and a cinnamon-flavored hot choco-
late. There was beef and wheat bread and pastries. And
there was traditional Mexican fare: *enchiladas, tostadas,
tacos, tamales, frijoles,* and more.

Nate's stomach was ready to burst when he pushed his
plate away and leaned back in his chair. "Francisco, if

I ate like this every day I'd be too heavy to climb on my horse.''

"We are strong believers in hospitality, my friend. While you are under my roof all that I have is yours."

Suddenly a servant appeared. Hurrying up to Francisco, he spoke urgently in Spanish.

"It seems my men have a problem, *señor*," Francisco addressed Nate. "Your gelding would not let them remove your saddle at first, and now he will not let them put him in our corral. Perhaps you would be so kind?"

"Gladly," Nate said, rising. He stayed on Gaona's heels as they went out the front entrance and around the side to where nine *vaqueros*, who had formed a large circle to prevent Pegasus from getting away, were laughing at the futile efforts of a tenth to get a rope around the gelding's neck. The *vaquero* was trying his best, swinging his *reata* with measured precision, but every trick he tried was foiled by the wily Palouse.

Pegasus would stand still and warily eye the roper until the instant the *reata* flashed out. Then the gelding would dash a few yards and watch as the *vaquero* coiled his rope for another try. Whether the *vaquero* hid the *reata* behind his legs or tried an overhand throw made no difference. Pegasus was always one step ahead of him, moving around the circle of *vaqueros*.

Francisco smiled. "Ignacio will be the brunt of many jokes in the weeks ahead. He is the best roper on the *hacienda* and until now there hasn't been a horse he couldn't catch. Perhaps you should spare him from further humiliation."

Nate stepped forward, between a pair of *vaqueros*, and straight over to Pegasus. The ranch hands all fell silent, observing with interest as the gelding snorted, then rubbed its head against him like an oversized puppy. He stroked Pegasus's neck and whispered in its ears.

Ignacio, a lean man with a wide black *sombrero*, a

brown jacket, and brown pants that flared out at the bottom, walked up and sadly shook his head. He glanced around as Francisco approached, and said something in Spanish.

"He would like to know where you obtained such a magnificent animal," Gaona translated. "None of my men have ever seen a horse such as this."

Nate briefly detailed how he received the gelding as a gift from the Nez Percé.

"It is unfortunate they saw fit to castrate him," Francisco lamented, "or I would be tempted to buy him from you so he can sire a line that would make my *rancho* the talk of New Mexico."

"I would never sell him," Nate said. "He means as much to me as my son's dog means to him."

"Then you are an *hombre* after my own heart," Francisco said. "I too love horses." He pointed at the corral. "Which is why I had this built a few years ago so we can keep watch over our best stock at night. The Apaches used to come in this close to Santa Fe quite regularly, but they no longer do. Still, I play it safe, as you say in your country. I have insisted that three or four *vaqueros* always go with my wife and daughter when they go for their daily ride."

Nate took Pegasus to the corral, then paused to admire the broad vista of beautiful countryside visible in all directions. The ranch was located in a lush valley watered by a swift running stream. From the abundance of green grass and trees the soil was ideal for tilling. To the southeast rose hills. Far to the south and west were more high mountains. "This land is almost as pretty as the northern Rockies," he commented.

"Almost?" Francisco said, and laughed. "There is no more lovely land anywhere as far as I am concerned. For four generations my family has lived here, has fought here, has died here. And through it all we have prospered.

When my time comes, I want to be buried on that hill to the west where my father and his father and his father before him are all buried, and on that day the son I hope to have before too long will take over this land and continue the good fight.'' His eyes sparkled as he spoke and his face shown with profound inner pride.

"I hope all that you wish comes true, friend," Nate said.

Just then the *vaquero* named Ignacio rejoined them and spoke to Gaona. Several minutes were spent in earnest conversation, and when Francisco turned to Nate there were worry lines around his eyes.

"This is not good."

"What?" Nate inquired.

"I have just been informed that during my absence the Apaches raided an estate twenty-five miles northwest of here and another fifteen miles to the southeast. Close to thirty people were killed, including women and children.''

"Do you expect trouble here?"

"Not really. My estate is one of the largest in the territory. I have forty-one *vaqueros* and they are all brave men. The Apaches know they would pay dearly for an attack." Francisco gazed at the distant mountains. "The estates that were raided are much smaller than mine. We have nothing to fear."

Nate couldn't help but notice that Gaona's tone belied his statement. He debated whether to stay at the *hacienda* or to return to the security of Santa Fe. There were plenty of hotels where they could stay. But he disliked doing so since it might hurt Francisco's feelings. As if Gaona could read minds, he unexpectedly spoke.

"I would not like for anything to happen while you and your family are my guests, *señor*. During your stay I will make certain all my men stay close at hand and I will have guards posted each night. You need not worry about your loved ones.''

''Thank you,'' Nate said, his mind made up. It was highly unlikely the Apaches would dare go up against such a large force of competent fighting men. He would stay.

''There is still some daylight left. Would you care to go for a short ride? I'll show you some of this land I hold so dear.''

''I'd be delighted,'' Nate said.

Vaqueros saddled fresh horses, and they were soon making a circuit of the thriving ranch, attended by six armed men. As they rode off Nate glanced back at the house, wondering what had happened to Shakespeare. The mountain man, he decided, must be entertaining the ladies with tall tales of his exploits, or else regaling Mrs. Gaona with quotes from old William S. He did see Zach and Juanita by a tree, talking and laughing and thoroughly enjoying one another.

The Gaona family had developed the land wisely over the years. They had dug irrigation ditches from the stream to water the tilled acreage, which was just enough to meet the food needs of the estate with a little extra produced to trade for needed goods. The rest of the land was maintained in its pristine state and afforded abundant grazing for a huge herd of cattle. There were also many fine horses and dozens of mules. Each year some of the best mules were culled and sold in Santa Fe for tidy sums since there was such a huge demand for the animals.

Wildlife was present in great numbers. Nate saw dozens of chipmunks and several colonies of prairie dogs. Rabbits often bounded off in alarm at their approach. He also saw coyote sign—and once, at the stream, the tracks of a bobcat, which he pointed out to Francisco.

''Are you a skilled tracker, *señor*?''

"Some might say so," Nate said, "but I don't hold a candle to McNair. That man can follow a fly across a desert."

"Really?" Francisco grinned. "I have a few good trackers in my employ, although I am afraid they have not yet learned how to track something through thin air."

"I'm sure Shakespeare would be willing to teach them," Nate quipped, and they both laughed.

A rosy twilight sheathed the verdant land when they made their way back to the corral and dismounted. Francisco gave orders to his *vaqueros*, then led the way inside, where they found the mistress of the house laughing over something Shakespeare had told them.

"What outrageous stories are you telling now?" Nate asked, seeking to bait his friend.

"I was just practicing my Spanish by informing Maria about the time you were being chased by a grizzly and you managed to ride smack into a tree limb and get knocked from the saddle."

"Oh."

"And how you thought you were going to die because you were sure your chest was caved in, but all you had was a tiny scratch," Shakespeare went on, eliciting smiles from the women.

"I wish you'd limit your yarns to ones about yourself."

"I would, but they're not half as comical."

"Where's Zach?" Nate asked to change the subject.

Winona rose. "He was playing out back with Juanita the last time I checked on him," she disclosed. "They have become very good friends in such a short time."

"Young'uns have that knack," Shakespeare said. "They're more open with each other than old coons like us. Since they don't put on airs, they have fewer walls to break down."

Taking Winona's hand, Nate walked down a long,

cool hallway to the sturdy back door. Outside was a carefully cultivated flower garden and several cotton-woods. Zach and Juanita were playing tag, chasing each other back and forth among the trees.

"Do you ever wish you were young again?" Nate asked softly, raising Winona's hand to his lips.

"Never," Winona said, leaning against him. "I have never been more content in my life than I am as your wife. You have brought me all the happiness I have ever wanted."

"Even though any of the bravest warriors in your tribe would have leaped at the chance to be your husband? Why, if you'd wanted, you could have married a chief. You'd now be living in the finest of lodges and own more horses than any other Shoshone woman."

Winona's teeth were white in the encroaching darkness. "Treasures of the heart, husband, matter more than treasures we can own."

"Is that a quote from William S.?"

She laughed lightly. "No. It is something I learned from my mother. She taught me that true love matters more than all the horses and lodges in the world. A woman who marries to gain such things goes through life as empty as one of those shells my people sometimes get in trade from the tribes who live close to the big water far to the west. She is lovely on the outside but inside there is nothing."

Looking both ways to be sure no one other than the children happened to be in sight, Nate drew Winona into the shadows, tenderly embraced her, and gave her a lingering, passionate kiss.

"What was that for?" she asked when he broke away.

"My love overflows my heart," Nate said, using the English equivalent of a Shoshone endearment. "You make me proud to be your husband, and I only pray I prove worthy of your trust."

"You already have."

Reluctantly, Nate stepped into the open and called out, "Zach, it's time to come in for the night."

His son stopped running and frowned. "Do we have to, Pa?"

"Yep. Let's go."

"But Juanita and I are having so much fun! She's been teaching me her language and we've been playing games."

"You can learn more and play more tomorrow."

"Awwww. I never get to do what I want."

Nate held the door for them, and gave Winona a peck on the cheek as she followed the youngsters inside. He was about to enter himself when from out of the night to the south came the faint cry of a bird, a warbling call he had never heard before. Pausing, he heard the cry answered from off to the southeast. New Mexico, he reasoned, must have night birds unknown in the northern Rockies. He made a mental note to ask Francisco about them sometime, then closed the door and caught up with his family.

Chapter Eight

Nate's eyes snapped wide open, and he lay in the inky darkness on his back listening to Winona's soft breathing at his side. What had awakened him? he asked himself. By his estimation it must be the middle of the night and everyone in the *hacienda* should be sound asleep. He listened intently but heard nothing. Slowly he started to drift off again, until a low growl sounded in the next room, the room containing Zach and Samson.

Easing quietly upward so as not to disturb Winona, Nate glanced at the closed door separating the two rooms. The mongrel never growled without a reason. Perhaps, he speculated, someone had risen to heed nature's call and Samson had heard them moving about.

The growl was repeated, louder this time.

Annoyed, Nate slipped off the soft bed and padded to the door. He opened it, and was able to distinguish Zach sound asleep on the bed and Samson standing over by the closed door to the corridor. Of half a mind to tie the

97

mongrel outside, Nate walked toward him, then halted in surprise on hearing the same birdcall he'd heard earlier. Only now the call was much louder, seemingly coming from right outside the house. And as before, the cry was answered by another, this time on the opposite side of the house.

A cold chill of premonition swept through Nate and he tensed, scarcely inhaling as he strained to hear more. What a dunderhead he was! Why hadn't he recognized the birdcalls for what they truly were before? Spinning, he hurried back and shook Winona to wake her, first placing his hand over her mouth to prevent an inadvertent outcry.

She woke up instantly, holding herself perfectly still.

"Apaches," Nate whispered. "Get your rifle and stay with Zach. I have to rouse the others."

Winona nodded and stood.

He already had on his leggings. Leaving his shirt and moccasins draped over a chair, he grabbed the Hawken, tucked both flintlocks under his belt, and tiptoed to the hall door. The latch gave without a sound. He peered into the murky corridor but saw no one. Unnerving total quiet reigned in the huge *hacienda*.

Moving in a crouch, he hugged the wall until he reached Shakespeare's room. Soundlessly he worked the latch and glided inside, stopping short on seeing McNair already up and holding a pistol. "I think we have some unwanted visitors," Nate said softly.

"I know. I was coming to fetch you."

"Watch over our wives and Zach. I'll warn Francisco."

"Be careful, son. Apaches are like ghosts when they're on the prowl."

Gaona's bedroom was at the west end of the hallway. Nate stayed low, his back to the wall, his thumb on the rifle's hammer, until he came to the door. Should he knock, he wondered, and risk being heard by the Apaches, or should he go right in? Recalling how handy Francisco was with those fancy polished pistols, Nate decided to lightly rap his knuckles on the smooth wood. He hoped Francisco would come to investigate and not give a shout demanding to know who was there.

There was no response.

Nate glanced at the spacious room fronting the corridor. He made out the outlines of several chairs and over in the corner stood a large bookcase, but nothing else. For a moment doubt assailed him. What if Shakespeare and he were wrong? What if there truly were night birds in the trees outside? He'd feel like an idiot if he was making all this fuss for no reason.

At that very moment one of the chairs abruptly moved.

Nate blinked, thinking his eyes were playing tricks on him, but the chair moved again, creeping a bit nearer to the hallway. His eyes threatened to bulge from their sockets as he probed the gloom to discern details. With a start he saw that the chair wasn't a chair after all but instead was a man hunched low to the floor. And not just any man. It was a stocky Indian naked except for a breechcloth. Even as the realization dawned on him, the figure surged erect and charged, venting a bloodcurdling shriek.

In pure reflex Nate leveled the Hawken, cocked the hammer, and fired from the hip, the gun recoiling in his hands. The onrushing warrior twisted as the ball ripped through him, but kept on coming, raising a knife on high. Nate hurled himself to the right, drawing a flintlock as he did, and got off his shot at the very instant the Apache loomed above him. This time the warrior staggered backwards, clutched at his belly, then collapsed.

The shriek had served as a signal for all hell to break

loose. War whoops echoed from all directions. Gunfire erupted outside. Men yelled and cursed in Spanish. Somewhere horses neighed in fright. From the rear of the house, where the servants were quartered, arose terrified screams.

Gaona's door was flung open and there stood Francisco, shirtless and barefoot, with a flintlock in each hand. He took a step, bumped into the slain Apache, then caught sight of Nate on the floor. "Are you all right, *señor*?"

"Yes," Nate answered, and started to rise.

"Good. I must direct my *vaqueros*. Stay here and don't let the savages get to our families."

Before Nate could say a word, Francisco dashed off. He saw Maria appear in the doorway holding a wrap tight around her body, her face unnaturally pale. "You're better off inside, ma'am," Nate advised, and then recalled she spoke little English. Motioning for her to go back into the room, he closed the door once she complied and turned, scanning the full length of the hall. How could he protect anyone when he only had one loaded gun left? He had to get his ammo pouch and powder horn.

The gunshots, shouts, and whoops outside had reached a crescendo; it sounded as if a war was being waged. But as yet no other Apaches had appeared at either end of the corridor.

Sticking the spent pistol under his belt, Nate drew the other one and ran toward his room. Shakespeare suddenly stepped out in front of him and they nearly collided. "Stand guard," Nate cried. "I'll be right back."

In four bounds he was at Zach's door. Winona, Zach, and Samson were clustered in a corner, Samson with his hair bristling and Winona with her rifle pressed to her shoulder, ready to fire. "Stay close to me," he ordered, not even slowing as he darted into the next bedroom and grabbed his powder horn and bullet pouch. He also scooped up his butcher knife and jammed it, sheath and all, under his belt. Then, running to the hall, he moved swiftly toward Maria Gaona's bedroom.

Blue Water Woman had joined Shakespeare and they were standing back to back, covering both ends of the corridor.

"We should get our families all together in one place," Nate said to McNair. "It'll be easier for them to defend themselves." He indicated Gaona's room. "We'll put them in there."

"Sounds good," Shakespeare replied.

From the rear of the house came a terrifying series of wails and shrieks mixed in with the rapid booming of guns, the din louder and nearer than anything Nate had heard thus far. He feared a large number of Apaches had gained entry and were wreaking havoc among the servants. Constantly glancing at the east end of the hall, he came to Gaona's room just as Maria, holding Juanita close, opened the door. She immediately addressed Shakespeare in Spanish and he answered.

"She wants to go to her husband," he translated, "but I told her we should wait right here."

Nate stood back so everyone could file in. He began reloading the Hawken, his gaze happening to fall on Samson. The mongrel was a yard off, staring intently down the corridor. Nate did the same, and felt his scalp prickle on beholding a bounding bunch of indistinct figures swarming toward them. "Here they come!" he shouted, his fingers flying, desperately striving to finish loading before the warriors reached them.

Shakespeare gave Zach a shove, propelling the boy into the bedroom. Then he faced their wives, both of whom were standing with their feet firmly planted and

their features as hard as iron. "Blue Water Woman,"
Shakespeare bellowed, "you and Winona get in there
and lock the door! We'll hold them off."

"No, husband," Blue Water Woman said. "Our place
is with you."

There was no time to argue. Shakespeare slammed the
door shut and turned to confront the onrushing Apaches.

As silent as a pack of marauding wolves, the warriors
swept down the hall two abreast, the leaders with uplifted
knives.

Nate rammed the patch and ball home, then yanked
out the ramrod and let go of it rather than try to reinsert
it. He whipped the Hawken up and cocked the hammer.
Suddenly Winona and Blue Water Woman fired, dropping the first pair of Apaches. Nate sighted on one of the
second pair and squeezed off his shot at the same instant
Shakespeare did. The second pair toppled.

Then the rest were on them.

In a flash Nate leaped in front of the women and drew
his loaded flintlock. A muscular warrior lunged at him.
He sent a ball tearing into the man's chest, then tossed
the useless flintlock down and reversed his grip on the
Hawken to use it as a club.

To his right Shakespeare was grappling with a robust
adversary while others tried to get past at the women.

Samson sprang at an attacker, his huge jaws closing
on the warrior's throat.

A knife nicked Nate's left arm, and he slammed the
rifle stock into the face of the warrior responsible. A
younger warrior darted in close and tried to rip open
Nate's abdomen. He just managed to deflect the blow,
then smashed the stock into the Apache's mouth. But
there was no respite. A pair of warriors sprang on him
at once. Nate went down under their combined weight,
jerking his head aside as a blade streaked past. A knee
gouged into his stomach. Something else rammed into

his groin. His vision blurred. All around was confusion as his wife and friends fought frantically for their lives. Someone—a small girl?—screamed in mortal terror. Samson was snarling fiercely.

"No!" Nate cried as a knife cut him in the side. He heaved, throwing one of the warriors off, but the other had snatched up his rifle and he saw the bloody stock sweeping down. Again he jerked his head to the right, but this time he failed to avoid the blow. Stars exploded before his eyes. A numbing jolt jarred his chin. He struggled to recover his senses, to stand, yet he did no more than touch an elbow to the floor when a great black wall crashed on top of him. The last thing he heard was a flurry of shots.

Someone was speaking in Spanish. The words were fuzzy, as if his ears were plugged with cotton. He heard the last one clearly, though. The word *"patron."*

A hand touched his shoulder. "Can you hear me, *señor*?"

Nate opened his eyes, and blinked in the sudden brightness of a nearby lantern. He was lying on the floor, but in the living room, not the hall, and next to him squatted Francisco Gaona, a very different Gaona from the self-possessed and confident host he had come to know and respect. Francisco's face was almost colorless, his eyes haunted by inner anguish.

"Thank God you have survived!"

"The others?" Nate asked, attempting to rise. Waves of pain pounded his head and he sagged, momentarily weak.

"Shakespeare is in a bedroom being tended to by one of my servants. He was stabbed in the shoulder and the neck. A *vaquero* is already on the way to Santa Fe for the doctor."

"Our wives? The children?"

"Gone."

Pain or no pain, Nate pushed to his feet. He swayed, and Francisco held his arm until he steadied himself. "The Apaches took them?"

"*Sí*. And two other women who have served my family faithfully for many years."

Nate closed his eyes to ward off the tidal wave of despair that threatened to engulf him. Winona and Zach in the hands of Apaches! He might never see them again!

"Are you sure you should stand?" Francisco asked.

"I'm fine," Nate lied, straightening and staring at his devastated friend. He touched his own forehead and felt a large bump. On his chin was a nasty welt. His left side, where the knife had cut him, had stopped bleeding. The cut itself was no more than an inch or two long and not worth being bothered about. "How long was I out?" he asked.

"Perhaps fifteen minutes, no more."

The room was filled with bustling *vaqueros,* most disheveled, many grimy and sweaty, at least half sporting minor wounds. Those with more serious injuries were being treated by their friends. Others were loading guns. Some were preparing packs for travel.

"Tell me everything," Nate said.

Francisco stepped wearily to a chair and sat down. The picture of dejection, he touched a bruise on his cheek while watching the swirl of activity. "From what I can gather, there were twenty to twenty-five savages in the band. A few went after the horses in the corral, but I suspect this was a trick on their part to keep my *vaqueros* busy while the rest broke into the *hacienda*. They were after captives, not horses."

"They like to take prisoners?" Nate asked, thinking that his loved ones would be gruesomely tortured and left to rot somewhere in the vast wilderness.

"Not prisoners as such, *señor*. They like to steal women to be their wives and children they raise as their own."

The mental image of Winona being molested by a leering Apache made Nate's blood boil.

"I was out near the corral, helping my men, when I heard a great commotion inside and guessed what the devils were up to. Right away I came back in, but I was too late. You and Shakespeare were both down. My bedroom had been broken into and Apaches were dragging off our wives and the children. We shot some of the *bastardos*. The others used our wives as shields until they got out the back door. Then they vanished as Apaches always do."

"Samson?" Nate asked, expecting to learn that the dog had sacrificed itself in their defense.

"Your great *perro*? I did not see him anywhere, my friend. Not even his body."

"Would the Apaches have taken him?"

"I don't see why. They would have no use for him except perhaps as food, and they can find plenty of that whenever they want. Apaches are masters at living off the land."

Nate glanced at a *vaquero* who was stuffing a pack with jerked beef and bread. "You're getting set to go after them?"

"At first light we will give chase. Tracking them is next to impossible but we must try. We must track them down before they reach the mountains or our loved ones will be lost forever."

"Count me in."

"I was hoping you would say that. It is most unfortunate that Shakespeare is not fit to travel. We could use another skilled tracker."

"How many men are you taking?"

"Twenty," Francisco answered. He stared at a groaning, bloody *vaquero* lying on the floor and scowled. "I can't afford to take any more. Six of my men were killed. Four have been so gravely wounded that they will probably not live through another day. In addition, three of the servants were slain."

"At least we made the Apaches pay dearly."

"Did we? All we found was one dead savage."

"With all the firing your men did? And I know that we accounted for five or six of them in the hallway, maybe more."

"That is good to hear. But there is no way of knowing for sure how many were killed because Apaches don't like to leave their dead behind," Francisco said. He slowly stood and licked his dry lips. "This is all my fault. I should have posted more guards. But I wasn't expecting much trouble after dark. Apaches rarely raid at night. They'll steal horses and property, but they don't like to fight once the sun goes down. It has something to do with a belief that the spirits of those killed after dark will wander the earth instead of going on to the spirit land. Or so I was told."

Nate was touched by Gaona's feeling of guilt for what had happened. "You should get some rest before we head out," he recommended.

"Could *you* sleep at a time like this?"

"No," Nate admitted.

Their discussion was interrupted by the skilled *vaquero* named Ignacio, who entered the room, saw Nate, and came over bearing the Hawken and the flintlock Nate had tossed to the floor during the heat of the battle. He said something in Spanish and held the guns out.

"Ignacio believes these are yours," Francisco related.

"Thank him for me," Nate said, taking the weapons. He still had his other flintlock and his butcher knife, each wedged tight under his belt, leading him to comment,

"I'm surprised the Apaches didn't take all the guns they could lay their hands on."

"They have little use for guns since powder and ammunition are so hard for them to obtain," Francisco said. "And too, they can shoot arrows far faster than we can shoot our rifles and pistols, in many instances with much greater accuracy."

Nate was thankful the Apaches had seen fit to use knives instead of bows in the house, no doubt so their hands would be free for in-close fighting or for taking captives. That made him think of his wife and son. "I'd like to see Shakespeare. Which room is he in?"

"Ignacio will show you," Francisco replied, and gave instructions to that effect in Spanish.

The bedroom was at the middle of the hall. An elderly woman admitted him, then politely stepped outside so he could be alone with the grizzled mountain man. McNair, flat on his back with his upper chest and neck heavily bandaged, looked up and mustered a lopsided grin.

"The next time I get a notion to go gallivanting around the country, shoot me."

Nate stared for a moment at the bright red stains on the bandages, then sat down on the edge of the bed. "Maybe you shouldn't do much talking. It looks like you've lost a lot of blood."

"I do feel a mite tuckered out," Shakespeare said. "Must be the worry. But it doesn't take much strength to flap my gums."

"We're going after them at dawn."

"Watch yourselves. They'll be expecting pursuit. You might wind up riding smack into an ambush."

"We'll do our best."

Shakespeare, wincing and grunting, shifted position. "Listen to me, son, and listen good. The lives of all those the Apaches took may wind up depending on you and you alone. Francisco is a good man, and his *vaqueros* are as brave as any I've ever met, but they're no match for Apaches out in the wild. They'll be out of their element.''

"Francisco says he has some good trackers."

"By his standards they are. But they can't hold a candle to you or me, and they're babes in the woods compared to the Apaches.''

"It doesn't matter how good the Apaches are. I'm not letting those bloodthirsty sons of bitches get away.''

"That's nice to hear, but don't be so hard on them. They're only doing what comes naturally.''

"Did I just hear right?'' Nate asked. "How can you defend them after what they've done?''

"You don't know the whole story,'' Shakespeare said with a sigh. He draped a forearm across his clammy brow and elaborated. "The Apaches weren't always so hostile. When the first Spaniards showed up in this region the Indians hereabouts were downright friendly. Then the Spaniards took to enslaving them, to forcing them to work in the mines and the fields, to treating them as no better than animals. Their women were abused, their children left to starve.'' He paused. "How would you react if that happened to your people?''

Nate said nothing.

"Ever since then the Apaches have hated all outsiders. They waged war on the Spaniards and they're waging war on the Mexicans because the Apaches see them as intruders who have mistreated their people and taken over their land. Branding them as bloodthirsty is a pure and simple case of judging another people's corn by your own bushel.''

"I had no idea."

"Now that I've said my piece, I have one thing left to add,'' Shakespeare declared, reaching out and grasping Nate's wrist. "Do whatever it takes to save our loved ones. Hound the war party to the ends of the earth if need be. Kill as many Apaches as stand in your way. But no matter what, *save them*.''

Nate simply nodded.

Weakened by his exertion, Shakespeare collapsed and closed his eyes. ''So tired,'' he said feebly. ''So tired.'' In moments he was sound asleep.

A long silence ensued as Nate sat and stared at his slumbering friend. At length he stood, gave McNair a pat on the leg, and hurried off to get dressed and load all his guns. Soon it would be morning, he reflected. Soon he must match wits with the fiercest warriors west of the Mississippi.

And all too soon he might well be dead.

Chapter Nine

They were a grim, determined group of men as they rode away from the *hacienda* before the sun even rose. A rapidly spreading golden tinge was brightening the eastern half of the sky and affording enough light for them to see the ground well enough to track the Apaches. From the southwest wafted a warm sluggish breeze promising a blisteringly hot day.

Nate rode at the front of the somber *vaqueros* between Francisco Gaona and Ignacio. Since they wanted to travel fast they were traveling light. Rather than slow all of them down by bringing along a string of pack animals, each *vaquero* had a small pack containing a meager food ration and extra ammunition tied securely behind his saddle.

A man named Pedro, the best tracker on the *rancho*, was a dozen yards in front of the main body, bending low to search for sign. The ground was relatively soft in the verdant valley so Pedro was having no trouble trailing the band, as yet. But once they reached the more arid hills and rocky mountains the chore would become extremely difficult if not almost impossible.

From what Nate could see as he scoured the soil ahead, the Apaches had made no effort to conceal the tracks left when they lit out with the captives and their spoils. While the *vaqueros* had prevented the war party from stealing any of the prize stock in the corral, the Apaches had taken some of the free-roaming horses and mules; a half dozen of the former and seven or eight of the latter. The hoof prints were as plain as the nose on his face.

He wondered about such apparent carelessness. From all he had heard about Apaches they *never* made mistakes. So why would they try to steal a small herd of stock when they knew the Mexicans would soon be in earnest pursuit, when they knew the tracks would lead the Mexicans right to them? There was only one answer as near as he could tell, which filled him with dread.

The tracks took them to the southwest, toward harsh, rugged country fit neither for man nor beast.

Within three hours they came to a narrow plain crisscrossed by shallow *arroyos* and deep ravines. Beyond lay a range of mountains, the peaks devoid of snow, thrusting stark and barren high into the dry air. Here Pedro slowed because reading the sign was much harder.

"It is too bad about the dust," Francisco abruptly commented. "They will see us coming from a long way off."

Preoccupied with his thoughts, Nate hadn't paid much attention to the body of *vaqueros* behind him. He now did, twisting to see the that a swirling cloud of dust was rising from under the hoofs of their many mounts. "You should string them out," he said.

"*Señor?*"

"Instead of riding all bunched up the way we are, you should have the *vaqueros* string out in a line with no more than two men riding side by side. We'll stir up less dust that way.''

Francisco seemed stunned by so obvious a suggestion. ''I should have thought of that myself, but I'm afraid that I am not thinking very clearly at the moment. I am too filled with worry. Do you realize that I know of only two times where women taken by the Apaches were ever recovered?''

''Then this will be the third,'' Nate said.

''I pray it is so, my friend,'' Francisco responded, and gave instructions in Spanish to Ignacio, who then slowed to mingle with the body of *vaqueros* and relay the orders. Presently they were strung out as Nate had advised, two abreast, and the telltale cloud of dust was drastically reduced.

The ground became harder, rockier. The hoofprints virtually disappeared. Several times Pedro held up a hand and called a halt; then he would dismount and get down on his knees to better check for sign.

While waiting, Nate would scour the ground himself, and he noticed that he was able to see nicks and scratches that Pedro apparently missed. At the third halt he turned to Francisco and commented, ''Maybe it would help matters if I gave Pedro a hand. Two sets of eyes are better than one.''

''Of course,'' Francisco said, and called out to Pedro.

Putting his heels to Pegasus, Nate joined the middle-aged tracker, who greeted him in Spanish, then gestured helplessly at the ground. This was the rockiest soil yet and there appeared to be no sign whatsoever. Nate stayed in the saddle and moved in a small circle, doubled over so he could search for smudges and other traces of the war party's passing. Seconds later he saw where a hoof had left the faintest of impressions, and he pointed it out to Pedro, who had to practically touch his nose to the rocky surface to see it.

Pedro glanced up, his expressive features betraying how impressed he was. Rising, he mounted and motioned for Nate to lead the way.

Now they moved much faster. Nate concentrated exclusively on the ground, tracking as would an Indian, noting spoor the average mountain man would miss. Which was understandable since he had been taught by Shakespeare McNair, whose tracking skills were legendary, and by some of the very best trackers in the entire Shoshone nation. Where other white men would see only a blank earthen slate, he saw a pattern of scratches and scrapes that plainly revealed the direction the Apaches had taken.

After a mile Pedro rode back and said something to Francisco that brought Gaona up to ride with them.

Nate hardly noticed, so intent was he on overtaking the band so he could free the captives. He did deduce that the trail was leading into a narrow notch between two of the mountains, and when he was a few hundred yards away he reined up.

"Is something wrong?" Francisco asked.

"I don't want to ride into an ambush," Nate said, pointing.

"It is an ideal spot," Francisco agreed. He waved an arm to bring the rest of his men forward. "But I see no way to go around. They have planned well."

"One of us should go on ahead and scout around."

"It would be suicide. They would kill him on sight."

"Maybe not. They wouldn't want to give us any advance warning. They might let a single rider go in and come back out without jumping him just so we'll think it's safe."

"You hope."

"There's only one way to find out for sure," Nate said, bringing Pegasus to a trot.

"Wait, *señor*!" Francisco cried.

But Nate merely gave a wave of his hand, hefted the Hawken, and rode straight for the mouth of the notch. The defile wasn't more than 20 yards wide. On the right was a gradual slope dotted with scrub trees. On the left was a steep stone face marred by countless cracks and fissures. The quiet was absolute; not so much as an insect buzzed.

Squaring his shoulders, Nate boldly advanced. The notch was in shadow, which was a welcome relief after he had been roasted by the blistering sun for so long, but it gave him an uneasy feeling. He swore he could feel hostile eyes on him every step of the way. Pegasus began acting skittish, confirming his hunch. Yet although he scoured the adjacent mountains intently, he saw nothing to show there were Apaches lurking in wait.

The notch curved at the middle, angling to the southwest. He stopped and looked back. Francisco and the *vaqueros* were still visible, but they wouldn't be once he rounded the curve. If he ran into trouble they wouldn't see it. He'd be on his own.

Gripping the reins tighter, he kept going. He tried to think like an Apache. If he was one of the band, where would he set up the ambush? Where else but right there? The *vaqueros* would be hemmed in by the slope and the cliff. And being halfway through the notch, they would have to run a gauntlet of arrows to get to safety at either end.

He scanned the cliff, then the slope. Even his keen eyes failed to detect tracks. Maybe he was wrong, he thought. Maybe the Apaches had gone on through and were miles off. Then he saw the dirt.

Five yards up on the slope to his left was a patch of bare earth bearing tiny lines that ran every which way. The lines were so faint that Pedro would never have spotted them. Clearly they were made by something rubbing back and forth across the patch. Lying a few feet from the spot was the answer: a handful of saxifrage that had been pulled out and used to erase the hoofprint or footprint that would have given the Apaches away.

Feigning a casual attitude, Nate stretched and gazed higher up on the slope. About 60 feet up was a sizeable group of large boulders, some as massive as a cabin, more than enough to conceal a dozen or so mules and horses. And captives.

He could have turned around. He could have left the defile without being harmed since he was right about the Apaches not wanting to alert the *vaqueros*. But he couldn't. Not when he knew with every atom of his being that his wife and son and Blue Water Woman and Maria and Juanita and the servants were right up there behind those boulders.

His next act took the Apaches completely by surprise. Call it stupidity. Call it brash recklessness. Call it a supreme act of human bravery. Whatever, Nate suddenly reined sharply to the left and raced right up the slope toward those boulders. He covered a dozen feet before the Apaches realized he knew they were there and guessed his intent.

A burly, swarthy figure popped up seemingly from out of the ground, directly in his path, and drew back a sinew bowstring.

Nate already had the Hawken to his shoulder. He fired before the warrior could, the ball catching the Apache in the chest, dropping him where he stood. Others materialized out of thin air like demonic wraiths from some nether realm. A shaft whizzed past his head. Another clipped his beaver hat.

He saw a powerful brave rise from behind a skimpy bush that wouldn't have hidden a rabbit. The man lifted a bow. Instantly Nate turned Pegasus ever so slightly, ramming into the Apache. The gelding's chest caught the warrior flush, sending him flying end over end.

Another arrow nicked his shoulder.

Then he was almost to the boulders, and he looked up to see a tall warrior about to leap from the top of one, a knife clutched in the man's bronzed right hand. His own right flashed to a flintlock, sweeping the pistol clear as the warrior sprang. In a blur he cocked the hammer and fired, and the Apache's nose splattered all over the man's face and the plummeting body missed the gelding by inches.

Below him the notch rocked to a flurry of gunshots. He didn't dare glance back to see what was going on because yet another Apache had stepped into view around a boulder. This one held a lance and he had it poised to throw. In a twinkling it was streaking at Nate. He ducked low and felt his hat swept from his head.

Then he was beside the warrior and leaning down to slam the flintlock into the man's face. The Apache's head snapped back, hitting the side of the boulder, and the man toppled.

"Pa! Pa! We're here!"

The cry electrified Nate. He raced around the boulder and saw them all: the horses, the mules, the servants, the Gaonas, Blue Water Woman, and those who meant more to him than life itself. The captives all had their wrists bound and were seated with their backs to the boulders, all except young Zach, who had leaped erect to shout and was now resisting the efforts of a sturdy warrior to shove him back down.

At the sound of Pegasus's hoofs the Apache let go of the boy and whirled, drawing a knife. Nate jumped down, jammed the spent pistol under his belt, and moved to draw his other flintlock. But he was too slow. The guard reached him in three prodigious bounds. Nate barely got the Hawken aloft in time to deflect the blade arcing downward. The force behind the blow knocked him backwards and he nearly lost his balance.

As stoically as if made of granite, the Apache closed, slashing wickedly, a swing that nearly ripped open Nate's stomach. He swung again, or began to, when suddenly he stumbled forward as if struck from behind.

Nate's heart leaped when he saw Zach behind the warrior, and he realized the boy had come to his rescue by kicking the Apache in the leg. The warrior coiled to lunge at Zach. Frantically Nate drew his pistol and without thinking shot the Apache in the back of the head.

All the captives were rising. Winona rushed toward him. From down on the slope came constant gunfire mixed with loud yells and fierce war whoops.

For the moment the area at the rear of the boulders was free of Apaches. Nate stepped to his son, his smile the only emotion he could show until they were safely in the clear. He jammed the second pistol under his belt, set down the rifle, and drew his butcher knife. In a thrice he had the boy cut loose, then he faced the others. "Hurry!" he said. "We'll take these horses and—"

"Pa!" Zach screamed, his wide-eyed gaze going over Nate's shoulder.

Nate tried to spin. He was halfway around when something smashed into the side of his head, knocking him sideways. The world swam, his knees buckled. He felt his brow hit the ground. Someone—Juanita?—screamed. He heard Zach yelling.

"No! No! Leave my ma be!"

Then he heard something else, a sound that froze his soul but galvanized him to grit his teeth and push up into a crouch. One of the stolen horses was in full flight up the slope, and mounted on it was a brawny Apache working the rope rein with one arm while holding Winona in the other.

Not again! Nate's mind shrieked. He shoved upright, aware of a sticky sensation where he had been struck, and stumbled toward Pegasus. As he lifted his foot to a stirrup his ears registered the drumming of heavy footfalls behind him. Pivoting, his vision still blurred, he extended the butcher knife.

"It's us, *señor*!"

Francisco and a dozen *vaqueros* poured around the boulder, immediately going to the assistance of the captives. Francisco himself dashed to his wife and daughter and tenderly embraced them.

Nate again began to mount, but a small hand touched his.

"Pa? You're hurt. Don't go yet."

"I've got to, son," Nate said, his head throbbing terribly.

"But you're bleeding bad. You should wait a bit."

"I have to save her," Nate said, finally getting his moccasin into the stirrup. He tried pulling himself into the saddle, but his traitorous head swam worse than before. Inadvertently, he groaned. Bitterly frustrated, he shook himself and tensed his legs. The next instant a strong arm looped around his waist and he was pulled away from the Palouse.

"No, my friend," Francisco said softly. "Your *hijo* is right. We must see how badly you are hurt before you go anywhere."

"They took her," Nate protested. He tried to pry Gaona's arm loose, but a firm hand gripped his wrist, stopping him. Ignacio was there, sadly shaking his head. Struggling to control his anger, knowing they were only trying to be helpful, Nate let them seat him on a flat rock. His vision abruptly cleared and he saw that the fleeing Apache and Winona had long since disappeared.

Only then did Nate learn another reason the Apaches had used the boulders for concealment. At the base of one was a small spring. A *vaquero* knelt there, soaking a strip of cotton he had torn from his own shirt. He gave it to Maria Gaona, who quickly wiped the blood off Nate's head.

"You have quite a gash, *señor*," Francisco said.

A sharp pang lanced Nate's skull and he winced. "It's nothing," he fibbed. "I'll be fit as a fiddle in no time."

"You took a great risk in what you did."

"It couldn't be helped," Nate replied. He felt Maria's slender fingers gently probing the wound. "But I sure am glad you showed up when you did."

"I was concerned for your safety. We came at a gallop the moment you vanished around the curve," Francisco stated. "By flushing the Apaches as you did, your shots forewarned us and gave us a fighting chance. Thankfully, we were able to drive them off." He shifted and stared to the southwest. "I am only sorry that our victory was not complete. If your wife was here all would be well."

"I'm not going back without her," Nate disclosed.

Francisco nodded. "I will send half of the men back to the *rancho* with the women and the children and the rest of us will go after her."

"No."

"No?"

"*I'll* save her. You'll need all of your men as escorts in case the Apaches regroup and try to stop you."

"Am I to understand you intend to go after your wife all by yourself?"

"Yes."

"I will not hear of it."

"What about your wife and daughter? Do you want to risk losing them again?" Nate asked, and saw anxiety flare in Francisco's eyes. "Of course you don't. So get them home as fast as you can and don't worry about me. I can go a lot faster and be a lot less conspicuous if I'm by myself. On Pegasus I have a good chance of overtaking the Apache who grabbed Winona well before nightfall."

Gaona frowned. "You are very persuasive. But I still do not like separating."

"If you won't do it for me, do it for Maria and Juanita," Nate said, and stood, unwilling to waste more precious time arguing. He gathered all his weapons and strode toward the Palouse, then halted. Zach and Blue Water Woman were next to the gelding, waiting. "I want you to go back with Francisco," he told his son. "Your ma and I will be along shortly."

"I'd rather go with you."

"Out of the question," Nate said, stepping over to grip the reins.

"I can help you."

"You'd only slow me down and give me twice as much to worry about," Nate declared, and promptly regretted doing so when Zach bowed his head, crestfallen. Squatting, Nate touched the boy's chin and tilted it upward until they were eye to eye. "I appreciate the offer. Any other time I might accept. But I need to ride like the wind if I'm to save your mother, and you know there's hardly a horse anywhere that can keep up with Pegasus." He paused. "Do you want to slow me down and give that Apache a chance to get away?"

"No," Zach answered contritely.

"Then do as I say. Go back. See if you can find out what happened to Samson."

"He's missing?"

"No one knows where he is. I half expected to find him trailing the band that took you, but I haven't seen hide nor hair of the ornery cuss," Nate said, trying his best to keep his tone lighthearted. "The last time I saw him was during the fight in the hallway."

"Me too."

"So we each have someone to find. I'll get your ma, you hunt down Samson."

Fired with a new purpose, Zach nodded vigorously. "You can count on me, Pa."

Nate leaned forward to give his son a hug and a kiss on the cheek. Rising, he saw that Blue Water Woman was staring expectantly at him. "Is anything wrong?" he inquired.

"Shakespeare?" she said, wringing her hands.

Insight brought a deep sense of guilt at his own neglect. He realized with a start that she had no idea what had happened to her husband and she must be tormented by apprehension. "He was stabbed twice. He's lost a lot of blood, but he's doing fine as near as I can tell. They've sent for a doctor from Santa Fe."

"I saw him go down," the Flathead said softly.

"What he needs most is you by his side," Nate said. He mounted, smiled at Zach, and nodded at Blue Water Woman. "You listen to her, you hear, son? Until we get back she'll look after you."

"I will, Pa."

Blue Water Woman gave Nate a meaningful look. "You need not worry. Your son will be our son until we see you again."

"Thank you. And be sure to tell that no-account husband of yours to quit loafing in bed. He does enough of that at home." Nate turned the Palouse, and was about to ride off when Francisco hurried up bearing one of the food packs.

"Take this, my friend. You might need it."

Inwardly chafing at every second of delay, Nate politely accepted the pack and secured it behind his saddle. Leaning down, he offered his right hand and said, "Just in case."

"May God go with you."

Finally Nate headed out, moving to where the fresh tracks of the Apache's mount led upward from the boulders. He followed them easily, and soon noticed that the left rear hoofprint bore evidence that the hoof itself was cracked, which was knowledge that might come in handy later should the Apache hook up with other mounted warriors. Since few horses went around with cracked hoofs, so distinctive an identifying mark would enable him to pick that horse out from any others.

He came to where the slope slanted westward. Drawing rein, he swiveled and looked down on the rescue party. Every single one of them was watching him, every man, woman, and child. Zach took a few steps and waved. His throat constricting, he waved back.

The breeze wafted the boy's yell toward the heavens. "Be careful, Pa! I love you!"

All Nate could do was wave again. He was afraid his voice would give him away if he shouted. For several seconds he lingered, burning the picture of his son into his memory. Then, facing front, he lashed the reins and galloped in lone pursuit of his wife and her wily, savage abductor, heading into the very heart of Apache country, into the very heart of a land no other white man had ever penetrated.

Chapter Ten

The mountain vastness of the Apaches was every bit as picturesque as the northern Rockies, but the harsh beauty was lost on Nate. He had eyes only for the tracks he followed. The trail took him ever deeper into the range, sometimes along animal trails where the going was easy, more often as not over rocky ground where reading the sign was supremely hard to do.

He didn't get the impression the warrior was in any great hurry. After the first mile the Apache had slowed his mount to a walk, evidently in the belief no one had given chase, and from there on the mount had been held to a leisurely pace.

Winona and the Apache were riding double, which upset Nate immensely. He didn't like to think of the Apache's hands on her body. But at least, he mused, she was safe as long as the Apache kept going. Not until they stopped would the warrior be able to have his way with her, if that was his intent.

The miles fell behind him. The sun climbed higher and higher. He was sweating more than he ever had before, and so was Pegasus. Late in the afternoon they were able to partially slake their thirst at another small spring nestled among rugged rock formations. The Apaches, it seemed, possessed an uncanny knack for finding water where none supposedly existed.

He saw wildlife here and there: several black-tailed deer, chipmunks, a coyote, and the ubiquitous rabbits. A hawk soared overhead for a while, perhaps studying him, and then flew on. At the lower elevations he saw some cactus and grama grass. Higher up grew scrub oak, piñon, and some ponderosa pine.

From the tracks he knew he was gaining on them, and he had every hope of spotting them when there was plenty of daylight left. He got his wish an hour before sunset, but under circumstances that compounded his fears for Winona's safety.

He was negotiating a switchback up a steep divide when he heard several whoops from the far side. Hurrying to the top, he hid behind a pine and surveyed the canyon below. To his consternation, the Apache he had been trailing had been joined by four tribesmen, and they were standing near the stolen horse talking excitedly. On the horse, her posture as defiantly erect as she could make it, sat Winona.

Nate's heart leaped out to her. He longed to spirit her away from there. But what could he do when the odds were so heavily against him? If he attacked when they were out in the open they'd see him coming from a long way off, and fill him with arrows before he got close enough to see the whites of their eyes.

His cause wasn't hopeless, though. The four newcomers were afoot, so if Winona's abductor wanted to stay with them he had to go at a much slower pace. Five minutes later the prediction was borne out when all five

Apaches hiked westward, the one who had snatched Winona leading the horse.

Nate never lost sight of them from then on. Using every available bit of cover, hanging far back to further reduce the risk, he dogged them until they made camp for the night in a gulch. He watched as they collected wood and made a fire. He observed two Apaches hasten off to the northeast, and was amazed when they returned within ten minutes bearing a slain deer.

Winona, much to his relief, was largely ignored. She sat by herself across the fire from the warriors. Every so often one or another of the men would try to engage her in conversation using sign language, but she always ignored them. Ignoring her captor proved impossible, however, when the buck was brought in. He marched up to her, hauled her to her feet, and through sign language directed her to cook their meal or he would cut off her ears.

From his hiding place in a dense thicket 30 yards from the camp Nate was able to make out what the warrior told her, and he tensed in nerve-tingling dread that she might refuse and be horribly mutilated. He held his breath until she moved her hands, signing she would comply. The Apaches settled down to talk and left her to carve up the buck.

Nate's stomach grumbled in protest when the heady scent of the roasting deer haunch was carried to his nostrils by the obliging breeze. He was famished, but he refused to eat until after he saved his wife.

Soon the Apaches were eating greedily, tearing into large pieces of meat with their fine white teeth, and occasionally wiping their greasy hands on their bronzed bodies.

All five were dressed similarly in that the lot of them wore breechcloths. Four of the five wore the distinctive style of high-topped moccasins unique to the Apaches, while the fifth went about barefoot. The long black hair of each man was parted in the middle and held in place by a headband. All five were armed with bows. One of them also had a lance.

And Nate finally had a good look at the weapon responsible for nearly splitting his head open earlier. Winona's captor had a stone-headed war club he carried wedged under a strip of leather wound around his muscular waist. Such clubs, Nate had heard, were often more deadly than tomahawks.

Once the Apaches finished their meal they sat around talking. The warrior who had grabbed Winona did most of it, leading Nate to surmise that he was telling about the raid on the Gaona *hacienda* and the subsequent battle in the defile.

Eventually, with the fire burning low, the Apaches retired by simply lying down where they were seated and going to sleep. Winona was bound hand and foot by her captor before he too turned in. Incredibly, they didn't bother to post a guard.

Nate couldn't believe his good fortune. They must be overconfident, he reasoned. Since no one had dared enter their country for so long, they considered attack unlikely. He bided his time, waiting until the fire was reduced to sputtering embers and all the Apaches were perfectly still before he inched out from his hiding place and crawled toward their camp.

He circled to the right, moving in a loop that would bring him around to the side of the fire where Winona lay. She was curled up with her back to the fire, her bound arms held close to her legs.

All the stories he had ever heard about Apaches went through his mind as he stealthily worked his way toward the woman he loved. It was claimed Apaches were men of iron resolve and constitution. They were able to cover 70 miles a day on foot without needing a single drop of water. When they wanted, they could vanish as if into thin air. They had the eyes of eagles and the ability to hear twigs snap a mile off.

Many of the tales were undoubtedly exaggerated. What bothered him was that at the core of every wildly embellished yarn was a kernel of truth. Apaches might not be the men of inhuman ability they were alleged to be, but there was no disputing they were among the finest warriors ever known. He must rely on all the skill he'd acquired if he hoped to effect the rescue.

He completed half of the circuit when the unexpected occurred. The stolen horse, which was tethered to the south of the fire, suddenly looked in his direction and nickered. Instantly flattening, he placed his face against his arm so the pale sheen of his white skin wouldn't stand out against the ebony backdrop of the night, and peeked over his wrist at the sleepers.

Only two of them were no longer sleeping. The Apache who had taken Winona and one other were both sitting up and gazing all around them. Both glanced at the horse, which had lowered its head and was nibbling at a patch of grass. They continued to probe the darkness for five minutes. Then, satisfied they were safe, they lay down again.

Nate stayed right where he was for almost half an hour. He wanted to be certain the pair were again sound asleep before going another foot. Now that those two had been unaccountably awakened, they would be more apt to jump up at the first unusual noise, no matter how slight. He must be especially careful from here on out.

He widened the circuit he was making to put more distance between the fire and himself. The horse appeared to be dozing, so he needn't fear in that regard. Winona still lay curled up in a ball. The fact that she hadn't even lifted her head when the horse whinnied indicated she might be asleep, although he would be surprised if she was. How could anyone sleep under such circumstances? he reflected. He knew he wouldn't be able to if the Apaches had caught him.

The time crawled by as if weighted with a ten-ton anchor. Nate's elbows and knees were sore when he stopped 15 feet from his wife and surveyed the sleeping figures yet again. The warriors seemed to be asleep. His nerves tingling, he edged nearer. Winona's long tresses were hanging over her face, obscuring her eyes. She wouldn't realize he was there until he touched her.

His eyes darted from Apache to Apache, constantly checking their postures for any hint that one was awake and aware of his presence. Ten feet separated him from the woman he loved. Then eight feet. Then five.

Suddenly an Apache grunted and rolled onto his back.

Freezing, Nate touched the rifle hammer and the trigger, prepared to try and slay them all rather than be thwarted when he was so close to freeing Winona. But the Apache was breathing regularly and deeply. Thus assured, he crawled another foot and reached out to touch Winona's shoulder, to shake her and to let her know he was there. As he did his roving gaze happened to fall on the horse, and he saw with a start that the animal was no longer dozing, that it was looking right at him again, and he intuitively knew the damn animal would neigh and give him away just as it had before.

The next moment it did.

This time three Apaches came instantly awake, two of them leaping to their feet and looking all about them.

Nate had nowhere to hide. He was caught out in the open, exposed and vulnerable. Only the fact that the fire had died out delayed his discovery for a second or two. In that span he saw Winona raise her head and their eyes briefly locked. Impulsively, he touched her shoulder. Then one of the Apaches bellowed and rushed at him with a drawn knife.

Twisting, Nate cocked the Hawken and fired when the warrior was almost upon him. The heavy gun boomed, the ball taking the Apache high in the chest and flipping him over. Even as the man went down, Nate was leaping up and backing away to give himself room to maneuver. In a flash he drew his right flintlock and leveled it, but there was no one to shoot.

The Apaches had disappeared into the night.

He paused, about to run to Winona and cut her loose when an arrow streaked out of the darkness and missed his head by an inch or less. He heard it buzz as it went by.

"Run, husband! Run!" Winona cried.

Under ordinary circumstances he would rather chop off an arm or a leg than desert his wife when she needed him the most, but now he had no choice, not with the Apaches liable to pick him off at any second. What good would he do her dead? Realizing he would be foolishly throwing his life away and consigning her to a fate worse than death if he stubbornly tried to fight it out, he reluctantly whirled and ran, shouting over his shoulder, "Don't fear! I'll be back!"

An inky form hurtled at him from the left.

Nate fired without aiming, the flintlock belching lead and smoke. The warrior twisted and fell, then quickly scrambled out of sight behind a nearby boulder. Behind him he heard one of the Apaches yelling, and off to the left was the patter of running feet. Looking, he saw no one.

Bending low, he skirted a tree and plunged into dry brush that crackled underfoot and caught at his buckskins. It was an obvious mistake. Stopping, he crouched and listened, hoping his pursuers hadn't located his position.

The hunter had become the hunted. He sank onto his hands and knees and worked his way forward until he was out of the brush. Turning to the left, he advanced until he came to a stunted pine. There, he halted to reload the Hawken and the pistol.

He was terribly upset. Everything that could go wrong had gone wrong. Now the Apaches knew he was on their trail, and should he be lucky enough to escape with his hide intact he would have to work twice as hard to free Winona since they would be on their guard at all times. All because of that lousy horse!

There was one small consolation. Quite by accident he was leading the Apaches away from Pegasus. Odds were they wouldn't find the Palouse, which was a blessing. If he was left afoot now, not only would any hope of rescuing Winona be gone, but his very survival would be at stake. A man needed a lot more water when on foot, which was more difficult to find since a man couldn't cover as much territory in search of it as a man on horseback. Nor could a stranded rider find game as readily. If the Apaches found Pegasus, Nate would be hard pressed to stick to their trail and still satisfy his hunger and his thirst.

The guns were loaded. With the Hawken in his left hand and the pistol in his right, he rose and warily hiked northward. The faintest noise was enough to make him as rigid as a tree until he felt safe enough to go on. Given all he knew about Apaches, he anticipated being transfixed or tackled at any moment.

Much to his amazement, he eventually worked his way around to where he had concealed Pegasus without incident. Mounting, he sat and pondered his next move. It would be wise, he reasoned, to seek high ground so he could spy on the camp come first light. Reining to the right, he had started to head for a rise when to the south-west he heard an almost inaudible sound that resembled for all the world the striking of a hoof against a rock.

Nate drew rein and gazed into the limitless gloom. A

troubling thought crept into his mind, a thought that blossomed into a certainty when the sound was repeated seconds later. Wheeling Pegasus, he galloped toward the Apache camp heedless of the noise he was making. If he was wrong he'd pay the price with his life. But if he was right—he had to know.

His hunch proved accurate. The Apaches were gone. Winona was gone. The warriors had taken their wounded or dead and lit out. Stunned, he stared at the remains of their fire and tried to make sense of their flight. Why would they run off when they outnumbered him? The most likely answer made him want to kick himself in the britches for not putting himself in their place and figuring out their next move in advance.

The Apaches had had no way of knowing how many enemies they faced. Since to their way of thinking no solitary white man would dare invade their mountain sanctuary, they must have figured there might be a large force closing in. Prudently, they had hastily departed with their captive.

Nate should have expected such behavior. Apaches, it was claimed, never attacked a larger opposing force unless they could do so from ambush with scant risk to themselves. They were raiders, first and foremost, men who preferred to strike fast and hard and then get out again before a counterattack could be launched. To the Apache way of thinking, a man who stole one horse without being caught or who killed an enemy without being wounded in return was a far better warrior than a man who stole 20 horses but who had to elude pursuers to do it or a man who killed five enemies but was wounded in the process.

Now he was stuck there until daylight. Tracking at night was next to impossible, and even if he could overtake them he didn't care to do so in the dark. Swinging down, he stripped off his saddle and saddle blanket and made himself comfortable. He was too overwrought to sleep but he had to try to sleep a little, if only so he'd be fully alert when he did catch up to them.

And catch up he would. To have been so close to Winona, to have touched her soft shoulder and gazed into her lovely, troubled eyes, had fanned the flames of love in his soul to a fever pitch. She was counting on him and he had let her down. But he wouldn't make the same mistake twice. The next time he would succeed!

His inner clock woke him when the eastern horizon was tinged with a pale pink glow. He sat straight up, surprised he had dozed off in the wee hours of the morning. The sleep had not done him much to relieve his fatigue, and his limbs felt sluggish as he stood and saddled the gelding. Swinging up, he rode in a southwesterly direction.

Now that the Apaches knew they were being followed they were doing their utmost to cover their sign. He went over a hundred yards before he found a partial hoofprint. Later on he found another. If not for the stolen horse, he mused, he wouldn't have a clue as to which way to go.

After the sun rose and he could see clearly he began to find small drops of blood here and there, which proved at least one of the Apaches was badly wounded. He suspected that he'd killed the warrior he'd shot with the Hawken, but he could be wrong.

His main worry was an ambush. One or two or all of the band might hole up somewhere until he came along and finish him off. Every tree, every boulder, every ravine might conceal a foe. His gut worked itself into a tight knot before he had gone a mile.

The morning dragged past. At noon it was blazing hot, and sweat caked his skin from head to toe. Shortly thereafter he came on the spring.

This was the largest so far, nestled in the shade of a bluff and ringed by grass. Although he burned with a keen desire to press on after Winona, common sense dictated he stop and rest, if not for himself then for the Palouse. Wearily dismounting, he again removed the saddle, then allowed the gelding to drink. Lying down, he touched his own lips to the cool water and drank greedily.

After their thirst was quenched he gave Pegasus a rubdown using handfuls of grass. Then he let the horse graze while he rested in the shade, occasionally dipping his hand into the pool to sprinkle water on his face and neck.

From the sign, he gathered that the Apaches had visited the spring at daybreak, but had stayed only a short while before hurrying on. The direction of their travel showed they were continuing deeper into the mountains.

He tried not to dwell on the unnerving fact that he was alone in the middle of a harsh land teeming with roving bands of savage Apaches. Should he be slain, no one would ever know exactly where or how he had met his Maker. Winona might hear of his death from a bragging warrior, but Shakespeare and Francisco would be left to wonder and reflect on the widely acknowledged futility of going against the dreaded Apaches on their own terms.

Presently he had Pegasus saddled and rode on. High peaks reared on all sides like the foreboding towers of a medieval fortress. The many boulders and rocky ground reflected the heat back at him, presenting the illusion he was riding through an enormous stone oven. Vegetation was sparse.

The tracks led him on a winding course through gorges and along dry washes, over ridges and around barren peaks. Several times he discovered clear hoofprints, and from the stride of the stolen horse, from the way it was dragging its hoofs now and then, he knew the animal was greatly fatigued. With ample cause, he decided. Its rest last night had been interrupted, and it had been unable to get a decent drink since the day before. Bearing Winona only added to its misery. How long, he wondered, could it hold out?

Nate thought of little Zach and how the boy would fare if a cruel fate made him an orphan. Shakespeare and Blue Water Woman would look after the child, Nate was sure. And under their guidance Zach would grow up to be someone his parents would be proud of. But Nate preferred to see Zach mature with his own eyes. There was no substitute for the first-hand joys of parenthood except the joys of marriage itself.

Mid-afternoon found him a thousand feet higher than he had been at the spring. The Apaches were steadily climbing. To where? Ahead lay massive ramparts shrouded in mystery.

He'd hoped to overtake the band before nightfall, which now appeared unlikely. Ceaselessly he scoured vantage points from which the Apaches might spy on him, but he saw nothing to show any were. Which proved nothing, since they were virtual ghosts when they wanted to be. They might know he was still after them; they might not. Regardless, he wasn't giving up.

By late afternoon a feeble but welcome cool breeze blew in from the northwest. He scaled a steep earthen slope and came out on top of a tableland covered with grass and dotted with trees, a virtual island in the midst of a sea of arid terrain, as unexpected as it was a joy to find. More so, for when he halted and scanned this oasis he spied a fair-sized lake off in the distance, its tranquil surface shimmering with the reflected radiance of the sun.

Were the Apaches here? he asked himself. The tableland was an ideal spot to stop for the night. For that matter, an Apache village might be situated close by. There was ample water for a large number of people, there was bound to be abundant game, and the isolated

location made random discovery by outsiders unlikely.
The place was perfect.

He must get under cover. Clucking the Palouse into
motion, he rode to a stand of aspens, then slid down. His
backside was sore, his spine stiff from all the time he'd
spent in the saddle. He stretched to remove the kinks,
tied the reins to a slender tree, and walked to the edge of
the stand for another look-see.

To the north lay undisturbed wilderness. To the west,
though, figures appeared, moving around the lakeshore.
There were at least a dozen and they were all on foot.

Suddenly he detected movement much, much closer.
He lowered his eyes to the southwest and inadvertently
gasped on seeing a stout Apache approaching at a dogtrot.
Instantly he ducked low, afraid he had been seen.

Behind the first warrior came others. Two, four, five,
seven all told, strung out in single file as was Indian
custom when a war party was on the prowl.

Nate huddled behind a screen of saplings and cocked
the Hawken. Although none of the Apaches had made a
sound, he was sure they'd spotted him. Why else were
they heading directly toward the stand?

Chapter Eleven

Nate hesitated, torn between an urge to fight and an impulse to flee. He might be able to shoot three of the warriors before the group reached him, but the rest would swiftly overwhelm him. It was smarter in his estimation to make a run for it simply because Winona's future depended on his staying alive.

He had started to back away from the saplings when a remarkable thing happened; the Apaches veered to his left to bypass the stand entirely. A smile spread over his face as it dawned on him that they had no idea he was there. He heard them talking among themselves as they went by on the far side of the stand.

What if Pegasus whinnied? The anxious thought brought him to his feet and he quickly made his way to the Palouse's side. He need not have worried. The tired horse was standing quietly, dozing. Breathing a bit easier, he moved next to the east edge of the aspens. From this vantage point he could see the Apaches clearly as they trotted to the rim of the tableland and there stopped.

As he studied their features he was stunned to recognize one of them as a warrior who had been a member of the small band he had tangled with. He knew it was the same man from the green headband the man wore, which was the only green one he had seen on an Apache thus far.

He abruptly realized what they were up to, and gave inward thanks he'd reached the hidden oasis when he had. His earlier assumption that there was a village nearby must be correct. The small band had hastened there after the fight, and now one of them was leading reinforcements back to find him and kill him or capture him for later torture.

The seven warriors were standing less than 20 yards from the spot where he had come over the rim. If, for whatever reason, they went north instead of going down the earthen slope, they were bound to see Pegasus's hoofprints and they'd know their quarry was much closer than they believed.

Nate watched expectantly until, at a gesture from the warrior with the green headband, the entire group vanished over the rim. He sat back, elated. Then a jarring insight sobered him. If those Apaches made straight for the site of the fight, they might not see the tracks he'd left as he'd made his way to the tableland. But if they used the very same route he'd used, they'd find the tracks in no time and immediately turn around to come after him.

What should he do? Standing, he hurried to Pegasus, untied the reins, and swung up. He couldn't afford to take chances. Time was now more crucial than ever before. Finding and freeing Winona must be done rapidly.

He swung to the south, and stuck close to the ragged rim on the assumption he ran less risk of encountering

Apaches there than in the midst of their verdant Garden of Eden. In this manner he covered over a mile.

Then he heard someone singing.

Nate instantly stopped and peered through the fir trees in the direction from which the merry sound came. Beyond the firs was a meadow. Crossing it were four young Apache women, all carrying baskets. They walked to the east, to a stand of bushes, where two of them knelt and commenced digging at the roots.

These were the first Apache women Nate had ever beheld, and he scrutinized them with interest. They were quite beautiful, what with their raven hair, smooth features, and decorated buckskin dresses. Being in their twenties, they had yet to acquire the many wrinkles that served as badges of distinction for older Indian women who lived hard but rewarding lives in devotion to their families.

They chatted gaily as they worked, feeling perfectly safe in their mountain retreat. All four were soon digging, and when their baskets were full of roots they rose and hiked to the northwest.

Nate waited until they were out of sight. Dismounting, he looped the reins around a low limb, gripped the Hawken in his left hand, and padded after the four women. He caught up with them in seconds, but kept far enough back that his chances of being spotted were remote. The women passed through a tract of trees, and emerged on the south shore of the sparkling lake.

Now Nate laid eyes on a sight no other white man had ever observed and lived to tell about. Spread out before him was a large Apache village, which in one respect was unlike any Indian village with which he was familiar. The lodges were totally different from those of the Shoshones. In fact, they were totally different from those of all the tribes living on the plains. Instead of dwellings made from buffalo hides, the Apaches lived in structures known as wickiups. Bowl-shaped, they were fashioned from slender poles and then covered with grass and brush.

There were 40 wickiups along the lakeshore. Among them played laughing, happy children. Women were engaged in a variety of tasks, everything from tanning hides to constructing baskets. The warriors sat around talking, sharpening knives, making bowstrings, or gambling.

Nate counted 27 men. The rest must be either out hunting or on raids. He scoured the village from one end to the other, but saw no sign of Winona. But he did spy the stolen horse, tethered beside a wickiup close to the lake. He settled down on his stomach and made himself comfortable.

Soon, with the golden sun perched above the western horizon, the women busied themselves preparing the evening meal. Cook fires were started. The children were called from their play, and the men went to their respective wickiups to await their food.

At last Nate saw Winona. The warrior who had abducted her emerged from the wickiup next to the stolen horse, turned, and motioned angrily. From inside came Winona, who was grabbed by the arm and rudely shoved to the ground. Through sign language the Apache ordered her to fix his meal. Then he stalked off to a nearby wickiup and began talking with another warrior.

As excited as Nate felt at seeing his beloved again, he was more worried about her welfare. That she had angered her captor was obvious. Why, he could guess. She would not submit meekly to being mistreated. Winona was a proud, strong-willed woman whose self-confidence was boundless. And knowing her as well as he did, he knew she would rather die than let herself be subjected to the ultimate indignity.

Her captor must be finding that out for himself. What would the man do next? Nate wondered. If the warrior was a fool he would try to force himself on her and risk having his eyes scratched out. Even if the man succeeded, he had to realize that at some point in the future, when least expected, he would wake up to find a knife buried in his throat.

Perhaps her captor was wiser than that. Perhaps he would take his time, try to seduce her gradually. If she eventually felt all hope of being rescued or escaping was lost, she might give in, if she didn't take her own life first.

A raging hatred burned in Nate's breast for the one who had taken her. He wanted to get his hands around the bastard's neck and squeeze, squeeze, squeeze until the Apache's tongue protruded and the man's face became as blue as that lake yonder.

Nate watched Winona cook the meal. Her captor returned, sat cross-legged, and ate without speaking. She took a small bowl and sat down several yards away, deliberately turning her back to him, which sparked an angry stare.

Keep it up! Nate wanted to shout, feeling a tight knot form in his throat. Swallowing hard, he scoured the entire village again, seeking evidence of dogs. The Shoshones and other tribes were partial to relying on dogs to guard their villages at night, so it was logical to expect the Apaches to do the same. Oddly enough, he didn't see a single one. Then he remembered being told by Shakespeare that the Apaches often *ate* dogs when other game was scarce, just like they ate horses and mules.

His stomach growled, reminding him of his own famished state. Steeling himself, he shut food from his mind and impatiently waited for the Apaches to retire. They seemed to take forever doing so. Once their meal was concluded, the women cleaned up while the men socialized. Parties of warriors gathered around various fires to discuss matters of importance.

As he lay there, an unusual and enlightening thought

occurred to Nate. For all their reputed ferociousness, the Apaches were much like every other Indian tribe. The men were born warriors, bred through countless generations to excel at warfare and raiding, and while they didn't count coup as did the tribes on the plains and those inhabiting the northern Rockies, they did take immense pride in their fighting ability. The women, like Indian women everywhere, lived what at first glance might appear to be lives of sheer drudgery, toiling from dawn to dusk at all the tasks necessary to feed and clothe their families, but they did so out of a sense of loving service, not because they were forced to. And the children were exactly the same as all carefree children everywhere, playing at the activities they saw the adults doing and hoping one day to be respected members of their people.

Viewing the Apaches as just another tribe gave him a whole new perspective. Yes, they were to be feared, but no more so than the Blackfeet or the Utes. Yes, the men were skilled warriors, but no more so in their way than the Shoshones or the Cheyennes or the Sioux were in theirs. The Apaches had adapted to the harsh land in which they lived just as the tribes living on the plains had adapted to the conditions there. Apaches were flesh and blood. They could be killed. They could be outfoxed. And he was going to prove it by freeing his wife from their clutches, by rescuing her from their very midst.

By the positions of the constellations the hour was nearly midnight when the last of the warriors turned in. The village lay serene under the myriad of shimmering stars. From the northwest came a strong wind, rustling the high grass and the leaves of the trees. Small waves rippled the surface of the lake.

Nate could wait no longer. Rising into a crouch, he stalked closer, his ears and eyes straining to their limits. From some of the dwellings came muffled snoring. Otherwise, all was as still as a cemetery. Near the first wickiups he paused and nervously licked his lips. Some of the entrances were covered with hide flaps or crude latticeworks, others weren't. Since he had no way of knowing if any of the Apaches were awake, he had to be careful not to walk past any doorways. A single warning shout would bring them all out like angry bees stirred from their hive.

He moved toward the wickiup by the lake, placing the soles of his moccasins down lightly with each step, wary of snapping a twig or causing a loose stone to roll. Close up, the wickiups were like great black turtles. Penetrating the darkness within each was impossible.

When he was halfway through the village he heard a grunt from a wickiup he was passing and halted, his scalp tingling until the grunt was replaced by low snoring. His palms slick, he crept past dwelling after dwelling until only one remained in front of him: the one where his wife was being held.

Suddenly he thought of the stolen horse. The animal was staring at him, but so far had made no sound. He tensed, dreading a whinny. A minute went by. Two. The horse lowered its head, disinterested. If he could, he would have given it a hug.

Nate leveled the Hawken and tiptoed toward the entrance. Suddenly something moved inside. In three quick bounds he was to the right of the opening, the Hawken upraised to bash out the brains of the warrior should the man step out. A heartbeat later someone did, only it wasn't the Apache.

It was Winona.

She backed out, her footfalls completely silent, and had begun to turn when she saw him. Her eyes widened and glistened as if from moisture. Her mouth forming a perfect oval, she threw herself into his arms and buried her face against his neck.

Nate smelled the scent of her hair and felt her warm

body pressed flush with his. He wanted to cry for joy, but he fought back the tears. Now was not the time, he told himself. Slowly he lowered the Hawken and gave Winona a fleeting embrace. Then he whispered in her ear, ''Did you kill him?''

She shook her head no.

Too bad, Nate reflected. Taking her hand, he stepped to the bay and carefully reached down to untie the rope. The animal looked at him but made no noise. Moving to the lake, he turned to the right, hoping the soft lapping of the waves would cover the dull plodding of the bay's hoofs. Proceeding cautiously, they covered 50 yards without mishap. Then a hundred.

Winona was giving his hand such a squeeze that it hurt. She unexpectedly leaned against him and give him a kiss on the cheek. ''I knew you would come, my husband,'' she whispered.

''I would never give up as long as I lived,'' Nate whispered back, and kissed her in return.

''I did not expect you so soon. I thought I would have to hide until the Apaches stopped looking for me, then try to find you.''

''I was lucky,'' Nate said.

''Naiche knew you would show up too, but not tonight. He thought it would take you two or three days if Naretena did not get you.'' She paused, then elaborated. ''Naretena and six others left this afternoon to hunt you down.''

''I saw them,'' Nate whispered. ''Who is Naiche?''

''The warrior who stole me. He was impressed by you, my husband, by the way you tracked us and fought them when you tried to save me. He said he had never known a white or Mexican who was a match for the Apaches, but you are.''

''*He* said that?''

''In his way he is an honorable man.''

Nate changed the subject. "Didn't he tie you tonight?"

"He did, but not as tightly as before." Winona grinned. "My teeth are as sharp as a beaver's."

By now they were well clear of the village and bearing to the south so Nate could reclaim Pegasus. He kept a vigilant watch on the wickiups, fearing the one called Naiche would awaken and discover Winona was missing. Truth to tell, he was surprised the warrior hadn't awakened when she snuck from the dwelling. Then he reminded himself that Naiche had just come back from a long, arduous raid during which the warrior must have gotten little rest. Secure in his own wickiup, Naiche must be sleeping as soundly as a hibernating bear.

"How are the others?" Winona asked.

"Francisco took Zach and Blue Water Woman back to the *hacienda*. Shakespeare was wounded but I expect him to pull through. He's as tough as a grizzly and three times as ornery."

"I feared you were dead until you showed up on the slope of that mountain, riding right into the trap the Apaches had set. Naiche said that what you did was one of the bravest acts he ever witnessed."

"It sounds like the two of you became fast friends," Nate commented testily, forgetting to whisper in his annoyance.

"I got to know him very well, my dearest," Winona said, relaxing her grip on his hand to rub her forefinger over his. "And I made it plain to him that you are the only man for me."

"Did he . . . ?" Nate began.

"He tried but his heart wasn't in it."

"No?"

"Apache men respect their women very much. They rarely hit them or mistreat them, even those they capture."

"They're regular saints," Nate muttered.

"Saints?" Winona repeated. "Oh. Now I remember the word." She laughed ever so lightly. "No, they are not saints. But they are men you would respect if you were not so jealous."

"Who's jealous?"

They fell silent, and presently reached the trees where Nate had left the Palouse. He stopped to survey the village one last time, then turned to go forward as a strident whoop rent the chill night air from somewhere near the lake. Seconds later there were more shouts and considerable commotion as roused Apaches spilled from their wickiups right and left.

"Hurry," Nate urged, giving the rope a sharp pull to hasten the stolen horse along. His own animal was right where he left it, and in moments both of them were mounted and moving slowly eastward so as not to make much noise.

"Naiche must have awakened and discovered I was gone," Winona commented quietly.

"Either that or one of them got up to heed nature's call and saw that the horse was missing, then woke Naiche," Nate said. From the uproar, the agitated Apaches were scouring the vicinity of their village for Winona. Soon, if they hadn't already, the warriors would fan out in all directions to try and find her.

"We should make a run for it," Winona recommended.

"I reckon," Nate said, although he had reservations. Once they broke into a gallop the enraged Apaches would hear them and give chase in force. With enough of a lead they could easily outdistance most of their pursuers, those on foot, but there had been several other horses in the village and they were cause for concern.

He poked his heels into the Palouse's flanks and angled

to the left, away from the rim, since a single misstep in the dark would plummet both horse and rider over the edge. Winona stayed at his side, her long hair flying.

Not 20 yards off there was a loud cry, echoed by another close behind him. More yells arose to the north.

Nate swallowed hard and leaned forward, making the outline of his body almost indistinguishable from that of Pegasus. Winona did likewise. It was an old Indian trick that rendered them less visible targets. At a gallop they crashed through brush and came out on an open stretch where he gave the gelding its head.

Suddenly a stocky figure materialized out of the shadowy murk, running to intercept them.

The Hawken was resting across Nate's thighs, the barrel pointing in the general direction of the Apache. It was a simple matter for Nate to swivel the rifle just so, cock the hammer, and fire without raising his body. The gun boomed, the warrior stumbled and fell. To their rear a chorus of shrill, bloodthirsty cries showed the Apaches were pursuing them in full force.

The thing Nate now dreaded most was that one of their animals would step into a rut or a hole or a wild creature's burrow and go down. The Apaches would be on them before they could mount double and continue their flight. Glancing over his shoulder, he saw a dozen or more ghostly shapes, all on foot but moving at an incredible speed. He'd heard tell that Apaches were some of the swiftest runners alive, and he was seeing that claim proved right before his eyes.

Still, the horses were faster and they began to pull ahead. He peered eastward, seeking some sign of the end of the tableland although he knew it was much too far off. A cluster of trees loomed in their path so he swung to the right, going around, then lashed Pegasus with the reins once they were in the open again. The bay, still fatigued from its long journey, began to flag, to drop back, forcing him to slow a bit to stay close to his wife.

With each passing moment the whoops of the warriors grew progressively fainter. He let himself relax a little, his confidence growing. Once they were in the maze of mountains bordering the Apache stronghold they would be safe. That is, if a roving war party didn't accidentally stumble on them.

At that instant a new sound was added to the frenzied racket to their rear, the sharp blast of a rifle.

Nate stiffened in dismay. He hadn't counted on the Apaches using guns, but he should have known better. Despite what he'd been told about the Apache preference for the bow and arrow, there were bound to have been warriors who, out of curiosity if for no other reason, had taken guns as part of their plunder from a raid and subsequently learned to use them.

"Husband," Winona suddenly said. "I think my horse has been hit."

He glanced at the bay, thinking she must be wrong because they were well out in front of the Apaches and the one who fired couldn't have seen them clearly. Odds were the warrior had tried to guess exactly where they were by the drumming of their mounts' hoofs, then fired blindly. Besides, he hadn't heard the bullet strike her horse. "Are you . . . ?" he began, and had to rein up sharply when the bay faltered and abruptly came to a stop.

Now that they were stopped, Nate could hear the stolen animal's heavy wheezing. Head sagging, it swayed. Quickly he moved Pegasus alongside it and held out his left arm. "Climb on," he directed.

Winona needed no encouragement, for now from behind them came the pounding rumble of pursuing horses, three or four at least. Her hand shot out and grasped his forearm.

With a surge of his powerful muscles, Nate pulled her up behind him. Her arms encircled his waist, her body molded flush with his. "Hang tight," he breathed, goading the Palouse into a gallop once more. Every second counted. The delay had proven costly, judging by the proximity of the horses after them.

War whoops confirmed the Apaches were close on their heels.

An arrow cleaved the air, missing Nate's head by a foot, but he paid it no mind. Fear for Winona eclipsed all else since she was more likely to be hit than he was. And he dared not ride a zigzag pattern to make aiming harder for the Apaches because doing so might enable the warriors to overtake Pegasus.

It was a furious race for life, with Nate keenly aware that both of their lives depended on the Palouse's performance. If the gelding faltered they were as good as dead. Or *he* was, anyway. Winona would wind up back in the clutches of Naiche.

He touched a flintlock, but decided against drawing it. Trying to shoot a gun accurately while astride the back of a moving horse was difficult under the best of circumstances. At night, at full speed, it would be a miracle if he scored a hit.

For the remainder of his life he would vividly remember those harrowing moments when fear dominated his being. Slowly, Pegasus increased the gap between them and the Apaches. The warrior armed with a rifle fired again, but this time he missed.

So intently was Nate concentrating on their pursuers that he was startled when suddenly a vast chasm seemed to materialize right in front of them. Too late he realized it wasn't a chasm at all. It was the earthen slope he had scaled to reach the tableland, but it might as well be a chasm because the very next second Pegasus plunged over the edge with a panicked whinny.

Chapter Twelve

They went down the steep slope on the fly, the gelding frantically digging its hind legs into the loose earth and then sinking down onto its rump as their momentum threatened to send them toppling end over end. A swirling gray cloud of dust enveloped them and spewed out to their rear.

Nate had to strain against the stirrups to keep from being unhorsed. One hand holding the reins and the Hawken, the other grasping Winona's arm, he barely stayed upright. The stinging dust got into his eyes and nose, and for harried seconds he couldn't see more than a yard ahead.

Somehow Pegasus saw they were near the bottom and gave a bound that brought them safely off the slope. In response to Nate's urging the Palouse raced off down a winding gorge, its hoofs ringing on the stony ground.

Were the Apaches still after them? Nate wondered. He looked back and spied a billowing dust cloud sweeping down the incline. The cloud parted enough to give him a glimpse of a single strapping warrior at its center. Apparently the rest had stopped at the rim, but for how long? He must lose this one Apache so they could make their escape.

Riding flat out over mountainous terrain in the dead of night is an unnerving experience at any time. Now, with the specter of a savage warrior close behind them and hot for his blood, Nate rode with his heart in his throat. The twists and turns of the high gorge slowed Pegasus down, allowing the Apache to keep them in sight most of the time.

What he wouldn't give for a level plain where the gelding could really move! But Nate knew that even Pegasus had limits. Eventually the Palouse would tire, giving the Apache the opportunity needed to overtake them. He must do something to stop the warrior and he must do it soon.

Around the next corner the gorge widened. Huge boulders dotted the ground. Nate cut Pegasus in behind one and reined up, then drew a flintlock. He didn't have long to wait. In the time it would have taken him to count to ten the Apache's mount clattered around the bend and swept abreast of the boulder. Nate promptly fired, rushing his shot. To his horror, he shot low.

The ball struck the Apache's horse, eliciting a terrified squeal, and the animal tumbled, its front legs buckling, sending the rider sailing. Arms out flung, the airborne Apache smashed with a sickening crunch into another boulder, then fell limp.

Nate couldn't wait to see if the warrior was truly dead. Others just might be coming. He rode on down through the gorge and out into the open. For the next hour he picked his way to the northwest. At last, positive they had eluded the Apaches, he wended into the middle of a tract of timber at the base of a flat-topped mountain.

There, as he suspected he might because of the trees, he found water in the form of an oval pool.

"You did it!" Winona said, touching her soft lips to the side of his neck.

"Pegasus pulled our fat out of the fire, not me," Nate wearily told her, and gave her a hand down. He swung his sore body to the ground, then stood aside as the Palouse stepped to the water to drink.

"Do you think they will find us?"

"Not if we're mighty careful," Nate responded. "At dawn we'll head for the *rancho*. If we keep alert we might make it back without any more trouble."

"You don't sound very confident."

"There must be thousands of Apaches in these mountains. Eluding them won't be easy."

"If anyone can do it, you can, my husband," Winona declared, stepping into his arms. They hugged and kissed. Then she rested her head on his shoulder and sighed contentedly. "No matter what happens, we are together again."

"As we'll always be."

He took her hand and walked over to the pool. Together they quenched their thirst. As much as he wanted to lie down and rest, first he stripped his saddle from the gelding, then reloaded the Hawken and the flintlock. "Sorry we can't have a fire," he remarked.

"I understand," Winona said.

They reclined on their backs on soft grass, linked their arms, and snuggled against each other. Nate thought of how close he had come to losing her, and uttered a silent prayer of thanksgiving for her deliverance. Somewhere in the wilderness an owl hooted. Elsewhere a coyote yipped and was answered by another. His eyelids became heavy and he had to shake himself to stay awake.

The gentle fluttering of warm breath against his ear caused him to look at Winona. He was amused to see she had fallen asleep so soon. Her ordeal had caught up with her, and after so many hours of uncertainty and peril she was resting peacefully at last. He lightly touched his lips to hers, then did the same to the tip of her smooth nose.

Feeling he must be the most fortunate soul on the face of the planet, he at length permitted sleep to claim him.

A low nicker from Pegasus brought Nate up in a flash. He stood still, listening, surprised to see the crown of the sun visible through the trees to the east. They had slept too long! They should have ridden out at first light!

Appalled at his oversight, he grabbed the Hawken and worked his way through the timber until he could view the land they had covered the night before. The three figures on horseback were over a mile off but there was no mistaking their identity. Apaches hounding their trail.

Back he ran to Winona. Shaking her gently, he said as soon as her eyes opened, "They're still after us. We have to push on."

Wordlessly she nodded, rose, and moved into the bushes.

Pegasus was saddled and Nate was mounted when Winona rejoined him. Sticking close to the base of the mountain, he rode until they were out of the high timber. A ridge afforded a convenient perch from which to check their back trail. There was no sign of the three warriors. By then, he reasoned, they were in the trees, close to the pool.

Since the Palouse was rested Nate had no qualms about pushing the horse for the next several miles. He wanted to get and keep a substantial lead, the more the better. In the meantime he had to do everything in his power to shake the doggedly tenacious trio.

For the life of him he couldn't figure out how the Apaches had tracked them so far. He's done his best to leave as few tracks as possible, but apparently all his efforts had been in vain. Or were the three warriors from another village? Maybe, he speculated, they had simply stumbled on the gelding's fresh tracks and decided to investigate.

Winona put her cheek on his back and kept it there for the longest while. She was strangely quiet, perhaps melancholy over being forced yet again to flee for their lives.

As the sun steadily climbed so did the temperature. It would be another unseasonably hot day, taxing the Palouse's strength even further. Nate wished he could stop every so often so the gelding wouldn't bake. Now and then he did pause for a couple of minutes, but it wasn't enough. Pegasus became caked thick with sweat.

When the blazing orb dominating the heavens was directly overhead, he halted in the shade of a cliff to give the Palouse an extended rest, whether it was wise or not. There was no water, no grass handy to rub the animal down. All he could do was loosen the saddle and stroke its neck.

"We must find more water soon," Winona remarked.

"First we have to shake these Apaches off our trail," Nate said. "Until then we can't take the time to hunt for water." He scanned the land they had just covered, but there was no trace of the warriors—yet.

"We could give them a taste of their own medicine and set up an ambush," Winona proposed.

"No."

"Give me a pistol, husband. Two of them will be dead before they know what is happening. The last will be easy to kill."

"No."

"Why not? The idea is a good one."

Nate looked at her. "It's too dangerous. We'd have to let them get too close. If they suspect what we're up to, if something gives us away, they'll take cover and we'll be in for the fight of our lives.''

''The real truth is that you are afraid harm will come to me.''

Her blunt assertion caught him flat-footed. Nate stroked Pegasus a few times before saying, ''Can you blame me? I nearly lost you once on this trip of ours, and I'm not about to risk losing you again.''

''We must make a stand eventually,'' Winona said.

''We'll see. If I become convinced we can't outrun them, then we'll pick our spot and fight. Until that time, we keep going.''

''As you wish, husband,'' Winona responded, although she did not sound pleased.

For half an hour Nate stayed there in the shade, giving Pegasus a chance to cool down and recover somewhat. Finally he climbed up and extended his arm to Winona. In minutes they were riding hard to the northeast.

On a rim of caprock that afforded a panoramic view for miles in all directions, Nate reined up. A frown creased his mouth when he spied the three Apaches nearing the spot where they had stopped to rest. ''Damn,'' he muttered.

''Do we ambush them now?''

''No,'' he said testily.

''As you wish.''

A bench took them to a lone peak. Once past the mountain they found themselves in a twisting series of canyons and draws. Far ahead appeared a divide at the center of which was a slender gap.

Nate was doing some serious pondering. Deep down he knew his wife was right; the only way they were going to shake the Apaches was by killing them. And if that gap should be what he thought it was—a pass to the other side of the divide—it might be just the place to hunker down and spring their trap.

He had to search some to find a relatively easy way to the top. In most spots the slopes were much too steep for the fatigued gelding. By using good judgment and climbing carefully he got them to the crown of the divide. Stopping, he twisted and saw the Apaches far below. The warriors had seen them and were coming on fast.

Nate entered the gap, which was no more than 40 feet wide and flanked by sheer stone walls impossible for a human being to scale. Three-quarters of the way through he found a crack large enough to accommodate a single person in the left-hand wall. Above the crack was a projecting ledge more than wide enough for someone to lie on. Here he halted.

"*Now* do we ambush them?" Winona asked.

"Yes."

"As you wish," she said impishly.

He rode on to the opposite end of the gap to confirm it was indeed a pass. From a spacious shelf he gazed down on a sprawling vista of spectacular mountainous landscape. Descending would pose no problem thanks to a game trail. "Here's where we leave Pegasus," he said.

Ground-hitching the gelding, they hurried back to the crack. Nate glanced up at the ledge, then stepped close to the wall, set the rifle down, and cupped his brawny hands. "Up you go."

Winona hesitated. "How will you get up there?"

"I won't. I'm hiding in the crack."

"Down here you will be at their mercy. Why expose yourself when there is enough room on the ledge for two people?"

"Now who's afraid?" Nate couldn't resist asking, and motioned with his hands. "Come on. You're wasting time. They'll be here soon."

Her displeasure transparent, Winona put her right foot in his upturned palms, tensed her legs, and surged upward when he gave her a boost. She easily caught the edge of the ledge and successfully pulled herself onto it. Turning, she lowered her hand.

"Take these," Nate said, holding up both the Hawken and one of the flintlocks.

Winona took only the rifle.

"This too," Nate prompted, wagging the pistol.

"You keep it. You will need it more than I will."

"I'll still have one flintlock, my knife, and my tomahawk. Take it. Please."

Winona made no answer. Instead, she positioned herself on the ledge so that she couldn't be observed from below.

"Contrary female," Nate muttered as he drew his other pistol. Easing into the crack as far as he could go, he held the guns at his sides and cocked both hammers. He was concealed well enough that a rider passing by would be unable to see him until the man was directly abreast of the crack.

Now came the hard part, waiting for the Apaches to appear and hoping against hope the warriors would think the two of them had gone all the way through the gap. The rocky ground helped since their footprints wouldn't show. Only Pegasus had left even partial tracks, which might deceive the Apaches.

Might, Nate reflected bitterly. He was realistic enough to fully appreciate that the Apaches hadn't garnered their justly deserved reputations as outstanding fighting men by foolishly riding into enemy traps. Another cause for worry was that some Apaches had undoubtedly developed the same uncanny sense of detecting impending danger he'd seen exhibited by several of his Shoshone friends and others. Men who lived in the world often acquired instincts the equal of the savage beasts with which they contended for mastery of the land, and snaring such men was often as hard to do as snaring a panther.

Beads of sweat formed on his brow and his palms felt clammy. No air got into the crack, so although the floor of the gap was in near constant shade it was still stifling in the confined space. Repeatedly he shifted the bulk of his weight from one foot to the other.

His thoughts strayed. Were Zach and Blue Water Woman back safe and sound at the *hacienda* by now, or had Francisco run into more Apaches along the way? What about Shakespeare? Did the doctor arrive in time to put the mountain man on the mend? And then there was Samson. The mangy mongrel had been part of the family for years. Zach would be devastated if it wasn't found.

Suddenly the awful quiet was broken by the sharp crack of a heavy hoof on a stone.

Nate broke out in gooseflesh. He lightly touched his fingers to the triggers of both pistols and girded himself for the fight. Speed would be the deciding factor. If things went as he planned, between Winona's rifle and his two flintlocks they would dispatch all three warriors with a single shot apiece. The Apaches would have no time to react.

The rattling of hoofs grew louder and louder. A horse snorted, perhaps having caught the Palouse's lingering scent.

Nate, through sheer will, calmed his jittery nerves. The Apaches were close, so close he heard words spoken softly in their tongue. Then there was a grunt, a single harsh exclamation, and total silence. The trio had stopped! he realized, his eyes glued to the section of the gap he could see. Why? Had they spotted Winona? Or were they so adept at reading sign that they knew he was in the crack? Dreadful uncertainty gnawed at him like a rat through cheese. He could barely stand the suspense.

Then he heard a peculiar sound, a sort of sibilant

hissing not unlike the noise made by steam escaping from a kettle. Cocking his head, he tried to identify what it could be. When he did, he nearly laughed aloud.

Soon the sound stopped, and the Apache must have remounted because the horses started forward.

Now Nate saw the brown nose of the foremost mount come into view. The head was next. Taking a breath, he took two bounds, bursting from the crack with his arms sweeping up even as from above him the Hawken thundered and one of the warriors was smashed to the ground by an invisible fist. He took a hasty bead on a second Apache and fired, but at the instant he squeezed the trigger the warrior began to lift a bow and his shot struck the man's arm, not the chest as he'd intended. The Apache jerked at the impact but didn't go down.

Venting a whoop in rage, the third warrior prodded his horse into a run and bore down on Nate with a war club raised on high.

Nate shifted and took aim, confident he would drop the man, and equally sure that if by some fluke he didn't, Winona would do the job. Then a thought hit him with the force of a bullet and made him blink in surprise. He'd forgotten to give Winona extra black powder and ammunition! Her rifle was now useless!

The oversight so distracted him that the onrushing Apache was almost upon him before he squeezed off his shot. A red hole appeared on the warrior's cheek and the man went down in a whirl of flying limbs. Nate had to leap out of the way of the Apache's charging horse, and he didn't entirely succeed. The animal clipped his left shoulder as it pounded past, sending him to his knees, and in the process jarring his left hand so badly that his unused flintlock went sailing.

"Husband!" Winona yelled.

He looked up to find the wounded Apache on the attack, galloping straight at him, hatred etching the warrior's swarthy face, a face he now recognized as being that of the man who had abducted his wife, none other than the Apache name Naiche. Releasing his spent pistol, Nate whipped his knife from its beaded sheath and pushed to his feet.

Naiche had let his bow fall. He appeared unfazed by his wound as, with both arms flailing, he tried to bowl Nate over. At the last instant Nate jumped out of the animal's path, then whirled to meet the next rush. Exhibiting superb horsemanship, Naiche wheeled his mount on the head of a pin and tried once again.

Nate frantically backed away, and felt his left heel bump an object lying on the ground. He tripped, falling backwards, and rather than fight gravity and be a sitting duck for Naiche he went with the fall, landing hard on his shoulder blades but quickly rolling to the right out of harm's way. Driving hoofs flashed on by.

Rising again, he saw that he'd tripped over the body of the first warrior he'd shot. Ten feet away lay one of the flintlocks, but was it the one he had fired or the other one? He started toward the gun, then stopped. Naiche was swooping down on him like a great painted bird of prey, trying to run him over. He feinted to the right, taking only two swift steps before reversing direction and darting to the left. His ruse worked. Naiche had angled his mount to compensate for the move to the right and was unable to swing it back before going past.

Swiftly Nate ran to the flintlock, grabbed it, and pointed the weapon at the Apache. Naiche didn't seem to care. Snarling, the warrior closed for the fourth time. Nate smiled in hopeful triumph as he cocked the pistol, but his expression was transformed into one of frustration when the hammer made a loud click and the flintlock didn't fire.

Naiche drew a large knife. He leaned down and lunged, lancing the blade at Nate's head, and Nate ducked down, narrowly evading the blow. Spinning, Nate did the unexpected. Instead of tiring himself trying to avoid the horse, he went on the offensive, dashing after the animal and leaping as Naiche, unaware of the bold gambit, was about to turn his mount for one more charge.

Nate's left arm closed around the Apache's waist and with his other he attempted to drive the knife into Naiche's side as the two of them began to fall. Somehow, Naiche blocked the swing. They landed next to each other, but promptly shoved apart and stood, each still holding his weapon.

For a moment they stood stock still, taking one another's measure. The Apache's eyes burned with inner fire as he contemptuously regarded Nate.

For Nate's part, he was noticing Naiche's exceptionally muscular build and the many scars on the warrior's body that bore eloquent testimony to the man's fighting prowess. Naiche was shorter but broader across the shoulders and hips, resembling a young grizzly in build.

The Apache struck with the speed of a striking rattler, his right arm flicking out at Nate's throat. Nate retreated a stride and countered with a slash at the warrior's stomach, but Naiche stepped to the left. Then they slowly circled, both seeking an opening.

Nate thrust out at chest height. The moment his arm was fully extended he arced the knife down lower, trying to slice open the Apache's stomach. Naiche twisted and the blade missed him by a fraction. Before Nate could regain his balance, the warrior lashed out, the blade of his knife striking the blade of Nate's so hard that Nate's arm was battered aside.

For a second Nate was wide open and Naiche promptly pounced, his left hand clamping on Nate's throat as his left knee slammed into Nate's groin. Together they went down, the Apache on top. Nate saw the tip of the warrior's knife sweeping at his face and he desperately wrenched his head aside. The blade nicked his ear, drawing blood.

Instantly Naiche raised the knife for another try. Nate bucked, striving to unseat his foe, but Naiche's knees pinned him in place. His own blade bit into the Apache's knife arm, not deep but inflicting enough pain to cause Naiche to jump up and take a bound to the right, out of range.

Nate rolled to the left, away from the warrior, and had started to rise when a foot caught him in the ribs, doubling him over. A second blow to the head knocked him flat. Dazed, he shifted, trying to stand, and glimpsed Naiche as the warrior leaped onto his back, pinning him again. He felt his hair gripped by iron fingers, and winced as his head was brutally bent backwards, exposing his throat to the Apache's blade.

Naiche gave a curt laugh that sounded more like a bark and went for the kill.

Chapter Thirteen

Nate stiffened as the terrifying realization that in another few seconds he was going to die coursed through him. He was totally at the Apache's mercy. There was nothing he could do to forestall the inevitable, but he refused to submit meekly. He reached up and tried to grasp the hand holding his hair to pry it loose even as he heaved his body upward with all the power in his legs and thighs.

Neither move accomplished a thing. His arm was swatted aside as casually as he would swat a fly, and the weight of the warrior combined with his own dazed state to prevent him from bucking Naiche off.

He struggled to pull his head down, to tuck his chin against his neck so the Apache would be unable to slit his throat from ear to ear, but couldn't. At any instant he expected to feel the cold steel slice into his soft flesh.

Then Nate heard a loud thump and the grip on his hair slackened. Naiche unaccountably sagged to one side. Seizing the advantage while it lasted, Nate strained with

all his might and threw the Apache off him. In the blink
of an eye he had scrambled to his knees and turned to
face his enemy.

Naiche was also on his knees and shaking his head to
clear it. In the middle of his forehead was a nasty gash
several inches long from which blood flowed down over
his nose. The warrior still held his knife, but loosely in
his lap.

For tense seconds neither of them moved as they both
mustered their reserve of stamina. At first Nate didn't
understand what had saved him, not until he saw his
Hawken lying on the ground a foot away. He didn't need
to look up at the ledge to know the answer. Winona had
hurled the rifle at the Apache just as the warrior was on
the verge of stabbing him, and the heavy gun had stunned
Naiche.

"Behind you!" she suddenly shouted.

Nate rose unsteadily into a crouch and twisted. A few
yards off was one of his flintlocks. But was it the one he
had already fired or the loaded pistol? He'd dropped the
useless one again and had no idea whether this was it.
The swirling fight had jumbled his sense of direction so
badly that he'd had no idea they were under the ledge
until just now.

Naiche also stood, his baleful eyes virtual slits as he
uttered a few stern words in the Apache tongue.

A threat, Nate figured, or a vow to kill him no matter
what. He looked at the warrior, then at the flintlock,
gauging whether he could reach the pistol before the
Apache reached him. Since there was only one way to
find out, and since any delay would give Naiche time to
recover, he took a swift step and dived with his left
hand outstretched. Behind him footsteps pounded and
something stung his left leg.

Nate landed with a jarring thud on his stomach. His
hand closed on the pistol and he whipped around to take

aim. But Naiche was already on him, straddling his legs, and the Apache knocked the gun to one side. He saw the warrior tense to stab downward, and in that instant when Naiche was concentrating on the gun and Naiche's torso was unprotected, Nate streaked his right hand up and in, sinking his blade to the hilt in Naiche's stomach. Without pause he bunched his shoulders, then drove the knife to the right and the left, ripping the Apache's abdomen wide open.

Naiche staggered backwards, his features ashen, and pressed a hand to his intestines as they spilled out of the rupture. He blinked, looked at Nate, and said something. Then his legs gave out as all his strength drained from him like water from a sieve. He lifted his face to the sky, voiced a piercing cry, and pitched over.

Nate had to scramble to get out of the way of the falling body. He sat up, staring at Naiche's blank eyes. A spreading pool of blood and foul intestinal juices was forming under the warrior and rapidly spreading outward. Abruptly nauseous, Nate got to his feet and shuffled to one side.

"Husband?" Winona said softly.

Turning, he met her anxious gaze. "I'm fine," he said softly, his voice oddly hoarse.

"You're bleeding."

That he was. In several places. But none of the wounds were life-threatening. "They don't hurt much," he mumbled, and inhaled deeply. "I'll be all right in no time."

"Help me down."

He wiped his knife clean on Naiche's leg first and stuck the blade back in its sheath. Moving closer to the rock wall, he positioned himself so that his shoulders were directly under the edge of the ledge. "Lower away," he prompted, lifting his hands overhead. She dangled her legs and he caught them and braced her feet on his shoulders. Then, ever so carefully, she climbed down using him as a ladder. Once her feet were on the ground she embraced him and locked her lips on his and for the longest time there was no sound or movement in the gap.

Winona went for Pegasus while Nate reclaimed his weapons and reloaded his guns. A close examination showed the Hawken to be intact. He sat down, his back to the wall, and gratefully let Winona clean and dress his wounds. As she closed the parfleche and began to stand, he gently took hold of her wrist and said in his best Shoshone, "You are pressed to my heart forever."

She smiled and responded, "And you to mine."

Two of the Apache mounts had run off. Nate mounted Pegasus and easily caught the third one, which Winona then climbed on. Together they rode out the far end of the gap into bright sunshine and a warm breeze that Nate found refreshing. He surveyed the beautiful but uncompromising land below and nodded, glad to be alive.

For the remainder of the day they pushed on toward the Gaona *rancho*. Twice they came on Apache sign, but the tracks were days old. Evening saw them camped beside a trickle of a stream that had satisfied their thirst and renewed their vigor.

Nate listened to their small crackling fire and held Winona tight as he stared at the stars filling the wide expanse of sky. He thought about the nature of love, and how men and women would do anything, including putting their own lives at risk, to save a loved one. Self-sacrifice was the cornerstone of a genuine commitment between two people, which explained why married men and women who always put their individual selfish interests first always had the most miserable marriages. His own parents, particularly his father, had been that way, and their family had suffered as a consequence.

Winona mumbled something and pressed her face to

his neck. Nate smiled, kissed the crown of her head, and
closed his eyes. If all went well they would be back at
Gaona's place within two days. He could hardly wait to
see Zach, Shakespeare, and Blue Water Woman again.
Provided, of course, they were all still alive.

Before dawn Nate was up and saddling Pegasus. He'd
had to tie the Apache horse to prevent it from running
off during the night, and now the animal acted up, balk-
ing when he led it to Winona and shying away when she
tried to mount. Afraid it might try to throw her, he
climbed on to see if it would buck. The animal looked
back at him as if wishing it could toss him clear to the
moon, but it gave him no further trouble. Satisfied that
it was safe for her to use, he slid down and let Winona
climb up. Then he stepped to Pegasus and did the same.

   This day was cooler and they made good time. At
midday they stopped in a tract of woodland to rest for
half an hour. Not until mid-afternoon did they come on
a spring, where once again they stopped to give their
horses a breather.

   Nate took a chance and shot a rabbit that evening for
their supper. While Winona skinned and butchered it, he
prowled around their camp, satisfying himself there were
no Apaches anywhere in their vicinity. The aroma from
the stew Winona was preparing, which would be his first
real meal in days, made his mouth water and his stomach
growl like a riled wolverine.

   He ate with relish, savoring every sip, slowly chewing
every morsel. Halfway through he saw Winona watching
him in amusement. "It's been a while," he said.

   "It has," she agreed.

   Nate noticed she had hardly touched her stew and
mentioned as much.

   "I was not talking about food, husband."

   "Oh."

The smile he wore the next morning rivaled the sun for brightness. This time the Apache horse was as gentle as a lamb. Toward ten in the morning, as they came to the top of a bench, he spied a thin column of smoke in the distance.

"More Apaches?" Winona wondered.

"Let's go see," Nate proposed.

From a rise they looked down on a tranquil scene. Three small wagons laden with bags of grain were parked under trees at the side of a rutted track. Four men dressed in the white shirts and pants of New Mexican farmers were lounging in the shade while two others worked at repairing a broken wheel.

All six stood and turned as Nate and Winona approached. He reined up, glanced at the dozing oxen hooked up to the wagons, and said, *"Buenos dios."*

A lean farmer beamed and launched into a short speech in Spanish. The only phrase Nate understood was *"con mucho gusto,"* which he knew to mean "with much pleasure." He racked his brain, trying to recall the words needed to explain he couldn't speak their language worth a hoot, when Winona spoke up and in short sentences answered the farmer. The skinny man then went on again at length.

"If we follow this road it will bring us to within a mile of the Gaona *hacienda* before nightfall," she translated.

Nate saw some of the farmers were smirking at him. *"Gracias,"* he said, and wheeled Pegasus. A few of them nodded and waved.

"Is something wrong?" Winona asked as they departed.

"No."

"Then why do you look as if you just swallowed a toad?"

"Sometimes I just can't understand why a brilliant woman like you married a dunderhead like me."

"I took pity on you," Winona joked, and laughed heartily.

True to the farmer's prediction, twilight bathed the countryside when they came into sight of the familiar buildings. Immediately they broke into a gallop. Several *vaqueros* were tending stock nearby, and while two of the hands came to meet them the third raced like the wind for the *hacienda*.

By the time Nate reined up in front of the house, Francisco and his family and Shakespeare and Blue Water Woman were all there, waiting. McNair wore clean bandages that evinced a professional touch. He grinned in delight and remarked, "About time you two got back. We were beginning to think you'd decided to pay Mexico City a visit."

Nate swung down and shook his mentor's hand. Then he looked around and asked, "Where's Zach?" The faces of all there clouded and Nate felt his pulse quicken. "Where's Zach?" he repeated urgently.

Francisco was the one who answered. "I am sorry, *señor*. It is all my fault."

"What is?" Winona inquired anxiously, her hand slipping into Nate's.

"Whoa there," Shakespeare said. "It's not what you think. You'll find your young'un out back under that tall tree with the fork at the top. We figured you'd want the honor of letting him know you're back safe and sound."

Without another word Nate hurried around the house, Winona at his side. They both stopped on seeing Zach on his knees next to a mound of recently dug earth.

"Oh, no," Winona whispered.

Nate bowed his head for a moment, then advanced quietly. They were close enough to touch their son before Zach heard their footsteps and turned.

"Pa! Ma!" the boy cried, and threw himself into their arms. He broke into racking sobs, his small frame trembling, and clung to them as if his life depended on it.

"We're sorry," Nate said. "So sorry."

Zach lifted his anguished, tear-streaked face. "Why, Pa? Why did it have to happen?"

"These sort of things don't *have* to happen. They just do."

"They shot him full of arrows, Pa. Shakespeare pulled out eleven." Zach sniffed and stared forlornly at the grave. "I found him back in a ravine. From the sign, Shakespeare thinks he killed two or three of them before they got him."

"He was a scrapper," Nate said huskily.

"Francisco dug the grave himself. Said it was all his doing because he didn't have enough men on guard when the Apaches attacked us."

"No one is to blame," Nate declared.

Winona tenderly put her hand on Zach's head. "If you want, my son, we will find you a new dog after we return home. I have a cousin who would be willing to give us one."

"No, Ma."

"It might—"

"No."

Nate stepped to the mound, sank to one knee, and picked up a handful of dirt. He let the loose earth run through his fingers, thinking of the many times the mongrel had come to their aid when they were in trouble. "So long, old friend," he said.

"It ain't fair, Pa," Zach said. "It just ain't fair."

"That's the way life is," Nate responded, rising. "Sometimes things work out the way we'd like and sometimes they don't. When the worst happens, you just square your shoulders and go on living the best way you know how."

Zach's forehead creased and he glanced skyward. "Do

dogs go to heaven like people do when they die, Pa? When I get up there will I see him again?"

"I can't rightly say, son," Nate said, and added quickly when tears filled Zach's eyes, "but if ever a dog deserved it, Samson was the one. You might see him again at that."

"I hope so, Pa. I truly hope so."

WILDERNESS

VENGEANCE TRAIL
DEATH HUNT

The epic struggle for survival in America's untamed West.

Vengeance Trail. When Nate and his mentor, Shakespeare McNair, make enemies of two Flathead Indians, their survival skills are tested as never before.

And in the same action-packed volume....

Death Hunt. Upon the birth of their first child, Nathaniel King and his wife are overjoyed. But their delight turns to terror when Nate accompanies the men of Winona's tribe on a deadly buffalo hunt. If King doesn't return, his family is sure to perish.

___4297-5 $4.99 US/$5.99 CAN

TWICE THE FRONTIER ACTION AND ADVENTURE IN ONE GIANT EDITION!

WILDERNESS

GIANT SPECIAL EDITION:

THE TRAIL WEST
David Thompson

 **David Thompson**

Follow the adventures of mountain man Nate King, as he struggles to survive in America's untamed West.

Wilderness #20: Wolf Pack. Nathaniel King is forever on the lookout for possible dangers, and he is always ready to match death with death. But when a marauding band of killers and thieves kidnaps his wife and children, Nate has finally run into enemies who push his skill and cunning to the limit. And it will only take one wrong move for him to lose his family—and his only reason for living.
_3729-7 $3.99 US/$4.99 CAN

Wilderness #21: Black Powder. In the great unsettled Rocky Mountains, a man has to struggle every waking hour to scratch a home from the land. When mountain man Nathaniel King and his family are threatened by a band of bloodthirsty slavers, they face enemies like none they've ever battled. But the sun hasn't risen on the day when the mighty Nate King will let his kin be taken captive without a fight to the death.
_3820-X $3.99 US/$4.99 CAN

Wilderness #22: Trail's End. In the savage Rockies, trouble is always brewing. Strong mountain men like Nate King risk everything to carve a new world from the frontier, and they aren't about to give it up without a fight. But when some friendly Crows ask Nate to help them rescue a missing girl from a band of murderous Lakota, he sets off on a journey that will take him to the end of the trail—and possibly the end of his life.
3849-8 $3.99 US/$4.99 CAN

Dorchester Publishing Co., Inc.
P.O. Box 6640
Wayne, PA 19087-8640

Please add $1.75 for shipping and handling for the first book and $.50 for each book thereafter. NY, NYC, and PA residents, please add appropriate sales tax. No cash, stamps, or C.O.D.s. All orders shipped within 6 weeks via postal service book rate. Canadian orders require $2.00 extra postage and must be paid in U.S. dollars through a U.S. banking facility.

Name_____
Address_____
City_____State_____Zip_____
I have enclosed $_____ in payment for the checked book(s).
Payment <u>must</u> accompany all orders. ❑ Please send a free catalog.

WILDERNESS

The epic struggle of survival in America's untamed West.

#16: Blood Truce. Under constant threat of Indian attack, a handful of white trappers and traders live short, violent lives, painfully aware that their next breath could be their last. So when a deadly dispute between rival Indian tribes explodes into a bloody war, Nate King has to make peace between enemies—or he and his young family will be the first to lose their scalps.

___3525-1 $3.50 US/$4.50 CAN

#17: Trapper's Blood. In the wild Rockies, any man who dares to challenge the brutal land has to act as judge, jury, and executioner against his enemies. And when trappers start turning up dead, their bodies horribly mutilated, Nate and his friends vow to hunt down the merciless killers. Taking the law into their own hands, they soon find that one hasty decision can make them as guilty as the murderers they want to stop.

___3566-9 $3.50 US/$4.50 CAN

#18: Mountain Cat. A seasoned hunter and trapper, Nate King can fend off attacks from brutal warriors and furious grizzlies alike. But the hunt for a mountain lion twice the size of other deadly cats proves to be his greatest challenge. If Nate can't destroy the monstrous creature, it will slaughter innocent settlers, beginning with his own family.

___3599-5 $3.99 US/$4.99 CAN

Dorchester Publishing Co., Inc.
P.O. Box 6640
Wayne, PA 19087-8640

Please add $1.75 for shipping and handling for the first book and $.50 for each book thereafter. NY, NYC, and PA residents, please add appropriate sales tax. No cash, stamps, or C.O.D.s. All orders shipped within 6 weeks via postal service book rate. Canadian orders require $2.00 extra postage and must be paid in U.S. dollars through a U.S. banking facility.

Name_____
Address_____
City_____State_____Zip_____
I have enclosed $_____ in payment for the checked book(s).
Payment <u>must</u> accompany all orders. ❏ Please send a free catalog.

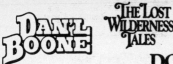

ARROW IN THE SUN
T. V. OLSEN

Bestselling Author Of *Red Is The River*

The wagon train has only two survivors, the young soldier Honus Gant and beautiful, willful Cresta Lee. And they both know that the legendary Cheyenne chieftain Spotted Wolf will not rest until he catches them.

Gant is no one's idea of a hero—he is the first to admit that. He made a mistake joining the cavalry, and he's counting the days until he is a civilian and back east where he belongs. He doesn't want to protect Cresta Lee. He doesn't even like her. In fact, he's come to hate her guts.

The trouble is, Cresta is no ordinary girl. Once she was an Indian captive. Once she was Spotted Wolf's wife. Gant knows what will happen to Cresta if the bloodthirsty warrior captures her again, and he can't let that happen—even if it means risking his life to save her.

__3948-6 $4.50 US/$5.50 CAN

KIT CARSON

**The frontier adventures of a true
American legend.**

#2: *Ghosts of Lodore.* When Kit finds himself hurtling down the Green River into an impossibly high canyon, his first worry is to find a way out—until he comes face-to-face with a primitive Indian tribe preparing for a battle in which, one way or another, he will have to take sides.
___4325-4 $3.99 US/$4.99 CAN

#1: *The Colonel's Daughter.* Kit Carson's courage and strength as an Indian fighter have earned him respect throughout the West. And when the daughter of a Missouri colonel is kidnapped, Kit is determined to find her—even if he has to risk his life to do it!
___4295-9 $3.99 US/$4.99 CAN

DAVY CROCKETT

Sioux Slaughter. With only his long rifle and his friend, Davy Crockett sets out, determined to see the legendary splendor of the Great Plains. But it may be one gallivant too many. He barely survives a mammoth buffalo stampede before he's ambushed—by a band of Sioux warriors with blood in their eyes.

___4157-X $3.99 US/$4.99 CAN

Homecoming. The Great Lakes territories are full of Indians both peaceful and bloodthirsty. And when the brave Davy Crockett and his friend save a Chippewa maiden from warriors of a rival tribe, their travels become a deadly struggle to save their scalps.

___4112-X $3.99 US/$4.99 CAN

Dorchester Publishing Co., Inc.
P.O. Box 6640
Wayne, PA 19087-8640

Please add $1.75 for shipping and handling for the first book and $.50 for each book thereafter. NY, NYC, and PA residents, please add appropriate sales tax. No cash, stamps, or C.O.D.s. All orders shipped within 6 weeks via postal service book rate. Canadian orders require $2.00 extra postage and must be paid in U.S. dollars through a U.S. banking facility.

Name_____
Address_____
City_____State_____Zip_____
I have enclosed $ _____ in payment for the checked book(s).
Payment <u>must</u> accompany all orders. ☐ Please send a free catalog.